Dear Reader,

Welcome to another fun-filled month of Duets!

Duets #31

It's babies and more babies, beginning with popular Kate Hoffmann and *Three Babies and a Bargain*. What's a single woman to do when she has to play nanny for three little mischievous nephews? Why, she strikes a bargain, *and fast*, with gorgeous handyman Nick Callahan! Next, Silhouette Romance author Sandra Paul delivers *Baby Bonus?*, a humorous tale about a sexy bank security expert dealing with five pregnant tellers—and one beautiful manager, Jessica—who have no time for his stuffy rules!

Duets #32

In *Tryst of Fate* talented Isabel Sharpe pens a delicious tale about an author who suffers lust-induced writer's block every time he encounters the woman of his dreams. Should he marry her or give up writing? Then Carrie Alexander is back with book two in THE COWGIRL CLUB m̶i̶n̶i̶s̶e̶r̶i̶e̶s̶ three lifelong female friends love horses an̶ ̶ ̶ ̶ ̶ ̶ ̶cowboys! *Counterfeit Cowboy* is a̶

Be sure to pick up bo̶

Birgit Davis-Todd
Senior Editor & Editorial Coordinator
Harlequin Duets

Three Babies and a Bargain

"The bargain's off!" Jillian said.

She crossed her arms over her chest. How could she have thought Nick Callahan attractive? And charming? And sweet? When the chips were down, physical perfection was no match for honor. Or trust. They'd made a bargain, and a good man would have respected the deal.

Nick glanced at his watch, then looked over at the boys. "I'll try to get back as soon as I can."

Jillian turned to the sink. "Don't bother. I'm sure we'll be just fine."

Suddenly she felt his hand on her shoulder. "I'm sorry," he said, his voice soft and warm. "But I wouldn't leave if I thought you couldn't handle it. You'll be just fine, Jillie." Then he turned and walked out.

Jillian rubbed away the traces of his touch. "Jerk," she muttered.

A chorus of "Nick's a jerk, Nick's a jerk" came from the back room where the boys were playing.

"I heard that," Nick called from the foyer.

For more, turn to page 9

Baby Bonus?

A big, fat toad stared out of the deposit box.

"Ribbit!" it declared, and leapt. Mitch caught it in midair—and then stood thanking his stars as the pregnant tellers shrieked and waddled for safety.

Jessica roused from her wide-eyed stillness and said briskly, "All right, show's over. Nothing to see but a man holding a toad." She shooed everyone away and smiled at Mitch dismissively—that serene smile that always made his teeth clench—before preparing to depart.

Without finishing their discussion about the tellers.

Without giving him a chance to ask her out.

Without settling one damn thing.

Just like after that video mishap, she'd left him holding the bag. Or in this case, the toad.

Not this time, sweetheart, he vowed silently. "Jessica!"

Her eyes narrowed. "Is there a problem?"

"No problem," he replied, stepping closer. "You've just forgotten something."

And he thrust the toad into her hands.

For more, turn to page 197

HARLEQUIN DUETS

ISBN 0-373-44097-9

THREE BABIES AND A BARGAIN
Copyright © 2000 by Peggy Hoffmann

BABY BONUS?
Copyright © 2000 by Sandra Novy Chvostal

This edition published by arrangement with Harlequin Books S.A.

® and TM are trademarks of the publisher. Trademarks indicated with
® are registered in the United States Patent and Trademark Office, the
Canadian Trade Marks Office and in other countries.

Visit us at www.eHarlequin.com

Printed in U.S.A.

Three Babies and a Bargain

KATE HOFFMANN

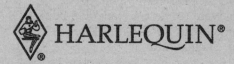

TORONTO • NEW YORK • LONDON
AMSTERDAM • PARIS • SYDNEY • HAMBURG
STOCKHOLM • ATHENS • TOKYO • MILAN • MADRID
PRAGUE • WARSAW • BUDAPEST • AUCKLAND

Dear Reader,

Though I don't have children of my own, I've heard many stories about the perils and pleasures of child rearing from friends and family. So when it came time to write my first Harlequin Duets novel, I decided to take a humorous look at children—from a single woman's viewpoint.

Of course, I couldn't give my heroine, Jillian Marshall, an easy time of it. Just one baby wouldn't do. So I gave her three...*three two-year-old boys!* And just when poor Jillie was certain she couldn't handle any more, I sent her a sexy-as-sin man to play nanny to her three rowdy nephews. What's a girl to do when she's faced with not one but four lovable males?

I should say a special thank-you to my friend Lori Handeland, whose own experiences with her son Alex inspired the incident in Chapter Three. I hope you enjoy reading *Three Babies and a Bargain* as much as I enjoyed writing it.

Best,

Kate Hoffmann

P.S. I love to hear from my readers.
You can write to me c/o Harlequin Books,
225 Duncan Mill Road, Don Mills,
Ontario, Canada M3B 3K9

To moms everywhere.

1

"Ayyyeeee!"

The high-pitched squeal hit Jillian Marshall's ears just as sticky fingers grabbed at the hem of her skirt, and she bit back a cry of dismay. She glanced down beneath the breakfast bar at the messy face of her two-and-a-half-year-old nephew, Andy. Dressed in his Dr. Denton's with the little elephants and the plastic feet, he held onto a soggy piece of toast covered with grape jelly.

"Jibby ee toad," he said, his mouth full of food. Slowly, he pushed the glob of half-chewed bread out of his mouth with his tongue and Jillian caught it just before it joined the jelly on her skirt.

"Jillie eat toast," he repeated, plopping the slice of bread facedown on her knee and rubbing it around for good measure.

The toast slithered down her leg and landed on her sandal before dropping to the floor, the jelly dripping between her toes. Jillian forced a smile, then pushed back from the counter. "I found Zach's missing breakfast," she said, holding the evidence up to her sister, Roxanne.

Roxy sighed. "I wondered where that went." She bent down and looked under the counter, growling playfully. "What else is down here? Are there monkeys under here?"

The other two members of her sister's terrifying trio giggled at their mother's silly faces, tumbling around amidst spilled Cheerios and colorful Legos beneath Jillian's feet. Zach, the most rambunctious of the identical triplets, wielded a wooden spoon and was about to bang on the bottom of a battered aluminum pan. Wearing the saucepan as a hat, his brother Sam sat placidly. A quiet, serious child, Sam was unaware of the enthusiastic military tattoo about to be played on top of his head until his mother plucked the pot from his head.

"You're not serious about taking care of the boys while Greg and I are in Hawaii, are you?" Roxy asked.

"Of course I am," Jillian replied.

Roxy looked up at her from the floor. "Jillie, you don't have to prove anything to me. I know you probably could do it. You can usually do anything you set your mind to."

If only that were true, Jillian mused, as she slid off the stool. She walked to the sink and tried to scrub the jelly stain from her skirt, her mind occupied with her sister's comment. She'd spent her entire life trying to carve out a place of her own in the Marshall family, trying to prove that she was as good as her sister. Roxy was the popular one, the cheerleader, the prom queen, the daughter who married a fabulous man and gave their parents not one, but three, grandchildren! Roxy was beautiful and witty and self-assured, a perfect copy of Jillian's mother and their father's pride and joy.

Jillian was the other daughter, painfully shy and gawky, a complete geek in high school. She had only one quality that had set her apart. She was smart—brilliant, by most standards. While Roxy had charmed boys and set fashion trends, Jillian had occupied herself with advanced calculus and computer programming, serving as president of the Math Club. By her sophomore year, she'd already begun taking college credit math courses.

And she had graduated a whole year early, sitting next to her sister at commencement—the ugly duckling next to the gorgeous swan.

Though she'd outgrown her gawky body and was now passably attractive, she still carried the scars of a clumsy and socially inept teenager. And she was still trying to prove herself to her parents. According to Sylvia Marshall, a husband and a family were the only true measures of success.

Unsure of herself in the social realm, Jillian hid behind her formulas and equations. Mathematics had become her life, bringing her recognition around the country as one of the foremost experts on number theory. She'd been the youngest person ever to be offered a tenured professorship at the New England Institute of Technology.

Though her mother still hoped for another wedding in the family, Jillian had grown satisfied with the course her life had taken...until now. Lately, her career was leaving her feeling strangely unfulfilled. She dabbed at the jelly stain on the cotton skirt, then gave Roxy a sideways glance. "Don't you think I'd make a good mother?"

"Maybe," Roxy said. "But you'll need to learn to roll with the punches a little more."

Punches? Roxy looked as if each day with her sons was a severe pummelling. At that precise moment, the Hunter home could have qualified for government aid as a national disaster area. But then, the house was always in a shambles—toys scattered everywhere, the sink piled high with dishes, the laundry room belching dirty clothes into the hallway and her beautiful sister looking like she'd slept in a wind tunnel.

"I'm sure if you put your mind to it, you could regain

control of your life,'' Jillian murmured. She had wanted to speak her peace on that matter for such a long time. It was clear Roxy had lost her ability to maintain any semblance of household order. In just an hour with the boys, Jillian could see a thousand simple ways to improve the living conditions in the Hunter household, starting with the judicious use of grape jelly.

Roxy laughed out loud. ''Triplets defy organization, the same way they defy eating their vegetables and taking a nap. It's genetic.'' She gave Jillian a shrewd look. ''Why do you want to do this? Are you thinking about getting married and having a few monsters of your own?''

Jillian paused before her next words, wondering if she should tell Roxanne about her plans. She *had* been thinking about children. A husband, on the other hand, wasn't a necessary factor in the equation. All that was required was a visit to a sperm bank, a test tube with a high IQ, and a simple withdrawal. ''No,'' she lied. ''I just want to spend more time with my nephews, that's all.''

In truth, there were three people in the world she felt completely comfortable with, three people who never judged her—Zach, Andy and Sam. Though she didn't always understand them, or the havoc they wreaked, they loved her unconditionally. They accepted her for the person she was and she returned their love in full measure.

Jillian sighed softly as she dried off her skirt. Perhaps if her life had taken a different path, she might have had her own children by now. But she was twenty-nine years old, with few prospects for marriage, though that was probably her own fault. When she'd finished her doctorate six years ago, she'd developed a list of standards for a potential mate—an IQ equal to or greater than hers, a successful career in the sciences and a belief that her work was as important as his. He'd have to be an extraordinary man, perhaps a Nobel prize winner.

She'd had a respectable number of male friends—successful intellectuals, most of them colleagues at the New England Institute of Technology. But after three or four dates, she found herself losing interest. Something was missing from her list, some element she couldn't describe, and Jillian was beginning to believe she'd never find it, even if she dated every Mensa member on the planet.

"It's hard work," Roxy warned. "It would be a big mistake for you to think it's easy. And ten days will seem like a lifetime."

"It just takes organiza—"

"I know, I know," Roxy interrupted. "Organization. Your answer to every problem. You're the only woman I know who keeps a schedule of housekeeping chores on a computer. Heck, if it's messy, I clean it. And if it's not, I catch a quick nap."

Jillian tipped her chin up stubbornly. "I'll bet if you gave me ten days with your boys, I'd have this house running smoothly." At first, she wanted to take the words back, knowing the statement might hurt Roxy's pride. But then, as the notion sank in, she began to realize that this would be an excellent opportunity to test her mettle as mommy material. And preempt any concerns Roxy might have over her baby plan.

"Mom said she'd take the boys," Roxy countered. "She's hired extra help, fortified the house, put away the good china and told Dad he can't play golf for an entire week. She's expecting her grandsons. It took me two months of cajoling to get her to agree so that Greg and I could go on this second honeymoon."

"I'm sure she won't be disappointed if you changed

your plans," Jillian replied. "I'm not teaching my seminar on transcendental numbers at the institute this summer. I've got my Goldbach research to work on, but I can do that in the evenings after the boys are in bed and while they're playing."

Babysitting the boys would also give her an excellent opportunity for empirical research. By the end of the week, she'd know just how her work and children mixed. "If I need help, I can always call Mom," Jillian added. "She's only ten minutes away. I know I can do this, Rox. Just give me a chance."

Roxy's expression softened and she nodded. "All right. But you have to promise, if things get bad, you'll call Mom immediately."

Jillian knelt down and the boys gathered around her, hanging off her arms. She gave them each a kiss, wincing at sticky fingers and dirty faces. "I promise. But I know we'll get along just fine. We'll have a wonderful time, won't we, guys?"

"ZACHSAMANDY! Put that down!"

Jillian groaned, then raced over to the entertainment center in the family room. Cereal crunched beneath her shoes as she dodged a pool of spilled milk and the sleeping form of Duke, the family's long-suffering Golden Retriever.

"You'd better stop that right away!" she warned. "That doesn't go in there!"

The little tyke watched her shrewdly, his mind calculating his odds of shoving the graham cracker into the VCR before she reached him. Jillian scrambled for a name, frustrated with her inability to tell her nephews apart. Roxy had taken care to identify each of the boys before she left for the airport, but, in a disciplinary pinch,

"Zachsamandy" had become her generic name for them all. She'd always thought Zach was the troublemaker. But after spending just one day with the boys, that theory had been disproved time and time again. They all had their destructive moments—together and separately.

She snatched the cracker from…"Zach," she muttered, putting a name with the red shorts he wore. "This is for tapes." She grabbed a Thomas the Tank Engine tape and pushed it into the VCR, only to hear the unmistakable sound of crumbling crackers.

"Poop!"

Jillian spun around to find another hellion standing behind her. By process of elimination, he had to be Andy or Sam. "Andy," Jillian murmured, recognizing the blue T-shirt. "Poop? Now?"

"Poop!" he repeated, patting his backside with a chubby hand. "Dirty diaper!" He punctuated each word with a hearty slap. "Change! Change! Change!"

"How could you do this to me?" Jillian cried. "I just changed you ten minutes ago." She crossed the room and grabbed Andy's hand, ignoring the strangled sounds coming from the VCR. "We are going to have to work on this," she muttered. "You're supposed to tell me *before* the actual act."

Andy looked up at her and grinned again. She was certain he understood her, but took some perverse delight in staring at her like she was speaking in some bizarre alien dialect.

She reached behind him and grabbed one of his toy trucks, then rolled it across the floor in front of him. A metaphor would be in order here, she mused, trying to gather her patience. Dr. Hazelton, the noted pediatrician and bestselling author of *Successful Child Rearing*—a book she'd read from cover to cover the night before last—recommended making potty training fun for the child with interesting examples.

"Pretend you're the dump-truck driver," she said, "and Auntie Jillie is the customer. You're supposed to let me know when you're coming so *Jillie* can tell you where to dump your load. The driver doesn't get to decide. And Aunt Jillie would really prefer only one load a day. All right?"

"Aw right," Andy replied, nodding, holding up his hand for a high five.

Jillian gave his paw a playful slap and struggled to her feet. But just as she was congratulating herself on her successful intervention, she saw Sammy wander into the room, a big piece of paper stuck to his cheek. Jillian plucked it off, then frowned. The pattern on the paper was oddly familiar. In fact, it looked just like—she groaned softly—the wallpaper in the powder room.

"What did you do?" Jillian asked. She raced to the bathroom, all three boys hard on her heels, only to find another disaster. The pretty wallpaper border that circled the room midway up the wall was now in shreds, tiny pieces scattered all over the tile floor. "I can't do this," she murmured, backing out of the room. "I give up. I can't keep track of all of you at once. You win. I surrender. I'm calling my mother!"

After only six hours as primary child-care provider to the Hunter triplets, Jillian was ready to give it all up. She felt as if she were the captain in a pediatric version of *The Poseidon Adventure,* trapped in an upside-down house that was about to sink to the bottom of the lake outside. If she didn't call her mother now, more serious disasters might await them all.

Of course, just when things couldn't get worse, they did. The phone rang.

"Phone!" Zach screeched, his attention diverted from unrolling yet another roll of toilet paper. He grabbed the end in his hand and ran toward the kitchen, a trail of white following him the entire way.

"I get it!" Andy shouted in delight, taking off after his brother.

Sam plucked another piece of wallpaper from the wall and handed it to her with an innocent smile, before joining the parade. Jillian sighed softly, her heart melting a bit at Sammy's little gift. How could she be angry at such a sweet child?

"Phone!" they all shouted.

Jillian palmed the scrap and took off after the boys, reaching the phone before they had a chance to climb up on the counter. "Hello?" she said breathlessly.

"Jillie? Jillie, is that you?"

Jillian winced at the sound of her sister's voice. Of all the times for Roxanne to call, why did she have to call in the midst of yet another calamity? Not that there'd been a break in the string of disasters that day.

Jillian schooled her voice into the essence of calm and control. "Hi, Rox. How are you? Are you there already?"

"Yes," her sister shouted, as if the distance between Hawaii and New Hampshire hadn't yet been conquered by the phone company. "It's incredible. Beautiful. I can't believe we're actually here!"

Jillian held the phone away from her ear. "I can hear you fine, Rox. You don't have to yell."

"How are the boys?" she asked. "Is everything all right?"

"Everything's just fine," Jillian lied. "We're all getting organized. It's going quite smoothly. No problems at all."

"Yeah, I bet," she said. "Let me talk to the little monsters."

As the boys took their turn with the phone, babbling their greetings to their parents, Jillian's thoughts wandered back to the conversation that had gotten her into this mess in the first place. "It's all a matter of organization," she had told her sister. Good grief, how could she possibly get organized when she couldn't even tell the boys apart?

"Jillie? Is everything all right? Jillian, are you there?"

Startled out of her contemplation, Jillian looked down to find Zach at her feet, bashing the handset of the phone against the leg of a kitchen stool. Her sister's voice was barely audible as she called out in alarm.

She snatched the phone from her nephew's hands, eliciting a shriek of disapproval from him. "I'm here," Jillian said over his cries. "Everything's fine. Don't worry."

"I'm not worried," Rox said. She paused. "Well, maybe a little. It's just that I've got the nagging feeling that I've forgotten to tell you something."

"I have an entire notebook full of instructions," Jillian said. "And I've practically memorized Dr. Hazelton's book. I can recite the phone numbers for the fire department, the police, the pediatrician and the poison control center and I have enough Huggies to last until the boys enter high school. Everything is fine. You and Greg have a wonderful time. And don't worry!"

She could almost see her sister's reluctant smile on the other end of the line. "You have our number," Roxy said. "Call if you have any questions. If not, I'll call back tomorrow or the next day."

"You and your husband should be spending time

thinking about each other," Jillian insisted. "I don't want you calling for at least three days."

"All right," Roxy said. "I'll try. Kiss the boys for me. And make sure Sam has his blankie before you put him down. And Zach won't sleep unless—"

"Good night, Rox. Go have wild hot sex with your husband now. And make sure you use protection or you may end up with another set of triplets on your hands." Jillian hung up the phone, then let out a tightly held breath. She glanced down at the boys. "That went well, don't you think?"

They all looked up at her and once again, she tried to put names to identical faces. With a soft oath, Jillian grabbed a laundry marker from the drawer beside the phone, then turned to the boys. "Sit," she said. They obediently did as they were told and Jillian smiled in satisfaction. She grabbed Zach's leg, tickling him behind the knee, then carefully wrote an initial on the top of both of his feet in thick black marker. She did the same for each of the boys. Z for Zach, A for Andy, and S for Sam.

Though the forehead might be better for quick identification, blond bangs would hide the initials. At least now, as long as they were barefoot, she'd be able to tell them apart. "See? Who needs Grandma now? Organization. That's the key."

JILLIAN WASN'T SURE what woke her, but some instinct deep inside told her something wasn't right. Her eyes snapped open and she listened for a long moment, holding her breath as she lay on the couch in the same spot where she'd thrown herself after finally getting the boys to bed. She tried to determine the time. Had it been minutes or hours since she'd lain down?

She expected to hear one of the boys crying or the dog barking, but that was not what she heard. She heard footsteps. Not the little patter of pajama-clad feet or the click of dog nails, but the distinct sound of heavy feet on a hardwood floor. Stifling a scream, she sat up and searched the family room for a weapon. But every item that might cause harm had long ago been put out of the reach.

She silently stood and tiptoed toward the phone, her mind racing to remember the number of the police station. But all she could recall was the number for poison control. If she could force the intruder to swallow Drano, she might be all right. On her way to the phone, she stubbed her toe on one of the boys' toys. Biting her bottom lip, she forced back the tears of pain, then realized she'd stumbled on exactly what she'd been seeking.

Jillian picked up the small xylophone and measured it for its heft and balance. For a weapon, it would have to do. And after she'd rendered her prowler unconscious, she could play a chorus of "Twinkle, Twinkle, Little Star" while she waited for the police.

The police! She had to get to the phone and call for help. But the instant she headed for the phone, she heard the footsteps coming nearer. Jillian crouched in the shadows beside the sofa and held the xylophone out to the side.

When the tall, dark figure passed, she seized the moment. Jumping up from her hiding place, she swung the instrument. The very highest note grazed his temple, then the xylophone smashed up against the wall in a bizarre chord. Duke, the guard dog, looked up from his spot in front of the fireplace, yawned, then put his head back on his paws.

The blow caused the prowler to stumble backwards.

When he caught his heel on the oriental rug, his feet flew out from under him and he landed on his back with a thud. A great whoosh of air left his lungs and as he gasped for breath, Jillian fumbled for the light switch.

Bright light flooded the room and he winced holding up his hand. It was at that moment that she realized she was staring at one incredibly handsome prowler. He had warm brown hair that was streaked blond by the sun. His face, all smooth planes and angles, was tanned and clean shaven. He wore a faded work shirt that revealed well-muscled arms. Blue jeans covered long legs. He looked up at her with surprised hazel eyes. Once he caught his breath, he tried to struggle to a sitting position, but she raised the instrument over her head again.

"Stay right there," she warned in a trembling voice, "or I'll sic my dog on you."

He groaned, then forced a smile and scoffed. "Duke? Unless you expect him to drown me in drool, I wouldn't bother." He flopped back down, placing his arm across his forehead. "What the hell did you hit me with?" he asked.

"A Toony Tots xylophone," she said. "And I didn't hit you. The high C just grazed your temple. Who are you? And what are you doing in my house?"

"This isn't your house," he said. "I know the people who live here and you're not one of them, lady."

Jillian shifted uneasily, then swallowed. "N-neither are you, so I guess I had every right to hit you."

"Maybe you'd better tell me who you are," he said.

"I'm Jillian Marshall. I'm Roxanne Hunter's sister."

He touched his temple and cursed, then pulled his fingers back and examined the traces of blood. "Ah, so you're the infamous Jillian," he muttered. "The math whiz. Your brother-in-law said you hated men, but I didn't think you'd take your feelings quite this far."

Jillian gasped. Of all the nerve! "I don't hate men! I can't believe Greg said that. When did he say that? And who are you that he would say something like that to you?"

He pushed himself up to a sitting position again, groaning as he moved. "Let me ask you something, Jillian. Do you make a habit of whacking your dates with musical instruments, too? No wonder you're still single."

How dare he speak to her so rudely? Was she now expected to defend her social life—or lack of it—to a complete stranger? "Who are you? And what are you doing in this house?"

"They didn't tell you I was coming?" He rubbed his head. "I'm Nick Callahan. I'm building bookshelves for Greg and Roxy in their library."

"Well, this is the first I heard about it," Jillian said. "How did you get in?"

"They gave me a key. I thought everyone would be gone. What are you doing here?"

"I'm taking care of the boys," Jillian replied.

Nick studied her for a long moment. "Did the rug rats do that to your hair or is that the way you usually wear it?" he asked.

Jillian's free hand fluttered up to touch her hair, the shoulder-length style now spiked up like she'd taken a bath with a plugged-in toaster. "I was just taking a—a nap." She frowned. "What time is it?"

"Around eleven," he said.

"Why are you here so late? Don't you—you carpenter guys work during the day?"

"Hey, I've got other jobs. I'm doing these shelves as

a favor to Greg and Roxy and they're letting me stay in the guest house. Now, are you going to put down that xylophone and let me get up, or am I going to have to find a trombone and challenge you to a duel?''

Jillian reluctantly lowered the xylophone. ''How do I know you're telling the truth? How do I know you're not some deranged psychopath who will murder me and my nephews in our sleep?''

''What do you want?'' he asked. ''Identification? I'll show you my hammer. Or how about my drill?''

''Your driver's license will do just fine,'' she replied.

Nick Callahan rolled to his side and withdrew his wallet from the back pocket of his jeans. Jillian watched him suspiciously, then realized that she was staring a bit too hard at his backside. She dragged her gaze away and met his eyes. A sardonic smiled curled his lips, a smile that told her he knew exactly what she had been staring at. He tossed his wallet at her and she caught it.

With fumbling fingers, Jillian found his driver's license and confirmed that he was indeed Nick Callahan from Providence, Rhode Island. She also confirmed that he was the only person in the United States who looked good on his driver's license picture. Very good. Incredibly sexy and handsome and—

''Are you satisfied?'' he asked.

She snapped the wallet shut and dropped it on his chest. ''You can wait on the porch while I call Roxanne. And don't try anything weird.''

''Don't worry,'' he muttered, as he pushed up to his feet. ''Right now you've got the corner on that market.'' He stood and stretched sinuously in front of her, the muscles of his chest bunching and rippling beneath the taut fabric of his shirt. Then he walked to the back door, rubbing the back of his neck. She slammed it behind him, making sure it was locked securely.

Fifteen minutes later, after frightening Roxanne half to death and disturbing her sister's late afternoon siesta on the beach, Jillian had confirmed that Nick was the "little something" Roxanne had forgotten to tell her about. Roxanne also added that this "little something" was handsome and available. But when Jillian opened the back door to let Nick back in, the carpenter was nowhere to be found.

She tracked him down in the library, where he'd already set to work. He'd moved most of the furniture to one side of the room and had begun to measure the empty wall. "I thought I told you to wait outside," Jillian said.

"I got tired of waiting," he replied through the pencil clenched in his teeth. "So I used my front door key." He snatched the pencil out and scribbled something on a piece of paper. "Did Roxy certify that I'm not a..." He turned to look at her. "What did you call me...a deranged psycho?"

Jillian tipped up her chin defiantly. "I was only protecting my nephews' safety. And she told me you were a good friend of Greg's and that you're supposed to be doing exactly what you said you are."

"Good," he replied. They stood there for a long moment, staring at each other. "Was there something else you wanted?" he asked. "Or do I have permission to get back to work?"

Jillian blinked, once again the first to look away, then shook her head. "Just try to keep quiet. It took me two hours to get the boys to sleep."

"I'll do my best," Nick said, giving her a devastating smile before returning to his measurements.

Jillian shot him an icy look before she walked out of the library. This was all she needed. Not only did she have to keep an eye on three energetic little boys, now she had to deal with Nick Callahan hanging around the house as well. How was she supposed to get things organized when all these unexpected events interfered?

Well, she'd just have to factor in Nick's presence. Perhaps he'd be an asset to her research. She could pretend he was a husband. He'd be there, but he wouldn't offer any help with the children, which probably would provide an average empirical model. She'd consider Nick Callahan the typical male. While he was working on the bookshelves she could make believe he was watching football or taking a nap on the sofa. In the end, he'd only serve to confirm what she already knew—that she didn't need a man around to raise a child.

An image of him flashed in her mind, broad shoulders and narrow waist, and she brushed it away. All right, there were other advantages to having a man around. But she shouldn't even be attracted to a guy like him. After all, he wasn't her type. Jillian preferred men with more brains than brawn, men who were a match for her on an intellectual level.

Sure, she had to admit that she could understand the fascination with a man like Nick Callahan. All that muscle and masculinity wrapped up in such a pretty package. So confident, almost arrogant, in his power over women.

But unlike the other weak-willed women in the world, Jillian knew what she wanted from life, and it wasn't Nick Callahan, or any other throwback to the Neanderthal age, who expected his women to be warm and willing and obedient. No, Nick Callahan definitely was not her type. She'd much prefer a pale, introverted Nobel laureate than a gorgeous Greek god with an inflated ego.

Jillian pinched her eyes shut and fought back a yawn. It was nearly midnight. The boys would be awake in six hours and she was exhausted. If she knew what was good for her, she'd leave Nick to his work and get some sleep.

But as she lay in the guest room, tossing and turning and trying to relax, thoughts of Nick Callahan teased at her mind. She pushed up and punched at her pillow, then flopped back down and began to methodically recite the prime numbers between one and five hundred.

Somewhere after eighty-nine, she fell asleep, drifting into restless dreams of muscled male bodies and crying children.

2

NICK STOOD at the kitchen sink, slowly sipping at his mug of coffee as he stared out the window. The rising sun sparkled on the surface of the lake and the trees blew in the soft morning breeze. Of all the houses he'd designed, he'd always liked this one best. Even better than his own house—or his ex-house. Though it rankled to admit it, for the near future, he was homeless.

His ex-house was currently inhabited by his ex-fiancée, Claire, and her son, Jason. It was the house he'd designed and painstakingly built on a vacant city lot in a trendy neighborhood of Providence, the house he'd thought had finally become a real home, inhabited by a real family.

Nick had never really wanted children, a fact he'd made perfectly clear to Claire early on in their relationship. But along with Claire, he'd gotten her seven-year-old child. At first, they'd kept a wary distance, Jason adamant that he didn't need another father and Nick certain that he didn't want a son. But it didn't take long for the walls to come crumbling down and for Nick to realize he'd been wrong about children, wrong about Jason. So, after going together for several months, Nick asked Claire to move into his house with her son.

They'd lived happily for nearly a year, but when he'd brought up the subject of another child to Claire, she'd steadfastly refused to consider the matter. This was not part of the agreement, she insisted. She had her child and no matter how much she loved Nick, she didn't want to have his. What had started as a minor disagreement over their future suddenly became a wedge, sharp enough to drive them apart.

It wasn't long before the fickle Claire had moved on to someone else, someone willing to give her exactly what she wanted—a glamorous, baby-free life. Nick sighed softly, then took another sip of his coffee. He'd walked out the instant he found out about the other man, unable to stay in a house full of anger and regret. He said a somber good-bye to Jason, the boy who had nearly become his son and told Claire she had two months to vacate. Luckily, the cottage on Greg and Roxy's property was vacant for the summer. Hoping that some solitude would put some perspective back into his life, he'd moved in about a month and a half ago.

Soft footsteps sounded behind him and he slowly turned to find Jillian Marshall standing in the doorway. She looked so soft and sweet-smelling, dressed in a pretty white nightgown and a robe with tiny flowers embroidered around the scooped neckline and around the cuffs of the wide, flowing sleeves. When she wasn't glaring at him, or whacking him across the head with children's toys, she was actually quite beautiful. He felt the faint stirring of desire, then brushed it aside. Though Jillian Marshall was pretty, he'd sworn off women, at least for the rest of the summer, and he was determined to keep that promise to himself.

She blinked, then frowned sleepily. "What are you still doing here?" she murmured, rubbing her eyes with her fists.

"Good morning," he said softly.

"I asked you a question," Jillian grumbled, hurriedly

combing her hair with her fingers. "Why are you still here?"

He bit back a sarcastic reply. Jeez, the woman was prickly twenty-four hours a day! "I just finished up for the night," he replied. "Would you like a cup of coffee? It'll do wonders for your mood."

Her brow shot up in surprise. "You—you made coffee?"

Nick turned and poured her a cup, then handed it to her. "Sleep well?" he asked.

She glanced at him over the rim of the mug. "No, not particularly."

He watched her gradually throw off her sleepiness. This was what he'd always imagined family life to be, sharing the first cup of coffee in the morning, starting the day together, quietly, with the little ones asleep upstairs. Not that he'd imagined a wife like Jillian Marshall—or triplet boys. It was just that Claire had always started her day fully dressed, makeup artfully applied, clothes neatly pressed.

"What about you?" she asked. "Don't you ever sleep?"

"Sometimes," he said. In truth, sleep had been hard to come by lately.

"You should always try to get eight hours every night," she murmured between yawns. "Usually, I keep a very strict schedule. I go to bed exactly at eleven and wake up exactly at seven. Once I get this household organized, I'm sure I'll be able to get back to my normal schedule."

"Really," Nick said. "Tell me, do things always go exactly according to your plans?"

"Of course," Jillian said. "It's all a matter of organization. For instance, the boys are supposed to sleep until six o'clock. It is now five-thirty. I'll have just enough time to eat my breakfast and take care of some household tasks before I go and get them dressed.''

The words were barely out of her mouth when Nick heard a wail coming from the direction of the boys' bedroom. He grinned. ''I guess you forget to tell the boys about your schedule.''

She shot him an irritated glare, then drew a deep breath and closed her eyes. ''They're supposed to sleep until six,'' she said. ''He'll just cry for a few minutes, and then go back to sleep.'' Another wail joined the first. ''Roxanne assured me they sleep until six.'' Soon the duet became a trio and Jillian covered her ears.

''Why don't you let me get the boys dressed?'' Nick suggested. ''Sit down and finish your coffee.''

She frowned at him in disbelief. ''You know how to change a diaper?''

''I grew up in a big Irish family,'' he said. ''The oldest of ten children. I think I can remember enough to get by.''

She studied him for a long moment, then shrugged. ''Go ahead,'' she said. ''They're yours, dirty diapers and all.''

Nick grabbed his coffee mug and headed upstairs. He found all three boys standing just inside their bedroom door, their faces screwed up in frustration, ready to start the day but unable to work the doorknob.

''Hi, guys,'' he said. ''You're up a little early.''

''Nick!'' Andy cried, his arms outstretched. ''Nick, Nick! Go up!''

''I want out!'' Zach cried. ''Now!''

Sam watched Nick from a safe distance, wide-eyed, his thumb stuck firmly in his mouth.

He picked Andy up and placed him on the changing

table, then took a quick survey of the situation. A search for diapers turned up a stack of Huggies with dancing bears across the front. "Disposable diapers," he muttered. "All I remember is plastic pants and pins." Plucking at the little tabs, he unfolded the diaper. "You've got a masters degree in industrial engineering, Callahan. You can certainly figure out a Huggies."

Nick went through six diapers before he managed to get Andy off the changing table and into a pair of shorts and a T-shirt. By the time he finished with Sammy and Zach, the mangled diapers made a rather impressive pile. He gathered them up and shoved them into a dark corner of the closet. The dirty diapers were another matter. After five minutes of tinkering, he managed to unlock the secrets of the Diaper Disposal, a finely engineered gadget that he found fascinating in its simplicity and practicality.

The moment he opened the bedroom door, the boys made a beeline to the kitchen, screaming all the way. Nick was the last to appear in the doorway, just in time to see Jillian's eyes widen with what appeared to be sheer terror.

"Come on, guys, let's give Auntie Jillian a chance to finish her coffee. I don't think she's ready to handle you until she's had a big dose of caffeine."

Jillian pushed up from the kitchen table, a look of exhaustion already flooding her face. "They're hungry."

"Sit down," Nick said. "I'll get them their breakfast."

She shook her head. "But you don't know what they eat. They have to have a nutritious balance and you have to cut up the food so—"

Nick chuckled. "I'm sure I can figure it out. It's got to be big enough to pick up with their fingers and small enough so it doesn't choke them. This isn't rocket science, Jillian."

She watched him suspiciously, her hands wrapped around her coffee mug. He plopped the boys into their booster seats and placed a bowlful of dry cereal, sliced bananas, and a spill-proof cup of milk on the breakfast bar in front of each of them.

"You're really good at this," she murmured.

He warmed under her unexpected compliment. "It just takes a little common sense," Nick replied.

"I'm not good at this," Jillian said, exhaustion tinging her voice. "Take the diapers. I figured if I fed and watered them all at once, they'd *go* all at once. But I changed diapers every half hour yesterday. By now, Dr. Hazelton says, they should be open to potty training."

"Who the hell is Dr. Hazelton?" Nick asked.

Jillian shot him a warning look. "Don't curse in front of the children," she whispered. "Dr. Hazelton says cursing can have a detrimental effect on their emotional well-being. And Dr. Hazelton happens to be the nation's leading authority on child rearing."

"Forgive me," Nick teased, snatching a cup out of Zach's hand an instant before he hurled it at Jillian's head. "But aren't they a little young for potty training? They don't even know how to pull their pants down yet."

"My nephews are more advanced than the average two-and-a-half year old."

Nick watched as Zach tried to stuff a piece of cereal up Sam's nose. "Yeah. I can see that."

The boys took only ten minutes to wolf down their breakfast. Nick wiped their faces and hands, then sent them off to play. All the while he felt Jillian's eyes on him, watching his every move.

"Tell me," she asked, after the boys had scampered out of the kitchen, "how much do you carpenter guys make? What's your hourly rate?"

Nick raised a brow at the sudden turn in conversation. "Carpenter guys?"

"Guys like you," Jillian said. "How much?"

He shrugged, too amused to be insulted. Though he'd always found great nobility in men who worked with their hands, his talents with a hammer and saw were merely a hobby. "I don't know. Union scale is around thirty dollars an hour for a journeyman carpenter. More for a master."

She gasped. "You make thirty dollars an hour?" He watched as she mentally did the calculations. "That's sixty-thousand a year for a job that requires absolutely no college education. That's half what I make and I've got a Ph.D."

"Supply and demand. I guess there are a whole lot more people that need carpenters than mathematicians. The invention of the calculator really cut into your business, huh?"

The color rose in her cheeks, and he smiled. God, he loved pricking her temper. She was such a snooty little thing when she wanted to be, full of herself and her prejudices. Just what would she say if he told her he held a master's degree in both industrial engineering *and* architecture and brought home ten times what a "carpenter guy" did? Right now, Nick thought it best to keep that information to himself. He might need it later to bring her down a few more pegs.

"For your information, number theory is a very complex science," she said.

"Something us working-class guys would never understand, right?"

"And I hardly ever use a calculator. All my calculations are done on a mainframe computer."

"Then why are you interested in my wage?" Nick asked. "Are you thinking of switching careers?"

Jillian shook her head and gave him a shrewd look. "No." She opened her mouth to speak, then snapped it shut.

"What?" he asked.

"Nothing." Jillian paused. "It's just that the boys like you so much and I thought it would be nice if you stopped by later this afternoon and visited—if you can spare the time."

"If you find caring for them so difficult, why did you ever agree to it?" Nick asked.

She shifted in her chair, straightening her spine. "I have my reasons. Besides, you said it. It just takes a little common sense. You watch, by the end of today, everything will be fine."

"I think you're being overly optimistic. Caring for three toddlers is very tiring."

She frowned, and then tipped up her chin, a stubborn gesture that had already become familiar to him. "I'm a highly intelligent woman, Mr. Callahan. Now, if you'll just be on your way, I can get started with my day."

A shriek split the air and Jillian's face went pale. She froze, her white-knuckled hands gripping the edge of the counter. Nick walked over to her and pulled her up out of her chair, then pointed her in the direction of the noise. He slowly rubbed her shoulders, like a trainer about to send a boxer back into the ring. "I've got some work to do," he said. "I can come back around three, if you'd like."

Jillian glanced over her shoulder and forced a smile. "I—I'm sure the boys would love that."

Nick steered her toward the stairs. When she'd taken the first step, he walked to the front door and opened it. He chuckled, wondering what scene would greet her when she reached the source of the scream. He suspected that by the time he returned, Jillian Marshall would be more than happy to see another adult. After all, common sense didn't always accompany a post-doctorate education in mathematics. And when it came to child care, Jillian seemed woefully short of common sense.

BY MID-MORNING, Jillian had managed to forget her earlier encounter with Nick Callahan, putting him and the memory of his hands on her body completely out of her mind. She'd never been touched by a man in such a casual, but powerful manner, and the thought of it disturbed her.

But by lunchtime, Jillian could think of nothing *but* Nick Callahan. She found herself counting the minutes until he reappeared, in between wiping macaroni and cheese and soggy saltines off the floor and walls. She'd taken great pains to prepare a nutritious, homemade sauce, a cheesy béchamel served with whole-wheat pasta, rather than feed the boys the boxed variety that Roxanne had recommended.

An hour later, after she'd cleaned the last trace of cheese sauce from the last little face, Jillian realized that the box probably was a better alternative—especially since half of it ended up on the floor anyway. Duke was the only one who got a nutritionally balanced meal! The dog plodded off for his nap, macaroni hanging from his left ear, and Jillian followed, looking for the boys.

She found them in the nursery. Sammy had already climbed into bed and was arranging his stuffed animals around his pillow. Andy was yanking books off the bookshelf, determined to find his favorite or make a mess trying. Jillian looked around for Zach and found him in the bathroom just off their bedroom, drenched in water and holding a tiny toy car over the toilet. Zach looked up at her as she came in, a devilish glint in his eye. "Boat," he said. He made a buzzing sound with his lips as the car circled the toilet seat.

Jillian glared at him. "That is not a boat and it doesn't belong in the toilet."

"Boat," he repeated stubbornly.

"Car!" Jillian insisted.

Zach watched her for a long moment and she could almost see the wheels turning in his mind. She crossed the bathroom in three short steps but before she had a chance to grab the little car, he dropped it in the toilet with a resounding "plunk" and yanked down on the handle. With a delighted giggle, Zach peered over the edge and watched the little red sports car circle the bowl for the last time. "Bye-bye, boat. See you later."

Jillian reached into the bowl and tried to catch it, but it was no use. The car was gone, along with her patience. "That was very bad," she said to Zach. "And you won't ever see that boat—I mean car—again!"

He nodded, frowning intently. "Very bad," he said, shaking his finger at her.

Jillian didn't have the energy to resort to Dr. Hazelton and his methods of discipline. Instead, she grabbed Zach by the hand and drew him back into the bedroom, firmly closing the bathroom door behind her and making a mental note to start closing doors more often. She changed his clothes, not even bothering to contemplate how he'd gotten so wet, then raced through *The Cat in the Hat* and *The Little Engine That Could*. Thankfully, they all retired without much fuss. Exhausted, she flopped down on the floor beside their beds and closed her eyes.

How would she ever make it through another eight days of this? Every time she thought she might have a moment to catch her breath, some new domestic tragedy rained down on the Hunter household. If she could just get a few steps ahead of the boys, she might be able to get things organized. But she always seemed to be lagging behind them, there to clean up after the latest disaster, yet never anticipating the next.

The only bright spot was the prospect of a visit from Nick. An image of him drifted lazily through her mind. Jillian rubbed her shoulders where he'd touched her, wondering at the warm tingle that still lingered on her skin. She'd nearly asked for his help that morning, but her pride had stood in the way. That, and the unbidden attraction she felt toward him.

She could rationalize the attraction, even ignore it. But it was the basics of child rearing she couldn't seem to get a grip on. No doubt if she asked for his help, he'd lord his superior skills over her. But she refused to admit failure so quickly. And calling in reinforcements, namely her overbearing mother, was not an option. At least not yet.

If only she could get him to stay in the house. Maybe she could fiddle with the plumbing in the cottage. Or cut the electrical line. She'd then magnanimously offer him a guest room and he'd be here when she got up in the morning and he'd be here when she and the boys went to bed. With another adult around, she'd at least be able to maintain a small measure of her sanity.

A shiver skittered through her at the thought of having Nick Callahan around twenty-four hours a day. She silently scolded herself. So he was attractive. Why not admit it? There was certainly nothing wrong with admiring perfection in the masculine form—broad shoulders, hair streaked gold from the sun, beautifully muscled arms and…

Her thoughts focused on more intimate territory. She'd had lovers in the past, but she'd never had one with a perfect body, a narrow waist and flat belly and a backside that just…

This time the shiver shot clear to her toes. "Nick Callahan is not your type," she muttered to herself. "He's arrogant and overbearing. He acts like a know-it-all. Besides, he's a carpenter. He works with his hands, not with his head. You've always preferred a great mind to a great body."

But, oh, what hands, she mused. Strong and warm. Jillian closed her eyes and thought back to the moment that those fingers skimmed along her shoulders, brushing briefly at the nape of her neck. Though his touch had been a purely innocent, casual gesture that meant nothing at all to him, she couldn't help but wonder what his touch might have done to her if he'd had other intentions, if he had really *wanted* to touch her.

She opened her eyes and sighed, then pinched them shut again, blocking out the handsome face that teased at her mind—and the mess that surrounded her. The nursery looked like a typhoon had roared through. She tried to push herself off the floor, knowing she should pick up the mess before Nick arrived. But she couldn't move and could barely keep her eyes open.

When she awoke some time later she wasn't sure how long she'd napped or what actually woke her up—whether it was the sound of Nick's voice calling from downstairs or the little face that stared at her from close range. She blinked, then reached up and rubbed her eyes.

But when her vision cleared, she could do nothing more than scream.

Zach held out a colored marker which he'd already liberally applied to his face. "Red," he said, holding it beneath her nose. "Smells like juice."

Jillian snatched the marker from his hand thanking the heavens Zach hadn't been suffering from severe facial lacerations. At the very same moment Sam and Andy jumped on top of her. They also clutched watercolor markers in their fists, only their faces looked much worse than Zach's, both sporting a collage of bright colors and swirling patterns to rival van Gogh.

"Jillian? Where are you?"

She jumped from the floor, frantically searching for the Baby Wipes. They were hidden under Sam's bed and once she retrieved a handful, Jillian immediately set to work scrubbing all three faces clean. She finished just as Nick appeared in the doorway of the nursery. Stuffing the crumpled Baby Wipes into the pockets of her sundress, she turned and gave Nick a nonchalant smile. "Hi! Look who's here! Uncle Nick!"

The boys screamed his name, then ran right past him out of the nursery, leaving the two of them alone. He gave her an odd look, part frown, part grin. "Is everything all right?" he asked.

"Just fine," Jillian said. "The boys had their nap and we were just...playing. I—I think we're finally starting to get organized."

He nodded, then looked around the room, his brow quirking up. "I can see that."

"In fact, you probably could have stayed away. I've got everything under control here." Why couldn't she just admit she was overjoyed to see him? She had nothing to prove to this man, to this stranger. She caught an odd expression on his face, half-confusion, half-amusement. Slowly, he reached out, as if to touch her cheek, but Jillian stepped out of his reach, afraid of the contact.

Nick forced a smile. "I'm sorry, I was just trying to— you have something on your—"

She reached up and smoothed her mussed hair, then straightened the neckline of her dress, disturbed by her reaction to his unbidden advance. This casual touching was completely inappropriate. "I realize we're in rather close quarters, Mr. Callahan, but I—I don't think we should...I mean, for the sake of the boys, we shouldn't..."

"I wasn't making a pass," he said with a grin. "You just have something on your face."

Jillian swallowed, heat rising in her cheeks as she rubbed them, finding a Cheerio stuck to her temple. "I know. It's fine," she said, popping the cereal into her mouth with as much nonchalance as she could muster. Dropping to her knees, she gathered the markers and started shoving them back into the box.

"So," Nick said, glancing around. "What would you like me to do?"

She looked up at him for a long moment, all manner of possibilities racing through her mind. He could touch her the way he had earlier that morning. Or he could stare into her eyes in that way that seemed to make her blood run warm. Or he could always just stand there and let her look at him until she had her fill of handsome carpenters with flat bellies and nice backsides.

"Well?" he prodded.

"I hadn't really thought about it," Jillian replied with a shrug. "Maybe you could play with the boys. Keep them out of trouble while I get some work done. It's a

beautiful day. Why don't you take them out for a walk?''
A long, exhausting walk, she thought to herself.

He grabbed her hand and helped her up from the floor,
then slowly reached out and brushed his thumb along
her cheek. Her body trembled, but this time, Jillian didn't
pull away, but just savored his touch. He allowed his
fingers to linger for a long moment, then he grinned.
''Why don't you come with us?'' he suggested.

She smiled hesitantly, tickled that he enjoyed her company enough to ask. ''All right. I think I will. I could
use some fresh air and exercise.''

''And I suppose I could use an extra pair of eyes and
hands,'' he said.

Oddly, it took Nick only five minutes to get the boys
into their shoes, a half-hour ordeal for her. He grabbed
a ball and headed outside, the boys at his heels and Jillian following close behind. She watched him as he
strode up the drive to the narrow road that circled the
lake. The boys romped after him, kicking the ball and
running along to catch it, the sun bright on their blond
heads.

Her gaze moved to Nick and fixed on his wide shoulders, on the muscles that bunched and stretched beneath
the taut fabric of his work shirt. Slowly, she let her eyes
drift downward until they stopped at his backside. She
took a long, slow breath as she admired the fit of his
faded jeans, his long, muscular legs and easy athletic
stride. Scolding herself, she hurried to catch up.

They strolled along the winding road, the five of them
causing mild curiosity for the people in the passing cars.
They waved at a few neighbors along the way and by
the time they'd turned back for the house, the exercise
had invigorated Jillian and brightened her mood.

''You really have a way with them,'' she said as Nick

hoisted Sam up onto his shoulders. The other two boys walked at his sides. He was completely at ease with them, as though acting the part of a father came naturally. Maybe it was a male thing, boys bonding with boys.

A sudden thought shot through her mind. "Do you have children of your own?" She groaned inwardly. Roxy had said he was single, but she'd never considered the possibility he might be a father.

He gave her a sideways glance, then shook his head. "I like kids, but no, I don't have any of my own."

"Have you ever been married?"

"Almost, once," he said. "But that didn't work out."

All the warmth had left his voice. Jillian crossed her arms in front of her, sorry for her curiosity. "Well, the boys certainly seem to like you." She cleared her throat, then glanced at him. "I've never been very good with children. I guess you've noticed that. That's why I decided to stay with the boys. I do like children. All it takes is time and practice."

"And organization?" he teased.

"Yes. I believe that," she said firmly. "Children need structure in their lives. Dr. Hazelton says that structure creates an atmosphere of safety and harmony in a child's life. You'll see, by the end of Roxy and Greg's vacation, I should have this household running like a well-oiled machine."

"And you think the boys are going to cooperate with this plan?" he asked.

"Why wouldn't they?"

He shrugged. "I think you might have overestimated your organizational abilities, Professor Marshall. Unlike those numbers you're so fond of, triplets defy organization."

She straightened her spine and gave him a stubborn look. "I'm perfectly able to achieve my goals with the boys. I've done my research and if I lay the groundwork properly, I'll—"

"If you're so capable, why did you invite me over for a play date?" he teased.

"You're good with the boys," she replied. "I'm not too proud to admit that."

Nick chuckled. "Gee, and I thought it was because you liked the way I wore my jeans."

She gasped and felt heat flood her face.

"Don't act so surprised," he said. "I noticed you looking."

"I was not!"

"Yes, you were," he countered.

"Why would I waste my time looking at your backside? You're hardly the type of man I'm attracted to." With that, she spun on her heel and headed back in the direction of the house.

"And what type of man *are* you attracted to?" he shouted, as he gathered the boys to follow her.

She turned around. "Certainly not a man with such a high opinion of himself—and his backside."

He laughed then, loud and deep, the sound echoing through the woods. The three boys giggled and clapped right along with him. Cursing beneath her breath, Jillian picked up her pace. By the time she reached the end of the driveway, they were nearly fifty yards behind her.

When she reached the house, she headed for the nursery, determined to clean up the mess that awaited her there. Dragging her fingers through her wind-tangled hair, she glanced at herself in the bathroom mirror, then stopped dead. The image that stared back at her brought a groan of mortification.

No wonder Nick had been looking at her so strangely! Her cheeks were covered with red and blue marker, the results of Zach's nap-time artistry. She looked like a reject from clown school! "You'll pay for this, Nick Callahan," she muttered. "Don't think you can make me look the fool and get away with it."

Jillian grabbed a bar of soap and scrubbed at her cheeks with a spongy bathtub toy. She dried her face with a wad of tissue, then dropped it in the toilet and flushed before scrubbing off a second layer of skin. But as she worked, the toilet gurgled and sputtered beside her.

She turned and watched as the water rose, higher and higher, until it began to flood over the rim. Screaming, she grabbed a towel and tossed it on the floor, then pulled a stack from the closet and scattered them at her feet. But nothing she did could stop the torrent. She clambered to the open window and shouted for Nick. To her relief, he'd reached the driveway.

An eternity later, Nick appeared at the door with the boys and calmly surveyed the situation. The floor had at least an inch of water on it and the flood had seeped out into the hallway. She didn't bother to chastise him for the marker incident. The disaster of her wildly colored face had now been replaced by a disaster of greater proportions. "Do something!" she cried as she mopped at the floor.

"Water!" Andy cried, patting his hands on the floor.

"Auntie Jillie make a mess," Zach added. "Clean up, clean up."

Duke appeared and began to lap up the water with great gusto.

"It looks like you need a plumber," Nick said, stepping over to the toilet. "I'm just a carpenter. Union rules prohibit me working on the toilet, unless you're willing to pay union wages."

"How much?" she asked through clenched teeth.

"Fifty dollars an hour should do it," he said.

Jillian stood up and tossed a soaked towel at his chest. It hit him with a loud "thwap." "Fix it," she said, as she shoved past him.

JILLIAN WAS SITTING at the kitchen counter when he and the boys came back downstairs. A bottle of wine was open in front of her, but Nick saw no evidence of a glass. *She must be feeling pretty badly to drink right out of the bottle,* he mused.

"You could have told me I looked like an idiot," she muttered, taking a slug of the wine.

"I tried," Nick said. "But then I figured you'd done it on purpose while you were playing with the boys. Besides, you looked kind of cute with scribbles all over your face."

Jillie groaned and cupped her chin in her palm. Sammy crawled up on the stool beside her and pointed to the wine bottle. "Juice?" he asked.

"Grown-up juice," she murmured, patting him on the head. She glanced over at Nick. "So, what was the problem with the plumbing?" she asked in a weary voice, no longer interested in blaming him for her short stint as a clown.

Nick held out a handful of toy cars he'd recently extracted from the toilet. "Major traffic jam," he said.

Zach screeched and reached out for the toy cars. "Boats!" he cried.

"Cars," Nick said, giving him a stern look. "And toys do not belong in the toilet. These are mine now."

Zach watched him suspiciously, deciding whether to

pitch a tantrum or accept his punishment. He finally shrugged and wandered off to find another source of entertainment.

Jillian looked at her watch, then sighed. "Two hours at fifty dollars. I owe you a hundred." She slid off the kitchen stool and grabbed her purse from the counter. "Will you take a check?"

"Actually," Nick said. "it's going to take more work. The water leaked through the floor into the ceiling below and the drywall needs to be replaced, along with the wallpaper border." He instantly regretted his words. She looked like she was about ready to cry. Instead, she grabbed the wine bottle and took another swig. "But, don't worry. I can fix it so Roxy and Greg will never even know."

Jillian lowered her head to the counter. "Have you ever heard of chaos theory?" she murmured, her cheek pressed against the granite, her glazed eyes staring off into space.

Nick's gaze was drawn to her hair. At first, he'd considered it a very ordinary color. But upon closer observation, he noticed how the warm brown hue glinted with red and blond. He reached over and plucked at a strand that threatened to slip into a puddle of orange juice. It felt like silk between his fingers. She moved slightly and he snatched his hand away.

"I'm not sure," Nick lied. In truth, he had read about chaos theory in one of his graduate classes, but he couldn't recall the particulars. All he knew was that, standing so close to her, he was certain chaos theory was at work in his body. He wanted to reach out to her and draw her into his arms, to bury his face in the sweet smell of her hair and run his hands over her soft skin, capture her mouth with his.

But his common sense told him that these protective feelings toward Jillie Marshall would only get him in trouble. Sure, he could play the hero for her, helping her with the boys, unclogging toilets and taking diaper duty. And she might need him, but not in the way he really wanted. "Why don't you explain it to me?" he murmured, unable to take his eyes off her.

Jillian looked up at him. "It's a modern area of mathematics. It tries to explain the erratic or irregular fluctuations in nature. When a system is chaotic, its behavior is only predictable if the initial conditions are known to an infinite degree of accuracy."

"In other words," Nick said, "you'd have to know precisely how many Hot Wheels a toilet could handle before you could predict whether it would overflow and ruin the ceiling?"

Her expression brightened and she straightened, managing a tiny smile. "Exactly! You see, I think this is where I've made my error. I neglected to apply chaos theory to child-rearing. I'm an expert in number theory. It's very orderly and predictable. Naturally, I wouldn't have considered chaos theory."

"So, what does this mean?"

"It means that it's not my fault that things seem to go wrong all the time!" Jillie cried. "It also means I should be prepared for things to lapse into chaos every now and then. It's all part of the natural order of this universe." She drew a deep breath. "I shouldn't let myself get too concerned about my mistakes. To this end, I'd like to pay you."

For a moment, he wasn't sure what to say, stunned by her direct statement. Hell, he'd be willing to do anything she wanted for free. "I'm not that kind of man," he teased.

A faint blush colored her cheeks through the faint streaks of marker still on her face. Nick couldn't help but notice how pretty she was—even when she was talking math. It wasn't just her body he found attractive. She had a curious and fascinating mind as well.

"I've got a deal I'd like to propose," she continued, "and I'm willing to pay you very well."

"What kind of deal?" Nick asked, curious and cautious at the same time.

"I want to hire you," Jillian said. "Just for a few days, until things get organized."

"Roxy and Greg already have hired me. Besides, I can incorporate the cost of the new ceiling into the price of the bookshelves. It's just a piece of drywall and some fresh paint."

She shook her head. "I—I'm not talking about the ceiling or the bookshelves. I want to hire you as a nanny."

Nick frowned. A nanny? He'd been propositioned by a fair number of women in his life, but he'd never heard this variation. And the fact that Jillian Marshall considered him on par with Mary Poppins certainly didn't do much for his ego! "I don't understand."

"It's quite simple. You appear to have a way with children, a way that I am still in the process of perfecting. Until I do, I'd like to hire you to help me care for the boys."

"Why not call your mother?" he asked. "She was supposed to take care of them in the first place, wasn't she?"

Jillian squirmed uneasily. "I have my reasons. I'll pay you six hundred dollars for three days. You'll come at three and work for me until eight, when the boys go to bed. After that, you can complete your carpenter duties."

Nick smiled. He'd been presented with a valid excuse to spend time with the beautiful, yet prickly Jillian Marshall and her exuberant nephews. And he'd get paid for it, to boot. He really couldn't afford to take the time away from work, but hell, he could work in the mornings and consider the afternoons a vacation. And what better way to spend a few free hours than with a gorgeous— and brilliant—brunette. This might be good for a few laughs, and God knew, he hadn't had a lot of laughs in his life lately.

He whistled softly. "Six hundred dollars for three days. Five hours each day. That's forty dollars an hour. You must be desperate."

"Actually, it represents a thirty-three percent raise above your normal wage. Fair compensation. And I am not desperate. I simply need an extra hand—or two. Just until I get organized."

He looked down into her indifferent gaze. She was trying hard to maintain an aloof air, but he could tell how much she needed his help. Should he agree now, or should he make her beg a little? Perhaps he might ask for a few fringe benefits to go with the hourly wage. A simple kiss, a quick taste of those perfect lips, one of which she was chewing on at the moment.

"All right," Nick said. "It's a deal." He held out his hand and she hesitantly placed her fingers in his palm. A warm tingle worked its way up his arm and without thinking, he reached out and touched her face. She blinked in surprise and drew back, her fingers fluttering to the very spot where his hand had just lingered. "You still have a little marker on your face."

Again, she blushed, her gaze flitting from his eyes to his toes. "Oh. I—I'm sorry."

"No," he murmured. "I'm sorry." He grabbed her

hand and dragged her out of the kitchen. "Since I'm officially on nanny duty, I think you can spare an hour to soak in a hot bath." She trudged up the stairs after him and he threw open the door to the master bathroom he'd designed especially for Greg and Roxy. Without a word, he bent over the whirlpool tub and flipped on the faucet, and then grabbed a bottle of purple bath salts and added a generous amount.

He turned and placed his hands on her shoulders, looking down into her eyes as he gently massaged her stiff muscles. "Relax," he murmured. "I'll scrape up something for dinner and get the boys fed. You have nothing to worry about now that I'm on the job."

Jillian gave him a grateful smile and nodded. "I don't think I'm paying you enough," she said.

"We can discuss a raise over dinner." With that he strolled to the door and pulled it closed behind him. Nick would have preferred to remain and scrub her back, but he'd have to wait to be invited into Jillian's bath.

3

JILLIAN STOOD IN THE SHADOWS of the hallway, wrapped in her robe, watching Nick and the boys playing on the nursery floor. The boys were dressed in just their diapers and Nick lay on the floor, shirtless. They were all so engrossed in make-believe, they didn't even notice her. Cars and trucks were spread out all around them and her nephews ran the little toys up and over Nick's body, giggling when he captured a little arm or a racing car in his hand. "So much for chaos theory," she murmured.

She distractedly rubbed the damp from her hair with a towel, feeling relaxed for the first time in two days. She felt as though she'd been on a forced march, exhausted and battered, scarred by battle. But the moment she'd sunk into the tub, her worries took flight and her aches were eased. *What a nice man Nick Callahan is,* she mused, listening to his deep laugh.

At first, she'd thought him to be a cad, a man concerned only with tweaking her temper and making her look like a fool. She scolded herself for jumping to conclusions. Now that their deal was in place, she found him to be completely charming. He'd been happy to offer his help with the boys and he'd generously drawn her bath. Sure, she was paying him for his help, but he could have refused her offer of employment.

Jillian frowned. Six hundred dollars was probably a lot of money to a guy like him. Maybe he hadn't accepted just because he wanted to be nice. Perhaps he had bills to pay, pressing financial obligations. It must be tough to make a living building bookshelves.

Whenever she met a man, she automatically held him up against her list of criteria. But since she'd met Nick, she'd begun to believe the list was just getting in her way. Though Nick didn't have the extraordinary, scientific mind she sought, he had his own special qualities, qualities she found very—

Jillian sighed softly. It wouldn't do to continue these silly fantasies. A sexy body and a smile that melted every bone in her body wasn't enough! For a relationship to be a success a man and woman had to be intellectually compatible as well. As for his intelligence, so far, she knew he could build bookshelves, change diapers and make coffee.

She watched as he grabbed Zach and held him above his head, pushing him up and down like a barbell, his biceps taut, the muscles in his shoulders rippling. He hugged the little boy to his bare chest and growled playfully, then tucked him under his arm and stood up. Andy and Sam each took a leg and Nick lumbered toward the bathroom, all three boys in tow. "Time for a bath," he said in a gruff voice.

Jillian's breath caught in her throat and she closed her eyes as she imagined the scene. Of course, Nick would look incredible with his clothes off. Just the thought of him naked sent a secret thrill through her body. She sighed softly and the boys faded from the scene, replaced by an image of herself, soaking amidst the Mr. Bubble with Nick.

He'd probably bathed with lots of women. With his experience, he'd know exactly where and how to touch her. He'd start slowly washing her back, kissing her neck, caressing her soap-slicked skin. His hands would be strong and firm on her body, his touch assured. And when she moaned his name, he'd...

She clutched her robe around her neck and opened her eyes. The thought of a little affair with Nick Callahan was tempting. Sex had always been rather uninspiring for her, ordinary, even. If she'd been more physically attracted to her partner, it might have been better. And she couldn't deny that she found Nick very attractive in that way. But Jillian had never chosen her companions for their physical appearance. She'd always looked for intellect first.

Jillian wandered back to the master bathroom and stood in front of the mirror, staring at her reflection. Good grief, what could she be thinking? She wasn't ready to throw herself into an affair with a complete stranger!—Especially with a man as unsuitable as Nick Callahan. She frowned. Besides, though she might find him attractive, he hadn't shown any sign of returning the sentiment.

She padded over to the wall and stared at herself in the full-length mirror. With hesitant hands, she opened her robe and looked at her naked body the way a man might. There wasn't much to recommend her. She had small breasts and narrow, almost boyish hips—but she did have a slender waist. With a soft oath, Jillian wrapped the robe back around her body. "You're seriously deluded," she muttered. "How can you even be thinking such a thing? He'd never find you attractive."

Putting all erotic thoughts of Nick Callahan out of her mind, Jillian grabbed a brush and began to tug it through her damp hair. She heard shouting and laughter from the boys' bathroom and smiled, wondering if Nick was as wet as the boys were. It really was sweet of him to give them a—

A sudden realization hit her. "Oh, no," she murmured. Nick was giving them a bath!

Jillian adjusted the gaping front of her robe, then ran down the hall and through the nursery, stubbing her toe on a vicious Tonka truck and leaping over a pile of dirty clothes. Cursing under her breath, she hopped along, rubbing her sore foot. When she reached the bathroom door, she sucked in a sharp breath at the sight of Nick, his hair drenched, his chest damp.

Nick glanced over at her and grinned, oblivious to the splashing of the three little naked boys in the tub. "Did you enjoy your bath?" he asked, raking his hand through his hair.

She knelt down beside the tub and reached into the water, snatching up a right foot from the nearest triplet. Jillian searched the water for another foot and when she saw six immaculately clean feet, she groaned, then sat back on her heels. "You washed their feet," she murmured.

Nick stared at her, his gaze drifting down to the gape in her robe, then back up to her face. She didn't bother to alter the view. She had other things on her mind besides modesty. "They were dirty. There was marker all over them."

"I—I put the marker there," Jillian said.

"You scribbled on their feet?"

"Roxy always dresses them in different colors so she can tell them apart. I didn't want to get them mixed up, so I—I wrote their initials on their feet. Oh, God, Roxy's going to kill me. We'll never know which is which. Dr. Hazelton says I have to make sure I never call them by the wrong name. It could cause irreparable harm to their developing individuality. Maybe we could take them to the hospital. They must have fingerprints or footprints or—''

"I know which is which," Nick interrupted. "This is Andy," he said, pointing to the triplet on the left. "This is Zach and this is Sam."

Her gaze darted from boy to boy to boy, seeing absolutely no difference in appearance. They all looked like little drowned rats. "How can you be sure?"

Nick shrugged. "I can tell. Sam hasn't said a word since I put him in the tub. Zach tried to shove Andy's hand up the faucet. And Andy told me that Aunt Jillie is the most 'bootiefull' aunt in the world." Nick smiled. "Either he means you're nice looking or that you have a pretty...backside."

Jillian couldn't help but laugh, his joke easing her worry.

"Besides, just ask them," Nick continued. "They know the difference." He bent over the tub. "Where's Sam?" Two of the boys pointed to another. "Where's Andy?" This time, they chose another triplet. "By the process of elimination, we can figure out who Zach is."

Jillian plopped down on the wet tile floor and sighed in relief. Once again, Nick Callahan had ridden to her rescue and saved the day. She was starting to become dependent on his help. He provided a calming influence in the house, a rational mind when hers was going haywire. "I can't tell them apart," she said. "If it weren't for the labels on their feet and the different clothes, I'd be lost."

"Just watch them," Nick replied, turning back to his job. "And use your instincts. If you'd stop trying to organize, Jillie, everything would become clearer."

Jillian did as she was told, sitting against the wall and

observing as Nick bathed the boys. She listened as he talked to them, participating in their conversations as if he truly understood what they were babbling about. When they got too rambunctious, a single warning was all it took to bring them under control. And when it was time to get out of the tub, they didn't whine or pitch a fit as they'd done for Jillian. They scrambled out and danced around Nick, three happy little naked boys waiting to be dried off.

"Look at how they respond to you," Jillian murmured. She drew a deep breath. "I'm such a failure at this."

Nick finished drying the last triplet, then sent them all running to their bedroom for their pajamas. When they were alone in the bathroom, he sat down beside her, leaning his back against the tub. He took her hand in his, giving her fingers a gentle squeeze. It was such an innocent gesture, but it revived her quickly sinking confidence. And she liked the rush of warmth it sent through her bloodstream.

"Somewhere along the line, you've made the mistake of thinking that child-rearing should be easy." He chuckled softly as he toyed with her fingers. "It isn't. And you don't learn it all in one day. It's a talent that comes by degrees. But you do have one thing that a good mother needs in abundance."

"What's that?" Jillian asked.

"Tenacity," he said. "You're not the kind of woman to give up, Jillian." With that, he bent closer and brushed a quick kiss on her cheek. Then he pushed up from the floor and wiped his damp hands on his thighs. "I better go see what the boys are up to."

Jillian sat in the bathroom for a long time after he left, staring at the empty doorway, her fingers pressed to her cheek. No matter how she tried to wrap her mind around his kiss, she couldn't seem to figure it out. Did he feel sorry for her? It could have been a pity kiss. Or maybe it was just a friendly gesture. It couldn't possibly be romantic, she mused.

Jillian buried her face in her hands and moaned softly. Trying to figure out the mind of Nick Callahan was almost as difficult as trying to figure out the minds of two-year-old triplets. Some things were simply beyond her capabilities!

"WHAT DO YOU MEAN you might not be able to come?"

Jillian stood in the kitchen, the boys sitting in their booster chairs, lined up along the breakfast bar. They'd been chattering away, guzzling orange juice from their tippy cups and stuffing their mouths with buttered toast. But when she'd screeched out her question to Nick, all three had stopped and watched warily, concerned by the desperate tone in her voice.

"I'm sorry," Nick said. "I've got an emergency at work. It can't wait."

"This is exactly what I should have expected," Jillian said with an edge of sarcasm. "You carpenter guys are all the same. Start a job, then disappear when it's half finished. When can I expect you back, next month?"

Nick gave her an irritated glare and she immediately regretted the comment. All right, perhaps she had been a little harsh, but they'd made a bargain and after only one day, he was reneging! She was his boss and she had a perfect right to be upset. After all, she'd come to count on him and the prospect of getting through an entire day alone with the boys was…daunting at best. Things went so much better when Nick was around.

She drew a ragged breath. "Can't you tell them you've got another commitment?" she pleaded.

"I would if I could, but I can't. I promise to be back by five or six. If you're that worried, call your mother. Have her take the boys for the day."

"No," Jillian said stubbornly. "I don't need my mother to bail me out."

Nick reached out and grasped her shoulders, catching her gaze with his. "Jillie, this isn't brain surgery here. You feed them, you change their diapers, you feed them, you put them down for a nap, you feed them, you put them to bed. You're a smart woman. Trust your instincts. Besides, you've weathered the worst of it. What else could happen?"

"All right, I'll trust my instincts!" she said. "And my instincts say that I don't need your help. In fact, the bargain's off! You can forget your career as a nanny and you can go back to your nails and your boards and your—your thing that makes holes in wood."

"My drill?"

"Yeah, your drill." She crossed her arms over her chest and leaned back against the edge of the counter, refusing to meet his gaze again. How could she ever have thought Nick Callahan attractive? And charming? And sweet? When the chips were down, physical perfection was no match for honor and trust. They'd made a bargain and a good man would have respected their deal. Nick Callahan was not a good man!

"Go ahead," she finally said.

Nick glanced at his watch, then looked over at the boys. "I'll try to get back as soon as I can."

Jillian turned to the sink and began to scrub at a stubborn grape-juice stain. "Don't bother. I'm sure we'll be just fine."

She thought he'd left, but then she felt a hand on her shoulder, his strong fingers branding her skin beneath the thin cotton of her dress. "I'm sorry," he said, his voice soft and warm. "But I wouldn't leave if I thought you couldn't handle it. You'll be just fine, Jillie." With that, he turned and walked out.

Jillian rubbed away the traces of his touch and bit back an oath. "Jerk," she muttered.

"Jerk!" Andy cried.

"Jerk, jerk, jerk!" Zach shouted.

"I heard that!" Nick called from the foyer.

She felt a blush warm her cheeks, then smiled at the boys and placed her finger over her lips to shush them. Just then, the doorbell sounded and all three of the boys shouted out loud, "I get it!" They scrambled down from their chairs, falling all over themselves as they raced to the front door, but Nick had already opened it.

"Nana!"

Jillian groaned inwardly when she saw her mother standing on the front porch. Dressed impeccably in designer golf clothes, she looked like she'd just walked off the pages of *Town and Country* magazine. Jillian frantically ran her fingers through her tangled hair, then tried to wipe an orange juice stain off the bodice of her dress.

But Sylvia Marshall didn't notice. After kissing each of her grandsons, she fixed her attention on Nick. Jillian could see her mind working, drawing the only conclusion that a nosy mother could. "And who are you?"

Nick smiled and held out his hand. "Mrs. Marshall. It's so nice to see you again. Remember me? I'm Nick Callahan."

Caught off guard by his charm, her mother took Nick's hand and gave it a feeble shake.

"We met a few years back when Greg and Roxy were building the house," he offered.

Jillian knew her mother didn't remember, but she acted like she did. Sylvia Marshall was always the picture of social grace. "Oh, yes. Nick, it's nice to see you again."

"I'm sorry I can't stay," he continued, moving to the door, "but I've got business in Providence. Say hello to Mr. Marshall for me." He nodded, then sent Jillian an apologetic look. "Good luck," he mouthed.

The door closed behind him, leaving Jillian to explain his presence and her general state of dishevelment. When her mother turned and stalked toward the kitchen, she grabbed her dress and tried to suck off the orange juice stain, then hurried after her. "Mother, it's not what you—"

Her mother had no patience for explanations. "I simply cannot believe what I see," she muttered, bending down to attend to the boys' appearance. She rebuttoned shirts and turned down socks and tied shoes. Before she finished, she fished a comb out of her purse and ran it through tangled hair. Then she sent the boys off to play and sent Jillian a withering glare.

She sighed. "Mother, he's just—"

"In front of the children! You're supposed to be caring for these boys, not entertaining your—" she lowered her voice "—male friends."

"He's not a male friend," Jillian said. "I mean, he is a male. An acquaintance. But he's not my friend. He's here building bookshelves in the library for Greg and Roxy. And he's staying down in the guest cottage. He just came up to the house for coffee."

Her mother slid onto a stool at the counter and stared

at Jillian for a long moment, an aristocratic arch to her eyebrow. "Then, there's nothing between you?"

"Of course not!" Jillian lied. She wasn't about to tell her mother the truth. That he'd kissed her on the cheek and told her she was cute, and that she'd spent most of last night in fitful dreams of his hands skimming over her body and his tongue following close behind. She drew a deep breath, banishing the residual images from her brain. "There's nothing going on."

Her mother sniffed, then heaved an impatient sigh. "And why not?"

Jillian gasped. "Why not?"

Sylvia clucked her tongue and shook her head. "He's a perfectly charming man, Jillian. And so handsome. And if he's a friend of Greg and Roxy's, then you know he's not some bum. You could do much worse. In fact, you have been doing much worse. How long has it been since you've had a date?"

"Mother, would you like some coffee?" Jillian turned and grabbed the pot from the counter, sloshing a fair amount on the front of her dress. But she was past caring. She'd almost welcome a domestic disaster with the boys right around now. At least she had a chance of handling that. But she'd never been able to handle her mother. To Sylvia Marshall, a successful career meant nothing unless there was a husband and children as well. In the pursuit of more grandchildren, she was ruthlessly outspoken and mercenary.

Jillian poured a mug of coffee for her mother, then handed it to her. "Why did you stop by?" she asked.

"Roxy called last night and she sounded worried. I wanted to see how you were doing."

Jillian glanced around the kitchen, then nodded at the boys who were gathered in the family room, watching the latest episode of *Barney* on television. "We're doing just fine."

"I could give you a break," she suggested. "I'll take the boys and you could go into town and get your hair done. Maybe get a manicure. There's a new little dress shop on Main Street." Her gaze drifted down to the huge stain on the front of Jillian's dress.

"Why would I need a new dress?" she asked.

Sylvia rolled her eyes as if she were talking to the village idiot. "He's coming back, isn't he? I really think you'd make a nicer impression on him if you weren't dressed in rags. You could cook him dinner, let him see the real you." She plucked her comb out of her purse and circled the breakfast bar. "Did you even bother with your hair this morning?"

Jillian brushed her hand away. "Believe me, Mother, he's already seen the real me. And it wasn't pretty. If you have any fantasies about Nick Callahan and me living happily ever after and providing you with additional grandchildren, then I'd warn you not to hold your breath. He's not my type."

Her mother looked at her long and hard. "Darling, I'm not a fool. That man is every woman's type. Those shoulders and those eyes. My goodness, I—"

"Mother! Stop!" Jillian gathered up the remains of breakfast and tossed them in the sink. She was so tempted to accept her mother's offer to care for the boys, but after Nick's challenge, she was determined to prove that she didn't need his help. She could get through the day. If worse came to worse, she could lock the four of them in the nursery for the next eight hours to avert disaster.

She wiped her hands on a dishtowel and turned to her mother. "I've got a busy day today, Mother, and I'd really love to sit and chat. But the boys and I are going outside to play. Why don't you get your hair done today?''

Sylvia reached up and patted her perfectly coiffed hair. ''Do you think it needs to be done?'' She grabbed her purse, pulled out a mirror and examined her reflection. ''Perhaps you're right.'' With that, she stood and bustled over to Jillian, then gave her a kiss on her cheek. ''If you need anything, don't you hesitate to call. There's nothing wrong with admitting that you aren't the motherly type. Your father and I love you anyway.''

Jillian walked her mother to the front door, then softly closed it behind her. ''Of course you do, Mother. But you'd love me more if I had the husband and kids.''

Why was it that her mother still had the capacity to make her feel like a failure? She was one of the most brilliant mathematicians on the east coast. She'd written two books and countless papers. She was on the verge of a major breakthrough in her Goldbach research. And just because she couldn't snag a wealthy husband and crank out a few babies, she was somehow worthless.

''Nag,'' she muttered at the closed door.

''Nag!'' Andy shouted from the depths of the house.

''Nag, nag, nag!'' Zach screamed.

Jillian giggled, then hurried back into the family room. She frowned at the boys. ''Who said that? Zach? What did you call Grandma?''

Zach pointed to Andy and Andy pointed to Sam. A sudden realization hit her, a bolt from the blue. She knew who they were! She didn't even have to look at the initials she'd redrawn on their feet. Jillian bent down and gathered the triplets up in her arms. They squealed and wriggled, but she managed to hold on to them. ''Listen to Auntie Jillie. Since Nick welshed on our bargain, I'm going to have to make a bargain with you." They all looked at her with angelic smiles and devilish eyes. Jillian took a deep breath. "No trouble today, all right? I want you to be good."

Zach nodded. "Be good," he said. He wagged a finger at his two brothers. "Be good."

Jillian sat back on her heels and watched them run off in three different directions, leaving a mess of toys scattered on the floor. If she couldn't trust a grown man like Nick Callahan to keep his promises, how was she ever supposed to trust two-and-a-half-year-old triplets?

She plopped down on the floor and leaned back against the wall. The coffee had seeped through her dress to her underwear and she just noticed she was wearing two different sandals. "Nick's desertion, my mother's visit and a ruined dress, all before 10 a.m. The day can't get much worse."

THE BOYS HAD BEEN way too quiet for way too long. Jillian had tried to keep them in the family room to limit the area of destruction, but they'd taken to running through the house, screaming like banshees. She'd attempted for the third time that day to clean up the mess, but it was impossible to collect all the Legos, Lincoln Logs, puzzle pieces and blocks before they came roaring back into the room to wreak havoc. If Greg and Roxy wanted to live in a perfectly clean house, Jillian suspected that they'd simply have to move and leave their sons behind with the mess.

They made it through lunch and nap time without any major disasters, and though she was exhausted, Jillian was starting to feel pretty proud of herself. She didn't need Nick Callahan! This mothering business wasn't that hard. In just three days, she'd nearly mastered it.

She'd learned to anticipate trouble and head it off before it blew up in her face. For lunch, she'd prepared hot dogs and sliced apples, very neat, very clean. She'd closed all the doors to the bathrooms to ward off toilet troubles and had hidden every marker and crayon the boys owned.

Jillian glanced at her watch. "Four o'clock," she murmured. "Four more hours until bedtime." And two more hours until Nick returned, she added silently. She pushed up from the floor and stumbled to the hallway where she found Zach and Andy sitting on the floor in front of the bathroom, shoving Hot Wheels beneath the door. Duke lay beside them, his nose pressed against the crack beneath the door. Jillian looked around for Sam, then called his name.

Jillian walked down the hallway and shouted up the stairs, but there was no answer. Her heart lurched and she ran to the front door, but she found it locked and secure. "Sam? Sammy, where are you?" She checked all the doors and windows, then ran upstairs and looked under every bed. But he was nowhere to be found. It wasn't like the boys to wander off. If they weren't playing together, they were usually in plain sight.

She raced back downstairs, then slid to a stop in front of the bathroom. "Where's Sammy?" she asked. "Tell Auntie Jillie where Sammy is."

Andy pointed to the bathroom door. "Sammy in there," he said.

"In the bathroom?" Jillian asked. "Sammy's in the bathroom? How did he get in there?"

Andy glanced over at Zach, then pointed to his brother. "Zach did it."

Jillian pressed her palm to her pounding heart. "How did you get that door open?" She reached out and turned the knob, but it wouldn't budge. Frowning, she gave the door a shove, then rattled the knob. Her stomach sank to her toes as she realized that the door was locked—from the inside.

"Sammy, honey, unlock the door for Auntie Jillie."

There was no sound from inside.

"Sammy, are you all right?"

Still no sound. With a groan, Jillian scrambled to find her shoes then slipped out the back door. She imagined all sorts of scenarios—Sammy unconscious from hitting his head on the toilet, Sammy munching on aspirin and guzzling cold medication, Sammy facedown in the bathtub.

The window to the bathroom was just above her reach, so she pulled a lawn chair over, shoved it through the bushes and climbed up. Through the screen she could see Sammy, sitting on the floor near the door playing with the Hot Wheels his brothers had offered up. Jillian called his name and he turned and waved at her, a wide smile on his face.

As if a ruined ceiling and torn wallpaper wasn't enough, Jillian contemplated breaking through the screen and crawling through the window. Nick could certainly fix a screen, and she had another hour or two to come up with a plausible excuse for why it had suddenly become broken. Drawing back her hand, she punched the mesh out of its frame, but the motion upset her balance and the chair beneath her wobbled.

Before she could catch herself, Jillian felt the chair tip and her body fall backwards. She had just enough time to scream before she landed hard on the ground between the bushes. Her ankle buckled beneath her and the sharp branches scraped her face. For a long moment, Jillian couldn't move. Then she heard Sammy's voice. He stood at the window, smiling at her from above.

"I—I'll get you out," Jillian called in a weak voice.

She managed to drag herself back into the house and, over the next hour, tried everything she could think of to free her nephew. She'd removed the doorknob to no effect, tried to jimmy the latch with a credit card, attempted to saw a hole in the door with Nick's tools, and finally began to pry the moulding off the door frame.

But Sammy was getting impatient and Jillian's ankle had swelled to the size of Andy's Nerf softball. When Sammy began to cry, she realized she had no choice but to call for help. She punched in the number for the fire department, then patiently explained the problem, asking that they send over a couple of discreet firemen with a short ladder. Then she limped back into the hallway to wait. But she didn't have to wait for long.

Within minutes, the sound of sirens drifted through the open window. Zach and Andy jumped up and ran to the front door, peering out through the screen. Jillian hobbled to the door and moaned. A long line of emergency vehicles snaked up the driveway. Two fire trucks, an ambulance, three police cars and the SWAT team had all turned out to witness her latest disaster, lights blazing.

A few moments later, they all hurried into the house with ropes and axes and handheld radios. Jillian explained the problem, then was shuffled aside. Within minutes, Sam was freed. Zach and Andy revelled in the excitement, falling all over the firemen and curiously examining all their equipment. Duke decided to take his guard dog duties more seriously and began an endless aria of howls and barks.

"Jillian? Jillian, where are you?"

She looked up from the chair in the family room,

where a female paramedic had insisted she sit while she wrapped Jillian's sprained ankle and tended to her cuts. Nick stood in the kitchen, dressed in a suit and tie and wearing a troubled expression. A tiny moan slipped from her throat as she stared at him and the paramedic stopped what she was doing.

"Did that hurt?" the paramedic asked.

Jillian smiled in embarrassment, then shook her head. She wanted to sink down into the chair and disappear into the upholstery. How would she ever explain the mass of emergency personnel that had descended on the house? Or the crowds of neighbors that stood on the lawn with concerned curiosity? Or the ravaged bathroom door and the broken screen? Her pride hurt worse than her ankle.

A policeman murmured a few words to Nick, then pointed to Jillian. He rushed over, then bent down and took her hand, lacing his fingers through hers. A frisson of electricity tingled through her arm. Why did it always feel so good when he touched her? She should have been angry. This mess was partially his fault for leaving her alone. But the genuine concern in his eyes banished the last trace of anger from her body and replaced it with a warm, cozy, safe feeling.

He reached up and gently touched the scratches on her face. "Are you all right? I saw the fire engines in the driveway and I—"

"I'm fine," Jillian said. "I just twisted my ankle."

The warmth of his fingers caused her heart to skip a beat and the paramedic who was now taking her pulse glanced up at her. She turned to look at Nick and then grinned at Jillian with silent understanding.

"Jillie, Jillie. What kind of trouble did you get into

now?'' His thumb brushed across her lower lip. ''It seems I can't leave you alone for a second.''

Jillian gave him a weak smile. ''It—it wasn't that bad. A simple little problem. Sam got himself locked in the bathroom and I tried to get him out. And then, things just got worse and worse and before I knew it I had another disaster on my hands.''

Gradually, the house cleared, and before long Jillian and Nick were left with just the boys for company. Nick took her arm and helped her out of the chair. She winced, the pain in her ankle much worse than it had been.

''I think you need to lie down and elevate that foot. You've had a very hard day.'' He slipped his arm around her waist, pulling her body up against his and taking some of the weight from her foot. If there was an upside to her sprained ankle it would have to be this, she mused—Nick touching her, his hands sliding over her, her body pressed to his.

''I'm just no good at this,'' Jillian murmured. ''The more practice I get, the worse I do.''

They passed the bathroom and Nick peeked inside, then frowned. ''What's the toast doing on the floor?''

Jillian turned her embarrassed face into his shoulder and groaned. ''When Sam started crying I thought he might be hungry, so I slipped him some food.''

''See,'' Nick said, touching the tip of her nose. ''You're using your instincts. I'm sure Dr. Hazelton didn't mention that in his book, did he?''

Jillian had expected to feel like a complete fool once Nick saw what she'd accomplished in his absence. But to her amazement, he was doing his best to make her feel better. She glanced up at him. ''You look very handsome in that suit. When you first walked in, I thought you might be from the FBI.''

Nick chuckled as he helped her up the stairs. "Promise me you won't do something so bad that it would bring the FBI down on us."

She paused on the stairs. "When chaos theory is at work, I can't make any promises."

With that, Nick scooped her up and carried her the rest of the way up the stairs. And when he set her gently down in bed, Jillian allowed her arms to linger for just a few moments longer, wrapped around his neck. When she drew away, her fingers brushed the hair at his nape and she fought the absurd temptation to pull him down onto the bed with her. She'd almost resolved to ask him to stay. But then he heard a scream from one of the boys and turned for the door.

"Don't go anywhere," he teased, his smile warming her blood. "I'll be back."

Jillian sank into the down pillows and sighed, pressing her palm to her chest. Her heart beat a rapid rhythm and she felt flushed all over. She wondered how long a sprained ankle took to heal. She'd never been one to malinger, but the chance to spend a little more time in Nick Callahan's arms seemed too good to pass up.

4

WHEN NICK FINALLY got back to Jillian, she was comfortably ensconced in bed, her laptop computer resting on her thighs and stacks of computer paper spread out around her. He pushed the door open with his foot and carried the tray inside. Jillian looked up and quickly took her glasses off, hiding them beneath her pillow.

"Men don't make passes at girls who wear glasses," he teased.

She blushed as Nick set the tray down next to her and sat on the edge of the bed. "The boys are already asleep and I surveyed the damage downstairs. It shouldn't take much to fix. I even found some extra wallpaper in the basement."

She chewed on her bottom lip as her expression turned serious. "I—I want to pay you. Whatever it costs. Just so Roxy and Greg don't know what happened."

"Jillian, this is a small town. I'm sure they'll hear from someone. Half the town was standing on the lawn and the other half was here with the volunteer fire department." The look of mortification on her face gave him pause. "It could have happened to anyone," he said.

A soft moan slipped from her lips. "But why does it always happen to me?" She grabbed her laptop and turned the screen toward him. "Look at this. I've been working on a computer model of my disasters. I've assigned a numerical value to each factor—time of day, severity of problem, length of predicament, cost of repairs. You'll see that things aren't getting better. They're getting worse. If the model is extended over the course of the week, I can expect to burn down the house sometime on Thursday. I may also be the cause of the first major earthquake New Hampshire has ever experienced.''

Nick held back a laugh. She looked so serious and solemn—and so incredibly sexy. Even with her scratched cheeks and her mussed hair, he fought the urge to push her computer aside and yank her into his arms. After all, they were in a bedroom and, right now, he was having some serious bedroom fantasies.

He wondered what the pulse point right below her ear might taste like. And whether the hair at the nape of her neck was as soft as the tendrils that framed her face. And whether her breasts would mold perfectly to his hands when he slipped off her cotton nightgown.

''And what if you factor me into your model?'' Nick asked, his gaze falling to her mouth. That incredibly sweet and tempting mouth, shaped like a perfect Cupid's bow.

''You?''

He could kiss her again, kiss away all her doubts and insecurities. He'd grown used to his role in the house—rescuing Jillie from her disasters, then reassuring her that she wasn't a complete failure. But words didn't seem to do the trick anymore. If he kissed her, then maybe she'd believe what a wonderful woman she was. She wouldn't have to turn to her formulas and charts and mathematical models for comfort. She'd turn to him.

But an ordinary kiss wouldn't do. This time he'd try a real kiss—long and wet and deep. A kiss that would bring a fierce blush to her cheeks and a breathless tone to her voice.

"Me," he said, letting his eyes drift along her neck to the spot at the cleft of her collarbone. "What if I help you out with the boys? How would that change things?"

She ignored his gaze and quickly typed the information into her computer, then studied the results. A slow smile curved her lips. "It would help. Look. The coefficient of disaster severity is nearly cut in half. But of course, I'll have to factor in the cost."

"I won't charge you." It wouldn't be the worst thing in the world to have Jillie Marshall indebted to him, Nick mused.

She blinked in surprise. "Oh, but I have to pay for your time. It wouldn't be fair. You have other work to do."

If accepting her money was the only way he'd get to spend more time with her, Nick wasn't going to quibble. "All right," he said. "What did we agree on? Fifty dollars an hour?"

"Forty," she said, her eyes turning suspicious.

"Right. Forty." He glanced down at the tray. "Forty dollars an hour for a jack-of-all-trades. Nanny, carpenter and general go-fer. At that rate, I probably should have spent more time on your dinner." He reached over and picked up the plate. "Grilled cheese, Tater Tots, and lime Jell-O."

"Umm, gourmet fare," she said, returning a bit of his teasing. With delicate fingers, she grabbed the sandwich and took a bite. Nick handed her a goblet. "Fine wine?" she asked.

"Fine grape juice," he replied. Watching her eat was almost as much fun as watching her try to diaper the boys. She did both with such concentrated enthusiasm that he made a mental note to provide better meals. Perhaps he could stop at one of the trendy delis in town and pick up something tasty for tomorrow night. Something suitable for eating by candlelight.

"What are you working on?" Nick said, anxious to continue the easy conversation. "I mean, besides your disaster model."

"An article on perfect numbers," Jillian said, glancing at her laptop.

"Tell me about it."

"Really?"

He nodded. She took a slow sip of grape juice while she collected her thoughts. "Perfect numbers are...well, they're perfect. A perfect number is a number whose factors add up to that number. Like six. One, two and three are factors of six, but they also add up to six."

"Is that what you study?"

"It's part of what I study. My area of expertise is number theory, which has to do with the properties of integers. Whole numbers. Like one, two, seven, thirteen."

"Were you always good at math?"

Jillian nodded, snatching up a Tater Tot and popping it into her mouth. "I was a real geek in high school. The smartest girl in the county. It didn't make me very popular with the boys."

"You've grown up," Nick murmured, mesmerized by the sound of her voice. He couldn't imagine that voice shouting over a roomful of college students or rapping out some mathematical formula. Her voice was made for more intimate encounters, soft conversations in bed and ragged moans in the throes of passion. "You must have plenty of men in your life."

Jillian smiled and leaned back into the pillows.

"When I first started working with perfect numbers, I had this silly theory that love was like a perfect number. You know, each person brings different factors into a relationship and when they all add up, they're... perfect."

"And do you still think that?"

She frowned and shook her head. "Now I think maybe love is more like an irrational number. Or a transcendental number. Like pi, it's unfathomable. And if you try to figure it out, you just go crazy."

Nick plucked a Tater Tot from her plate and considered her view on the matter. His opinion of love wasn't much different. After he'd left Claire, he'd driven himself mad trying to figure out where it had all gone wrong. "Have you ever been in love?"

She shook her head. "Not the perfect number kind of love. How about you?"

Nick considered her question for a long moment. He'd thought he was in love with Claire, but now he wasn't sure. He'd said it enough times, but looking back on it all, it seemed like another man's life. The intensity of his feelings for her had faded over the weeks they'd been apart, so much so that he hadn't thought of her in—in forty-eight hours, exactly the same amount of time he'd known Jillian Marshall. "No," he finally said. "I don't think I've ever been in love."

A long silence grew between them and Jillian focused her attention on finishing her dinner. He wanted to kiss her again, but for some reason, the time didn't seem right. Thoughts of Claire nagged at his mind. How could he have forgotten so quickly? He was supposed to have loved her! And now, all he could think about was Jillian and her sweet lips and tempting body.

"I should go," he murmured, when she'd finished her

meal. "You need your rest. You've had a very busy day." He stood up and took the tray. "I'll make breakfast tomorrow morning. Why don't you sleep in?"

"But you're not due to stay with the boys until three."

"Call it a favor. You'll have to factor favors into your computer model."

A winsome smile touched her lips and she snuggled down in the bed, tugging the comforter up to her chin. "If you were a number, you'd be a perfect number."

Nick turned and walked out of the room, balancing the tray beneath his arm as he shut the door. When he reached the solitude of the kitchen, he slid the tray onto the counter and stared out the window above the sink. The full moon glimmered gold on the black surface of the lake. He wandered over to the door and pulled it open, then stepped outside to draw a deep breath of the balmy night air.

He'd promised himself that he wouldn't jump into another relationship. He'd been burned badly by Claire and he never wanted to go through that again. A relationship with Jillian, however short and sweet, promised to be complicated. She was Roxy's sister, for one. And—and she didn't like carpenters. And—he tried to come up with another reason. She'd make a horrible mother?

Nick knew that wasn't true. Though luck hadn't been with her the past few days, he had no doubt that she'd treasure her children and make a wonderful home for them. But he just couldn't picture her children as *his* children, too.

So if he couldn't imagine a future with her, what was the attraction? Maybe it had to do with her helplessness, her vulnerability. He liked rescuing her. Claire had never needed anything from him. She had her own money, her own friends, a great job and a son she adored. That's probably why he'd been so determined to have children with her—it was the only thing he could give her that she didn't already have. Jillian, on the other hand, seemed to spontaneously combust every time he walked out of reach. She needed him.

How could such a brilliant woman have so little common sense? Nick should have found that trait irritating, but in truth he found it quite charming. He pulled the door closed behind him, then strolled down the lawn toward the lake and his cottage. When he reached the water, he turned around and looked back at the house. Her window was still illuminated and he wondered if she was working or if she was dozing off to sleep.

Nick closed his eyes and imagined himself lying next to her, touching her, inhaling her scent and listening to her soft and even breathing. He saw her kneeling before him on the bed, the hem of her nightgown bunched in his hands. Slowly, he'd pull it up, the fabric brushing along her thighs, skimming her backside and belly, rising to reveal the soft swell of her breasts. And then, he'd tug it over her head and her hair would fall loose and free around her naked shoulders.

His fingers clenched with instinctive anticipation and he allowed a long breath to slip from his lungs. Nick opened his eyes and the vision was still there, behind the lacy curtains. But then, her bedroom light went dark, startling him out of his reverie.

He cursed softly, then turned away, frustrated by the errant path of his thoughts. If this was the way he put women out of his life, then he was doing a damned poor job of running his life!

THE NEXT DAY DAWNED hot and humid. As he'd promised, Nick appeared before breakfast. After bringing her coffee in bed, he got the boys dressed and fed, then suggested they all spend the morning down at the beach. Hobbled by her sore ankle, Jillian was looking forward to the solitude. She'd been far too anxious for a few stolen moments with her nanny, caught up in disturbing fantasies that always involved a semi-naked Nick.

Later, from her spot on the family room sofa, she watched him finish cleaning up the remnants of the boys' breakfast. A morning all alone would do her some good. She had planned to spend the time with her computer on her lap and an ice pack on her ankle. But after Nick had slathered sunscreen on every body, snapped every life jacket, tugged on every beach shoe and blown up every water wing, he had scooped her up in his arms and carried her down to the water's edge, the boys racing ahead of him.

She hadn't realized that "they all" included her as well. Secretly pleased that he expected her company, she didn't bother to protest. After all, she was supposed to be in charge of the boys. She couldn't abdicate all responsibility. Nick settled her on the cushions of a chaise lounge just a few yards from the water, fetched her a glass of iced tea from his cottage, then raced into the lake with Zach, Andy and Sam. Jillian laughed as she watched the four of them splashing and shouting and jumping up and down.

At any other moment, Jillian might have considered sunning herself in a lawn chair to be the ultimate waste of time. But here, in the eighty-degree heat, her sundress clinging to her skin and her iced tea sweating in her hand, she didn't even want to think of work. Her research on the Goldbach conjecture could wait. Her paper on perfect numbers didn't need to be done for a month. Right now, she'd much rather enjoy the sight of Nick

Callahan, dressed in a pair of baggy shorts and nothing else.

The wide brim of her straw hat shadowed her face, hiding the fact that her eyes remained on Nick. He had incredibly broad shoulders and finely muscled arms, probably from carrying all that wood, she mused. His smooth chest gleamed in the sun and Jillian allowed her gaze to drift downward, following the narrow dusting of hair that began at his collarbone and ended beneath the waistband of his shorts.

She continued her survey of his physical attributes with a study of his lower body. A flat belly, narrow hips and long legs. Jillian had always believed only women could boast of attractive legs, but she'd now be forced to change that opinion. Nick Callahan had great gams.

Her mind flashed back to the moment when he'd tugged his T-shirt off, the way the muscles in his torso bunched and twisted. A silent thrill had raced through her at the notion of watching him undress. Now, as he emerged from the water like some Greek god, Jillian grabbed his T-shirt from the blanket beside her chair and stuffed it beneath her. If he wanted to cover that wonderful body, he'd have to use a towel.

Jillian sighed softly. What was this sudden obsession with the physical? Did all women go through this when they came across a stunningly handsome man? Or was she a special case? She'd just never noticed the male physique before and like a child deprived of sweets, she was now stuffing herself with candy.

The boys stayed in the shallow water and Nick kept a careful eye on the triplets, easing her mind. If she knew nothing else about Nick Callahan, she knew he could be trusted to take care of Zach, Andy and Sam. And the boys revelled in his attention. They'd made a game of

Nick grabbing each boy around the waist, tossing him up in the air a few times, then suddenly dunking him. Though they coughed and sputtered and wiped water from their eyes, they came back for more with cries of "Do again, Nick, do again!" And he was happy to oblige.

There were times, when Nick was with the boys, that she saw such childish exuberance in his face, such joy for the simple act of play. And then, she'd see him in another light, as a man, strong and sexy and completely aware of his charms. Such a contradiction, Jillian mused. A woman would never be bored by him.

The splashing stopped and Jillian watched as Nick and the boys stumbled from the water. He paused when he reached the sand and raised his arms to rake his fingers through his wet hair. Her eyes fixed on his chest, on the tiny rivulet of water that ran down his belly. Nick bent over and grabbed a stack of beach towels. He handed one to each of the boys, then took one for himself, draping it around his neck.

Jillian knew she shouldn't stare. But from beneath the brim of her hat, who would know that she'd developed a lustful nature? Or that she possessed such voyeuristic tendencies? Nick looked over at her and she quickly closed her eyes, pretending to nap.

"The water is great, Jillie," he called.

She looked at him just in time to see him rubbing the towel over his sun-streaked hair. It stood up in spikes, making him look as cute and boyish as Zach, Andy and Sam. "You should go in," he added, slowly approaching her.

"I didn't bring a suit," Jillian said, grateful that she'd managed to forget that little item. In truth, she didn't even own a bathing suit, at least not since high school swimming class. She'd never had the courage to put one on after that.

"I'm sure Roxy has one you can borrow," Nick said.

Jillian chuckled. "I don't think we want to expose the boys to the sight of me in a bathing suit. It might scar them for life."

He plopped down on the blanket beside her chair. "Why?" he asked, surprised by her comeback. "You have a great body. You'd look incredible in a bathing suit."

He said it so casually, as if it were a known fact throughout the civilized world. "Jillian Marshall" and "great body" had never appeared together in the same sentence to her recollection. She opened her mouth, ready to brush aside the compliment with a silly joke. But then she merely smiled. If Nick really thought she had a great body, who was she to disabuse him of that notion? She rather liked the thought that he considered her sexually attractive.

Nick crossed his arms over his bent legs and stared out at the water. "I don't ever want to go back to Providence," he murmured. "I'm beginning to get used to this place. An endless summer."

"Is that where you usually work?" Jillian asked. "Providence?"

Nick nodded. "My office is there, but I work on projects all over, mostly up and down the east coast."

"A lot of people must want bookshelves, huh?" Jillian said.

He glanced at her, frowning, then broke into a soft chuckle. "Yeah, lots of bookshelves just waiting to be built."

"Actually, bookshelves are a very important thing. Look at libraries, universities. I have some very nice bookshelves in my office. Where would the world be without bookshelves?''

"I never really thought about it," he said, rubbing his palm over his damp chest. "Although with the advent of the Internet, I guess my job might be obsolete before long."

Her eyes followed his every move, imagining the contours and curves of his body beneath her own hands. "Oh, I'm sure you could do something else," Jillian said, her voice cracking slightly. He glanced her way and she quickly averted her eyes, ashamed to be caught gawking.

An odd silence hung between them for a few moments, then Nick called out to the boys and they scurried over. He grabbed up a bottle of sunscreen and liberally applied it to every inch of exposed skin, then sent them on their way to build sand castles on the narrow strip of sand at the edge of the water. "You should put some of this on yourself," he suggested.

"I'm all right," Jillian replied. "What about you?" His skin was already burnished a deep shade of gold. As he leaned forward to wipe his hands on a towel, she noticed the contrast between his tanned back and the skin that peeked from beneath the waistband of his shorts. He'd obviously spent a fair amount of time outside, with his shirt off.

He sat up, then twisted to look over his shoulders. "Maybe I ought to put some on." But rather than squeeze a blob of lotion into his hand, he handed her the bottle. "Do you mind?"

Jillian swallowed hard. Had it sounded like she was looking for an invitation? "No!" she said, her voice cracking again. The bottle nearly slipped from her trembling fingers.

"No?"

"I—I mean, no, I wouldn't mind. Where would you like it?" She said a silent prayer that he didn't sunburn in intimate spots, places on his body that she wouldn't be able to touch without swooning.

"Shoulders," he said, turning his back to her.

With shaky hands, she flipped open the top and squeezed the bottle, but it had been sitting in the sun for too long and the lotion squirted out, spraying all over her hand and arm and the front of her dress. "Oh!" Jillian cried.

Nick glanced over his shoulder. "Is there a problem?"

Of course, there was a problem! She been invited to touch him, to run her palms over the taut muscles of his back, to enjoy the smooth expanse of his naked skin. And she wasn't supposed to enjoy it! Slowly, she moved her hand toward him, then with a silent oath, slapped the lotion on his back and began to rub.

At first, she moved frantically, as if desperate to finish as quickly as possible. But then, as her fingers became aware of the pleasant warmth of his skin, the hard muscle and sinew beneath, she slowed down, grazing her hands over his shoulders and memorizing the feel of him.

She couldn't remember the last time she'd touched a man the way she was touching Nick now. In the past, foreplay had always seemed so perfunctory, the touching and caressing an obligation to be performed before the actual event could take place. Perhaps she'd ignored it all out of nervousness, or the knowledge that she probably wouldn't enjoy the encounter as much as she was supposed to.

But now, as she touched Nick, every nerve in her body stood on edge. Her skin crackled with strange new sensations, like tiny electric shocks racing from her fingertips through her arms and ending somewhere deep inside her, in that place where desire had lain dormant for so long. Gently, she kneaded the muscles near his neck.

"That feels nice," he murmured.

Jillian wasn't sure what to do next. She could lean closer and let her hands slip over his shoulders to his chest. Or she could allow her fingers to drift lower on his back to his narrow waist and tempting backside. She'd never seduced a man before, never felt bold enough to try. Maybe she should just kiss him, brushing her lips along the skin below his ear. She closed her eyes and bent forward, but before she could reach her target, his voice startled her.

"Are you almost done?" he asked.

Jillian's eyes snapped open and she drew back, snatching her hands from his skin as if it had suddenly turned hot to the touch. "Yes," she murmured. "You should be fine."

The expression on his face was uneasy yet intense and, for a moment, she thought he might be angry with her. Then, he sighed softly. "I—I think I'm going to go back in for a swim." He grabbed his towel and levered to his feet, then walked away from her without looking back.

When he reached the pier, he dropped the towel. Jillian's breath caught in her throat as she caught a glimpse of the bulge in the front of his shorts. A mortified moan slipped from her lips and she pulled her sunhat lower over her eyes. Good grief, what had she done to him?

Jillian slouched down in the chair and tried to quell her humiliation. She'd just assumed that her touch wouldn't have any effect on him at all. She'd never been adept at the sexual arts. But then men did have involuntary responses to…stimulation, whether intentional or not.

She watched him swim laps from the pier to the small raft that floated a good distance out into the lake. "Oh, God," she muttered. "What must he think? I've completely embarrassed him."

Jillian thought about making her escape, but the boys were playing a few feet away in the sand, and Nick was too far away to watch them. She'd just have to stay and face him again. Perhaps if she pretended she hadn't noticed his...discomfort, everything would be all right.

"From now on, just keep your hands off him," Jillian muttered to herself. Though that vow might be hard to keep, she had no choice. Nick Callahan already believed she was a complete nitwit when it came to child care. She didn't want him thinking she was a sex-starved spinster as well.

THE SUN WAS HIGH in the sky before Nick could finally pull the boys away from the water for lunch. They'd put up such a fuss that he decided to scratch up something to eat from his refrigerator instead of heading back up to the main house. The boys usually weren't allowed to play in the cottage, so when Nick pulled the screen door open, they tumbled inside, sandy feet and all. Jillian preferred to wait on the threshold, hesitant about entering.

Since Nick's rather deflating dip in the lake, an uncomfortable silence had descended around them. Hell, his reaction had surprised him as much as his hasty retreat had surprised her. He'd always had such ironclad control around women. But the feel of her hands on his skin, the warmth of the sun and the slippery lotion, had been more than he could handle. At least he'd managed to hide the evidence of his arousal with a well-placed towel.

"Come on in," Nick murmured, snatching up rolls of

blueprints and tossing them in a corner. "Sorry about the mess."

"What are all these?" Jillian asked, limping as she entered. To his relief, she'd refused his offer of transportation across the lawn and had tested her ankle instead. If lotion application had caused such an unbidden reaction, he wasn't sure what having her in his arms might do.

"Just some plans. For a new project."

She picked up a blueprint and stared at it. The design for a new auto assembly line probably looked like Greek to her—or maybe like bookshelves, Nick mused. But when she picked up his sketch pad, he held his breath.

"What's this?" she asked, pointing to a drawing of the front facade of a house.

He'd been thinking about building another home, ridding himself of the place that he and Claire had shared. Sleeplessness the previous night had produced a few interesting ideas, in between fantasies of Jillie. This home would be different, set on a wooded lot, perhaps beside a lake, constructed of stone and natural woods with a wide porch and a spacious, but cozy interior. "Just a hobby," Nick replied. "I like to draw houses."

"This is very good. You should think about becoming an architect—you know—go back to school and study."

Nick took the sketch book from her and shoved it beneath a stack of blueprints. Though he basked in her compliment, he knew it was based on a perception of him that was less than accurate. To Jillie, he remained a simple carpenter. How could he possibly possess the talent to design a house? "Nah, I think I'm finished with school."

He really should tell her the truth. At first he'd kept his background from her on purpose, hoping to use the revelation to tweak her temper. But now his decision to hold back the truth just stood in the way. Deceiving her about who and what he was would only cause trouble in the future. She'd been completely open with him and he hadn't returned the favor.

But then, what future did they have together? He'd been to hell and back trying to come to terms with Claire's desertion. He didn't want to go through that again. And the fastest way to repeat his mistakes was to fall in love with another woman—with Jillie Marshall. It was better to let her believe he was a working-class guy, the kind of man she could never love. His little lie could be used to his advantage, to protect his heart from more hurt. For if Jillie had any lustful fantasies the reality of his professional prospects would make her quickly push them aside.

"Sit down," he said, shoving the rest of the blueprints off the table.

She did as she was told, perching on the edge of her chair and folding her hands in front of her. It felt so odd to have her here, in his temporary home. He'd imagined her here a number of times, when he'd lain in bed and let his mind wander. He'd pictured her sitting across a candlelit table from him, seen her slow dancing barefoot with him on the porch. And he'd also imagined her lying on his bed, wrapped in his embrace, her naked body pressed against his.

Nick turned away from the table and began to busy himself with lunch preparations. Why couldn't he stop fantasizing about her? Every shred of common sense told him Jillie wasn't his type—and he certainly wasn't hers. Hell, Claire *had* been his type and look at what happened to them. Falling for Jillie Marshall was a one-way ticket to heartbreak.

"Can I help?" she asked.

"I think I have everything under control. How about SpaghettiOs and hot dogs?"

"You have SpaghettiOs?"

Nick smiled. "I've always considered them one of the major food groups. A boon to bachelors everywhere." He held up the can. "Nutritious and great-tasting. Plus they only take a minute to heat up in the microwave."

"You need a wife," Jillie teased.

Nick knew she'd meant it as a joke, but when his eyes met hers, he couldn't keep himself from speaking. "Are you volunteering?" A deep blush stained her cheeks and he instantly regretted provoking her.

"You wouldn't want me as a wife," she said. "I'm a terrible housekeeper, I don't cook very well and I put my work before everything else. And you've certainly been witness to my skill with children."

Her words should have confirmed his feelings, that Jillie wasn't his type. But instead, he found himself even more attracted to her, to her plain-spoken honesty, to her ability to recognize her flaws and face them. "I think any man would be lucky to find a woman like you."

She smiled uneasily, then glanced around the room. "Don't you think it's a little quiet?" She pushed to her feet and when he moved to help her, she waved him off. "I'll go find the boys. I don't want disaster to strike your house, too."

She limped across the tiny living room and peeked inside the bedroom door. A few moments later, the boys came running out, smelling of Nick's cologne. Jillie appeared hard on their heels, the empty bottle clutched in her hand. "Disaster on a small scale," she said. "They dumped this all over your bed. It's so strong in there, it'll make your eyes water."

"No problem," he said. "I've been sleeping on the screened porch lately. In the hammock. I like listening to the sound of the water and the night birds."

"Maybe if we drag the bed outside and air it out, the smell will—"

"Don't worry about it," Nick said with a shake of his head. "If it doesn't go away, I'll buy Greg and Roxy a new bed. This wasn't your disaster."

Jillie took her place at the table, keeping one eye on the boys, who were hitting each other with rolled-up blueprints.

"How's your ankle feeling?" he asked.

She held out her leg, turning it from side to side. "It's feeling better, but it's still a little swollen. It doesn't hurt too much when I walk. By tomorrow I should be back to normal."

He took a moment to admire the trim curve of her calf and her pretty ankle, before turning back to the SpaghettiOs. He'd grown so used to having her near that he'd begun to look forward to any situation that might put them together. Baby-sitting the boys was just a convenient excuse. But what would happen when Greg and Roxy returned? Would she just walk away, never to see him again?

Nothing in her manner gave him a clue as to how she regarded him. Even when he'd kissed her, he'd been met with an uneasy silence. He was tempted to kiss her again, right here and now. They'd grown closer since that night in her bedroom, yet it was becoming harder and harder to make a move, more difficult to predict her reaction.

Why? Was it because now there might be some real desire behind his kiss? Or was he just afraid? Hell, he wasn't sure what he wanted. Rejection would be impossible to handle, yet capitulation would be even worse.

Perhaps it would be more sensible to stop thinking about kissing Jillian Marshall altogether.

When lunch was ready, Nick gathered the boys and set their bowls on the plank floor of the porch. He and Jillie grabbed a pair of wicker chairs and sat down to iced tea and ham sandwiches. "I was thinking, if your ankle is better by tomorrow, we could take the boys into town. The volunteer fire department is having their picnic this weekend and they have pony rides and cotton candy and clowns."

Jillie smiled. "That would be nice." She took a tiny bite of her sandwich, then set it down. "I want to thank you again for helping me with the boys. I don't know what I would have done if you hadn't been here. I can't chase them down with this bad ankle."

He leaned back in his chair. "Why were you so determined to take care of them?" Nick asked. "It's hard enough for Roxy and you haven't had any experience with kids."

"That's why I volunteered," Jillie said. "Because I wanted to see what it was like."

"Why? Are you thinking of adopting triplets? If you are, I'd seriously question your sanity."

Jillie paused. "Actually, I have wondered what it would be like to be a mother. But after this week, I think it's pretty clear that I should put it out of my mind."

"I wouldn't use this week as an example. Most women don't have to care for three. Three boys are even worse. I grew up in a family of ten and we didn't enjoy as many disasters in an entire year as you've had this week. It just takes—"

"Organization?" she asked, a grin curling the corners of her mouth.

Nick laughed. "Yeah. Organization."

Slowly, the easygoing banter between them returned and the morning's events were forgotten. But Nick knew his desire for Jillie Marshall lurked just below the surface. All it would take was another touch, an inadvertent caress, and he'd be faced once again with the inevitable proof that when it came to Jillie, he wasn't sure where friendship ended and passion began.

5

BY THE NEXT DAY, Jillian's ankle felt almost normal. The scratches on her face had faded and Nick was hard at work fixing the window and the ceiling of the downstairs bathroom. Had Roxy and Greg walked in that evening, they'd have believed that everything had run smoothly during their time away.

Only she and Nick knew differently. And maybe the boys, although they wouldn't be doing any talking. She planned to brainwash them with as many pony rides as possible at the Firemen's Picnic so the experience would be the only thing they'd talk about for days. Nick had promised he'd finish up after lunch so they could all head into the village for the festivities.

She wiped her hands on a dish towel, then followed the sound of a power drill as she went to find Nick. But she was stopped by the ring of the phone. She grabbed the receiver before the boys noticed a second ring, then froze when she heard her sister's voice.

"Roxy! I didn't expect you to call again," Jillian said.

"It's been four days. Is everything all right? I've just had these strange feelings, like something was wrong."

Jillian put on a light-hearted tone. "I told you I'd call if anything went wrong. I didn't call, did I?"

A long silence travelled over the phone lines from Hawaii. "Are you sure? I mean, you haven't had any experience with babies," Roxy said. "Things can't be going that well. There must be at least a few problems. What about Zach's allergies? And Andy had that scrape on his knee. That's not infected is it? And Sammy can never sleep when it's windy."

Jillian detected the desperate edge in Roxy's voice. Her sister wanted to know that she was irreplaceable, that no one could take care of the boys as well as she could. Guilt niggled at Jillian's mind and she considered telling her the whole truth—that the past five days had been one disaster after another, punctuated only by interludes of lusting after the family carpenter.

But then, knowing Roxy, she and Greg would be on the next plane home if she told the truth. Maybe it would be best to soften it just a bit. "Well, I did slip and fall while I was playing with the boys," she said. "I twisted my ankle. But I'm fine. The boys are fine. Here, I'll let you talk to them."

Jillian called the boys from the family room where they'd been watching *Sesame Street.* Zach grabbed the phone first and began to babble to his mother. Jillian sat on a stool and listened distractedly as she sipped her coffee.

"Jillie fall down," Zach said. "Jillie have owwee."

She set her cup of coffee on the counter where it sloshed over the side, then pried the phone out of Zach's hand. "Roxy, I'll put Andy on now."

Andy grabbed the phone and laughed as he listened to his mother's voice on the other end. Then he went silent for a moment. "Jillie fall down," he said. "Fire truck. Fire truck!"

Jillian took the phone again and pushed it into Sammy's hand. At least she could trust Sammy not to talk. He just listened to his mother, nodding and saying "Uh-huh." When he finally handed the phone back to

Jillian, she figured her secrets were still safe. The boys ran back into the family room and she prepared for damage control with her sister.

"Jillie, what happened?" Roxy demanded. "Andy was talking about fire trucks."

Jillian cleared her throat. "Yes. I—I tripped over his little toy fire truck."

"The boys don't have a fire truck," Roxy said.

"They didn't," Jillian said, her voice cracking slightly, "until I bought them one. Tell me, how is Hawaii? Are you having fun?"

"Sure, sure," Roxy said. "Palm trees, white sand beaches, flowers everywhere. It's a damned paradise. I miss my boys. I want to come home."

"Don't be silly," Jillian said. "We're all getting along so well. In fact, we were about to go down to the Firemen's Picnic in town. Nick says they have pony rides."

"Nick? Nick Callahan?" Jillian could almost see the sly smile curling the corners of Roxy's mouth. "So, how is Nick?"

At that very moment, the man in question strolled into the kitchen, shirtless, his jeans and his tool belt hanging low on his hips. He smiled at her, then moved to the sink to get a glass of water.

"He—he's been great with the boys," Jillian said distractedly, admiring the smooth expanse of his shoulders, the fascinating curve of his back. "And he's a wonderful carpenter. Your bookshelves are looking just…fine. Everything's just fine."

"So what do you think of Nick?" Roxy asked. "You know he's not just a—"

"Roxy, I've got to go," Jillian said, unwilling to discuss Nick Callahan's particular attributes in front of the man himself. She wasn't sure she'd be able to hide her true feelings about him, or keep her voice from trembling. "We'll discuss this when you get home. I've got to get the boys ready for the picnic. Bye-bye. See you soon." She hung the phone up, then sank down onto a stool and drew a shaky breath.

Nick watched her from over the rim of his water glass. "How's Roxy?" he asked.

"Fine," Jillian replied.

Nick nodded. "Did you tell her about the water problem? And the twisted ankle? And the—"

"Of course, I did," Jillian lied with a weak smile. "Right before you walked in."

He chuckled. "So when does her plane come in? Should we leave for the airport now or do we have time for lunch?"

Jillian couldn't help but laugh at his gentle teasing. "All right, so maybe I didn't tell her everything. She'll find out soon enough. There's no need to ruin a perfectly lovely vacation."

He sent her a smile so charming that she wondered if she'd be able to stand upright again.

"Are you ready to go?" he asked.

She nodded. "Are you planning to go like that?" Her gaze drifted down his body and her fingers twitched as she thought about touching him. The feel of his warm skin still lingered on her fingertips and, standing so still, his hip cocked against the edge of the counter, he looked like he'd been sculpted by Michelangelo, muscle carved from fine marble.

"I'm going to run down to the cottage and take a quick shower," he said, interrupting her little fantasy. "I'll be back by the time you have the boys' shoes on."

Jillian grabbed the damp dishtowel and tossed it at him as he walked to the back door. Determined to prove him wrong, she rounded up the boys, lined them up on the sofa and pushed their shoes on, one after another. Then she went back down the line and tied the laces. "See. It's just a matter of organization," she murmured, her hands braced on her hips. "Time for pony rides!"

Andy looked up at her and frowned. "No ponies in van," he said.

"Ponies go *nnnnneeeeeeaaaay,*" Zach shouted.

"I kiss ponies," Sammy said.

Jillian smiled. "No ponies in van. We're going to ride on top of the ponies, not drive them around in the van. And as for kissing the ponies, we'll have to see about that, Sammy. Now let's go. We don't want to keep Nick waiting."

The boys jumped down and ran to the front door. Grabbing her sun hat, Jillian followed after them. They only waited outside for a few minutes, before Nick appeared from around the corner of the house. His hair was damp and he wore a fresh T-shirt and clean jeans. Jillian couldn't help but think, dressed as he was, he was the handsomest man she'd ever met.

He grabbed Sammy and swung him up on his shoulders. Zach and Andy climbed into the wagon and they set off on the short walk toward town. The tiny village of Dunsboro was only a mile down the road, set on a serene inlet of the lake. The boys were so filled with excitement that Jillian couldn't help but be caught up in it as well. That is, until she recognized some of the firemen who had rescued Sammy from the bathroom. She expected some joking and teasing, but to her surprise, the volunteer firemen considered her emergency the most excitement they'd had since Ed Ridley's horse got loose in the town square.

Nick and Jillian strolled through the arcade, observing

the games and trying to keep the boys from running off.
There were pennies to throw into goldfish bowls and
balloons to pop with darts. There was even a sledgehammer challenge with a weight that flew up a pole and
measured masculine strength in terms of "Mama's
Boy," "Girly Man" and "Hercules."

A volunteer fireman she didn't recognize lured them
over with a colorful pitch and a wave of his hand.
"Come on, lad. Show your little wife the limits of your
strength. Hit the bell and win a teddy bear."

Jillian opened her mouth to correct his mistake but
Nick stepped up to accept the challenge. He plucked
Sammy off his shoulders and handed him to Jillian. With
a playful grin, he spit on his two palms and rubbed them
together, then offered his palms to each of the boys so
they might participate with a good spit of their own.

They all watched Nick heft the sledgehammer over his
shoulder. And then with one smooth motion, he brought
it down on the anvil. The ball rose like a rocket and
struck the bell and the boys squealed in delight. Nick
paid four times and each time, he hit the bell. In the end,
he presented them each with a tiny stuffed bear.

"You've got quite a husband there," the fireman
called, slapping him on the back.

"He's not my husband," Jillian said.

The fireman looked at the boys, then back up at her,
a questioning arch to his eyebrow.

"And they're not my children," she added.

"You're not the little lady staying out at the Hunter
house, are you? My goodness, I heard all about your
little emergency. Sorry I couldn't respond, but me and
the missus was over in Nashua visiting her sister. Heard
it was quite the to-do."

Jillian politely listened to a recap of her "emergency,'' before Nick found a way to excuse them. But again and again, as they walked through the amusements at the picnic, people either assumed she and Nick and the boys were a family or they knew the truth and had heard about her disaster at the lake house. She couldn't seem to escape embarrassment, no matter which way she turned.

But oddly, she didn't feel the need to defend herself or to retreat behind the facade of the esteemed Professor Jillian Marshall. Perhaps it was because Nick was holding her hand, giving her confidence. Or maybe she was beginning to "roll with the punches." There were even times when she laughed along with the stories, finding her actions genuinely amusing.

After three hours at the picnic, they started for home. The boys, filled with cotton candy and corn dogs, were placed in the wagon where they dozed, a tangle of arms and legs and sticky faces.

Jillian and Nick walked along the road, hand in hand, commenting on the flora and fauna they passed and enjoying the late afternoon sunshine, dappled by the trees overhead.

The air buzzed with insects and birdsong filled the woods. Though Jillian's ankle ached, she barely noticed. Instead, she enjoyed the perfection of the afternoon, the easy camaraderie that had developed between Nick and her, the feel of her fingers laced through his.

It was no wonder people assumed they were married. She'd even caught herself pretending they were a couple a few times during the afternoon. It wasn't hard, with Nick treating them all to games and food, gathering up the boys like a watchful father and inquiring about her comfort like a doting husband.

She'd seen so many sides of Nick over the past few

days. The carpenter who competently cleaned up after her disasters, the father figure who looked after the boys, the sexy male who piqued her passion and the boy inside the man who played with her nephews in the lake. And now, she saw him as he might be—as a husband.

How strange that her little list of criteria for a mate now seemed utterly ridiculous. She'd always thought she'd have the power to choose the man she'd fall in love with. But it had become obvious to her that she had no more control over her feelings than she had over the rising of the sun and movements of the moon.

She was falling for Nick Callahan and there was nothing she could do about it.

JILLIAN SAT at the long table in the mahogany-panelled conference room at the Institute. She was dressed in a tailored suit and a silk blouse, her typical wardrobe for work. Yet, she felt oddly uncomfortable. She fought the urge to kick off her shoes and wiggle her toes, to unfasten the buttons of her blouse and free herself from the tight collar.

She'd been summoned back to Boston by a phone message, left for her while she and Nick and the boys had been at the picnic. At first she'd thought about ignoring the message, but then her professional ethics overruled her initial reaction. Nick had graciously offered to watch Zach, Andy and Sam, but Jillian had adamantly refused and called her mother instead.

She glanced at her watch and wondered what the boys were doing at home. It was just about nap time and Sylvia had probably put them to bed. Nick was no doubt busy in the library. Or perhaps he was fixing the evidence of her disasters.

As soon as the interview was over, she'd find a phone

and call home, just to check on everything. Though she'd learned to expect the unexpected from Zach, Andy and Sam, her mother hadn't a clue as to what the boys were capable of. Jillian smiled, thinking back to the sticky kisses the boys had pressed on her cheek that morning. The thought that they missed her, even a little bit, warmed her heart. She also imagined that someone else in the house might notice her absence. Would Nick think of her while she was gone?

She'd certainly thought about him more than a few times over the past hours. On the drive down to Boston, she'd been caught up in a careful review of their time together, from the moment she'd hit him on the head with the xylophone to the quick kiss she'd brushed across his cheek before he'd returned to the cottage the night before.

She now listened with only halfhearted interest as the chairman of the Committee for Academic Excellence droned on and on about the merits of an association with the institute. The entire committee was there, dressed in their very best suits, determined to impress Dr. Richard Jarrett. Jarrett, a well-known physicist, had expressed an interest in a faculty position at the New England Institute of Technology and had promised to bring considerable research money with him. The committee had convened to discuss the possibility of a tenured professorship and to interview the candidate.

As Jillian listened to the committee's questions and the physicist's answers, she realized how quiet the room was. Besides the soft-spoken voices, the only thing she could hear was the whir of a ceiling fan. She'd grown so used to the chatter of childish voices that she almost missed it.

In truth, Jillian should have been captivated by this

entire process. Here was a man that fit all her criteria for a husband. Richard Jarrett was relatively attractive, although not nearly as handsome as Nick Callahan. She scanned his curriculum vitae, noting the long list of publications and awards. He was obviously brilliant and with a teaching position at NEIT, he'd be close at hand.

Jillian groaned inwardly. So why did she find him so incredibly boring? Why did she find this entire meeting excruciatingly dull? Everyone in the room seemed to operate in slow mode, their questions carefully worded, their answers deliberate. She'd been operating at such a high speed lately that her co-workers, men and women she admired, now appeared almost lifeless.

"Dr. Marshall?"

Yanked out of her thoughts, she looked up. "Yes?"

"Do you have any questions for Dr. Jarrett?"

"Ah...no," Jillian said. "Actually, all my questions have been answered. Thank you...sir."

The chancellor frowned at her for a moment, then went back to his agenda. Jillian felt a trace of embarrassment. She probably should have asked something, just to appear interested. But it was patently clear that Richard Jarrett was eminently qualified and anyone who didn't think so didn't have a bit of sense. The interview was simply a formality and had she been in charge, she might have stood up and adjourned the meeting.

A few minutes later, the chancellor did just that. Jillian got out of her seat, but rather than join the group gathering around Dr. Jarrett, she wandered to the door, hoping to sneak back to her office and call her mother. But the chancellor caught her eye and before she could make her escape, she found herself cornered.

Dr. Leon Fleming's ruddy cheeks were flushed with excitement. "Well, Dr. Marshall, what do you think? A fine addition to our staff. No doubt about it. Now we just need to hope he accepts our offer."

Without giving her a chance to render her own glowing recommendation, he drew her aside and spoke in a hushed tone. "Dr. Marshall, the committee would like to ask a favor of you. Dr. Jarrett is staying the night in Boston and, as he's unfamiliar with the city, we'd like you to show him around, take him out to a nice restaurant, maybe for a stroll along the Charles."

Jillian forced a smile and tried to appear grateful that she'd been chosen for such an important task. "I—I'm afraid I can't, Dr. Fleming. I've got…family responsibilities."

"Family?" the chancellor asked. "I don't understand. I didn't think you had a family."

"Oh, I don't," Jillian replied. "It's just that I'm taking care of my nephews for a few days while their parents are away and they're quite a handful. I really don't like leaving them with someone else."

"I'm sure they'll be fine. They won't even realize you're gone." He cleared his throat. "I don't think you understand how important this is to the committee, Dr. Marshall."

"Why don't you send someone else? Dr. Wentland is much more familiar with the city than I am. And he and Dr. Jarrett are both graduates of Stanford. Or Dr. Symanski. She's quite a gourmet. I'm sure she'd choose a wonderful restaurant."

"But we all think you would be the better choice," Dr. Fleming insisted.

Realization slowly dawned as her gaze flitted amongst the members of the committee. She was the better choice because she was a young, relatively attractive, single woman! Good grief, wasn't this against some institute policy? Using her as bait to lure in a hot physicist with loads of research money? Jillian weighed her options. Refusing the request would probably result in her being dropped from the prestigious committee. But then, she never really wanted to serve in the first place.

Still, what harm could it do to take Dr. Jarrett to dinner? On any other day, she'd be thrilled to spend time talking research work and grant proposals and Nobel prizes. "All right," she said. "But it will have to be an early evening. I've got a long drive back to New Hampshire."

The chancellor grinned and gave her hand a squeeze. "Now, I've heard that Dr. Jarrett is quite the ladies' man. I expect you to keep things strictly business. Try to pump him for information about his time at Oxford. I'd like to know the real reason he decided to leave, not the reason Oxford is peddling."

"I'll do my best, sir. Now, if you don't mind, I really should call and make sure the baby-sitter can stay with the boys."

"You do that," the chancellor said.

Jillian glanced over at Dr. Jarrett and he looked up at that very second and sent her a warm smile. Her heart should have skipped a beat, but instead, it sank. This promised to be a very long evening, an evening that could have been spent with Nick and the boys.

She found a pay phone just outside the meeting room and Jillian quickly dialed the lake house. Her mother answered on the third ring. She expected to hear chaos in the background, but the line was silent. "Mother, it's Jillian. How's everything going?"

"Oh, everything is just fine, dear. I'm just having a cup of tea."

"And the boys?"

"They're with your friend, Nick. He's got them in the library."

Jillian sighed. "Mother, you really shouldn't let them play around in there while he's working. He has to finish those bookshelves for Greg and Roxy before they get back."

"He's not working, dear. He's reading to them. They've been so quiet, like little angels." She lowered her voice. "Your friend is such a nice man, Jillie. So kind and patient with the boys. You'd never guess that he didn't have children of his own. Or that he's not even married."

"And how do you know that mother? Did you interrogate him?"

"We ate lunch together. I made him chicken salad with roasted pecans and grapes. He was very appreciative. And he's got wonderful table manners."

Jillian groaned. The last thing she needed was her nosy mother pumping Nick for information——or trotting out all of Jillian's personal and professional accomplishments for a potential husband, which she could just imagine her doing. "The reason I'm calling is that I need you to stay a little longer. I've got to take Dr. Jarrett out to dinner and show him the city."

"Dr. Jarrett? Is he single? Handsome? Rich?"

"He's not married, marginally attractive and we're not close enough yet for me to ask to see his stock portfolio."

Sylvia sighed. "Oh, dear, I can't stay. Even though I'd love to give you and Dr. Jarrett an evening to yourselves, Daddy and I have plans at the club. But I'm sure Mr. Callahan would agree to watch the boys. Here, I'll let you talk to him."

"Mother, no, I can't——"

"Jillie?"

She drew a ragged breath. An image of Nick flashed in her mind. He was probably dressed in his jeans and a T-shirt. And his hair was probably mussed from rolling around on the floor with the boys. She could picture his smile, the easy way he moved. "Nick. Hi, how are things going?"

"No problems. When are you coming home?"

"Actually, that's why I was calling. I'm going to be late. I have to go to dinner with Dr. Jarrett. Hopefully, I'll be back by nine or ten. Mother can't stay. I hate to ask you but—"

"Sure," he said. "We'll be fine."

"Roxy would probably have a fit that I asked you. You signed up to build bookshelves, not to ride herd on the boys. But I trust you and you're so good with them and I can't get out of this dinner date."

"Date?" he asked.

Jillian sucked in a sharp breath. "Not exactly a date."

"You're going with a group?"

"No," she said. "Just me and...him. But it's not a date. It's strictly professional."

"He's bringing his wife?"

"He doesn't have a wife," Jillian said.

Her statement was met with a long silence. Was he angry? Or just curious? Jillian couldn't gauge his mood over the phone, but she couldn't imagine that he'd be jealous. "Nick?"

"I'll see you when you get home. Have a good time, Jillian."

She slowly hung up the phone, letting her hand linger on the receiver as she tried to figure out what had just happened between them. He'd called her Jillian. To her memory, he only called her that when he was angry or frustrated. Lately, it had been the more informal "Jillie."

"Well, Professor Marshall, I understand we're going to dinner. Are you ready?"

Jillian jumped slightly as Richard Jarrett touched her shoulder, then she turned and forced a smile. She tried to summon some enthusiasm for spending an evening in such illustrious company. But in truth, she'd much rather choose a root canal over an endless evening with Dr. Jarrett. Jillian grabbed her purse. Maybe it wouldn't be so bad, she mused. He might even turn out to be a nice guy.

Twenty minutes later, after a quick stop at her nearby apartment to change, they were comfortably seated at a trendy restaurant just off Kendall Square. The waiter hovered over them as he explained the evening's specials and, though Jillian insisted she didn't care for wine, Jarrett ordered a bottle anyway. She soon found out that his lengthy perusal of the wine list was only to show what good taste and exacting knowledge he possessed. She tried to pay attention as he catalogued the qualities of every single wine the restaurant offered. But instead, she busied herself with pulling a dinner roll into tiny bits.

"Wine is a great passion of mine," Jarrett said. "I just bought a case of '90 Chateau Margaux at an auction that is simply marvelous. At $5000 a case, it should be. You must share a bottle with me sometime. It has a deep plum color with an exquisite bouquet. Aromas of roses, cherries and blackberries. Opulent, full-bodied and harmonious. A very nice structure. The first time I tasted it, I knew I had to have it." He reached over and covered her hand with his. "And when I see something I want, I go after it."

Jillian pulled her hand away and tried to steer the conversation toward more innocuous subjects, like the weather. But Jarrett continued his monologue and somewhere around the time he began talking about the silky texture of his favorite wine, Jillian's mind began to drift away from the droning one-sided conversation and back to the lake house. She glanced at her watch and noticed it was about time to put the boys to bed.

After just a few short days, she'd grown accustomed to the ritual and actually believed she might be getting more efficient with the drill—wrestling the boys into their pajamas, gathering them all on Sammy's bed for stories, then tucking them each into their own beds with a kiss goodnight. Suddenly she longed for those chubby little arms around her neck, for the sweet smell of their bodies after their baths, for their silly, fractured sentences.

How easy it was to love them, Jillian mused. Even through all the trouble, she couldn't stop caring. The disasters had all been her fault, due entirely to her lack of preparedness. She had already learned to anticipate problems at mealtime and playtime. And though chaos theory could never be completely discounted, she was beginning to understand the conditions that created chaos—open doors, messy food, available art supplies and little boys with too much energy.

Jillian smiled to herself, then let her mind drift to Nick, to the moments after the boys went to sleep, when she'd wander downstairs and hope to find him waiting for her. It had never really happened that way, except in her imagination. She imagined him waiting now, wondering when she'd get home, ready to yank her into his arms and kiss her "hello."

Had the cool tone of his voice really indicated jealousy? Perhaps he'd just been maintaining an indifferent attitude toward her because her mother had been standing right there. "That's it," Jillian murmured to herself.

"I thought so, too," Jarrett said. "Three hundred dollars a bottle was my top price for that Bordeaux."

Jillian groaned inwardly and willed the waiter to hurry with the entrées. The sooner she got out of this restaurant, the sooner she'd be on her way back to Nick and the boys. She wondered about the reception she'd receive when she got home, wondered how Nick really felt about her "date."

Only a lovesick fool would be jealous of a dinner with the esteemed but pompous Dr. Richard Jarrett. And if Jillian knew one thing about Nick Callahan it was that he was no lovesick fool.

SOMEWHERE, DEEP in the house, a clock chimed midnight. Nick set his level down and stepped back from the shelf he'd been hanging. Every hour on the hour, the clock reminded him that Jillie was out with another man, sharing an intimate dinner, perhaps dancing—and God only knew what else.

Nick cursed beneath his breath. Hell, by this late in the evening, they could have hopped into bed as well! He shouldn't have felt anything at the prospect of Jillian Marshall with another man. He'd already written her off as a woman wholly unsuitable to his tastes. Yet even the mere consideration of her kissing this—this Dr. Jarrett caused his gut to twist and his temper to flare.

He raked his hands through his hair, brushing out the sawdust. This was his fault! He should have refused to baby-sit for the boys—then she would have had to come home directly after her meeting. He thought he'd been doing her a favor, for professional reasons. But after he'd hung up, Sylvia Marshall had informed him, with great relish it had seemed, that Dr. Jarrett was just the type of man Jillie found attractive—a brilliant scientist, who just happened to be single and handsome.

Nick stepped away from the bookshelves that now lined an entire wall of the library. He'd thought to do the project slowly, but in his anger, he'd been working for nearly four hours without pause. At this rate, if he stayed angry with Jillie, he'd have the project finished sometime tomorrow morning.

Wiping his hands on his jeans, Nick headed for the door. He'd check on the boys, then get himself a beer before he finished installing the crown moulding along the top of the cases.

He walked silently up the stairs. Jillie couldn't stay away the entire night. Not without calling. He mentally calculated the time it took to drive from Boston to the lake house—two hours by his count. Dinner with a business associate shouldn't last any longer than nine o'clock. That meant she was already an hour into something much more than pure business.

When Nick reached the bedroom, he found the boys sound asleep, curled into impossible positions, their faces sweet and innocent, their breathing even. Outside, the distant rumble of thunder signalled an approaching storm. His thoughts went immediately to Jillie, wondering if she was driving home in the dark, on the winding road that led to the lake. Driving would be more dangerous with a storm upon her.

He bit back an oath, resolving to put Jillie and her safety out of his mind. She was adult. She could make her own choices. And if those choices included an affair with Dr. Jarrett, so be it.

Nick carefully covered each boy with the light blankets they'd managed to kick off, then tiptoed to the door.

Watching Zach, Andy and Sam sleep brought a stark realization to his mind. He had no right to worry. These were not his children, no matter how much he wished they were.

And Jillie Marshall was not his wife. He had no claim on anyone in the house. And no reason to be angry with Jillie.

He took the stairs slowly, and when he was nearly to the bottom, he looked up to see the front door quietly swing open. Nick froze, standing in the shadows that kept the stairs in near darkness. By the feeble light from the porch, he could see that she'd changed out of her prim suit and into a form-fitting black dress with a scooped neck and short sleeves. Her hair, which had earlier been pulled back into a neat knot was now loose and falling in soft waves around her shoulders.

He wasn't surprised by her beauty, though the dress and her hair did take his breath away. The woman he saw entering the house was not the Jillie Marshall that he'd come to know. This woman was almost a stranger, aware of her beauty and willing to use it to her advantage.

"I bet that dress wowed them at the institute," he said.

The sound of his voice coming out of the darkness startled her and she jumped, then pressed her hand to her chest. "Nick?" Jillie squinted up the stairs as she stepped nearer. "What are you doing?"

He slowly descended the last five stairs, emerging from the shadows to stand in front of her. "I could ask you the same. It's past midnight. Awfully late for a business dinner, isn't it?"

Jillie gave him an uneasy look, confusion mixed with an apologetic smile. "It did go on a lot longer than I thought it would. I almost decided to stay in the city, but then I knew you were here alone with the boys. I figured you'd want me to come home."

"This isn't your home," Nick said, his voice cold and dispassionate. "And why should I care whether you spend the night here or at your place in Boston? Or even in a hotel room with some stranger you just met?"

Jillie gasped. "What? Some stranger? What are you talking about?"

Nick brushed by her and stalked back to the library, ready to pick up where he had left off. But Jillie wasn't about to let his comment go by without a response. She hurried after him, tossing her purse onto a hallway table as she passed.

When she reached the library, she braced her hands on her hips and glared at him. "Are you angry that I stayed out so late?"

"I didn't say I was angry."

"Then why won't you look at me?"

Nick glanced up at Jillie to find her expression filled with apprehension. But it didn't dilute his anger. Damn, she was so beautiful and so vulnerable. Yet she was also a woman and, right now, he wasn't sure he could trust his feelings about any woman, especially Jillie. "Did you enjoy your dinner?" he asked, his words sharp and biting.

She blinked, unnerved by his tone. "Not really. I found Dr. Jarrett egotistical, self-aggrandizing and boorish."

"Did you kiss him?"

A faint blush worked its way up her cheeks and her gaze darted to her feet, then back up again. "Kiss him? No, not exactly."

"Ah, here we go. This wasn't exactly a date. And he didn't exactly have a wife. Come on, Jillie, you're a mathematician.What can you tell me that might be exact?''

She narrowed her eyes, apprehension slowly replaced by indignation. ''All right. He kissed me. It lasted exactly 3.8 seconds, he used exactly this much of his tongue—'' she held out her fingers to demonstrate ''—and on a scale of one to ten, I felt exactly zero attraction to Dr. Jarrett.'' She paused. ''But why should that make a difference to you?''

Nick stared at her for a long moment, his anger subsiding with every passing second. And then, without thought, he crossed the room in three easy strides and yanked her into his arms. His mouth came down on hers, first punishing, then probing and then sinking into pleasure. This was more than just a kiss. It was an end—and a beginning. An end to the little dance they'd been doing since the night they'd met. And the beginning of something real and passionate between them.

He pulled back and look down into her flushed face. With his thumb, he slowly traced the remains of the scratches on her pale complexion, then moved to touch her bottom lip, still damp from his kiss. ''It makes a difference,'' he murmured before kissing her again.

But this time the kiss didn't last for long. With a soft cry, Jillie pulled away, squirming out of his embrace until she stood a safe distance away. ''What are you doing?''

''I thought it was obvious,'' he said with a satisfied grin. ''Would you like me to do it again, just to clear up any confusion?''

''Stop it!'' she snapped. ''You—you just can't kiss me and expect me to forgive you.''

''You're the one who stayed out late, wining and dining another man.''

"And you're the one who was angry! You have no right to be angry. And certainly no right to kiss me."

"I didn't hear you complaining," Nick said, sauntering toward her.

"It's a little hard to talk when you're—when you—when I—"

His arm snaked around her waist and he pulled her hips to his. Then he bent lower, until his lips were just inches from hers. "I think we've said everything that needs to be said. At least I have."

"Then let me go." Her gaze met his, defiantly, daring him to try again and warning him that he'd be rebuffed. But Nick wasn't about to give her the last word. He waited, his breath soft on her lips, his eyes scanning her face. Then he suddenly let go of her and stepped away, glancing around the room.

"I think I'm done here," he said.

With that, Nick slowly walked from the room. He smiled to himself as he heard her moan of frustration. Hell, he didn't care what she thought of him. One kiss was all it had taken to change the stakes between them. And whether she wanted a man with a Nobel prize or an Einstein IQ, Jillie Marshall was about to find herself caught up in an affair with a lowly carpenter. Because, if Nick had anything to say about it, there would be more to this than just one or two passionate kisses.

Maybe they didn't have a future together, but that didn't mean they couldn't have a present. He wanted Jillie Marshall more that he had ever wanted a woman in his life. He wanted to kiss her whenever the mood struck, draw her into his arms on a whim.

And he wasn't going to let the chance to have her pass

him by. From now on, the gloves were off. There was going to be so much more between them—just as soon as Jillie faced the fact that she wanted him as much as he wanted her.

6

JILLIAN STOOD in the middle of the library, stunned into both silence and immobility. Her breath had caught in her throat when he'd kissed her and she wasn't sure that she had drawn another breath since. Slowly, she raised her fingers to her lips. "Oh, my," she sighed, her heart pounding in her chest, her mind spinning.

If she had any doubt at all about Nick Callahan's feelings, those doubts were erased the moment he kissed her. This hadn't been a kiss between two friends. There was passion and need, an almost desperate will to possess her. A shiver ran down her spine.

Wasn't this exactly what she'd been fantasizing about? Jillian racked her brain to recall some of those fantasies. How had she responded? If this were one of her fantasies now, what would she do? Would she follow him and throw herself back in his arms? Or would she wait in the library until the house grew silent and she could sneak up to bed?

Even with her limited experience with the opposite sex, Jillian sensed that the next move was hers. Nick was probably waiting for her to follow him, waiting for her to make her own feelings known.

"This would never work," Jillian muttered. "We have absolutely nothing in common."

She could just picture it now. Walking into a faculty reception with Nick Callahan. Everyone might act pleased to meet her new escort, but she knew the gossips would start speculating. "What could Professor Marshall possibly see in a man like that?" they'd say. "A great body and even better sex," they'd say. "Outside of the bedroom, he's probably a crashing bore."

But that wasn't true! Jillian had spent five days in the company of Nick Callahan and she hadn't once been bored. In truth, she found him exciting and interesting and enormously intriguing. They never ran out of things to say to each other and even when they weren't saying anything, he was the most fascinating man she'd ever met.

"So what does this mean?" Jillian murmured, still frozen in place. "Does this mean that you like him? That you're falling in love with him?" She moaned softly, then covered her face with her hands. She drew a ragged breath and straightened. "Maybe it's about time you found out."

Jillian hurried to the library door, then raced through the house to the kitchen. But Nick was nowhere to be found. She yanked the back door open and saw him, his head bent to the rain, heading toward the cottage. She stepped out onto the deck.

"Nick Callahan, we need to talk!" she shouted over the sound of the rain.

He stopped, but didn't turn around. "I'm tired," he called over his shoulder. "You're getting wet. And we're done for the night."

Jillian's temper flared and she walked to the edge of the deck. "Damn it, get back here! I'm not leaving the boys alone to chase you!"

Nick turned to face her, walking backwards as the rain soaked his jeans and washed the dust from his bare shoulders and chest. He held his hands up in a nonchalant gesture, his T-shirt clutched in his fingers. "Then you're stuck, aren't you?"

Jillian knew if she didn't go after him, this thing would lie unresolved, nagging at her all night and keeping her awake until sunrise. She needed to know where things stood between them and she needed to know now! Jillian glanced up at the boys' bedroom window, then stepped off the deck. She'd seen Roxy work in the garden when the boys were napping. Taking that as her cue, she strode across the slick grass, her heels sinking into the soft turf. With a vivid oath, she kicked off her shoes and proceeded in her bare feet until she reached Nick.

"This can't wait until morning?" he asked with a self-satisfied smile.

"No, it can't," Jillian replied.

"You don't want to hear what I have to say, Jillie."

"I'm not afraid of you," she said.

Nick stared into her eyes, causing a shiver to skitter down her spine. "Maybe you should be."

As if it wasn't raining hard enough already, water began to come down in torrents. Thunder cracked and rumbled and Jillian was certain the storm was right on top of them. She stared up at the sky, the raindrops pelting her face and drenching her hair. "We're going to get struck by lightning standing out here!"

"Go back in the house, Jillie."

Jillian didn't listen to him. In truth, she wasn't even listening to her own common sense. She didn't want to listen, she just wanted to feel—the warm rain on her skin, the heat from his body as she moved closer, the damp of his naked chest beneath her palms. Without speaking another word, she wrapped her arms around Nick's neck and pulled him nearer. And then she kissed him as if it were the most natural thing in the world for her to do.

The rain poured over them as their mouths searched and their tongues probed. Jillian's blood ran like liquid fire through her veins, tingling the nerves in her fingertips and toes, and warming the gooseflesh from her skin. If she hadn't known better, she'd think that lightning had struck them both, sapping the breath from their lungs and causing them to gasp.

"We shouldn't stay out here," Nick murmured, his mouth tracing a damp path from her lips to her jawline.

"I've heard that you're supposed to stay low," Jillian replied. She grabbed his hand and tugged him down on the slick grass. Nick rolled until he'd pulled her beneath his body, their legs tangling, his hips pressed against hers. With a low moan, he grabbed the neckline of her dress and tugged it off her shoulder, then softly nipped at the skin he revealed.

"What do you want from me?" he asked, his voice tinged with anger.

This was exactly what she wanted, this fire and lust, this uncontrollable passion that seemed to consume them both. She'd never felt more alive in her life, the storm raging around them, his body heavy upon hers. "Just this," Jillian murmured, arching against him as his mouth drifted lower. "All I want is this."

"But you don't want a man like me," he said, his breath hot on the skin above her breast. His teeth grazed her flesh, causing a flicker of pain. Did he mean to punish her, or had he been swept away by pure sensation as she had?

"And you don't want a woman in your life," she challenged, nipping at his neck.

"You want someone brilliant and driven," he said,

nuzzling at her cleavage. "Someone with a scientific mind."

"And you want someone sweet and compliant," Jillian countered. "A woman who'll let you be the boss."

"A man who'll play second fiddle to your work."

"A woman who'll be at your beck and call, in bed and out."

"Then we're agreed," Nick said, his hand slipping beneath the neckline of her dress. "There can't possibly be anything between us."

She furrowed her fingers through his hair, then pulled his mouth against hers. "Except this," she said against his lips.

The sounds of the storm faded into the background and all Jillian could hear was his breathing, harsh and quick, and her pulse pounding in her head. The rain made her sense of touch even more acute and as she ran her hands over his naked chest and back, she could feel every taut muscle beneath his smooth skin.

She didn't care about the consequences of what they were going to do. She just wanted to feel his hands on her body, to taste his mouth and to hear the sound of his moans, soft in her ear. Why bother thinking about the future? For Jillian, this was enough.

Nick slipped his fingers under the edge of her bra, following an inexorable path. A moment later, he cupped her breast in his palm. And then his mouth closed over her nipple and Jillian cried out. But the sound was swallowed up by the storm.

Time seemed to slow, measured only by the exquisite sensations that pulsed through her body. Jillian ached to be possessed by him, giving herself over to his touch, to the power of his hands and his lips on her body. Any inhibitions that she had were gone, replaced by undeniable need.

She no longer wanted to resist, no longer cared what loving him might cost her. Nick held her heart in his hands and even if they only shared this one moment, Jillian knew it would be a moment that defined the rest of her life. There would never be another man like Nick Callahan.

"Is this what you want, Jillie?" he murmured, his mouth pressed against the curve of her breast. "Do you want me to make love to you right here? In the rain and the wind?"

Though Jillian wanted to shout out her assent, his words tripped a circuit in her mind, an instinct all but forgotten beneath his gentle seduction. Faced with the choice, apprehension stole into her thoughts. Was this really what she wanted? Overwhelming lust followed by meaningless sex followed by ultimate desertion? She swallowed hard and closed her eyes. *Yes, yes, yes.*

But her single moment of indecision was all it took for Nick to roll off her. "Maybe we should go inside and check on the boys," he murmured.

Jillian tugged at her dress and sat up, the fire between them suddenly doused by the rain. Why didn't he want her anymore? Why had he been so willing to put a stop to it? And where had this wanton behavior come from? Was it simply a physical reaction to his touch or were these feelings racing through her true and real? "Maybe we should."

Nick levered to his feet, then reached down for her hand. He gently pulled her up and began to walk toward the house, silent, indifferent. He pulled the door open and stepped aside to let her pass.

As Jillian stepped inside the house, she rubbed the

water from her face and ran her fingers through her hair. "I'll just go upstairs and see how they are," she murmured, glancing over at him. "And I'll bring us a few towels."

Nick smiled, then nodded. But as Jillian walked through the darkened hallway, she knew when she returned to the kitchen, he'd be gone. Her tiny moment of indecision had ruined everything. She stopped halfway up the stairs and listened, just in time to hear the back door open and then close. With a soft sigh, she walked back down to find the kitchen empty. All that was left of him was a puddle of water where he'd stood.

She blinked. Droplets of rain blurred her eyes and ran down her cheeks. With a soft oath, she brushed at the water, determined not to give in to tears. Instead, she sighed softly and tried to banish every memory of his touch from her mind.

"Well, Jillian, you wanted to know if you were falling in love with him," she murmured. "I guess now you have your answer."

HE COULDN'T SLEEP. The rain continued on through the night, driving away the humidity and freshening the air that blew through the screened porch. Nick lay in the hammock, his arm thrown over his eyes, his mind occupied with thoughts of Jillie Marshall. The taste of her damp skin still lingered on his tongue and the feel of her warm flesh had branded his palms.

Every instinct had told him to make love to her there in the grass, and then later, in the house. But when it came to Jillie, he couldn't trust his instincts. He had to walk away or risk making a mistake he could never take back. A mistake he'd regret for a long time.

After Claire, he'd believed that no woman would ever

hold the power to hurt him. But then he'd met Jillie, a woman determined to keep him at arm's length, and all that had changed. With a soft curse, he swung his legs over the edge of the hammock, then furrowed his hands through his damp hair. The light from her bedroom window had gone dark hours ago. Nick wondered if she, too, lay awake with thoughts of what they'd shared.

Now, in the deepest dark of night, he could almost believe it had all been a dream. That first kiss, borne of frustration, her passionate response, and the desire that had driven them to grasp and gasp as the rain poured down on top of them. Her flesh in his hands, her hands on his body, her body beneath his. And then, that tiny moment of hesitation, the doubts and insecurities apparent in her eyes.

Though he'd wanted her in the most intimate way, Nick knew, in the end, he couldn't have made love to her. With Jillie, he needed more than just a one-night stand, more than a night of meaningless passion. He needed her to want him, the *real* him. Hell, if she couldn't accept him completely, both body and soul, then he couldn't have her at all.

It wasn't an easy thing to admit, this power she unwittingly held over him. But Jillie was special, a woman who hadn't been molded by the same forces that other women in his life had. She was the most intelligent woman he'd ever met, yet she lacked basic common sense at times. And though some men might pass her by as too plain, Nick had immediately seen the beauty in her features.

He smiled. She was opinionated and independent, yet sweet and vulnerable at the same time. Every time he advanced, she'd retreat, hiding behind the proper facade of Professor Marshall, refusing to acknowledge the passionate side of her nature. But tonight he'd seen it, felt the fire that burned deep inside of her. And he knew in a single moment, that he wouldn't be satisfied with just one night.

He pushed to his feet and paced the length of the porch, his bare feet cool on the painted floor. "This will have to stop," he murmured. "Needing Jillie Marshall has already cost you more than you can afford." Every minute of every day had been consumed with thoughts of her, questions about her desires and speculation about what they might share.

With a sigh, he shoved the screen door open and stepped outside. As he strode down to the lake, Nick unbuttoned his jeans, then kicked them off, along with his boxer shorts. The moon was just beginning to break through the clouds when he jumped off the end of the pier and sliced into the black water.

The lake was still warm from the hot day and he swam back and forth between the end of the pier and a raft that bobbed thirty yards away. If only he could exhaust himself, perhaps he could sleep. He swam and swam, the water rushing by his body until his breathing grew labored. When he couldn't go any further, he pulled himself up onto the raft and lay on his back, naked in the moonlight, the cool breeze drawing a shiver over his skin.

He closed his eyes and images of Jillie floated in his brain. But this time, he didn't push them aside. What if he had no control over his fate? What if he and Jillie were meant to have this undeniable passion? Stranger things had happened.

Nick sighed, then raised his hands over his head. His muscles were tired but his mind was even more exhausted. Every ounce of his energy had been used to walk away from Jillie and the intimacies they'd shared. It would have been so easy to make love to her...so easy, he mused as he closed his eyes.

The sun was just beginning to lighten the eastern sky when he finally dived off the raft and swam back to shore. Nick grabbed his jeans and boxers, then strode into the cottage, sleep now unnecessary. The sooner he finished the library, the sooner he could go back to his life in Providence. He'd gotten over Claire. Hell, he'd even managed to ward off a wicked case of lust for a near stranger. Surely, he'd had enough of women by now, hadn't he?

He quickly dressed, then walked up to the house in the dark. When he opened the back door, he'd expected silence to greet him. But instead, he found Jillie, perched on a stool, sipping a cup of coffee and lost in her thoughts. She was illuminated only by the light from above the sink and, for a moment, he was afraid to make a noise. She looked so tiny, so alone, wrapped in her robe and clutching her mug as if it offered some solace.

"I didn't think you'd be up," he said softly.

Startled, she turned to him, her eyes wide. He remembered that first night, when he'd walked in on her and she'd hit him with the xylophone. Had that really only been six days ago? Lord, it felt as if he'd known Jillie for a lifetime.

"I—I couldn't sleep," she murmured, flustered by his appearance, her hands fidgeting with her hair.

Nick shrugged. "I couldn't either. I thought I'd get an early start in the library." In truth, he didn't care when he got the library done. The moment he saw her, he knew he didn't want an excuse to walk away.

"I—I'm glad we have a chance to talk," she said. "I

mean, while the house is still quiet." She picked up an envelope from the counter and held it out to him.

Nick took it from her fingers. "What's this?"

"It's your pay. For your services as a nanny. I've included extra for the overtime you worked yesterday evening."

Nick tossed the envelope down in front of her, his jaw tight, anger surging up inside of him. Was this supposed to solve everything between them? A quick paycheck and a pink slip. "I don't want your money."

"We had a bargain," she said in a small voice.

He cursed softly, trying to control his fury. "What is this really about?" he demanded. "Is this about our bargain? Or is it about last night? Are you angry because I wanted to make love to you? Or because I wouldn't."

She toyed with the handle of her coffee mug, refusing to meet his gaze. "I don't even want to talk about last night," Jillie said. "We made a mistake. We got carried away. Both you and I know that."

"I don't know anything," Nick said. "I don't think you do either. Except that from the moment we met, we've been heading toward this."

"I know that you're not the kind of man I belong with," she said, her words lacking complete conviction.

"Why? Because I'm just some carpenter guy who makes a living with his hands instead of his head. Is that all you care about, Jillie? Because if it is, then I'm glad we didn't make love. Because you're not the woman I thought I knew. And you don't know me at all."

She sighed deeply, then met his gaze. "I'm just being realistic," she said, her chin tipped up defensively. "Admit it, Nick. You don't really think I'm your type either. I'd make a terrible wife and a worse mother. You couldn't want that, could you?"

He cursed softly. "I don't know what I want right now. Except to get those bookshelves finished so I can get the hell out of here."

"I think that would be best," Jillie murmured.

Nick gave her a long look, trying to see past the indifferent expression and the icy composure, looking for some sign of the passionate woman he'd kissed last night, the woman who had moaned his name and arched against his body. But she wasn't there—she'd hidden herself behind the condescending facade of Professor Jillian Marshall, calculating female and cold-hearted realist. He shook his head and walked out of the room.

When he reached the library, he closed the door behind him and leaned back against it. He still had at least a day, maybe two, of work ahead of him, though he could always leave and come back after Roxy and Greg were home. They'd given him the cottage for the entire summer if he wanted it that long, so there was no need to put himself through this torture.

But he'd started a job and Nick knew if he didn't finish it now, he'd never come back. He glanced around the room. This wasn't the only thing left unfinished. Though Jillie had given him his walking papers, he still felt as if there was something left between them unresolved.

Had Nick known building a set of simple bookshelves would completely mess up his life, he might have chosen a different project. He still had a new house to design for himself. Next month, he was due to travel to Tennessee to firm up plans for the new auto plant he was designing. In two or three months, he had a canning plant in Florida that he'd have to start. There was plenty to keep his mind off Jillie Marshall once he escaped her presence.

But he'd gotten a taste of something here, something he never thought he'd have. He and Jillie and the boys had fallen into the rhymes and rhythms of a makeshift family. It wasn't surprising that everyone at the picnic believed Jillie to be his wife. And Zach, Andy and Sam, his sons. He'd imagined it that way himself. So much, that now he could barely picture a family that didn't include Jillie Marshall at his side.

But he'd thought the same of Claire and Jason, that they'd be his family and his future. And how quickly they'd been forgotten. And this from a man who, until a few years ago, had been determined to remain single.

"I don't need a woman in my life," Nick murmured, as he reached for a shelf bracket. "There are some numbers that aren't meant to be perfect. And I'm one of them, Professor Marshall."

Jillian stood in the kitchen, watching the boys as they picked at the hot dogs, apple slices and Cheese Nips she'd offered them for lunch. They'd passed the entire morning without catching sight of Nick. He'd shut himself in the library and hadn't come out. Zach had knocked on the door, then tried the knob, but found it locked. Jillian had even prepared a sandwich for him, certain he'd emerge for lunch. But the only evidence that he was still in there was the occasional sound of a hammer or a power drill.

With a soft sigh, she reached out and stole a Cheese Nip from Andy's plate. He giggled in delight, then offered her a soggy one from his mouth. Jillian smiled to herself. At one time, she would have recoiled in horror at the offer, but now, she bent down and let Andy put the cracker in her mouth, smacking her lips and sending him a rapturous smile.

"It hasn't been so bad, has it?" she asked. "None of us has been seriously injured or emotionally scarred. We've managed to follow most of Dr. Hazelton's advice. And we're starting to know each other pretty well, don't you think?" All three of the boys nodded in unison.

"So what if Nick is mad," she continued. "We're better off on our own anyway. There won't be anymore disasters, will there?"

They nodded their heads again, clearly confused by the question. Jillian laughed. "What shall we do today?" she continued. "I thought we could play outside, perhaps a little ball toss to work on your eye-hand coordination. Dr. Hazelton says that's very important at your age."

"Play ball," Andy said, milk dripping from his upper lip.

Jillian reached out and swiped at his mouth with a damp paper towel. "Now that you're the only men in my life, I guess you have my full attention."

She slipped off the stool, then helped them down from their booster chairs. They ran to the back door and Zach worked at the doorknob. "Go out," he cried.

"Out, out, out!" Andy shouted.

Jillian collected the shoes and socks which had been scattered around the family room during the morning playtime. When she managed to get them all on the correct feet, she sat back on her heels and grinned at the boys. "Zach, Sammy and Andy," she said, pointing to each one in turn. "How could I have not known the difference?"

She opened the back door and the boys went tumbling outside, tripping over themselves as they ran. Jillian grabbed a ball from the bin on the deck and tossed it out on the lawn. They kicked it back and forth, then fell on top of it in a pile of legs and arms. Jillian ran over to them, ready to pull them apart. But when she saw how much fun they were having, she fell into the pile, tickling and teasing them.

Their play was rough and tumble, nothing like the sedate dolls and puzzles that she'd enjoyed as a child. The boys seemed to push themselves to near exhaustion, then, somehow, find a bit of reserve energy to go even further. After fifteen minutes with the ball, they moved on to the sandbox, then back to the ball, then to the tire swing hanging from a huge maple. Like little bees buzzing from flower to flower, they never seemed to light for more than a few minutes.

As Jillian stood off to the side, watching the boys chase a butterfly, she felt someone watching her. She slowly turned and looked up at the library window only to see the curtains flutter slightly. Had it been her imagination, or had Nick been looking down on them? Everything had been settled between them. There was no room for regret or doubt. So why couldn't he just leave her alone?

Jillian thought about all that had passed. It seemed like weeks ago when she'd arrived to care for the boys, not just a few days. Nick had walked into her life as a stranger, but in such a short time, they'd nearly become lovers. But what had she really learned about him? And could she trust her judgment when desire affected every thought of him?

This week was meant to be an experiment in motherhood, not in moral fortitude. She'd expected it to be so easy. But now she realized she'd been a fool to believe anything involving a lifelong commitment could be simple. Falling in love, having children, building a future with a family. None of it was meant to be easy.

She'd lived in her protected little world of numbers

and theories and formulas. In truth, she'd hidden herself there, away from love and commitment. Now, for the first time in her life, she'd met a man who stirred her senses and made her heart soar. And she didn't want to go back to her orderly little life. Instead, she wanted to rush headlong into chaos.

"There is another man out there for you," Jillian murmured. "A man who fits into your life-style." But was that what she really wanted? Order and predictability? Settling for half-hearted passion and unfulfilled desire with a man like Richard Jarrett?

"I always have my work," she said. In truth, she'd barely thought of work in the past few days. Her time had been consumed by Nick and the boys. She'd always thought it weak when a woman gave up a career to raise a family and take care of a husband. Why couldn't all women have both—career and family life?

But now she saw that it wasn't necessarily a choice made for lack of time or energy to do both. It came from priorities, from listening to the heart. She now understood why Roxy had given up her career in law to raise her boys. Zach and Andy and Sam were a piece of Roxy's soul come to life and watching them grow was a miracle unfolding before her eyes.

"Chaos theory," Jillian murmured. "One never knows what to expect."

The boys came running toward her and she braced herself for an assault on her knees. But when they raced right by, Jillian turned to see Nick striding across the lawn.

"Nick! Nick!" the boys shouted, then threw themselves against his legs. His expression, at first fierce, softened and then broke into a grin. He placed Zach on his shoulders, poking and grabbing at Andy and Sam as they frolicked alongside. When he reached the spot where she stood, he set Zach down.

"Hi," she murmured.

"Hi," he replied.

Jillian took a deep breath and pasted a bright smile on her face. "You've been working hard," she said, nerves making her voice a little breathless. "We haven't seen you all morning."

He shifted his gaze from her eyes to a point somewhere over her shoulder. "I've nearly finished in the library. I just have a little more work to do this afternoon and that will be it."

"Well," Jillian said, twisting her fingers together and staring at her toes. "That's good, then. I'm sure Greg and Roxy will be pleased."

She groped for something more to say. How had they suddenly become strangers after all the time they'd spent together, the intimacies they'd shared? The barriers that had first stood between them had been rebuilt in less than a day.

"They've hired someone else to do the finishing," Nick continued. "I'll collect my tools from the house after I'm done and I'll be leaving tomorrow morning."

Jillian shouldn't have been surprised by his revelation, but she was. Her heart twisted in her chest and, for a moment, she couldn't breathe. "Then you'll have to have dinner with us tonight—seeing as it's your last night with the boys." She didn't ask for herself, preferring instead to issue an invitation that couldn't be refused.

But Nick shook his head anyway. "I've got too much packing to do. And I have to clean up the cottage."

"Don't you have the cottage for the rest of the summer?"

His gaze met hers. "I've had enough of vacation," he said. "I need to get back to Providence."

Jillian clutched at the skirt of her cotton dress, bunching the fabric in her fists. "It doesn't have to be this way," she murmured. "This hostility between us isn't necessary. We're both reasonable adults."

"I think that's the problem," he said with a dry laugh. "We're adults and we're entirely too reasonable. I'll be out of your way before you know it." With that, he continued to walk toward the lake, leaving Jillian and the boys to stare after him. A few moments later, he disappeared into the cottage, the crack of the screen door splitting the air.

"Nick mad," Andy said, taking her hand.

"Jillie bad?" Zach asked, looking up at her with questioning eyes.

Jillian shrugged, then sent them a little smile. "Nick is just preoccupied," she said. "Busy," she amended, noticing their blank looks. "Very, very busy."

"Sad," Sammy said.

She reached down and ruffled his hair. "No, not sad."

She sat down in the grass and the boys, sensing her mood, gathered around her. They held her hands and curled up beside her in the warm sun. Jillian stared out at the lake, watching a small sailboat glide by on the soft breeze. She'd come to love this place, the quiet, the serenity of the woods and the water. But how would she ever be able to come back without thinking of him?

Could she walk through the house and not remember the disasters he'd saved her from? Could she stand on the lawn and not recall the touch of his hand or the warmth of his kiss? Maybe she ought to think about getting back to her real life, her research and her plans for next semester, and resolve to put this week in the past.

She looked down at the boys. "We only have a few days left," she said. "I say we should have all the fun we can. What would you say if I filled up the pool and we could go for a swim?"

"Fill the pool!" Andy cried.

If only life were so simple that a summer afternoon splash in a plastic pool could solve all her problems. Jillian wondered if she'd ever come to terms with what had happened between her and Nick. These ten days at the lake house might very well haunt her for the rest of her life.

7

JILLIAN SLEPT FITFULLY, completely exhausted, yet on edge at the same time. She'd close her eyes, certain that this time she'd drift off, only to be frustrated with hazy images of Nick teasing at her mind. Again and again, she found herself reliving the previous night, when they'd nearly made love in the storm. And each time the memories came back so vividly that she could almost feel the cool rain on her face and his warm hands on her body.

Her thoughts were interrupted by a quiet cry from the boys' room. Jillian pushed up from the bed and listened. Over the past six nights she'd learned to wait, rather than run in. They often woke from a dream, then fell back asleep again a few minutes later. She glanced at the clock—it was just past midnight.

When the crying continued, Jillian rolled out of bed and pulled on her robe. She turned on a small lamp on the dresser in the boys' room and moved to the bed against the wall. To her surprise, all three boys were curled up in Sammy's bed. They wore only their Huggies, pajamas discarded sometime after she'd put them to bed and closed the bedroom door. "What's wrong?" she murmured, picking up the triplet closest to the footboard. He looked like Sammy, but Jillian couldn't be sure.

She placed her hand on his cheek, then snatched it

away. His face was hot and as she walked him around the room, he began to cry inconsolably, a plaintive sound that woke his brothers. "Are you sick?" she murmured, putting him down on the changing table and pressing her lips to his forehead.

Her brain scrambled to remember Dr. Hazelton's advice as she ticked off his symptoms. Flushed cheeks, glazed eyes, warm to the touch, tugging at his ear. Could he have an earache? Jillian looked into his eyes. "Does your ear hurt?" He burst into a fresh round of tears without answering.

She glanced around the room. Should she call the pediatrician? What if it was just a little sniffle? Maybe she should take him to the emergency room. "I don't know what to do," Jillian said. The only thing she really did know was that she needed help. She couldn't possibly take care of a sick child and watch the other two boys at the same time. There was only one place to turn for help.

Jillian put the boys back in their own beds, kissing each on the head. "I'll be right back," she murmured. "I promise."

She hurried downstairs and slipped into her sandals before stepping outside. The night air was warm, but a shiver still rocked her body as she ran toward the lake. The cottage was dark, and though going to Nick for help rankled her pride, the boys were the most important thing on her mind. Nick would know what to do. When it came to the boys, he always knew what to do.

A bright moon illuminated her way and when she reached the cottage, she knocked on the screen door, but after a few long seconds, there was no answer. Jillian turned to look back at the house, but a movement caught her eye. She stared into the darkness at the edge of the lake and watched as a figure rose from the water in slow motion, then levered up onto the pier.

Moonlight gleamed off wet skin and a tremor of fear raced through her body. But then she realized it was Nick who had emerged from the water, long limbed and slender hipped—and completely naked. She stepped into the shadows near the doorway, her gaze transfixed by the sight. He grabbed a towel and ran it over his body before draping it around his shoulders and she held her breath as he made his way toward the cottage.

When he was nearly to the porch, Jillian stepped from the shadows. Her heart pounded in her chest and she shifted uneasily from one foot to another, clutching at the front of her robe and trying to keep her eyes on his face.

"Jillian?" He peered through the dark at her. "What are you doing out here?"

"I—I need you," she said, her voice trembling.

"Jillian, we talked about this. I—"

"No!" she cried. "I need you because one of the boys is sick and I don't know what to do. I don't know if I should call the doctor or take him to the hospital. He's so hot and I think his ear hurts. Please, can you help me?"

He took a step toward her, unfazed by his nakedness, then cupped her cheek in his hand. His cool touch immediately soothed her nerves. "Just let me get dressed. I'll come right up."

Jillian nodded in relief, then turned and ran back to the house. On her way upstairs, she grabbed Dr. Hazelton's book and was frantically paging through it outside the bedroom door when Nick appeared beside her. An image of his naked body flashed in her brain, but she pushed it aside.

He took her hand and, together, they slipped into the boys' room. "Over here," Jillian whispered, moving to the bed in the far corner. "I—I think it's Sammy. They took off their pajamas, so I can't be sure." She clutched the book in front of her. "I don't even know who it is. What am I supposed to say to the doctor? How is he supposed to treat him if he doesn't know which triplet it is?"

Nick bent down beside the bed. "It's Sammy," he said softly. He reached out and stroked Sammy's tousled hair. "He does feel warm. Find a thermometer and let's take his temperature first."

Jillian rushed to the bathroom. She struggled with the child-proofed cabinet door before she managed to get it open. A few moments later, she returned with the thermometer. She held it out in front of Sammy's mouth but he turned away, whimpering in protest.

Nick smiled and shook his head. "Jillie, that's the wrong end."

Jillian frowned and flipped the thermometer around, the silver end pointing toward her. "That can't be right, can it?"

"No," he said, taking it from her hand. "The wrong end on Sam." He grabbed a jar of Vaseline from the dresser and took off Sam's diaper.

"Do you know what you're doing?" she said, peering over his shoulder, wincing.

"Pretty much. Why don't you read me directions out of Dr. Hazelton just to be sure."

Jillian held the book up and slowly recited the section on thermometers while Nick calmly responded. His composure both surprised and steadied Jillian. When she'd found Sammy ill, she'd panicked, but now she knew with Nick at her side, everything would be all right.

Sammy watched them silently, his characteristic quiet interrupted only by the occasional whine. Zach and Andy were both lying in their beds, observing the action with their eyes half-closed. "Well?" Jillian said. "The book says a normal temperature…er, on that end is 99.6."

He held the thermometer up to the light. "It's high," Nick said, placing it on the dresser before fastening the tabs on Sammy's diaper.

She grabbed up the thermometer and squinted to read it. "It's 103.4. That's bad."

"What does Dr. Hazelton say?"

Jillian scanned the book. "Temperatures of up to 102, monitor closely. Between 102 and 104, give medication, a sponge bath, and call a pediatrician if it persists. Over 104, take to doctor or emergency room immediately."

"Do you have the pediatrician's number?"

"No," Jillian said. "I mean, I do, but I don't want to take any chances. I think we should take Sammy to the emergency room."

Nick took her hand and gave it a squeeze. "If that's what you want to do, then that's what we'll do, Jillie."

"You don't think I'm over-reacting?" she asked, her mind spinning with indecision. "I just don't think I can trust a book to tell me what to do. He looks so flushed and what if he gets worse? We're a half hour away from a hospital. By then, it might be too late. Do you think I'm over-reacting? Dr. Hazelton says there can be convulsions. If you think we should keep him here, we won't go."

Nick stood, then pulled her over to the door and placed his hands on her shoulders. He gazed down into her eyes. "I can stay with the boys, while you take Sammy in. Or I can take Sammy in while you stay with the boys. What do you want to do?"

"I—I want to go and I want you to come with me. We'll take the boys with us."

"All right," Nick said. "I'll get Zach and Andy up and dressed, you take care of Sammy. See if there's any Children's Tylenol in the medicine cabinet, and if there is, give him a dose. Then get him dressed." He bent lower and gave Jillian a gentle kiss, his thumb hooked beneath her chin.

Time seemed to stand still and, for a long moment, neither one of them moved. Jillian risked a look up at him, expecting to see desire in his eyes. But instead, she found concern and care, and what she'd always thought love might look like. She wanted to break down and cry, to throw herself into his arms and have him assure her that everything would be all right.

Nick brushed his hand over her cheek and smiled. "Kids are resilient, Jillie. Everything will be all right. I promise."

"Roxy is going to kill me," Jillian said, fighting back tears. "Nothing was supposed to go wrong."

He smiled. "This happens with kids. It's not your fault. You didn't give him a fever."

"I let him play too long in the pool. He got cold water in his ears and now he has an ear infection. It *is* my fault." She drew a ragged breath, needing him to kiss her just once more. "I'm sorry to get you mixed up in this. I should be able to handle this on my own. What if you weren't here? What if you'd finished the library and left? I should be able to handle this."

"You would have. And you are, Jillie. Now, go get dressed and then find the Tylenol for Sammy. I'll get the boys ready."

The next few minutes passed in a blur. Zach and Andy weren't too happy about being roused from sleep a second time and fussed as Nick pulled on shorts, T-shirts and shoes. She gave Sammy the medicine, then quickly dressed him, wrapped him in a light blanket and brought him downstairs. Nick had already fastened Zach and Andy into their car seats and took Sam from her arms to do the same.

Jillian hopped in the front seat and closed the door. She took a deep breath and Nick started the van. "Wait!" she cried. "I should go back and call Roxy. What if she calls and we don't answer?"

"Sweetheart, it's past midnight. I don't think she'll call. And we can call her after we find out what's wrong. If we call her now, she'll just worry."

"You're right," Jillian said. She sent him a nervous glance. "Did—did you just call me 'sweetheart'?"

Nick shrugged as he pulled away from the garage and steered the van down the driveway. "Yeah. Sorry. It just slipped out."

"No," Jillian said, secretly pleased with the endearment. No one had ever called her sweetheart before— besides her father. It made her feel safe and cherished, something she needed right now. "It's all right. I—I liked it."

They drove silently for a long time, all three boys drifting off to sleep in their car seats. She reached back and stroked Sammy's cheek and he felt cooler to her touch, but Jillian didn't know whether the fever had subsided or she was engaging in wishful thinking. "Did I thank you?" she murmured.

"Yes, you did," Nick said. He reached over and slipped his arm around her shoulders, gently massaging her nape. "But I don't need thanks. I want to help you, Jillie. You and the boys are important to me."

She sank back in the seat, all the emotions welling up

inside of her. Tears pressed at the corners of her eyes and she fought them. She didn't deserve a man like Nick, especially after she'd been so cold to him. He was kind and thoughtful and any woman, including her, should be happy to have him in her life. "I—I just feel so helpless. Sammy can't tell me what's wrong and my mind is coming up with all these terrible possibilities. And—"

"You're getting a taste of what it's like to be a mother," he said.

"I don't think I like it," Jillian said, shaking her head. "My stomach is in knots and my head hurts and I feel like I'm going to throw up. And I can't stop shaking."

"I think that's normal."

"But I'm not even Sammy's mother. What would it be like if he were really my son?"

Nick drew a finger along her jaw. "You love Sammy. You have every right to be worried."

Jillian stared out at the road in front of them, wishing they were already a the hospital. Nick easily maneuvered the van around the sweeping curves and she sank down in the seat and crossed her arms over her chest, trying to still the tremors that wracked her body.

All her problems with Nick had dissolved in the midst of this new crisis and she took comfort in his touch, in the gentle way he consoled her, in the warmth of his fingers laced through hers. He drew her hand up to his mouth and kissed her wrist. Jillian glanced over at him and smiled.

"Everything will be all right," she murmured. But she wasn't talking only about Sammy. Things had been set right between her and Nick as well. The anger and confusion that had marred their last day together was gone and, once again, they were friends.

THEY ARRIVED at the hospital in thirty minutes, a quick ride from the lake house to the small city of Rochester. They could have driven another twenty minutes to Dover and a regional medical center, but Nick thought Jillie might not survive the ride. Though she tried to maintain her composure, beneath the surface she was a nervous wreck. He saw it in the way she gnawed on her fingernails and checked on Sammy every five seconds, in the way she kept glancing at the clock in the dashboard, then at the speedometer, mentally calculating their exact time of arrival.

Nick had offered encouraging words, but he knew they'd gone in one ear and out the other. He was tempted to pull over to the side of the road and yank her into his arms until she quit trembling. Instead, he kept driving, nodding whenever required. In truth, he was glad Jillian had decided to take Sammy to the emergency room. Once a qualified medical professional pronounced him out of danger, she could stop beating herself up. Had they kept Sammy at home, Jillian probably would have driven him crazy second-guessing Dr. Hazelton.

The emergency room was empty when they arrived, but getting Sammy examined was a complicated affair. Jillie had forgotten to bring health insurance information for the boys and had also left the number to Roxy and Greg's hotel at home. The admitting nurse hassled her over parental permission but Nick suggested they call the boys' pediatrician whose number Jillie had committed to memory. A quick phone call and the emergency staff was satisfied with the medical permission slip Roxy had left with the pediatrician.

A few moments later, another nurse appeared to whisk Sammy away. The little boy was barely awake and put up no fuss. Jillie wanted to accompany him, but the doctor assured her that they would call her if she was needed. In truth, Nick could understand why they didn't want her in the examination room. She was nearing the edge of hysteria caused, in part, by the pamphlet on encephalitis she'd picked up as she paced the waiting room. Zach and Andy, on the other hand, seemed to be taking the whole night in stride. They'd discovered a play area in the corner of the waiting room and were busy poring over new and exciting toys and puzzles.

Nick drew Jillie over to a pair of chairs near the boys and they sat down. He held her hand, gently stroking the inside of her wrist with his thumb, hoping to divert her attention, yet also happy just to touch her. "Don't worry," he said. "I think Sammy looked better already."

"You're just saying that to calm me down," Jillie replied morosely.

"No, I wouldn't lie to you. He felt cooler to the touch and he wasn't so flushed. Little kids get fevers, sometimes for no reason."

"Maybe we should call Roxy and Greg. You could drive home and get the number."

"Let's just wait and see."

Jillie drew a ragged breath. He slipped his arm around her shoulders and pulled her against him. She pressed her face into his chest and closed her eyes, her teeth chattering. "I can never be a mother. This is just too hard." She glanced up at him and gave him a rueful smile. "Maybe I should get a cat."

Finally, a smile, Nick mused. Physical contact seemed to soothe her so he rubbed her arm, her skin like silk beneath his fingertips. "You'd always have a husband to help."

"No," she said.

Nick pulled back and looked down at her in confusion. "No? What do you mean?"

She laughed and shook her head. "Nothing. It was just...stupid."

"Tell me," Nick said.

Jillie sighed softly. "Actually, *I* was stupid. Stupid enough to believe I could have a child on my own. That's why I volunteered to take care of the boys. I figured if I could handle three boys for a week, then I could take care of one child for eighteen years. I worked it all out on my computer, work hours, home hours, school expenses, college fund. I wanted to show Roxy I could have it all."

Nick stifled a chuckle. He never knew what to expect from Jillie. The way her mind worked was sometimes a complete mystery, yet he found that quality endlessly intriguing. He could spend a lifetime with her and never be bored. "Your computer told you you could have a child of your own? I hate to tell you this, but I think it takes more than just you and your computer to have a baby."

"I know that," Jillie said. "I would have gone to one of those banks...and made a withdrawal. They have them, you know, where all the...depositors are Mensa members."

"There are much more interesting ways to make a baby."

She sighed. "It's a moot point, anyway. I thought I could do it, but this past week proved me wrong. Don't you agree?"

Nick pressed a kiss to her forehead. "You're an amazing woman, Jillie Marshall. I think you could do pretty much anything you set your mind to—including becoming a mother."

"Mr. and Mrs. Hunter?"

Jillie jumped out of her chair, nearly clipping Nick's chin. He rose to stand beside her, then grabbed her hand so she wouldn't twist her fingers together. Instead, she shifted from foot to foot. "I'm Jillian Marshall. This is Nick Callahan. We're not married—"

The young female resident glanced around the waiting room, frowning. "Mr. and Mrs. Hunter?" she repeated.

"They're in Hawaii," Jillie said. "And we're the baby-sitters, not the parents. We're not married. A lot of people make that mistake but we're just..."

"Friends," Nick finished, putting an end to her babbling.

"Yes," Jillie said. "Friends." She swallowed hard. "Is—is Sammy all right?"

The doctor nodded, glancing down at her chart. "He's fine. He doesn't have a fever anymore. The Tylenol must have done the trick. But he does have a little ear infection. I've called his regular pediatrician and he suggests that you monitor him for the next day or two. If the fever returns or the ear seems to give him problems, then we'll put him on antibiotics. But let's give it a little time to clear up on its own."

Jillie sagged against Nick and he caught her around the waist, certain her knees were about to give out. "Then he's all right?" she asked. "It's not pneumonia? Or encephalitis?"

The doctor chuckled. "No, his lungs are perfectly clear. You probably didn't have to bring him in, but if it eased your mind, then it was the right thing to do. You can talk to the admitting nurse about the bill. I'll just go get Sammy and you can take him home."

When the doctor disappeared behind the automatic doors, Jillie moaned softly. "The bill. What does an emergency room visit cost? Two, three thousand dollars. Roxy is going to kill me. What if their insurance doesn't cover this?''

''Don't worry, I don't think it's quite that much. And I gave them my credit card,'' Nick said. ''Everything will be taken care of.''

Jillie turned to him, suddenly frantic. ''No! You can't keep rescuing me like some white knight. And you can't afford this. By the time you're finished paying for my mistakes, all your profits from the bookshelves will be gone. I have to learn to handle my own problems.''

Nick hooked his thumb under her chin and forced her gaze to meet his. Her eyes were rimmed red with exhaustion and her face was pale and drawn. The sooner he got her home and to bed, the better off they'd all be. ''Jillie, if you haven't noticed yet, I like helping you. I like being around you. And I'm getting used to your little disasters. I can certainly afford to help you out. That's what friends do.''

She frowned. ''You find this all entertaining?'' Anger flickered in her eyes. Considering the stress she'd been under, he wasn't surprised by her behavior. Just then, the automatic doors opened and another nurse emerged with a sleeping Sammy in her arms. ''Mr. and Mrs. Hunter?'' she whispered.

This time Jillie didn't bother to correct her. ''I'm Mrs. Hunter,'' she said, her anger suddenly evaporated. The nurse held her finger up to her lips, then put the boy into Jillie's arms. ''He'll be fine,'' she said. ''The nurse at the desk has his discharge papers. You'll need to read them and sign. And make sure to call us if there are any further problems. Or you can call Sammy's pediatrician.''

Jillie pressed her lips to Sammy's forehead, but he

continued to sleep. "He feels nice and cool. Thank you. And thank the doctor for us."

They completed all the paperwork, Nick collected Zach and Andy from the play corner and they headed back out to the van. It was nearly two in the morning and the parking lot was silent, the town around them asleep. They settled the boys in their car seats, then Nick reached out to open Jillie's door, but at the last minute she turned to him.

"I'm sorry I snapped at you," she said, staring up into his eyes. "I should thank you for helping me. And tell you that you're a—a good friend, Nick Callahan." They stood looking at each other for a long moment, then she pushed up on her toes and kissed him, softly, sweetly, her lips warm against his.

Nick's hand drifted from the van door to her face and then to the nape of her neck. When she pulled back, he wasn't ready to let her go and he leaned forward and captured her mouth again. She seemed to melt into him and he slipped an arm around her waist and drew her nearer.

The kiss spun out, growing more passionate with every passing second. For a moment, he forgot where they were and what they'd just been through. All he could focus on was the taste of her, the way she fit perfectly in his arms. But what he really wanted from Jillie he couldn't have here in the parking lot of a hospital at two in the morning with three sleeping boys in the back seat.

He wanted time—minutes and hours, days even. The time to slowly undress her, to learn the angles and curves of her body, to memorize her scent until he could recall it at a moment's notice. He wanted to make her gasp and moan at his touch, to bring her to the edge, then carry her over.

Nick brushed his lips against hers, then looked down into her eyes. "I think we better get you and the boys home."

Jillie nodded, then turned to climb into the van. He closed the door and drew a long breath of the night air. Though Jillie might think of him as a friend, he just couldn't reciprocate. In truth, he'd stopped thinking of her as a pal a long time ago. She was a woman he needed. A woman he couldn't afford to lose. And a woman he'd grown to love. Nick knew it like he knew his own name.

But there was one thing he didn't know. He didn't have a clue whether Jillie Marshall felt the same way about him.

JILLIAN DIDN'T REALIZE she'd fallen asleep until she woke up in Nick's arms. He was gently lifting her from the van when she opened her eyes. "Are we home?" she asked, raising her hand against the soft glow of the porch light.

He nodded. "I took the boys upstairs and got them to bed. They're already sound asleep. You drifted off right after we left the hospital."

"I—I can walk."

"And I can carry you," he said. "You've had a rough night and I don't want you to trip and sprain your ankle again. Then what would we do?"

She wrapped her arms around his neck and snuggled against him. After what she'd been through tonight, it felt good to be indulged. And she wasn't certain she would be able to walk into the house and up to her room.

She felt as if she'd been run over by a cement truck, every muscle in her body completely spent.

He carried her, as if she weighed nothing more than a feather, to the porch, then through the door and up the stairs. He didn't pause until he'd dropped her gently on the bed. "My hero," she said sleepily, lying back against the down pillows.

"Can I get you anything?" he asked, taking a step back from the bed.

She stared up at him in the dim light from the bedside lamp. Lord, he was handsome. Her mind drifted back to the moment he'd stood in front of her naked, dripping with water. A shiver ran over her body and she remembered the sheer masculine beauty of his physique, the unbidden desire it awakened in her.

But there was more than just physical perfection to Nick. He wasn't her Nobel prize-winning scientist, but he was strong and kind and capable, a man she could depend on in a crisis, a man who truly cared about her. He watched over her and the boys when everything seemed to be falling apart. And she could trust him like she'd never been able to trust a man before.

How had she managed to overlook these qualities? She'd been so set on maintaining her silly standards, certain that only a man who fit her criteria would be worthy of her love. But here was a man who protected her, who cherished her, and she'd so steadfastly refused to see him for what he was. Nick Callahan was a man she could love. In truth, he was a man she *did* love.

"There is something I need," Jillian murmured, suddenly emboldened by her revelation. She needed to touch him, to brush aside his clothes and revel in the sight of his body. Jillian pushed up on her knees, then motioned him to come closer.

He did as she asked and before Nick had a chance to react, Jillian wrapped her arms around his neck and kissed him again. But this time there was no gratitude in the kiss. Instead, it was filled with unrestrained desire, passion that had simmered inside of her for so long. "Stay with me tonight," she whispered, her lips trailing along his jaw.

"Jillie, I don't think—"

"Don't say anything. I don't need to hear any promises. I just want to be with you. We don't have to—you know."

His eyebrow arched. "We don't have to?"

Jillian sighed. "When you're with me, I feel safe. I don't worry and obsess. I'm not going to be able to sleep if I'm alone. And right now, I just want to be with you."

Nick hesitated for a moment and Jillian's heart sank. But then he kicked off his shoes and socks and sat down on the edge of the bed. Jillian lay down on her side and softly stroked his back. "Did you mean what you said, earlier in the emergency room?"

He glanced over his shoulder. "What was that?"

"That we were friends?"

He bent his head and she heard a soft chuckle slip from his lips. "I suppose so."

"Good," she replied. "I'm glad." It felt good knowing that the man she loved was also her friend.

After a long moment of silence, Nick reached down and grabbed the hem of his T-shirt, then yanked it over his head. When he turned to Jillian and stretched out beside her, she couldn't help but notice the pained look on his face. "Are you all right?" she asked.

"Fine," he said in an edgy voice. "I guess I'm just tired, too."

He slipped his arm beneath Jillian's head and she

snuggled up against him, pressing her face against his bare skin, the soft dusting of hair on his chest tickling her cheek. "This is nice," she murmured, raking her nails softly along his collarbone.

Jillian splayed her hand over Nick's chest. Beneath her fingers, she felt his heart beating, strong and sure. She tipped her face up to look at him and found him staring at her, a look in his eyes that she'd never seen before, fierce, unyielding, predatory. A shiver raced down her spine and she wasn't sure what to do.

Then ever so slowly, he brought his mouth down on hers and kissed her with such tenderness she could do nothing but respond. As his tongue gently invaded her mouth, Jillian mused at how right this felt. Different than the frantic passion they'd shared that night on the lawn. All her apprehension vanished, all her inhibitions receded and she allowed herself to enjoy the taste of his mouth.

She ran her hand along his chest, skimming her fingers lightly over his skin. The male body had never intrigued her as much as it did now and she relished the feel of muscle and bone, his broad chest and his washboard belly. Her fingers trembled slightly as she accidentally brushed the hard ridge of his desire, evident through the worn fabric of his jeans.

Jillian sighed softly. She didn't think of herself as a sensual person, but with Nick's hands on her body, she was more of a woman than she'd ever been, acutely aware of her power over the man beside her. But all her power seemed lost when he began a lazy exploration of her body. His lips trailed after his fingers, first to her collarbone, then to the cleft between her breasts, and then to her stomach, her clothing pushed aside to reveal bare skin for Nick to taste.

Jillian knew this could only lead in one direction, but she was past worrying. She'd been fighting her feelings for him since the moment they'd met and she simply didn't have the strength to continue the battle. They'd been moving toward this moment all along and she was glad it had finally come.

Before long, her top became a barrier and he gently tugged it over her head. Jillian expected to feel embarrassed, but then she saw the pleasure in his gaze as he fingered the lacy edge of her bra. Jillian reached up and slipped the satin straps off her shoulders. He took his cue and nuzzled at her breast, capturing her nipple through the damp fabric of her bra.

Jillian's breath caught in her throat at the intimate contact, a current shooting through her body, setting her nerves on edge. How could she have lived for so long and never experienced this with a man? This pleasure was so intense it bordered on pain. "Oh," she murmured, furrowing her fingers through his hair.

Nick looked up and gave her a sleepy grin. "Does that feel good?" he asked, teasing at the nub with his thumb.

"Umm," Jillian murmured, arching beneath his touch.

"Jillie, maybe we should—"

She pressed her finger to his lips and shook her head. "You don't have to ask me if this is what I want. It is."

Perhaps she'd been waiting for this her entire life, for a man like Nick. She felt scared and reckless and completely exhilarated, as if she were about to step off the edge of a cliff without knowing what lay below. Her life up until this point had been so carefully planned that she'd even imagined a moment like this. But nothing in her past had prepared her for the sheer power of his touch, the warmth of his body next to hers, a raging need to make him ache for her touch.

For the first time in her life, she didn't have a plan. Logic had been discarded and she now operated on pure instinct. She couldn't reach for her computer and predict how this was all going to turn out. Would this be the first of many nights together? Or would it be all over tomorrow or the next day, when their time at the lake house ended? She should have been more concerned, but Jillian didn't care. All she cared about was the flood of exquisite sensation that surged through her body every time he touched her.

With hesitant hands, Jillian smoothed her palms over his shoulders. Muscle rippled beneath her fingers as he moved above her. Jillian's eyes drifted over his body, mesmerized by the sheer perfection of his broad chest and narrow waist. "I—I'm not sure what to do," she murmured. "I've never been—I mean, I have done this before but—"

With a low groan, he grabbed her around the waist and rolled her over on top of him, pulling her legs alongside his hips. He pushed up, then nuzzled the soft cleft between her breasts. "We'll just take it slow and figure it out as we go along."

A flood of relief washed over her and she smiled at him. Reaching around her back, Jillian unclasped her bra, then let it slide down her arms. A long sigh slipped from his lips as he took in the sight of her. Suddenly, she wasn't nervous anymore. The trust she'd come to have in Nick wasn't limited to their lives outside the bedroom.

"You're so beautiful," he murmured. Tenderly, he cupped her breast in his palm, his touch so stirring it took her breath away. "I knew you'd be beautiful."

Jillian closed her eyes and tipped her head back, enjoying the caress of his hands. Nick made her feel cherished and protected, and she could believe that he loved her, even if it wasn't really true. But it didn't matter, for nothing could make her turn back now. This was what mattered, this was what she needed. "Love me," she murmured. "Now."

"Now," he repeated, drawing her back down to the soft folds of the sheets. His mouth covered hers, his tongue urgent, his kiss insatiable. They fumbled with each other's clothes, hands frantic, limbs tangling, breathlessly anxious to do away with any barriers between them.

When they were finally rid of the last barriers, Jillian stilled, letting her gaze drift over his naked body, stretched out beside her. Her gaze fell on his hard shaft, fascinated by the beauty of his desire.

"Touch me," he said, his voice low and ragged with need.

She reached out and drew her fingers along the length of him, lingering there as his breathing quickened. Nick moaned softly as she closed her fingers around him and began to stroke him gently. This was how she'd always imagined true passion to be, inhibition tossed aside, desire like wildfire out of control.

Nick drew in a sharp breath, then grabbed her wrist. At first, Jillian thought she'd done something wrong, but the look on his face told her she'd brought him too far, too fast. He smiled then pulled her arm over her head. He raised the other one, then cuffed her wrists in his hand.

With a low growl, he let his other hand drift down along her body, lower and lower until he reached her moist core. Patiently, with exquisite tenderness, he touched her there, teasing at her until Jillian arched against his hand. If she'd been surprised by the powerful sensations before, those that coursed through her body now made her nearly mad with need.

As gently as his seduction had begun, it now slowed, as he twisted on the bed, reaching for his jeans and pulling a condom out of his wallet. He tore the foil packet open with his teeth, then watched, eyes half-hooded as Jillian sheathed him.

His eyes fixed on hers as he pulled her beneath him and settled himself between her thighs. Jillian had lost herself in his gaze so many times, but now she felt as if he'd opened the doors to his soul. As he gently probed at her entrance, she watched as raw emotion glittered in their blue depths. He loved her and though she'd never expected to hear the words, the feeling was evident in his eyes.

A soft moan slipped from her lips as she wrapped her legs around his waist. He began to move inside of her and slowly she lost touch with reality. But one clear thought still remained in her mind. Jillian loved Nick. And whether they parted for good in a few days or became lovers for a lifetime, it didn't matter. She'd always know, in her heart, that he'd loved her, too.

8

AFTER MAKING LOVE to Jillie until the predawn hours, Nick should have fallen into a deep and dreamless sleep. But instead, he lay awake, Jillie wrapped in his arms, her body tucked in the curve of his. The first light of day had just begun to illuminate the windows and he knew they'd have only an hour or so before they'd have to face the morning and three sleep-deprived boys.

These were their last hours together. Nick had no choice but to head back to Providence and the responsibilities of his work there. Had he known he was going to meet a woman like Jillie Marshall, he might have passed on some of the projects he had pending. Another day with her was all he wanted—all he needed.

Though they'd given in to their passion, things still remained unsettled between them. Where would they go from here? She'd been clear last night that she didn't expect any promises. And with any other woman, Nick might have been relieved. But if Jillie really thought their lovemaking was all about physical gratification, she had another guess coming. When he touched her, when he moved inside of her, it only confirmed what he knew. He was in love with Jillie Marshall. But did she love him?

At first he'd thought his little deception was standing in the way of something more serious between them. But now he was glad for it, glad that they'd made love while she still believed he was a working-class guy. What better way to test the strength of her feelings? He wanted Jillie to want him for who he was, not for what he'd made of his life. He didn't want to be just a line of check marks on her list of requirements for a husband. Acceptable job, decent education, good professional prospects, passable manners. His IQ and his bank account had nothing to do with the man he was.

Nick sighed softly, a strand of Jillie's hair tickling his cheek. But now that he knew she cared enough for him to make love with him, it was time to tell her the truth. When she woke up, he'd come clean. If she truly loved him, then the deception wouldn't matter. He was still the same man, just with slightly better prospects. She might be angry, but she'd understand why he'd done it. Hell, look at his history with long-term commitment. He hadn't taken the time to be sure of Claire's feelings before he proclaimed his own.

This time he'd be sure. If Professor Jillian Marshall could love a simple carpenter, capitulate to an emotion that went against everything she'd ever wanted, then maybe there was a chance she could love Nick Callahan for the rest of her life. And that's what he wanted with Jillie—a lifetime.

Settled on a course of action, Nick closed his eyes and tried to fall back asleep. But lying in bed with Jillie naked in his arms didn't exactly promote healthful rest. He slowly slid his palm over her hip and down her thigh, enjoying the feel of her skin beneath his fingers. Memories of their lovemaking teased at his brain. Flashes of sensation still pulsed through his body.

Loving Jillie had been a revelation. It was obvious that she'd never had a lover who had taken time with her, who had let her passion unfold slowly. She was nervous and clumsy, then eager and excited, and finally bold and unbridled. And though she knew the technical workings between a man and a woman, she had no idea of what she'd missed beyond that.

The first time, it had been all about need and release. But the second time they made love, Nick had shown her the true depths of her passion. He'd brought her to the edge again and again, before gently retreating. And when she finally came, any memories she had of previous lovers had been permanently erased from her mind.

Nick smiled to himself. He wanted to be the only man in her life, the man she woke up with in the morning and fell asleep with at night. He'd always thought falling in love would be difficult, finding a woman who captured his heart and his mind. But loving Jillie was so simple, so natural.

He pushed up on his elbow and peered over her shoulder at her face. She was beautiful. He'd never known a woman who could stir his senses with just a coy look or a simple smile. Reaching out, he gently skimmed his fingers over the dark circles beneath her eyes. He'd let her sleep, confident in the fact that they'd make love again very soon.

A soft cry broke the morning stillness and Nick glanced at the bedside clock. The boys were up. He pressed a soft kiss to Jillie's shoulder, then rolled out of bed. If he could keep them quiet, maybe she'd have a chance to catch up on all the sleep she'd missed the night before. Nick grabbed his jeans and tugged them on, not bothering with underwear. Then he softly padded out of the room.

Though he tried to keep the boys quiet over the next hour, lack of sleep and childish energy made that nearly impossible. He was just about to take them outside when

Jillie wandered downstairs, her hair tousled and her slender body wrapped in a disheveled robe. She headed right for the coffeemaker and poured herself a mug.

"Good morning," Nick said.

She glanced up at him over the rim of the mug. He saw wariness in her eyes, as well as a good measure of exhaustion. "Morning."

"I made French toast for the boys. There are a few pieces still warm in the oven if you're hungry."

"Thank you," she said. "I—I am a little hungry."

Nick grabbed a pot holder from the hook near the stove and removed the plate from the oven. He set it in front of her on the breakfast bar. "Syrup or jam?"

"Syrup," she said.

"Butter?"

Jillie nodded. He stood back as she picked up her fork and sliced into the French toast. Geez, what was wrong with them? They'd just shared the most intimate moments of their lives together and all he could talk about was condiments! He strode around the end of the breakfast bar and spun Jillie's stool until she faced him. She stared up at him with wide eyes as he grabbed her fork from her hand and set it behind her. Then he cupped her face in his palms and gave her a gentle but passionate kiss. "There," he said, when he pulled back. "That's the way we should start the morning."

A pretty blush slowly stained her cheeks. "About last night, I—"

"I know," he said, slipping his arms around her waist. "It was pretty amazing." He kissed her again, this time on the tip of her nose. "You were pretty amazing."

"That's not what I—"

"Jillie, we don't have to discuss it to make it real," he said, nuzzling her cheek. "What happened between us happened for a reason. It was meant to happen all along. And I'm glad it did.''

He took her hands and wove his fingers through hers. ''We do have to discuss a few things, though.'' He slipped onto the stool beside her. ''I have to leave this morning,'' he said. ''I've got a business meeting early tomorrow and I've got a presentation to prepare. But before I leave, I wanted to tell you something.''

''I don't need to hear anything,'' she said. ''There's nothing to talk about.''

''Actually there is. And it's kind if important. You might be upset and I—''

She forced a smile, then jumped to her feet and began to wipe off the counter. ''You—you don't have to worry about me,'' she said. ''I'm perfectly capable of taking care of the boys on my own now. Besides, my mother said she'd come over tomorrow morning to watch the boys until Greg and Roxy get home. I—I have to get back to my life, too. I have some important…meetings tomorrow myself.''

Nick sat back. Did this mean she wouldn't talk to Roxy before he saw her next? If that were true, then maybe he could delay a bit, lay a little more groundwork before confessing to his little lie. ''Jillie, are you all right?''

''Of course,'' she snapped.

''Are you angry with me?'' he asked, trying to capture her gaze with his.

''Don't be ridiculous! You have to leave. So do I. We both knew this would all come to an end sooner or later.''

''It's not coming to an end, Jillie. We will see each other again.''

"Sure," she said in a cheery voice. "We'll probably run into each other at Greg and Roxy's Christmas party. Maybe sometime next summer. It's not like we're going to go back to being strangers. That's not what I meant."

"It's not what I meant either." Nick shook his head. "We're damn well going to see each other again—and within the next twenty-four hours."

Jillie blinked in confusion. "What do you mean?"

Nick bit back an oath. "What the hell have we been doing here, Jillie? Playing house?"

"I—I don't understand," she said. "We've been taking care of the boys."

"Did you expect that I'd just walk out on you and never see you again? If you did, then you don't know me at all."

She looked up at him, the first time this morning that she'd met his gaze directly. A tremulous smile curved her lips. "That's right. We don't know each other at all. So I have no right to expect anything from you. I don't think you should feel obligated to—"

"You don't want anything beyond what we shared last night?" he asked.

"What I want doesn't make a difference. You see, it's all a matter of mathematical probabilities," she said.

Nick looked at her, dumbfounded. Whenever she felt nervous or ill-prepared, she always retreated to her ordered little world of formulas and computer models. But what the hell did math have to do with what they shared in bed? "All right, I'll bite. Explain, Professor Marshall."

"Over the past few days, I've been working on a probability table. I found some data on the Internet and I created a model using divorce rates. Did you know the most prevalent reason for divorce is incompatibility?''

"So?"

"Well, we're clearly incompatible," Jillie said. "You know nothing about the Goldbach conjecture and I know nothing about power drills."

"What the hell does this have to do with anything? From where I sit, we get along pretty damn well."

"Maybe we get along now, but sooner or later, we won't. According to my charts, the probabilities of our forming a lasting relationship are approximately nine thousand, six hundred and thirty-seven to one. It—it's simple mathematics," she said. "I can show you the charts if you want."

"Forget the charts, Jillie," he said. "Tell me how you feel."

"About what?"

"Us. Together. Jillie, last night we made love. More than once, if you remember."

"My research says that when good sex is factored into a relationship, it doesn't significantly affect the compatibility ratios."

"All right," he said, his frustration nearing the breaking point. "Let me make it very plain. Are we going to see each other again after I walk out today?"

"Do you want to see me?" Jillie asked.

"Do you want to see me?" Nick countered. She thought about her answer a bit longer than he would have liked and Nick sighed. "What are you afraid of?"

"I'm not afraid," she answered, her chin tipped up defiantly.

"You hide behind all your numbers and formulas. Why don't you just say it? You don't want to fall in love with some working class slob who gets his hands dirty at work. You're a snob, Jillie.'' He pushed out of his chair and paced the length of the kitchen.

"I'm just a realist," she murmured.

"Hah! You're a fraidy-cat," he said.

Jillie gasped. "A fraidy-cat? Where did you get that from? Andy?"

"Let's be honest, Jillie. You're afraid of how you feel. You're falling in love with me and you don't know what to do. How will you introduce me to your egghead friends? What will you do if we can't discuss irrational numbers over breakfast? How will we ever live on my measly salary building bookshelves?"

"That's not the reason," she said. "I'm simply using my common sense."

"I think the past week has proved one thing and that is, you don't have an ounce of common sense—not when it comes to the boys and certainly not when it comes to me."

"We barely know each other," she snapped. "I met you nine days ago. How can you possibly expect me to make a life decision based on nine days?"

"I'm not asking you to marry me," he said. "I just want a damn date."

This stopped her cold. She opened her mouth, but it took a few seconds for the words to come out. "A—a date? Like dinner or a movie?"

"That's a start," he said. "Maybe if we did something more than just change diapers and sweep up Cheerios, we might find we're pretty compatible after all."

"All right," she said. She grabbed a pad of paper from beside the refrigerator and scribbled down her address. "I'm going to be home tomorrow night. Pick me up at seven. We'll…go out. And I'll prove to you that I'm right. This will probably be the worst date you've ever had.''

Nick grinned, satisfied that he'd finally gotten through to her. One date was all he needed to prove his point. They belonged together. "It's a plan, then." He stepped in front of her and grabbed her around the waist, yanking her body against his. Without giving her a chance to speak, he kissed her long and hard, making sure it was a kiss that would last until they saw each other next. When he pulled back, he reached up and cupped her cheek in his palm, forcing her eyes to meet his.

"As hard as you'll work to prove that you're right," he murmured, "I'm going to work twice as hard to prove that you're wrong."

JILLIAN OPENED HER EYES long after the sun had peeked over the horizon. She'd had trouble sleeping and drifted off sometime in the wee hours of the morning. After only one night in Nick's arms, she suddenly found it difficult to sleep alone. Maybe it was more than that. After all, he'd been close by for all those days and now he was miles away. She didn't feel as safe and secure without him near.

She rolled over and groaned softly. She shouldn't have worried about sleeping alone. The boys had been awake before dawn and she'd brought all three into bed with her as well as Duke, who had taken up Nick's spot, his big head resting on the pillow. Even with a bed full of warm bodies, she still missed him.

In truth, Jillian half-expected him to be there when she wandered downstairs, a coffee mug in his hand and a boyish grin on his face. He'd be dressed in his typical jeans and T-shirt, casual yet incredibly sexy. She'd been so accustomed to the rumpled look of academia, the tweed jackets and khaki pants, the dull colors, that she found Nick a refreshing break in a world of rather mundane men.

But was that all he was? A break? A brief interlude? A vacation fling? Now that he was gone, Jillian had expected to put him right out of her mind. But instead, she couldn't stop thinking about him. Suddenly all the reasons for not loving Nick had turned into the exact reasons why she loved him so deeply.

They had absolutely nothing in common, yet she found him endlessly fascinating. Though he was just a regular guy, she'd come to see him as a hero of sorts, a kind and honorable man, a man she could count on in a crisis. And there was no denying that the physical aspect of their relationship was as close to perfect as she could imagine.

So what was holding her back? Why had she fallen back on her formulas to scare him away? And why was she so uneasy about their date tonight? They were the same people they'd been all week. The only thing that would change was geography. Perhaps it was because their week at the lake house had been like a week on a deserted island. The real world had been kept at bay, and they'd been able to enjoy each other's company without life interfering.

Back in Boston, she wouldn't be Aunt Jillie, inept baby-sitter and instigator of domestic disasters, damsel in distress. She'd be Dr. Jillian Marshall, brilliant mathematician, career woman. And he wouldn't be her white knight, riding in to the rescue. He'd just be...

Jillian cursed softly, then punched at her pillow. The

truth was, she didn't know him at all, beyond the fact that he made her knees weak with his kisses and her body burn with his lovemaking. Maybe she'd been right to accept a date with him. By the end of the evening tonight, her doubts should be put to rest. And then she could go on with her life as if she'd never met him…and never fallen in love.

She snuggled back down beneath the covers and closed her eyes. There was no use worrying about that now. She'd have plenty to worry about once her mother arrived. She'd have to clean up the house and dress the boys and get them ready for Greg and Roxy's arrival this afternoon. Though she'd first intended to leave before they got home, Jillian had decided to cancel her afternoon appointments with her graduate students and face the music like an adult. She owed Roxy a big apology and she intended to tell her sister everything that happened—except all the parts about Nick.

Jillian only wanted to doze for a few minutes but the next time she opened her eyes, she found Roxy and Greg standing in the doorway of the bedroom. "We're home, we're home!" Duke lifted his head and barked, and the boys pushed up from the bed and rubbed their sleepy eyes. A few moments later, screams of delight filled the room, and Roxy threw herself onto the bed and hugged her sons.

Stunned, Jillian ran a hand through her tangled hair. "What are you doing home so early? I thought your flight didn't get in until two."

"We caught an earlier flight," Greg said, grabbing Andy and tossing him up, before giving him a bear hug. "Rox couldn't stand to be away a moment longer, so we took the red-eye from L.A. How have my boys been?"

Zach and Sam scrambled over their mother and threw themselves at Greg. "I see the house is still standing," he said with a grin.

Jillian smiled sheepishly. "I'm sorry about the mess. Mother was going to come over and watch them so I could clean up. I wanted to have them all bathed and dressed in their best."

Roxy rolled over on her back and laid her head on Duke's hip. "Don't be silly," she said. "The house looks fine, and so do the boys." She leaned over and hugged Jillian. "And you look good. You've got some color."

Jillian reached up and touched her cheeks. "We—we spent a lot of time outside. The weather was perfect."

Roxy frowned, fixing her with a shrewd look. "There's something else," she said.

Jillian threw the covers back and jumped out of bed. Running her fingers through her tangled hair again, she searched for her robe, tripping over the boys as they scampered around the room. Was it that obvious? Could Roxy tell she'd made love to a man the night before last? Or was her sister sensing something else? "So how was your flight?" Jillian asked, deftly changing the subject.

"Endless," Roxy said, snagging Zach around the waist and nuzzling his neck. "I am so glad to be home. Paradise is nice for a few days, but the silence was beginning to drive me crazy." She sighed contentedly. "So, how were they? Tell me the truth."

"We had a great time," Jillian said, picking up a brush. "They're a handful but we got along fine."

Roxy raised her eyebrow. "Is there anything else you'd like to tell me about?"

Greg cleared his throat, then gathered up the boys.

"I'll get the monsters some breakfast while you two talk."

Roxy sent him a grateful smile, then turned her attention back to Jillian. She pushed up from the bed, crossed the room to the dresser and stared at Jillian's reflection in the mirror. Jillian kept brushing her hair, thankful for the distraction. "I didn't notice Nick's truck in the driveway. Is he gone?"

Jillian shrugged nonchalantly. "I don't know. I think he finished the library, but I don't keep track of his schedule."

Roxy grabbed the brush from Jillian's hand, set it on the dresser and drew her over to the bed. "Talk," she ordered.

Jillian took a deep breath, then forced a smile. "There is one thing I should say to you right away. I'm sorry I underestimated what it takes to be a mother. And if I said anything to make you feel bad, I'm sorry for that, too. It takes so much more than organization to keep this household running and I know that now." Jillian bent forward and hugged Roxy. "And I'm so glad you're back."

Roxy chuckled. "I noticed the downstairs bathroom ceiling was freshly painted and I've got a new wallpaper border. Let me guess. The bathtub upstairs ran over and wrecked the ceiling?"

"The toilet," Jillian said. "Hot Wheels."

"Hmm. Three weeks ago it was every towel in the linen cupboard tossed into a tub full of water and bubbles. That's the closest I've ever come to putting all three of them up for adoption."

"Really?" Jillian said, warmed by the news that she wasn't the only one to suffer the occasional domestic meltdown. "That makes me feel better. I might as well tell you that I've also become intimately acquainted with the volunteer fire department. They rescued Sammy when he got locked in the bathroom. After I tried to crawl through the window, wrecked the screen and sprained my ankle."

"Sounds like it was a pretty normal week around here," Roxy said.

"I don't know what I would have done without Nick," Jillian murmured, staring down at her fingers.

Roxy leaned down and caught Jillian's gaze with hers. "I was wondering when you were going to mention him," she said.

"He did a great job on the bookshelves," Jillian said. "He's a very good carpenter."

"Yeah," Roxy said. "And the fact that we don't have to pay him makes him even better."

"What?" Jillian said. "You mean you didn't hire him to build the bookshelves?"

"If I paid him what he was worth," Roxy said with a chuckle, "those bookshelves would have cost about as much as the house. We invited him to stay in the guest cottage after he broke up with Claire and he returned the favor by building the bookcases. I guess he likes to work with his hands every now and then. It probably relaxes him."

"I—I don't understand," Jillian said. "I thought he was a carpenter. And—and who is Claire?"

Roxy blinked in surprise, before an uneasy look crossed her face. "Didn't Nick tell you what he does?"

Jillian shook her head. What was he hiding? Was he some kind of criminal, a drug runner or a mob boss?

What could be so bad that he'd keep it from her? And who the hell was Claire?

"That's odd," Roxy said. "He's not a carpenter, he's an industrial engineer and architect. Pretty famous, too. He designs factories all over the world. A few years ago he designed a vehicle assembly building for NASA. He designed our house as a wedding present when he couldn't be here for the wedding."

"But—but, I thought he was just some ordinary guy."

Roxy giggled. "Nick? Ordinary? Oh, he must have found that amusing. He can be such a tease. And he hates it when women go on and on about all his fame and fortune. I think if he could have been a carpenter, he would have. He just likes to build things for relaxation. He has a pretty high-powered job."

Jillian felt a surge of anger burn in her brain. Was that what this had been to him—an amusement? A little charade? She'd admitted that she barely knew him, but now she wondered if anything she'd believed about him was true. Jillian swallowed hard. "Who is Claire?" she demanded. "His wife? His mistress? Or is she like me—someone he sleeps with on occasion?"

"You slept with Nick Callahan?" Roxy asked, with a gasp.

Jillian jumped up and paced the room, her hands twisted in the belt of her robe. "God, I can't believe I was stupid enough to go to bed with him! I—I thought he was sweet and honorable. And now I find out he was lying to me all the time!"

Roxy reached out and grabbed her hand, stopping her restless movement. "Jillie, what's going on between you two? Are you in love with Nick Callahan?"

"I—I thought he was just some ordinary guy, a guy

I could never be serious about. And I was going to write the whole thing off as a little fling. But then I let myself believe that he was something more.''

She snatched up her clothes from around the room, then stripped off the bathrobe and nightgown. "In love with Nick Callahan?'' Jillian laughed sharply as she began to dress. "I may have thought I was—for a few minutes. But now that I look back on it, maybe it was just temporary insanity.''

A GRAY MIST SKIMMED across the choppy surface of Narragansett Bay and clouds hung low in the sky, threatening a warm summer rain. Nick stood on a bluff above the water, breathing deeply of the tangy salt air. His thoughts drifted back to the lake house and he glanced at his watch. By his estimate, Jillie should probably be on her way back to Boston by now.

In a few hours, he'd drive up to Cambridge, ring her doorbell and they'd begin their future together. Thoughts of Jillie had teased at his mind constantly over the past twenty-four hours. During daylight hours, he'd lapse into silly fantasies, and last night, those fantasies had become his dreams. Already, he missed having her in his bed, close enough to touch in his sleep.

Even this morning, during his business meeting, he'd caught himself wondering what she was doing, whether the boys had woken her up before dawn, what they'd eaten for breakfast, whether she'd bothered to comb her mussed hair before coming downstairs. He'd finished his meeting in Hartford before noon, a successful presentation for a new bottling plant he'd been hoping to design, and then moved on to an appointment with his real estate broker, Ken Carlisle, that he'd arranged long before his visit to the cottage.

"What do you think?" Ken now asked.

"It's a beautiful piece of property," Nick replied. In truth, he could already imagine the house sitting high above the water. He'd use stone and cedar, as if it grew right out of the rugged landscape. But the more he tried to convince himself that he'd found exactly what he was looking for, the more doubts he had.

"I'm not sure," Nick murmured.

"You're not going to find a piece of property this large on the Bay," Ken said. "If we don't make an offer today, it will be gone tomorrow."

"It's just so…" Nick sighed. What was it? So secluded? There were houses just down the road. And it was a quick drive in to Providence. It would be the perfect spot for his new home, except…

"How far would you say we are from Boston?" Nick asked.

"Boston?" Ken shrugged. "I don't know. Maybe an hour. Probably a lot longer in rush hour."

Jillie lived in Boston. If he was at all optimistic about a future with her, then this would be the wrong choice. Sooner or later, he'd grow impatient with the hour wasted in the car, an hour not spent in Jillie's arms, an hour wishing they were already together. And she might not want to stay overnight with him, not on nights when she had classes the next day. Rush-hour traffic into Boston would turn a one-hour drive into two or three. And what if she didn't like the property? Or the house he'd built? Building something new was an awfully big investment for a guy who wasn't sure what the future held.

Maybe he was being too optimistic. After all, they'd

only known each other a little more than a week. A person couldn't make life decisions after such a short time—isn't that what she'd said? He'd seen her in just one situation and she barely knew anything about him. Hell, this whole thing could fall apart after just one date.

"Even if you don't build, this could be a great investment," Ken said. "You could hold it for awhile, then sell it at a profit."

Nick shook his head. "I don't think this is the right place for me."

"Well, I suppose you don't have to make a move right away. It's not like you're homeless since Claire moved out of the house a couple of days ago."

Nick glanced over at him, startled by the mention of her name. He'd lived with her for nearly a year, and now, after only a couple of months apart, her name brought absolutely no feelings at all—no anger, no regret, nothing. "Actually, I'm glad you brought that up. I want you to list the Providence house. Price it to move quickly."

"But where are you going to live?"

He shrugged. "I've been sleeping on the sofa in my office since I got back from New Hampshire. I'll look for an apartment in a few days. I just don't want to go back to that house. It's like another man's life and another man's home. You can sell it, can't you?"

Ken frowned. "Sure. It's a very desirable piece of property. In the meantime, I could show you some condos downtown. It's got to be better than sleeping on your office sofa."

Nick shook his head. "Nah, I think I'll wait. I'm not ready to make any permanent decisions right now."

Damn it, he hated living in limbo. He wanted his life settled, his future laid out for him. Was what happened with Jillie just a passing fling? Or was the emotion he saw in her eyes when they made love meant to last? Nick knew what he wanted. He wanted Jillie Marshall in his life. Now, next week and for years to come.

He wasn't quite sure when he'd fallen in love with her, but it was probably in the midst of one of her disasters. He knew it for certain a few nights ago in the hospital, when he realized he never wanted Jillie to feel scared or worried again. He wanted to be there to protect her—for the rest of her life.

How he knew this was a complete mystery. Hell, he'd lived with Claire for a year and he'd never been quite this sure of his feelings. He'd known Jillie for nine days and there was absolutely no doubt in his mind that she was the one he was supposed to spend his life loving.

Her feelings were another matter. In bed, her passion took over and he could easily believe that the feelings were mutual. He *wanted* to believe. But the next morning, nothing had seemed the same. When he'd touched her, she stiffened slightly and when he'd tried to bring up their future, she found some math topic to discuss.

At first, he'd thought she was simply keeping their relationship from the boys. But now he wasn't sure. Knowing Jillie, she'd probably convinced herself that what they shared was only possible in the atmosphere of the lake house and nowhere else. In the outside world, she was a respected mathematician with high standards for a potential mate. And he was just a…a "carpenter guy."

Nick cursed beneath his breath. He'd tell her tonight and let the chips fall where they may. But would the truth be good enough for her? After all, he wasn't a rocket scientist, although he had designed a building for

NASA a few years back. And though he'd gone through his college level math classes with ease, he couldn't do quadratic equations in his head.

He would tell her tonight, over a candlelit dinner and good bottle of wine. He'd patiently explain himself, his concerns, his doubts about her feelings, and then he'd get her to admit her feelings for him. Only then could their life together really begin.

9

THOUGH SHE'D BEEN expecting the sound for the past half hour, Jillian jumped when she heard the intercom buzz. She sat in the center of her bed, her knees tucked up under her chin, waiting, wondering how many times Nick would buzz before he went away.

She felt like a fool, a naive twit who had been duped by a more worldly and sophisticated man. To hear Roxy tell it, Nick Callahan was quite the ladies' man. He'd dated all types of beautiful women, from models to flight attendants, even an actress from New York. Sure, he'd settled down with Claire what's-her-name for a year or so, but, after that ended, Jillian had become just the first in what would undoubtedly be another long line of lovers.

Though she didn't consider herself beautiful, Jillian knew she'd at least been convenient. A willing woman close at hand, a plaything for Nick Callahan's amusement. At first, she'd been hurt, but now she was just angry. How could she have let herself believe that they could share anything worthwhile? She should have trusted her instincts.

Roxy had a completely different opinion of the situation, a view that Jillian couldn't understand. Maybe her sister chose to give Nick the benefit of the doubt because they were such good friends. But Jillian couldn't believe that Nick deceived her for anything but perverse motives.

Sure, she may have been a little pretentious, a little snooty at first. But after they'd become friends, he could have told her the truth. It certainly would have saved her making a fool of herself time and time again.

She thought back to all the conversations she'd had with him. "Oh, God, I told him he should go back to school and become an architect. He must have gotten such a laugh. And all that babbling about the importance of bookshelves. He must have thought I was such a dope."

The buzzer sounded again and she ground her teeth and fought the urge to let him in. She'd love just two minutes to tell him exactly what she thought of his little games. Jillian hugged her knees to her chest and slowly counted to ten, then twenty and thirty. The apartment remained silent.

Relief mixed with disappointment. Jillian was happy that he'd finally gone, yet strangely frustrated by the fact that he hadn't tried just a little harder to see her. In truth, she had wanted to be pushed, to find an excuse to see him again. She missed his handsome face and the warmth of his smile. With a soft sigh, she crawled off the bed and wandered toward the kitchen. But as she passed the front door, a knock rattled the hinges. Startled, she cried out, then pressed her hand to her rapidly thudding heart.

"Jillie?"

The sound of his voice, even muffled by the door, still had the capacity to turn her knees weak and make her head swim. The memory of that same voice, deepened by passion, flitted through her mind and she blushed as she recalled the things he'd said to her as they made love.

She tiptoed up to the door and peeked through the

peephole. A soft moan slipped from her lips. Why did he have to look so damn handsome? Jillian spun away from the door, her emotions at war inside her. Could there be an explanation for his lies? She tried in vain to think of a reason she might find forgivable, but she couldn't come up with anything even remotely plausible.

He knocked again. "Jillie, are you in there?"

"Go away!" she called. "I don't want to talk to you." The moment the words were out of her mouth, she regretted them. She should have remained silent. Sooner or later, he would have given up.

"Jillie, let me in. Come on, I thought we were supposed to have a date."

Her temper tested, Jillian flipped the locks, pulled off the chain and yanked the door open. Her breath caught in her throat the moment her eyes came to rest on Nick. Gone was his usual wardrobe of faded jeans and a form-fitting T-shirt. Instead, he was dressed in an impeccably tailored suit, a white shirt that set off his deep tan and a conservative silk tie. But then she shouldn't have been surprised, since Nick really wasn't the carpenter she'd believed him to be.

With a charming smile, he produced a huge bouquet of flowers from behind his back. "I've been thinking about you every minute since we last saw each other." His gaze scanned her outfit, baggy sweatpants and an old cotton sweater. "You look beautiful."

Jillian grabbed the flowers from his hand then swung them at him, hitting the top of his head with a shower of petals and leaves. "You can take your flowers and your devil-may-care smile and your—your handsome face and you can leave!" She grabbed the edge of the door, intending to slam it in his face, but his hand shot out to stop her.

He gave her a long look. "Would you like to tell me what's wrong?" he asked, in a deceptively even voice.

"I only opened the door because I wanted to tell you face-to-face that we won't be going on any dates. Not now. Not ever."

A frown marred his perfect features. Then he drew in a sharp breath and took a step back. A soft curse slipped from his lips. "You talked to Roxy and Greg."

"Of course I did," she sneered. "What did you expect? That your little joke would just continue? Is that why you asked me out? So you could make an ever bigger fool out of me?"

"Jillie, that's not what I meant to do. And I was planning to tell you this morning. But then, when you said you'd be leaving before Greg and Roxy got home, I decided we should be alone when we talked." He raked his hands through his hair. "Hell, maybe I wanted them to tell you—to spare me from having to tell you myself."

"I don't want to hear anything you have to say!" She made to close the door again, but this time, he stepped around her and walked into her apartment.

"Don't you want to hear my explanation?"

"What possible reason could you have for lying to me?"

He slowly walked around the perimeter of her living room, gazing at paintings and knickknacks and the wall of awards above her desk. The mere presence of him in her apartment, so strong and determined, caused a shiver to run down her spine.

"At first, I didn't think it made a difference," he said, picking up a small plaque and examining it closely. "I didn't expect to fall in love with you."

His admission struck Jillian like a punch to the stomach. She opened her mouth to draw a breath, but she couldn't. Her head began to swim and, at first, she thought she must have misunderstood. Nick Callahan loved her? Jillian shook her head, unable to believe what he'd just admitted. If he loved her, then why had he lied?

"But you made it clear, time after time, that you couldn't possibly love me," he continued. "Not just me, the carpenter, but Nick Callahan, the man. So I let it go on. And when I fell in love with you, I thought I could use it to prove that you truly loved me." He glanced up at her and for a moment all her anger dissolved as his gaze probed hers. "I figured if you could love a man that you were dead set against loving, then maybe we had a chance."

He'd been right. She'd fought against loving him, convinced herself that nothing they'd shared was meant to last. And yet now, even after his deception, she still fought it. Why couldn't she keep herself from loving Nick Callahan?

Nick stared at a painting on the wall. "I know this doesn't make a lot of sense, but everything happened so fast and I wasn't always thinking clearly when it came to you. I just didn't want it to make a difference, and I convinced myself it wouldn't."

"Is—is that it?" Jillian asked.

"Not by a long shot." He loosened his tie, then unbuttoned the collar of his shirt. "I'm not going to leave until we get this settled."

Jillian shook her head, confused by all that had passed in such a short time. "As far as I'm concerned, it is settled. I don't have anything more to say to you."

"Why not? Because your computers and your number theories and your probabilities have already written us off? Or is it because this is something you can't control? Chaos theory at work again."

"I can trust my numbers. I can't trust you."

"Come on, Jillie, you know that's not true." He slowly made his way across the room, taking a few tentative steps at a time toward her. "We love who we love. Do you think I planned to fall in love with a woman who has already decided what she can and can't tolerate in a mate? Do you think I like being held up to some list of qualifications? Hell, I just broke up with Claire a few months ago. The last thing I expected—the last thing I *wanted*—was to have another woman in my life."

"I never made you any promises," Jillian said.

"No, you didn't. To you, I was just a working-class guy. It didn't matter how I made you feel or what we shared when we were together."

"Can't you see that we just weren't meant to be together?"

He slowly reached out and touched her hand, covering her fingers with his. Warmth seeped up her arm, like a drug, lulling her into a false sense of security.

Nick sighed. "The only thing I see is a woman scared of her feelings. You hide behind your numbers because they're orderly and logical. Love isn't logical, Jillie."

She took a ragged breath. How could these feelings be real? She and Nick had known each other barely ten days. A person couldn't fall in love that fast. *That* wasn't logical. "I think you should go," Jillian murmured, pulling the door open further. "I—I want you to go. Now."

Nick stared at her for a long moment, a mix of emotions flooding his expression. At first, she thought he might stay and press his point, but then he just shook his head and walked to the door. But as he passed, he stopped and turned to her.

A split second later, she was in his arms. His mouth covered hers and he kissed her like he'd never kissed her before. Jillian's legs went boneless and though she wanted to push him away, she couldn't seem to make her body do what her mind commanded. So she did the only thing she could do. Jillian kissed him back.

When he finally let her go, she stumbled, then grabbed onto the door. A slow smile curled the corners of Nick's mouth. He grabbed the bouquet from her white-knuckled hand and nodded. "I guess I found out what I needed to know," he said. "The next move is yours, Jillie."

With that, Nick turned on his heel and walked out, leaving Jillian to wonder just how she'd managed to do without his kisses for a whole twenty-four hours.

NICK GLANCED UP at the clock on the microwave, then rinsed his coffee cup in the sink. The boys were asleep in bed, tucked in by Roxy before she and Greg had left for a night out at the movies. The lake house was silent and he stretched out on the sofa and linked his hands behind his head.

He'd been at the lake for the past few days, soaking up the last rays of summer and helping Greg out with a few projects. In truth, he'd come hoping to run into Jillie again. He'd considered paying a visit to the college or her apartment in Cambridge, but had decided to leave that as a last resort. For now, he was counting on Roxy's help. In the spirit of familial interference, Roxy had extended an invitation to Jillie to join the family at the lake house for the Labor Day weekend. Of course, she hadn't mentioned that Nick would be there.

Unfortunately, Jillie had begged off, citing an overwhelming work schedule. Disappointed, Nick had decided to make the best of the holiday weekend. The boys had been thrilled to see him and he and Greg had taken them for endless rides around the lake in Greg's speedboat. Roxy had chatted on and on about Jillie, filling him in on her life since he'd seen her last, almost three weeks ago.

Nick closed his eyes, listening to the soft whir of the ceiling fan above his head. He'd have to come up with another plan, a way to convince Jillie that they belonged together—that they were *good* together. He allowed his thoughts to drift to more sensual subject matter. An image of Jillie swam in his mind, her body naked, moving sinuously above him, her hair tumbled around her face. Nick sighed softly, remembering the silken feel of her skin, the sweet taste of her mouth....

He wasn't sure whether he'd fallen asleep or not, but he sat up when a thudding sound from the front of the house interrupted his nap. He glanced at the clock and noticed that only fifteen minutes had passed. Greg and Roxy weren't due home for an hour or two.

He levered off the sofa and quietly walked to the stairway, listening for the boys. But another thud from the direction of the living room drew him into the dark foyer. He peered inside the archway to see a shadow dance by one of the windows. "What's this?" he murmured. He strode back to the kitchen and dialed the police, gave his location and explained the situation.

As he hurried back to the living room, Nick grabbed the first weapon he could find, a plastic baseball bat. He got there just in time to see the sash being raised. He thought about heading to the boys' room and protecting them until the cops came. Or turning the lights on and trying to scare the intruder away. But what if the guy had a—

A tightly held breath slipped from his lips as a head popped through the window. Soft brunette hair shone in the feeble light from the porch. She grunted, then cursed softly. "This is what you get for changing your mind," she muttered to herself.

"Jillie," he murmured, so softly she didn't hear. His heart twisted in his chest and Nick fought the urge to cross the room and pull her into his arms. He'd missed her so much and now that she was near, he wanted nothing more than to kiss her and touch her without hesitation.

She struggled through the window, tumbling onto the floor, her feet flying above her head. Another curse reverberated through the silent room. Her eyes hadn't adjusted to the light by the time she stood up and she tripped over a footstool. Nick took a quick step toward her, catching her in his arms before she fell. "You could have rung the bell," he said.

Jillian screamed and threw her arm out, whacking him in the nose. Nick let out a vivid oath, dropped the bat and cupped his nose with his hand. He felt the warmth of blood on his palm and groaned. "Damn it, Jillie, either you're going to kill yourself or you're going to kill me."

"Nick?" She stumbled over to a nearby lamp and flipped it on. Light flooded the room and he squinted. "You're bleeding!" she cried. Jillie rushed to his side, then tried to staunch the flow with the cuff of her jacket.

Nick gently pushed her arm away. "I'm all right." He tipped his head back and pinched his nose. "What the hell are you doing here?"

"What the hell are *you* doing here?" she countered.

"I was invited," Nick said.

Jillie frowned suspiciously. "So was I."

"Usually invited guests come through the front door."

"I—I didn't think anyone was home," Jillie said. "Roxy called me yesterday to ask if I'd come up for a visit. When I arrived, all the lights were off. I didn't realize until I got here that I'd left the key to the house back at my apartment. I figured everyone was in bed and I didn't want to wake the boys and—'' She drew in a sharp breath. "Did you know I was coming?"

"I knew you were invited," Nick replied. "But until you broke in and—damn!" He turned and ran back to the kitchen, then dialed the police again. While he was waiting for the operator, he grabbed a paper towel and held it up to his nose. But before he could ask the operator to call off the squad car, he heard the sound of sirens out on the road.

Jillie came rushing in. "You called the police?"

"I thought you were a burglar! But then I don't have to explain that mistake to you."

"I don't believe this," Jillie said. "This just gets worse and worse."

Nick stepped around her and walked back to the foyer. Jillie followed hard on his heels. They both walked outside to meet the police. To Nick's surprise, the police recognized him from the last time they'd visited the Hunter household. A quick explanation was all it took to send them on their way. Jillie waited until they'd turned out of the driveway before she headed to her car.

"Where are you going?" Nick called.

"Back to Cambridge. I'm not staying here—not with you."

"Jillie, it's late. Don't be silly. You'll be staying in the house and I'm in the cottage."

"Don't be silly?" Jillie repeated. "Isn't that what you counted on? A few more laughs from Jillian Marshall."

He reached out and grabbed her arm. "Jillie, don't do this. Just stay, get a good night's sleep and tomorrow we'll talk. I'm glad you came."

Jillie stared up at him for a long moment, then nodded. "I am tired."

Nick opened the car door, reached in and grabbed her bag. Then he slipped his arm around her shoulders. "Roxy will be glad to see you. And the boys have been in fine form. They gave Duke a new look."

"Duke?"

"They smeared his fur with a jar of marshmallow cream. Roxy didn't find out until it was dry. The boys were covered with sticky dog hair and Duke looked as if the Sta-Puf man just exploded in his dog house."

Jillie smiled. "I'm glad things haven't changed around here. Now that I've arrived, it's bound to get more interesting."

They reached the bottom of the stairs and Nick gave her the overnight bag. Then he pressed a quick kiss to her forehead. "I really am glad you're here," he murmured. "I was hoping I'd see you this weekend."

Jillie nodded, then turned to climb the stairs. The temptation to follow her up to the bedroom was undeniable. He'd gently push her back onto the bed and make love to her until the sun came up in the morning. But he wasn't about to take a chance. He would let Jillie come to him. And when she did, he'd never let her walk away again.

JILLIAN STOOD in the window of the guest bedroom and stared down at the lake. It was nearly midnight and the moon was just coming up over the water. Roxy and Greg had come home a half hour ago. Her sister had peeked in the room and called her name, but Jillian had pretended to be sleeping. Jillian could almost imagine the smug smile on her sister's face, her attempts at matchmaking a rousing success. A few moments later, she'd crawled out of bed and hurried to the window, hoping to watch Nick walk back down to the lake.

The light in the cottage was already on and Jillian tried to picture him inside, undressing for bed. The night was warm. Maybe he'd sleep outside as he had the last time he'd been to the lake house. She thought of the time she'd caught him swimming in the lake, how he'd emerged from the water, wet and naked, like some ancient Greek god. And how they'd made love later that night.

Drawn by some invisible force, Jillian tugged off her nightgown, then rummaged through her bag for the light cotton dress she'd packed. When she found what she was looking for, she pulled the dress over her naked body and ran her fingers through her hair. She couldn't sleep. Perhaps a short walk and some fresh air would help.

The house was silent as she tiptoed down the stairs and through the kitchen. She slowly opened the back door and stepped out into the warm night, the breeze fluttering over her skin. The grass was damp beneath her feet as she strolled toward the lake. She paused near the spot where they'd first discovered their desire for each other, remembering how they'd nearly made love right there in the middle of a thunderstorm.

She'd come here now looking for the moon on the surface of the lake, for the sound of the water lapping at the shore. But she'd really hoped to find Nick. Jillian stepped up onto the dock and walked to the end. But the dock was empty and the raft bobbed silently on the surface of the lake. With a soft sigh, she sat down and dangled her feet in the warm water.

A few minutes later, she heard footsteps. Jillian didn't turn around, just waited, her eyes closed, her heart slamming against the inside of her chest. She knew he'd come. She'd been counting on it. When she felt his presence behind her, she spoke. "I couldn't sleep." The words sounded so contrived, but she was past caring. She'd done everything she could to push him away, but no longer.

"Neither could I," Nick replied. He squatted down beside her, clasping his hands in front of him as he stared out at the lake. He was wearing a pair of jeans but no shirt. The soft light from the moon gleamed on his smooth skin and Jillian fought the urge to reach out and touch him.

"It's a beautiful night," he said. "There's an owl up in that tree. He'll hoot all night and keep me awake. Listen."

Jillian closed her eyes and let the night sounds penetrate her brain. Like a drug, the sounds soothed her nerves and focused her mind. "I can hear him." She glanced over at Nick. "When Greg and Roxy bought this property, I thought they were crazy, living way out here, away from the city. But now I can see the appeal. I was glad when Roxy invited me out for the weekend. I really wanted to come."

"A few weeks ago, I looked at some property on Narragansett Bay," Nick said, sitting down beside her. "I was thinking of building a new house." He glanced over at her. "But then I changed my mind."

The conversation came so easily between them. Gone was the tension and the apprehension. Jillian loved to listen to the sound of his voice and she wondered if they'd ever run out of things to talk about. She couldn't imagine a time like that. "You don't want to build a new house?"

Nick shook his head. "I do. But not that house. Not there."

"Then where?" Jillian asked.

"Closer to Boston," he said, reaching out to take her hand. "Closer to you."

Jillian swallowed hard, tears suddenly pushing at the corners of her eyes. Why had this taken so long? Had she simply needed to come to it on her own? The short time they'd known each other suddenly didn't make a difference. If she'd known Nick for ten years, she wouldn't feel any less love for him. "Really?"

"Jillie, I was standing on this gorgeous bluff overlooking the Bay and, suddenly, I realized I didn't want to build a house that you weren't going to live in. I didn't want to make decisions about cabinets and fixtures and appliances because I wanted you to make those decisions with me. I wanted to build a home for us both."

"Nick, I—"

"I know," he said, pressing a finger to her lips. "We barely know each other. But I do know that I've never felt this way before. And I never will again."

"I—I've never felt this way either," Jillian said softly, staring down at the water. She pulled her legs up and wrapped her arms around her knees. "Remember when I told you about the perfect numbers. How I thought that was what love was like?"

Nick nodded.

"Maybe I was right all along. We were two factors just waiting to meet, waiting to become a perfect number. With someone else, we would have been ordinary. But when we're together, we become something special."

"And I was thinking it might be fate that brought us together," Nick said.

"Actually, I was hoping you'd be here this weekend,"

Jillian said with a smile. "In fact, I kind of figured that we'd probably...run into each other."

"This is where it all started," Nick said, looking up at the sky, "and ended."

"Maybe we could start over again?" Jillian asked, hope flooding her voice until it nearly trembled with emotion.

"Maybe we could," Nick said. He held out his hand to her. "Hi, I'm Nick Callahan. I'm a friend of Roxy and Greg's. I'm an industrial engineer from Providence. I have no idea what my IQ is. I got an A in college calculus but I have to use a calculator to divide eighty-four by six."

She laughed. "Hi, my name is Jillian Marshall. I'm Roxy's sister and I'm a college mathematics professor. I don't care what my IQ is, I dropped out of my college calculus course and I think it's charming that you can't divide."

He leaned closer and brushed a kiss across her lips. "I'm Nick Callahan," he murmured, "and I'm in love with you, Jillie Marshall. And sometime soon, after we've had a few days to get to know each other, I have every intention of asking you to marry me."

Jillian reached up to touch his face, her palm soft against his beard-roughened cheek. "I'm Jillian Marshall and I love you, Nick Callahan. And sometime soon, when you ask me to marry you, I just might accept."

"So I guess that's all settled," Nick said. "Now what should we do?"

"I'm not sure," Jillian said.

"We could always take a swim," he teased, pulling her down onto the dock and nuzzling her neck.

"I don't have a suit," Jillian replied, wriggling against him.

Nick gave her a wicked grin. "You don't need a suit, sweetheart."

"I'm not a strong swimmer," she lied.

"Jillie, if you go under, all you have to know is that I'll always be there to hold you up."

Jillian smiled, then wrapped her arms around his neck. With deliberate leisure, she kissed him, nibbling at his lower lip before trailing a line of kisses along his jaw. How quickly her life had changed. One minute she was alone and the next, her whole life lay before her, Nick Callahan at the center of it. She had found a man whom she could love forever and all she wanted now was for their life together to begin.

"I love you, Nick," she murmured, kissing him softly.

Nick pressed his forehead to hers and stared into her eyes. "And I love you, Jillie."

With a laugh, Jillian pushed up to her feet and began a tantalizing striptease for Nick. Bunching her skirt up in her fists, she slowly raised it along her thighs. Then, in one quick movement, she tugged her dress over her head. "Race you to the raft," she said in the moment before she jumped in the lake.

Nick shouted her name as she smoothly cut through the water. Jillian glanced back over her shoulder to watch him strip out of his clothes and dive into the lake. In a few short strokes, he caught up to her. Grabbing her around the waist, he pulled her body against his.

"I thought you couldn't swim."

Jillian splashed water at him. "There's a lot you don't know about me, Nick Callahan."

"I've got plenty of time to learn. I'm never going to let you get away from me again, Jillie."

She laughed, tipping her head back in sheer joy, the

sound echoing off the water. Nick needn't have worried. Jillian didn't plan to do any more running. She'd found her future in the arms of Nick Callahan and nothing could be more perfect than the love they shared.

Baby Bonus?

SANDRA PAUL

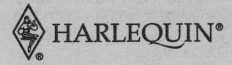

HARLEQUIN®

TORONTO • NEW YORK • LONDON
AMSTERDAM • PARIS • SYDNEY • HAMBURG
STOCKHOLM • ATHENS • TOKYO • MILAN • MADRID
PRAGUE • WARSAW • BUDAPEST • AUCKLAND

Dear Reader,

Like many writers, I tried various jobs before discovering my true "calling," and being a bank teller was a favorite. Not that I was good at it. Despite the patient tutoring of my best friend, "balancing out" my cash box each night was a "cross-your-fingers-and-hope" exercise. When distracted, I sometimes tossed money into my wastebasket, and I soon learned to protect my trash can as zealously as my teller cart.

Of course, avoiding distraction would have been better—but impossible. The customers were so interesting. Big-eyed children who'd plop down rolled pennies to exchange for cash. Young couples solemnly saving for a house. Diminutive jockeys in colorful silks with long-legged blondes from the nearby racetrack. And my favorite customer, a little old lady who'd escape from her nursing home to deposit her Monopoly winnings. With a fur stole around her shoulders and Winnie-the-Pooh slippers on her feet, she'd count out the colorful bills with dignified glee, accept my receipt for "Monopoly money" and shuffle out again.

Like me, my heroine Jessica enjoys people, too. And she's pretty good at handling them all. Then Mitch Flaherty arrives and Jessica discovers she's now the one being handled—in more ways than one!

I hope you enjoy their story, and I thank you sincerely for picking up my book.

Happy reading,

Sandra Paul

Dedicated to
Jackie Radoumis,
who has done so much for so many.
Thanks for all the help and encouragement, Jackie.

Prologue

THE FIRST SAVER'S BANK was just begging to be robbed.

Crossing his arms, Mitch Flaherty leaned back against a black marble counter in the service lobby. Some banks reminded him of solid gold bars—smooth, gleaming and impenetrable. Others he equated with new bills, crisp and still gritty enough to catch on his callused fingertips when shuffled through his hands. This bank reminded him of a twenty he'd once found not far from here on the streets of downtown L.A. The flat face of Jackson had peered up at him through the sludge—exposed, vulnerable, there for the taking.

Vulnerable. Mitch rolled the word around in his mind. Yeah, that described this bank perfectly. It was vulnerable. The unexpected splendor of a mural of angels high on one wall and the chubby cherubs depicted in the ornate molding along the vaulted ceiling probably distracted most people from that fact, but Mitch wasn't most people. Discovering the weaknesses hidden beneath the facades was what he did best.

Narrowing his eyes, he assessed the worn and faded red carpet, the even more worn and faded customers wending their way between dusty velvet ropes to the tellers' windows. Conversations, held in the hushed tones reserved for churches and banks, were punctuated by faint *dings* as the tellers hit small bells signaling their readiness for another customer.

Two outdated cameras perched high in the corners on

both sides of the mural provided a record of the banking transactions. Not a security guard was in sight. On his first visit two days ago, Mitch had figured the guard was on a break. It wasn't until his second visit that he realized the bank didn't have a guard. The only male employees in the place were the portly, gray-haired manager absorbed in a fishing magazine and a pretty-boy loan officer who'd spent the past twenty minutes on the phone.

Yet, the lack of a guard didn't surprise him much. Guards, especially good ones, were expensive, often earning as much as three tellers. What did surprise him was that five of the seven women working the line were pregnant.

Hugely, obviously, ready-to-give-birth pregnant.

He stirred restlessly and the blunt edge of the Colt stuck in his rear pocket jabbed his hip as someone bumped into him. He glanced sharply down. A bent, white-haired lady clutching her purse and social security check timidly met his eyes. Nodding in response to her faint "Excuse me," he pushed his sunglasses higher on the bridge of his nose as she scurried away.

It was almost time to get started. Searching for the person in charge, his gaze moved dismissively past the manager. The true power in most banks wasn't the manager, but the operations officer who oversaw the employees and handled the day-to-day security measures. Mitch looked over at the two employees seated by the file area behind the tellers. It wasn't the plump, older woman on the phones, he decided. She was too isolated; none of the employees had approached her since he'd been in the lobby. His gaze lingered on the younger woman constantly being interrupted.

He hoped it wasn't her, but the sinking feeling in his gut told him it was. Damn it, she looked too young to be an operations officer—no more than twenty-four or

-five judging by her smooth skin and thin figure. He estimated she'd weigh a hundred and ten pounds dripping wet and that ten more pounds in the right places would be of benefit. If she had anything on top, it sure wasn't noticeable beneath her serviceable gray suit and white blouse.

From this distance, he couldn't tell the color of her eyes, but her hair was brown and cut short, exposing her slender neck. Another woman handed her a piece of paper. As she signed it she smiled, and two shallow dents flashed in her soft cheeks.

Dimples. Mitch's jaw tightened. *Give me a break.* No doubt about it, he'd been set up. "It's an easy job," his partner Raul had assured him. "No complications, no problems." Yeah, right. A bad area, a run-down building, pregnant tellers and an operations officer who looked too damn naive and trusting to be for real.

Well, that last fact would soon change. He crossed his arms again and settled back to wait a few minutes longer. Mitch Flaherty was here to educate her.

1

"HE'S HERE AGAIN!"

The strident whisper broke Jessica Kendall's concentration and the numbers she'd been mentally adding dissipated in her mind. She looked up.

Pamela Frost, one of the tellers at the bank, pressed her seven months pregnant stomach against the opposite edge of the oak desk. Balancing slightly on it, the redhaired teller stood on tiptoe, rolling toward her operations officer as she hissed, "I'm sure he's a robber, Jessie. Look at him! Just look at him!" A half-excited, half-frightened expression covered Pam's round, freckled face. "He's casing the joint right now!"

Casing the joint? Jessica suppressed a groan. Pam must have been watching old James Cagney movies again. "Who's a robber?" she asked, weariness combining with her Southern accent to slur the words a little.

"That man! Right over there!"

In response to Pamela's furtive pointing, Jessica began searching with her stocking-clad toes for the high heels she'd slipped off under her desk. She wasn't surprised when she couldn't find them. It was one of those days.

Not that anything unusual had happened. The bank was busy, but that was typical of June, especially when the third of the month struck on Friday, and the social security recipients crowded in. No, it wasn't any major problem stressing her out, but rather the small irritations that threatened to overwhelm her by sheer number. Like the hole in her stocking just large enough for her little toe to get caught in. Or the melting ice-cream cone stuffed in the instant deposit box. Then there was the toilet in the women's rest room that wouldn't stop leaking no matter how many times she called out a plumber, and the ancient air-conditioning that was no match for the humid summer heat.

But most of all, it was the interruptions that tried her patience—the never-ending, sometimes important but usually idiotic, interruptions that kept her from finishing anything and made her long to be back home in Crab Apple, Texas. Nothing ever happened in the small brick bank when she'd worked there. Of course, the pay had only been half as much as she made in L.A., too. Stifling a sigh at the thought, Jessica bent down and snagged her shoes from behind the trash can. Slipping her aching feet into them, she stood up for a better view of Pam's "suspect." Her gaze brushed over Lupe and Maria, two more of her pregnant tellers who were gossiping in fluent Spanish in between customers, and fastened on the man leaning against a service desk.

Trouble, she thought, immediately understanding why he made Pam nervous. He made her nervous, too. Adrenaline flushed through her, erasing her tiredness and causing the fine hairs on her nape to lift in an atavistic signal of danger. Her muscles tensed, her skin prickled with awareness. Yes, the man was definitely trouble. Whether he was a robber or not was a different story.

She studied his face to commit it to memory for a possible police report. He wore sunglasses, dark enough for anyone working the line to suspect they were intended for a partial disguise. His short dark hair was combed back from his forehead, emphasizing rugged cheekbones and finely cut lips. His nose wasn't overly large, but had a bump on the bridge, as if it had been broken.

She tried to estimate his height. Six foot? Six-one? Faded jeans encased lean hips and powerful thighs before tapering down to black running shoes, negligently crossed at the ankles. His tanned arms were folded across his chest, his bulging muscles displayed beneath the short sleeves of his untucked black T-shirt. Despite those muscles, something in his build gave the impression of flexible power, like a man who did physical labor for a living—like a carpenter, or maybe a roofer—rather than one who spent his days bulking up in a weight room.

Jessica knew some of the tellers would be big-eyed over those sculpted biceps. Others would appreciate his broad chest. Personally, she wanted to admire his cute behind—as it headed out the door.

"When was he in here before?" she asked, looking back at Pam.

"This morning. I'm sure I saw him because I told Kathy he looked like a fighter with that broken nose and square chin." Waving her plump hands in an expressive gesture, Pamela rolled her eyes heavenward. "And those arms! He wore sunglasses this morning, too, but it didn't strike me as being odd then 'cause he just got change for a fifty and left. Now he's probably come back to make a hit." She shuddered, and her frizzy red curls seemed to quiver with excitement. "There's something about him that worries me."

And when Pam worried, anything could happen, Jessica added silently.

To be fair, the teller had reason to be nervous. In the past few months the bank had been hit three times, an unusually high average even for this run-down section of the city. But ever since she'd been robbed six weeks earlier, Pam constantly "spotted" criminals, twice set-

ting off false alarms, and once almost causing a bearded
old man with a cane—"I swear the beard looked fake,
Jessica!"—to nearly have a heart attack when he walked
out of the bank to face hard-eyed police with their weap-
ons drawn.

The police hadn't been pleased to discover they'd
been called out by a nervous teller with an overactive
imagination. One more false alarm, the stern-faced sergeant had warned Jessica, and the bank would be fined.

Which meant, Jessica thought, biting her lip, that she
couldn't afford to make any mistakes now. Her gaze returned to the man in the lobby. He should have looked
relaxed as he lounged against the counter, but the taut
readiness of his powerful body negated the casual stance.
His concentration on the tellers' activities was also suspicious. The bank was crowded, yet he appeared oblivious to the ebb and flow of people around him.

Better to be safe than sorry. Reaching a decision, Jessica said, "You take down his description." She walked
around the desk and, grasping the other woman's arm,
led her to the chair she'd just vacated. "And don't get
so excited. Because a man looks tough—" and dangerous and sexy "—doesn't mean he's a bank robber. Half
the men whose paychecks we cash fit that description.
But I'll speak to him."

She turned away, only to be stopped short by Pam's
clutch on the back of her straight-cut gray skirt. "But
what if he is a robber, Jessica? Promise me if he does
anything suspicious—*anything!*—that you'll touch your
ear and I'll push the alarm under the desk."

"I'm almost positive he's not. He probably just needs
some information." She tugged at her skirt, but Pamela
refused to loosen her grip.

"Promise to give me a sign," Pam insisted.

Jessica closed her eyes a second, summoning patience.

Opening them again she focused on the other woman's face. Pam's cheeks had whitened until her freckles stood out in stark relief. Her blue eyes were crinkled with worry. Jessica's irritation disappeared. She couldn't be angry with someone who was only concerned for her safety.

"All right, I'll touch my ear if I think he's a bad guy," she conceded. "Now, for heaven's sake, let me go!" She pulled insistently, tottering backward a couple of steps on her two-inch heels as Pam released her. Regaining her balance, she warned, "But don't jump the gun, Pam. We can't afford another false alarm."

She had started his way, when a deep angry voice at the other end of the line shattered the hushed atmosphere.

"Give me my money!"

Immediately forgetting the robber suspect, Jessica whirled around, heading to where a man stood shouting obscenities at Diane, her youngest teller. Heads were turning; a little old lady hurried out the door.

Approaching the altercation, Jessica recognized James Edwards. Edwards was tall with a once-muscular frame that had melted into fat. Judging by his angry tone, Diane had refused to cash his weekly construction paycheck. Usually when his check was bad, Edwards left grumbling. No such luck today. Diane, who'd been pale all morning from a vicious bout of morning sickness, looked even more drawn now. When Edwards lost his temper, he definitely wasn't easy for anyone to handle.

Maria offered to try. As Jessica rushed past, Maria hissed in Spanish, "Let me help that..." Jessica wasn't fluent enough to translate the final word, but the gist was more than clear. Shaking her head reprovingly, she kept moving.

The stench of beer and stale sweat hit her as she

reached the window where Edwards stood, half sprawled on the counter. Her heart sank. Oh, great. He'd been drinking.

"Give me my money, damn it! I've been waiting in that line forty-five minutes and no snot-nosed little b—"

"Excuse me." Jessica's deliberately soft voice interrupted his tirade. Taking advantage of his momentary silence, she gestured the younger woman away from the window and stepped forward. "Keep your voice down, please. What is the problem, Mr. Edwards?"

Red-rimmed, watery eyes glared down at her. "The problem is this stupid girl refuses to give me my—"

"Sir." Jessica lowered her voice even further, her words as curt as her Texas drawl would allow. "If you can't be civil, then my employees are not required to help you." She paused. "Neither am I."

He glared at her. Keeping her expression impassive, she gazed back. A fine gray film of plaster sprinkled the top of his thinning brown hair and his stained coveralls. Additional flecks dotted the darkening red of his fleshy cheeks. His thick eyebrows bristled together. Hiding her escalating tension beneath a deliberately cool mask, Jessica glanced fleetingly at the manager's and loan officer's desks. No help there. John's and Rod's seats were both empty.

Shoving aside the uncharitable suspicion that they'd fled at the first hint of trouble, she looked back at Edwards. "May I see your check, please?"

Scowling, he shoved it across the counter, subsiding into a sulky silence as she punched his employer's account number into the computer.

Insufficient funds.

For a brief second Jessica considered cashing the check anyway, counting on the construction company to make it good, but pushed the temptation aside. Edwards's employer was poised on the brink of bankruptcy, ready to go under at any time in the uncertain California economy. She couldn't afford to take a chance on a loss from this check. Besides, Diane had been doing her job and deserved to be backed up.

Squaring her shoulders, she held the check out across the counter. "I'm sorry, Mr. Edwards. This check isn't good at this time. If you'd like to try tomorrow—"

"What!" Bursting into another rage, Edwards ignored the check. His meaty hand jerked out to grab Jessica's wrist.

She stiffened, but displayed no other sign of alarm. It was Edwards who appeared surprised, as if he'd been unaware of his action. "What in the hell…" he muttered. Jessica saw his bloodshot eyes widen slightly as he met her gaze. His grip tightened for a brief second, then his glance slid away, his hold loosening. Before he could release her completely, however, a deep voice intruded.

"Let her go."

Jessica and the man holding her turned startled eyes to the newcomer. Sunglasses still in place, the robber suspect she'd been watching earlier stood next to Edwards with his arms down by his sides, his jaw squared at an unrelenting angle.

Unconsciously, Edwards's grip tightened again. "Who's gonna make me?"

"I am."

"Who the hell are you?" Edwards demanded.

The man pushed the concealing sunglasses up over his dark hair. Jessica barely had time to notice the white scar etched in his right temple before his gaze snared hers. His eyes were blue—a deep, compelling blue. Something in that heavy-lidded gaze caused her to tense, and her stomach muscles clenched even more when he shot her a narrow, warning glance. *Oh, God, he was going to do something stupid.*

She yanked on her wrist, but Edwards didn't let go. The newcomer turned fully toward the heavier man, saying, "I'm Mitch Flaherty, the man who's going to break your arm if you don't release her. *Right now.*"

"Damned if I will—"

"Hold on, both of you!" Rising tension made Jessica's voice sharp. This was ridiculous. A small incident was escalating into World War III. She looked at Flaherty. "Thank you for your—" she bit back the word *interference* "—help, Mr. Flaherty, but I assure you everything is fine."

2

SURPRISED, Mitch stared at the woman. She spoke with a soft drawl that was as sweet as maple syrup. Too bad what she was saying didn't make sense. Didn't she understand he wanted her to stay out of this now? That he was helping her? Why the hell didn't she back off?

He shot her another warning glance. Big brown eyes met his, filled with anger.

Mitch stifled a twinge of irritated amusement. *So what did you expect, Flaherty? Gratitude? When will you learn that women these days aren't looking for help— that they think they're tough enough to handle problems on their own? Like Bambi Eyes here.*

"It's no problem, Miss..." His gaze lingered on the badge pinned to her breast. "*Ms*. Kendall," he corrected, his tone mocking.

He watched with interest as she took a deep breath, causing the badge to lift and fall. He'd done the woman an injustice. Soft breasts curved enticingly beneath that unappealing suit. Not large ones, but still...

"Mr. Flaherty." He looked up. Her gaze met his. Enunciating each word clearly, she said, "Please step away. Believe me, everything here is under control."

Edwards smirked, making no move to release her, and Mitch's irritation hardened into anger. At the top of the list—a very long list—of things that made him angry were bigmouthed bullies. But also high on the list were women who didn't know when they were in over their heads.

He looked pointedly at her wrist, still trapped by the other man's huge paw. "Yeah, I can see things are under control. The only question is, whose control? Yours? Or King Kong's here?"

Her brown eyes blazed. *"Mr. Flaherty—"*

"Hey! You calling me an ape?" Suddenly rousing from his openmouthed stupor, Edwards swung a meaty fist at Mitch's face.

Taken off guard, Mitch ducked reflexively, but wasn't fast enough to avoid a glancing blow to his nose. There was a distinct crunching sound. Pain and rage blurred his vision. "Damn! You son of a—"

Another huge fist came at him. Mitch blocked it. He stopped another before Edwards managed to land a right to his jaw. Mitch's teeth snapped together. His glasses went flying. Adrenaline pumped through his veins. He fought back as massive fists hammered at him with unrelenting determination.

"Stop it! Both of you!" Jessica demanded.

Dimly, Mitch was aware of people gathering around and a woman—there was one in every crowd—screaming. Then someone shouted, "He's got a gun!" and everyone scattered.

Mitch realized his shirt must have lifted to reveal his pistol, but he was too busy trying to subdue the mountain of flesh attacking him to do anything about it. He landed a jab to the man's fat belly. Edwards's stale breath gusted out as he doubled over, but the hit didn't take him down.

Changing tactics, Mitch took a couple of steps back. Edwards lunged after him. Hooking his foot around the bigger man's ankle, Mitch toppled him to the floor, quickly following up his advantage by forcing Edwards onto his stomach. He secured the man's hands behind him. A well-placed knee in the small of Edwards's back kept his groaning victim in place.

Things finally under control, Mitch looked up—directly into the bore of the HK.40 pointed at his head.

A smart man didn't argue with the business end of a gun. Mitch cautiously raised his hands in the air. He was familiar with the procedure, and the four police officers surrounding him were definitely experts. Thirty seconds later, he was lying facedown, hands and legs spread, his head tilted back at an awkward angle to keep his sore nose and swollen jaw from bumping the dusty marble floor.

He waited while the police confiscated his gun. He waited until Edwards's howling protests ceased. He even waited until the pregnant teller shrieking, "He's a robber! He's a robber!" finally shut up.

But when his gaze swept the crowd and met a pair of condemning brown eyes, Mitch's patience finally snapped. "Damn it, I'm not a robber," he growled. "I'm the new security advisor for this bank."

AN HOUR LATER Mitch stood with the manager, John Smith, in the loan department, nodding now and again as the older man rambled on. Carefully, Mitch felt along his jaw, wincing as his fingers touched swollen skin. He didn't even try to examine his nose. The throbbing he felt there probably meant he'd broken it again.

Smith paused in his tale about "the history of our bank" to inquire, "Are you all right, Flaherty?"

"Yeah. Fine."

"Your nose—it looks a little…er, crooked. Are you sure…"

"Positive," Mitch said curtly.

Satisfied, the older man nodded. "Good, good.

Well...harrumph, as I was saying, in the fifties the same artist who painted the scene in the church down the block, created our mural, too. I think you'll agree his work is extraordinary...."

Mitch cast a cursory glance at the mural and the myriad of angels pictured there. All wore the same golden curls and bored expressions as they lolled among doughy clouds, gazing indifferently down at the people in the lobby below. Mitch's gaze turned to the lobby, too, fastening on the person he blamed for this whole fiasco.

Jessica Kendall.

She stood several yards away, talking with the last remaining police officer while Edwards hovered in the background. She was good at controlling her expression, Mitch gave her that. She looked as calm and aloof as any of the celestial beings hanging above her head. Not many people would realize she was even upset. For the past hour as she comforted hysterical customers and nervous tellers, she'd worn that same soothing smile—as serene as a nun at morning prayers. Still, the signs of anger were there. Flushed cheeks, overbright eyes. The Southern drawl that sounded almost clipped. Her slender spine couldn't get any straighter and her shoulders looked stiffer than a three-day corpse.

Propping his hip on the new-accounts desk, Mitch shut his aching eyes, suddenly realizing he'd never picked up the glasses he'd lost in the scuffle. Opening his eyes again, he met Jessica's gaze. He lifted an eyebrow. Her lips pressed together and she turned away. Yeah, Jessica Kendall was a wee bit pissed.

Good. So was he.

She should have backed off when he'd told her to. She could have been seriously injured. As it was, *he'd* been injured. He carefully touched his jaw again. Edwards was a menace. It would do him good to spend a few days in jail. Although the police still hadn't cuffed him. Why the hell not?

The old man was finally winding down. "...So, Flaherty, anything you need, just ask Jessie. She's the best operations officer I've ever worked with, as I'm sure you'll soon agree. And I hope, despite this inauspicious beginning, that you'll enjoy your stay with us."

Mitch straightened to accept the proffered handshake and Smith wandered back to his desk, absentmindedly tapping his coat pocket to ensure his fishing magazine was still in place. Mitch immediately headed toward Jessica to find out what the deal with Edwards was. As he neared the small group, he heard the sergeant ask, "Are you sure you don't want to press charges, Ms. Kendall?"

"I'm sure, Officer," she replied.

Mitch couldn't believe his ears. What the *hell* was she doing now?

From the corner of her eye, Jessica saw Flaherty approaching. The sergeant flipped his notebook shut while Edwards gave her a look of bleary-eyed gratitude. She smiled back, then stiffened as she noticed the angry, determined look on Flaherty's face. Her eyes narrowed. Great, the new security advisor was coming to "rescue" her once again. Hadn't he done enough damage for one day? Starting a fight and then making his dramatic announcement, as if that excused his behavior?

She didn't like security advisors. They always upset the smooth rhythm of the bank. She'd learned the best way to deal with them was to keep them on a short leash and get them out as quickly as possible. All too often the men were tactless alarmists, constantly stirring things up—and this one appeared to be the worst of the bunch. She didn't have time right now to explain—in words of one syllable so he'd be able to understand—that his job was merely to advise. That *she* was the one who made the decisions—and that, unlike him, *she* managed to enforce those decisions without any bloodshed.

She glared at him, trying to make him back off, but wasn't really surprised when it didn't work. His expression told her he was on the rampage again, and she turned her shoulder to him, hoping he would realize—this time—that his interference was neither wanted nor needed.

No such luck. He stopped right next to her, demanding in his authoritative baritone, "Hold on a second. Do you know what you're doing?"

She met his gaze. "Yes," she said, then deliberately looked away.

Edwards relaxed and the officer frowned. From the corner of her eye, Jessica noticed with satisfaction that Flaherty's jaw had tightened.

"Speaking as security advisor—and as an ex-cop—I suggest you press charges," he said between clenched white teeth.

The officer reopened his book. Edwards's shoulders slumped.

Jessica lifted her gaze to meet Flaherty's again. The man was dense, no doubt about it. She smiled, as if she wasn't simmering inside with the urge to pop him in his swollen jaw. "As operations officer, I disagree. Mr. Edwards is sorry for his actions. Pressing charges would serve no purpose."

"It would serve the purpose of making him think twice before he tries anything like that again," Flaherty replied.

Jessica's eyebrows rose. She sensed her smile annoyed him, so she made it even more serene as she answered, "Mr. Edwards is a valuable and longtime customer of this bank. I refuse to take any action against him."

Edwards and the officer turned expectantly to

Flaherty. He leaned forward, his hands on his hips. "If you don't press charges, then I will."

Her eyes didn't waver. "Then I will press charges against *you*. In my opinion, you were as much to blame for the fight as Mr. Edwards."

Her voice rang out in the suddenly quiet bank. A long silence followed. Edwards and the sergeant seemed to hold their breath, while customers and tellers cast discreetly curious glances their way. Even the angels in the mural above appeared to be watching, waiting to see what would happen.

Jessica kept her smile firmly in place, but with an effort. Mitch Flaherty suddenly looked...different. The planes of his face had tautened, the muscles in his arms were bunched. But it was the expression in his blue eyes that caused her throat to go dry. The piercing rage there pinned her in place. *My goodness,* she thought. *The man hadn't looked that angry when he was fighting Edwards!*

After what seemed like an eternity, Flaherty's lids dropped, shielding his gaze. He turned to the police officer. "Thank you, Sergeant. We won't take up any more of your time."

Jessica's shoulders relaxed, although until then she hadn't even been aware that she'd braced them. For a moment, she'd thought she'd have another major argument on her hands and relief trickled through her that she'd been wrong. Flaherty wasn't going to be troublesome, after all. He might come on like Mr. Macho, but obviously, she'd just needed to make it clear that she was in charge to make him back off.

She started to escort the officer and Edwards to the door when Flaherty's low-pitched voice stopped her. "Ms. Kendall, we need to talk."

Jessica smiled—naturally this time—no longer worried about the implied threat in his tone. "Certainly. Follow me."

Nodding goodbye to the other two men, she headed through the loan department with Flaherty at her heels, forcing herself to subdue the extra sway that triumph threatened to add to her hips. Opening a door in the corner, she began climbing the narrow stairs inside.

"Your conference room is on the second floor?" he asked, his deep voice echoing in the empty stairwell.

"No, I thought we'd talk in the break room. In case you wanted to put some ice on your jaw. Or nose."

He merely grunted, so she kept climbing. At the top, she led him into an open room with a chipped Formica table in the center, surrounded by metal chairs. Jessica flicked on the overhead light and Flaherty winced, narrowing his eyes.

Catching his involuntary movement, she paused. "What's wrong?"

He shrugged. "Bright lights bother my eyes sometimes."

"Oh." She reached into her pocket for his sunglasses. "I'm sorry. I forgot all about these."

"Thanks."

"I didn't realize you wear them to protect your eyes," she added apologetically.

"No problem." His face expressionless, he looked down, polishing the lenses on the edge of his black T-shirt. He started to put them on, then obviously remembered his sore nose and simply held them instead.

Feeling a twinge of remorse, Jessica yanked open the refrigerator door, mentally berating herself for assuming he'd worn the glasses for intimidation purposes. The least she could do was to get him some ice. The poor man had been hurt—not just in the fight, but apparently before that as well. Of course, the injury to his eyes was no excuse for not telling her who he was immediately when he arrived at the bank, but then again, John shouldn't have forgotten to tell her that a security advisor was expected either. But that wasn't too surprising. All John thought about these days was his retirement and plans to go fishing.

Frowning a little over the elderly manager's lack of interest in bank matters, she pulled out an ice tray and shut the refrigerator door. She turned on the faucet at the sink, and held the tray under the running water. Flaherty's deep voice rumbled behind her. "If that's for me, don't bother. I'm fine."

"It's no trouble. There's no reason you should suffer while we talk things out," she said. "Your poor nose—"

"I said I'm fine."

She paused and glanced at him. He was half sitting on the edge of the table, his eyes hidden as he stared down at the glasses in his hand. The bruises on his jaw had darkened and the bridge of his nose looked swollen. Despite his surly tone, sympathy again surged through Jessica. His judgment had been bad, but after all, the man had only been trying to help—in his own heavy-handed manner.

She turned away to crack the cubes out onto the counter, asking, "How long do you expect the security review to take?"

"A couple of months."

"A couple of months!" She whipped back around. "In the past, our security advisors completed their reviews in a week or less."

"In the past, your security people have done a damn poor job," he said evenly. "The board is tired of losing money in penny-ante holdups."

"Surely you're not blaming me or my staff for the fact we've been hit so often recently." Jessica tossed the cubes into a plastic bag, her sympathy for his injuries rapidly disappearing.

"Someone's to blame, that's for sure," he said. "The major problem with this bank is that it has a reputation for being an easy target—a reputation that having five pregnant tellers on the line sure as hell doesn't help."

She glared at him. "It's not my fault they happened to get pregnant at the same time."

His mouth quirked. "Mine either."

"Of course not." Jessica forced herself to calm down. Walking over, she offered Flaherty the ice bag. He didn't take it. When he'd ignored it for another ten seconds, her patience evaporated and she dropped it into his lap. Let him try to ignore that!

He couldn't, of course. He picked it up in one hand, watching her from beneath hooded eyes. He gingerly laid the bag along his jaw.

Hiding her satisfaction, she said, "I realize having five pregnant tellers in one bank is a little inconvenient. Especially since I'm the one who'll have to find replacements when they go out on maternity leave." Her tone firmed. "But that's my job, Mr. Flaherty. It's also my job to handle troublesome customers and any problems my employees may have."

"And you must be damn good at it," he said unexpectedly, "seeing as how you've reached such a responsible position at—" his gaze roved over her, then lifted to lock with hers "—twenty-four? Twenty-five?"

"Twenty-eight," she admitted stiffly.

"That's still rather young to be an operations officer." He lifted an eyebrow questioningly. "Friends in high places?"

She flushed with annoyance. "Of course not. I stepped up into the position when Nita Burns, our regular operations officer, had to go out on—"

He lifted a hand to stop her, a sardonic expression on his hard face. "Don't tell me, let me guess. She went out on maternity leave."

The dry irony in his tone irritated Jessica even more. "That's right," she conceded stiffly. "But all that really doesn't matter. The fact is, *I'm* the acting operations officer, and until that changes, I'm the one who decides what's best for my employees."

He didn't answer, just watched her with that unblinking stare. Encouraged by his silence, she added in a lighter tone, "But I know our security equipment is out of date, and perhaps it is time that we had a change of advisors. We'll have to wait and see how well your firm does."

Again, no response. Jessica finally released the breath she'd been holding. He wasn't going to argue. As she'd thought before, Mitch Flaherty appeared a bit rough, but underneath his rugged exterior he wasn't at all as dangerous as she'd first supposed.

Why, he couldn't even keep his ice bag in the right position. While she'd been talking, he'd let it slide to one side, apparently thinking over what she'd just said. Impulsively, Jessica stepped forward and gently eased the ice to a better position along his jaw, her gaze drifting over him.

He was close, so close that she could see the individual long, dark lashes curving along the heavy eyelids that gave him a slightly sleepy look. His poor nose definitely looked broken, but the rest of his skin was tanned and smooth, with the exception of the faint whiskers shadowing his chin and bruised jaw, and the white scar along his temple. The mark curved in a wicked "C" shape from the corner of his eye along his cheekbone. She wondered how he'd gotten it. He'd said he was a cop...maybe from a bullet? Or in a knife fight? She was staring at the scar, trying to decide, when she became aware of his slow smile.

She stiffened, suddenly realizing what an intimate position they were in. She stood in the vee of his thighs only inches away from...trouble.

Heat rose in her cheeks. Instinctively, she took a step back and he laid his hand over hers on the ice bag to stop her. Except for his hand, he wasn't touching her, but his scent surrounded her, rising on the heat of his body, a spicy mixture of soap and clean male sweat. She was acutely aware of the breadth of his shoulders, and the strength in his muscular arms. But more than anything else it was his measuring stare that held her in place.

"Where are you from, *Miz* Kendall?" he asked.

"Texas," she said, slightly surprised at the question. She coughed a little, trying to clear an unexpected huskiness from her voice. "Crab Apple, Texas."

"Never heard of it."

Although familiar with the response, Jessica eyed him suspiciously, sensing disparagement of her birthplace. "It's a small town," she conceded, "but one of the nicest, friendliest you could find anywhere."

He tilted his head, apparently considering that statement, then nodded. "I'm sure it is. In fact, I'm sure it's much, *much* different from L.A."

That should have been a compliment to Crab Apple, but for some reason, it didn't sound like one. Jessica's lips pressed together. She stirred restlessly, and began to pull away. "Mr. Flaherty—"

"Oh no you don't," Mitch said, his grip tightening on her fingers. "It's my turn to do the talking and your turn to listen."

Something in his tone caused a flutter of warning in Jessica's throat. Warily, she searched his expression. Beneath his sleepy lids, his eyes were disconcertingly keen. There was amusement in his face. Maybe even a hint of anger; she couldn't be sure. But one thing was unmistakable. Determination was etched in every rough-hewn angle.

Jessica swallowed, suddenly aware that she'd been wrong. Very wrong. He wasn't going to passively accept what she'd said at all.

Her chin lifted. Again she tried to pull away. Again he wouldn't release her. His gaze still locked with hers, her slender fingers still sandwiched between his warm, callused palm and the chilling ice, he added, "I'm here to do a rundown on bank security. The bank has given me complete authority to do whatever's necessary to ensure the job's done right. If that includes teaching a small-town girl about the dangers of the big city, then that's how it's going to be."

Jessica opened her mouth to protest the "small-town girl" crack, then closed it again as the rest of his statement sunk in. Dismay washed over her. Complete authority? Surely he didn't mean...

He studied her aghast expression and his lips curved into a sardonic smile. "Yeah, that's right, Bambi Eyes. I'm calling the shots now. Not you."

3

"I'M GOING TO KILL HIM," Jessica announced to her senior vault teller a week later, sending a narrow-eyed glance over the low merchant-room walls to where Mitch Flaherty was adjusting a security camera tucked in a corner of the vaulted ceiling. "I'm going to go over there and shake that ladder he's on until he falls smack on his stubborn head."

"Now, Jessica..."

"I mean it, Linda. That man is the most aggravating, annoying, bullheaded—" Running out of adjectives, Jessica snapped the rubber band off a thick bundle of twenties. Propping the bills in the money counter, she switched the machine on. "He's making me crazy."

Looking up from the bills she'd been shuffling expertly through her swollen fingers to check for counterfeits, Linda sent her an amused glance. "What's he done now?"

"What hasn't he done? Every time I turn around, I practically trip over the man. He meddles in everything and is constantly giving me orders." Raising her voice to be heard over the happily whirring machine, Jessica mimicked Flaherty's no-nonsense baritone. "'Marked bills aren't good enough, *Miz* Kendall. We'll go with the dye-release bait money from now on.'"

Linda's slight smile widened at the disgust on her boss's face. Shifting her heavily pregnant body to a more comfortable position on the small stool she'd pulled up to the counter, she asked, "Does he know Pam keeps setting that kind off in her cart and what a mess it makes?"

"He knows—doesn't care," Jessica answered. The machine in front of her whined to a stop, and she scooped up the twenties, taping and marking them with her initial. She plopped in another bundle. "He told me to *teach* her to handle it." She gritted her teeth as she remembered his rejoinder—*Surely someone as good at her job as you claim to be, Miz Kendall, should have no problem with that small chore.*

Simmering at the memory, she told the pretty brunette, "He's changing the vault code again, too," and derived gloomy satisfaction from the way her friend's smile immediately disappeared.

"Oh, no!" Linda exclaimed, looking up with dismay on her face. "Can't he just wait until John leaves?"

"No—that would be too easy." Jessica knew that Linda—along with everyone else involved—hated changing the code at the best of times. The combinations were long, and memorizing them an annoyance. The first half of the sequence was given to Jessica and Linda; the second half to John and Rod, thus ensuring that no one person had the entire sequence. The last few times they'd changed the combination, however, had been a real pain since John kept forgetting his half. Instead of opening the vault at eight as usual, the women had to wait until Rod arrived at work, which held everyone up for at least an hour or more. Which made Jessica's job that much harder.

She sent another narrow-eyed look in Flaherty's direction. He was wearing a white T-shirt today, which made the tan on his face and arms appear an even darker bronze. As usual, the sleeves were rolled up over his biceps and as he reached up to remove the back of the camera case, the cherub in the plastered molding nearby seemed to watch approvingly, its chubby cheeks plumped out in a vacuous smile. Despite her disgust with his decisions, Jessica watched Flaherty too, unwillingly fascinated with the way the sculpted muscles of his arms bulged and contracted with each powerful turn of the screwdriver in his hand.

She forced her gaze away as Linda demanded, "Didn't you tell Mitch that John has a hard time memorizing new numbers and that Rod is always late?"

"How could I?" Jessica asked. "It would hurt John's pride, and I couldn't do that. And Flaherty already seems annoyed with Rod."

Linda nodded, saying merely, "Well, you can't really blame Mitch for changing the code if you didn't tell him the problem, Jessie." She tilted her head to the side and eyed her boss questioningly. "Do you think he suspects you tried to have him removed?"

"Probably," Jessica replied, but she really had no doubts at all on the matter. She'd practically stormed out of the break room that day he'd arrived to corner John, who'd mumbled apologetically that what Flaherty claimed was true—he was in charge of all security measures. She'd then called up the board of directors to double-check John's assertion and received the same unsatisfactory response. Flaherty would remain until the job was done to his satisfaction.

And so she'd tried to make the best of the situation. Except for letting off steam occasionally to Linda—a trusted friend—she backed him in every decision he made, smoothing the feathers he left ruffled in his wake without once letting the other tellers know how she really felt. But she wasn't sure how much longer she could keep up the pretense of total support.

After all, announcing a new policy wasn't hard; implementing it was where the real work came in. Every change Flaherty made meant more work for her—explaining, reassuring, reteaching the women until the procedure became second nature. And keeping them calm in the process. Jessica had worked hard these last few months to create a pleasant and peaceful environment for the women, to eliminate as much stress as possible so they could concentrate on their jobs more easily. Her goal was to keep things running calmly and smoothly; Flaherty's seemed to be to keep stirring things up.

Jessica slapped down another bundle of twenties. "The main trouble with the man is he's simply too addicted to giving orders."

Linda shifted again on her stool and stole a glance across the room, sighing with feminine pleasure at the sight of Flaherty's broad shoulders and lean buttocks. "Well, no matter how bossy he is, you have to admit the man's a hunk."

"He sure is," Jessica agreed readily. "A hunk of pure male cussedness."

"Jessie," Linda said in a scolding tone. "I know you got off on the wrong foot with him, but he can't be all bad. At least you can admit he's handsome."

Jessica paused to stare at her friend, raising her eyebrows.

"Okay, maybe he's not *conventionally* handsome," Linda conceded. "Not with that broken nose and that scar. But he is all male."

"So's my sister's pet jackass. And he wants his way all the time, too."

Linda chuckled but added protestingly, "C'mon, Jessie. Don't you think he's even a little sexy?"

"No," Jessica lied promptly, too smart to fall into that trap. Aware of Linda's speculative look, she was careful to keep an indifferent expression on her face. Okay, maybe Flaherty did have an aura of…of virility, for want of a better word, that made her pulse beat a little faster whenever she saw him. So what? That didn't mean she was interested in the man. When she was ready to settle down, she planned to go back to Texas and find a husband. Probably someone like Tom Hutchinson, the nice, if unexciting, owner of a ranch near her mother's who'd indicated he'd be waiting for her return.

Besides, if she showed even the least little hint of agreeing with Linda that Flaherty was *somewhat* attractive, the brunette would pounce on her faster than a prairie dog on a juicy June bug. In spite of being nearly seven months along with twins, and in spite of the fact that the father of her two toddlers and unborn babies was a stout, bald man who's idea of bliss was an easy chair, a baseball game on TV and a six-pack of beer at his side, Linda was an incurable romantic and an avid matchmaker.

All the mamas-to-be were avid matchmakers, Jessica thought wryly, wrapping up another bundle of twenties. In fact, the whole teller line was, including Norma and Thelma, both happily married for over thirty years. And with the scarcity of single women in the bank, they all were practically panting for victims to practice their skills on.

Not that they bothered Dorothy, the other single woman, much. Dorothy—with her big hair, big eyes and artificially enhanced, great big breasts—didn't seem to arouse quite the same maternal instincts in the women that Jessica did. In vain had Jessica protested over and over again that she wasn't interested in meeting men right now. That she didn't plan to stay in L.A. longer than it took to make enough money to help her mother, recently widowed and with three kids still living at home, get the family's ranch on its feet again. The tellers had simply refused to listen.

For the past few months Jessica had been quietly amused by their subtle—and sometimes not-so-subtle—machinations to get her to date Rod. Primarily to get them off her back, she'd even gone out with him once—and once had been enough. Despite his man-of-the-world airs, the loan officer reminded Jessica of an immature boy with his restless eyes and whiny voice. The other women must have secretly agreed with her evaluation, because once Mitch Flaherty swaggered through the door, they abandoned Rod as a possible match for Jessica quicker than a pack of hounds turning tail on a porcupine, concentrating all their efforts on corralling Mitch.

Jessica could have told them they were wasting their time there, too. She might have been a small-town girl, but her mother had raised eight kids—five of them girls—with not a fool among them. Despite the heavy-lidded glances he kept throwing her way, Jessica knew the only thing—well, the major thing anyway—on Flaherty's mind was making the bank secure.

Her lips tightening, she snapped a rubber band around another bundle of money and tossed it on the growing pile on the cart. The ironic thing was, she wholeheartedly backed Flaherty in his goal—or she would have if the idiot man hadn't decided that the only way to accomplish it was by creating as many new procedures as he could, as quickly as possible.

"If the women can't handle changes, they should leave now," he'd said implacably. He'd even suggested getting rid of some of the pregnant tellers and replacing them with a security guard.

Twice this past week, he'd cornered Jessica and brought the subject up. Both times, she'd firmly told him no, she wasn't pushing any of the women to go out on leave until they were ready. None of the women were working for the fun of it; they all needed to help support their families, especially with brand-new babies on the way. Besides, if she cut back on tellers, everyone else's workload would be that much heavier, since the bank board had refused to increase the budget to hire more employees.

Flaherty hadn't taken her refusal with especially good grace and Jessica was positive he was merely biding his time before trying again, but at least he hadn't yet said anything to worry the women that their jobs might be at stake.

She paused, struck by a sudden doubt. Or had he? She gave Linda a considering glance and asked casually, "Flaherty hasn't upset any of the girls in any way, has he?"

Linda gave a low chuckle. "Quite the reverse."

"What do you mean?"

In an effort to ease her aching spine, Linda heaved her bulk off the stool and stood a moment, her hand pressed to her lower back as she replied, "Haven't you seen how tense the man gets around any of us pregnant women? Pam noticed it first. I thought she was imagining things—as usual—but when I was talking with him yesterday about the possibility of raising the wall around this room—remember how that one robber climbed right over it?—one of the babies suddenly kicked so hard my stomach shifted. It startled me, but Mitch— Good Lord! The man practically jumped a mile. And when Maria moaned the other day in the lunch room—you know, that way she does when she's eating anything especially good—he backed away as if she was a balloon about to pop."

Jessica frowned. "So?"

"So, since then I've noticed he's always nervous around any of us. I think he's kind of—you know. Shy."

Shy? The heated memory of standing between Mitch's hard thighs rushed over Jessica. A flush burned in her cheeks as she thought about how she'd just stayed there—like a deer caught in the headlights—frozen in place by his intent blue gaze and warm callused palm. Bambi Eyes, indeed. A man didn't acquire that kind of sheer male dominance—never mind the sex appeal he exuded—by staying at home alone, knitting knee socks. Flaherty—nervous around women? The idea was almost laughable.

"Mitch Flaherty doesn't have a shy bone in his entire body," she said flatly.

Linda refused to be daunted. "You can't be sure of that, Jessie. If he isn't shy, then why hasn't he asked you out? Pam found out that he isn't married, or even dating anyone steadily, and I swear, there's no way on earth that man is gay. I'm sure he's interested in you. Lupe told Maria who told Norma who told me that he asked— in the casual way men do when they think they're being clever—if you were seeing anyone on a regular basis."

"Well, that certainly sounds like proof positive he wants me," Jessie said dryly. "That's assuming, of course, that Lupe, Maria, Norma or you haven't somehow misinterpreted his question—or if he even really asked it at all."

"He did!" Linda said indignantly. "Besides, he watches you all the time— Why, he's watching you right now!"

Involuntarily, Jessica's gaze flew to the corner where Mitch was working. Her heart skipped a beat. He *was* looking in their direction, his eyes hidden behind those infernal sunglasses. More than once during the past few days she'd looked up to find that predatory gaze upon her. Each time, she had the irrational, almost panicky impulse to run and hide, like a small animal sighted by a hungry hawk.

The sensation made her angry. Who did he think he was, to try to intimidate her like that? Ignoring the way her pulse speeded up and the dampness of her palms, she said stoutly, "All he's doing is trying to unnerve me—or catch me making a mistake." Her mouth tightened in disapproval. "Let's get this money into the vault before he comes over with another complaint."

Jessica concentrated on the task at hand and Linda followed suit, efficiently stacking the remaining money on the small cart. When they were done, Jessica hid the pile of money beneath a canvas cloth, then grabbed one end of the cart. While Linda pushed, she pulled. The darn thing wasn't especially heavy, but possessed a renegade wheel that made it balk and buck like a recalcitrant mule. Jessica sighed in exasperation as it rolled over her toe, and tugged harder. Shopping carts had the same tendency to fight her, and she'd learned through experience that, as with other things in life, sheer grit often triumphed where finesse failed.

The cart certainly wasn't aiding in their efforts to be discreet. Closing time was near and customers sparse, but almost all those remaining were looking their way. As quickly as possible, Jessica and Linda laboriously maneuvered their burden across the teller section to the vault at the other end of the bank. Jessica studiously ignored Mitch, who was still staring at them from his high perch, but from the corner of her eye she could see his darkening frown.

"I can feel another lecture coming," she breathed to Linda, trying not to move her mouth as she talked. With the luck she'd been having lately, Flaherty could probably read lips. She could almost feel his disapproval radiating at her across the bank, and she tugged harder, exasperation giving her added strength. "He told me he doesn't want us to move money while the bank is open—yet he has a fit if the merchants overload you all with cash."

They'd reached the foot-thick steel door of the vault now, and they paused to check that no customers were inside. The vault itself was actually a small, shoe box–shaped room lined with the customer safe-deposit boxes. Two doors were placed at either end—the heavy one at the entrance, and a thinner door opposite, which led to a storage room beyond.

No customers were around, so they started to enter, but as Jessica passed the portal, she stumbled and caught hold of the cart to keep from falling.

"What the—" She glanced down, grimacing at the brick that her foot had struck. Due to faulty hinges, the vault door had the disconcerting habit of swinging shut. The brick was John's solution to the problem. Already, the huge door was starting to move and Jessica hastily shoved the makeshift doorstop back in place. The last thing she wanted was to be trapped inside.

Once the door was secured again, they didn't linger, but pushed the cart through the vault to the second locked door that led to the storage area. The musty storage room didn't look like much—filled with shelves containing old boxes of papers and faded Christmas decorations—but it was in here that the tellers' carts were stored overnight. It was also in here—and not the vault itself—where the majority of the bank's ready cash was actually kept, locked in an old metal cabinet that took Jessica less than fifteen seconds to open.

"It wouldn't take much effort for a thief to break into this," Jessica said, helping Linda pile the money on one of the cabinet's lower shelves. "If that so-called security expert is so hot to fix things, then why doesn't he get rid of this old cabinet and that darn brick as well?''

"It's on his list," Linda said. Meeting Jessica's questioning look, she admitted, "He asked me about the brick the first day he was here."

"Then why hasn't he done anything about it?"

"Good grief, Jessica, he's only been here a week— those hinges have been loose over three months. He's already repaired the ATM machine that keeps jamming and the toilet in the women's rest room that overflows. Give the man a break."

"Et tu, Brutette?" Jessica said sadly, but felt her attitude toward Mitch soften just a bit. A lot could be forgiven of a man who knew how to wield a wrench. "He fixed the toilet, huh?"

Linda nodded vigorously. "Yep. And the leaky faucet in the break room, too." She thrust the last bundle of money into the cabinet, slammed the door shut and spun the lock. "Honestly, Jessie, you might like the guy if you just gave him a chance. See what a little friendliness accomplishes. At least call him by his first name, like you do everyone else."

Jessica didn't answer, but as they wheeled the cart back through the main vault room, she thought about what the other woman had said. Maybe Linda was right; maybe she hadn't given him enough of a chance. They had gotten off on the wrong foot, after all. Maybe the dark glasses he often wore were to blame for the tension she felt around him. It was hard to feel at ease around someone whose eyes were hidden. And could he really be nervous around the pregnant women? That would explain why he often seemed so abrupt. Or maybe—

"Hurry up, guys," Pam urged, popping her head around the huge steel door for a moment. "The bank has closed and Mitch wants us to watch a training video. Number 617.''

—or *maybe* the man was simply insane. *Number 617? That* was the video he was planning to show? Was he *crazy?*

Pam took off again, and Jessica hurried after her, leaving Linda to deal with the cart. All the employees were heading toward the stairs leading up to the break room where the training videos were shown. When she spotted Mitch's tall figure striding in that direction, too, Jessica quickened her step to intercept him.

''Mitch,'' she called breathlessly, remembering Linda's admonition to try to be friendlier. His name seemed to linger on her tongue, emerging on a husky note that she had certainly never intended. She cleared her throat and tried again. ''Mitch,'' she said more briskly.

He turned and lifted a questioning eyebrow. ''Jessica,'' he responded, drawling her name out slowly.

Jessica repressed a little shiver of awareness. Everyone called her by her given name—so why did it sound so intimate when he said it? She brushed the disconcerting thought aside as she paused and glanced up at him. His lips were set in their usual stern line, but when he shoved his sunglasses up on his head to meet her gaze, Jessica could see a sardonic glint in his eyes. Nope, the sunglasses weren't to blame for her tension. Her nerves were already tightening just from him standing so near.

''Is there a problem—again?'' he asked.

She ignored the provocation in his question and eyes, and got right to the point. ''Pam says that you're planning to show video 617.''

That aggravating eyebrow lifted even higher. ''That's right,'' he replied evenly as the last of the tellers flowed around them heading toward the stairs. "Those videos are supposed to be viewed at least twice a month."

"I know," Jessica said. "And I've been showing them—"

"Then why hasn't number 617 been viewed since December?"

"Because—as I was about to tell you," Jessica said, holding on to her patience. "I've been using the other films instead. You see, number 617 upsets the pregnant women."

"But that's the one that deals with hostage situations."

"I know, but as I just told you, that's also the film that upsets my employees," she repeated. "It appears to be very realistic."

He took a deep breath, and Jessica's gaze fastened involuntarily on the rise and fall of his broad chest. She wrenched her gaze away as he began speaking again, his tone slow and reasonable, like a man talking to someone who wasn't too bright. "Of course it seems realistic. If the situations aren't portrayed accurately, the tellers won't learn precisely what to do."

"I understand that," Jessica replied between clenched teeth, in a tone even more slow and reasonable. "But they already know what to do. They've seen the film."

"Six months ago."

"Believe me, they haven't forgotten." She could tell by the expression on his face that he wasn't convinced, and knew she'd have to try harder. She couldn't let him show that tape.

Impulsively, she touched his arm—and almost jumped at the small jolt that shot through her fingers. It unsettled her somehow to have her hand on him. Which was ridiculous. She was comfortable with people, easy with the small pats and soothing strokes that persuaded and calmed. But touching Mitch wasn't calming at all. His skin was warm, the muscles beneath firm and unyielding. Heated currents of energy traveled up her arm, zipping down to just below her belly to bloom in a fireworks display of warmth. Just your imagination, she told herself firmly.

Ignoring the strange sensation, she concentrated on the subject at hand. "Please," she urged softly. "I just don't want them to have to go through that video again."

He hesitated, and his hand came up to cover hers. The currents tingling along her nerves increased, the fireworks in her abdomen burned hotter. Jessica fought to maintain a calm expression as his eyes roved over her face. "Look, Jessica," he said slowly, "I'm not out to upset anyone, but according to the procedure manual—"

Jessica stiffened, then snatched her hand away, half-thankful for the anger that gave her a reason to escape that tantalizing touch. "Forget that darn manual. I'm talking about people here."

His dark eyebrows lowered over his eyes. "And I'm talking about doing what's best—"

"Hey, Jessie. Flaherty," Rod said, interrupting Mitch in midsentence as he joined them. He dropped a casual arm around Jessica's shoulders and nodded in the other man's direction. "What's going on?"

"Flaherty is planning to show the tellers video 617," Jessica said impatiently. "And I was trying to explain to him why it isn't a good idea."

She turned back to Mitch to continue the argument, but before she could, Rod started talking again. "Better listen to her, Flaherty," he advised. "You're still new around here, but if you do what Jessie suggests, you'll soon get the hang of things."

Mitch's gaze settled briefly on the arm still encircling Jessica's shoulders, then lifted again to pin Rod in place.

It didn't take Jessica more than a glance at his hardened expression to realize she'd lost this battle, too. Forget her explanation, forget what was best for the employees. Once again Flaherty had made up his mind.

He confirmed her suspicion immediately as he said to Rod in a hard voice, "Unlike you, Merckle, I don't need anyone telling me how to do my job. I'll see you both upstairs."

"Whew," Rod breathed as Flaherty strode away. "What's his problem?"

"Mass hysteria. He just doesn't know it yet," Jessica replied, staring after Flaherty's rapidly retreating figure. Her fists clenched at her sides. He hadn't even given her a chance to tell him what would happen.

Becoming aware suddenly that Rod still had his arm draped around her shoulders, she shrugged it off impatiently, adding, "And you certainly didn't help by interrupting us like that."

"Why, Jessie," Rod began. "I didn't mean…"

But Jessica didn't wait to hear his excuses. She headed for the stairs. So Flaherty thought he knew it all, did he? Good, because she'd lost all desire to help him out, to warn him of the consequences of showing video 617. Now she simply wanted to be there when he did.

She reached the stairwell and began climbing, her high heels stamping on the old oak, her anger and disquiet growing with each step. Partly because Mitch had refused to listen, but even more because her fingers still tingled from the contact with his warm skin.

4

"I'M GOING TO KILL HER."

"Now, Mitch..."

"I'm serious, Raul," Mitch told his partner in their security business the next afternoon over the phone. He gripped the receiver tighter, half wishing he had his hands around a certain someone's slender neck instead. "Jessica Kendall is the most obstinate, difficult, *aggravating* woman I've ever tried to deal with."

Swiveling his chair away from the empty desk he'd appropriated in the loans department, he glared across the room at the woman under discussion. Unaware of his regard, Jessica stood by a counter with a red pencil in her hand, concentrating on the papers spread out before her. She had on another suit today—laboring, no doubt, under the misconception that it made her look more businesslike—but, in deference to the summer heat and ancient air-conditioning had discarded the gray jacket. She'd also undone the top buttons of her blouse, revealing the lacy edge of whatever underwear thingy she was wearing beneath—perfectly evident to any guy who stared hard enough.

Gritting his teeth, Mitch swung away from the sight as his partner asked, "What has she done?"

"What *hasn't* she done? She questions every change, every decision that I make. She won't even consider letting a couple tellers go and hiring a security guard instead. Now she has all the employees acting as if I'm

Attila the Hun—most of the employees, anyway," Mitch amended, inadvertently meeting the eyes of Dorothy, sitting some twenty feet away at the new-accounts desk.

The big-busted blonde waggled her fingers at him. He nodded politely in response, then turned away quickly as his partner drawled in his ear, "What? You mean all those women aren't eating out of your hand by now? What's going on? You losing your touch, buddy?"

"They're pregnant."

"What! C'mon, not *all* of them."

"Near enough." Mitch ran his hand through his hair before admitting in a low growl, "And I scared them."

There was silence at the other end of the line. "That's a new one—especially considering how spooked you get if a pregnant woman even looks at you cross-eyed."

Mitch's jaw clenched. He'd known Raul since they were kids and had even lived with his family for a while. They'd joined the military, then the police force together before starting up their security business. There wasn't another person on the face of the earth that Mitch trusted more.

But there were some things he refused to discuss— even with his best friend. "Raul…" he said in a warning tone.

"Okay, okay. Never mind about that. Just tell me how you managed to frighten them. I know you don't have the handsomest mug in the world, but still—"

"I did it with a training video," Mitch interrupted before his partner could really get started. "Number 617." The numeral felt as if it was permanently etched on his brain.

It rang no warning bells in Raul's mind, however. He asked, "What's the big deal about that one?"

"It deals with hostage situations, and apparently it terrifies the pregnant women," Mitch said, giving the explanation he'd refused to listen to the day before. Taking off his glasses, he leaned back and rubbed the bridge of his nose. "I put it on, and when it came to a part showing a woman with a baby being held at gunpoint, everyone in the room—even the women who aren't pregnant— started crying. And I'm not talking dainty little sniffles here, pal—I mean full-blown wailing." Mitch swallowed, his throat going dry at the mere memory. He shoved his glasses back in place. "One even latched on to my arm and wouldn't let go, just kept begging me over and over to do something, *please.*"

"Holy crap."

Gratified at finally hearing some honest horror in his friend's voice, Mitch confirmed, "You've got that right. Now none of them will cooperate with anything I suggest. All day long they've been sending me dirty looks, and the redhead who grabbed me—Pam—starts whimpering and holding her stomach if I even glance her way. She acts like I'm going to yank her kid out of there and make a run for it."

Raul preserved a moment of sympathetic silence, then said, "That's tough, bro. But how is all this—what's her name again?—Jessica Karmel's—"

"Kendall's."

"—fault?"

"Because she *knew.*" Mitch straightened in his seat, outrage simmering as he remembered the look on her face just before he'd switched on the tape. "She *knew* I was setting the scene for a riot and she didn't even try to stop me." Innate honesty made him add grudgingly, "Not as hard as she could have, anyway. And she certainly didn't stay to help me calm down all those hysterical women," he added, his voice hardening again at the memory of how she'd slipped out the door with that puppy, Rod, at her heels. But not before sending him an "I told you so" look.

"Like I said, pal. That sucks," Raul said. "She sure sounds like one tough old broad."

Mitch turned his chair, glancing in Jessica's direction again. Her attention still absorbed by the papers, she was absently running the pencil across her soft palm, alternating the movement now and again by threading it through her slender fingers. Those slim fingers that had felt so gentle and cool touching his arm.

Honesty nudged him again, and he admitted, "Well, she's not exactly what you'd call a broad...." His gaze roamed her face. The humid heat in the building had tinted her cheeks a delicate pink, and fluffed the baby-fine strands of hair at her temples into wavy curls. "And she's not all that old either," he added dryly.

"No? How old is she?"

Raul's tone suddenly sounded very interested; Mitch's turned abruptly casual. "Late twenties."

"She's in her *twenties?*"

"*Late* twenties," Mitch corrected firmly.

"So what does she look like?"

Smooth skin. Soft hair. Enticing dimples bracketing kissable lips. "I dunno. Average, I guess."

"Average? What kind of answer is that? Average like Rosie O'Donnell, or average like Catherine Zeta-Jones?"

Purely for the sake of discussion, Mitch stared at Jessica again. Still absorbed in her reading, she slowly...oh, so slowly...lifted the pencil to her mouth. She tapped the pink tip against her lush lower lip, then stroked it back and forth along the sweet curve. Back and forth. Back...and...forth.

Oh, God. She apparently had some kind of oral fixation. Mitch swallowed heavily at the thought and glanced away. "Somewhere between the two."

Raul let out an exasperated huff of breath. "C'mon, buddy, you can do better than that. She a big woman?"

Mitch considered the question, remembering how little she'd seemed standing between his thighs as he'd leaned against that table in the lunch room. The top of her silky brown hair had barely reached his chin, and she'd had to tilt her face back to meet his eyes with her deceptively demure brown ones. "Nah. In fact she's kind of short."

"Hefty?"

Mitch slid her another sidelong glance. The pencil was still at her mouth, not moving now as she concentrated intently. Her lips parted. Mitch held his breath. She bit down gently on the pink tip, and he released the breath on a groan.

"What was the question?" he asked thickly, watching as she nibbled absently on the eraser.

"What's the matter with you, buddy? You losing it or something?"

Forcing his gaze away from Jessica's lips, Mitch swung back to the desk. "I just didn't hear you."

"I asked what her figure looks like? Big hips? Big breasts?"

Taking a deep breath, Mitch chanced another look in her direction and exhaled on a sigh of relief. Thank God. She'd set down the pencil. His gaze surveyed her figure from her hand-span waist to her breasts. "She's on the slim side."

"Kind of mannish, though, right? One of those die-hard feminists who's always barking out orders and ripping at a man's ego?"

Reluctantly, Mitch lifted his gaze from Jessica's breasts to her face. She wore a sweetly serious expression as she listened to John, who—judging by the way he was holding his pudgy hands apart at chest level—had launched into another fish story. The fluorescent light above her flickered across her short curls, highlighting them with shades of gold as she nodded now and again, encouraging the elderly man to talk.

"She's not really mannish," Mitch admitted, remembering how enticingly feminine she smelled—like flowers and baby powder and stuff like that, all mixed together. He leaned back in his chair as he considered the second half of his partner's query. "As for barking...she *does* give a lot of orders, but she doesn't bark exactly. She's got this drawl..."

He tilted back farther, half closing his eyes as he tried to describe Jessica's voice. "It's one of those slow, sexy drawls that, even when she's only talking about ATM deposits or employee rights, kind of flows over you like warm, melted honey."

The silence at the other end of the line was even longer this time. "She sounds like a real ball-buster, all right," Raul said dryly. "Maybe I should come and take over. See what a little Latin charm can do."

Mitch's eyes snapped open and he straightened abruptly, his chair creaking in protest at the sudden movement. Jessica Kendall was a problem, all right, but she was *his* problem. His jaw tightened. He certainly didn't need Raul—the lady-killer king—hanging around making trouble. "Thanks, but no thanks. Despite the lack of cooperation around here, I should have things wrapped up pretty much on schedule."

His partner didn't appear convinced. "If you're sure..."

"Positive."

Mitch hung up before Raul could argue any further. He grabbed the list he'd been compiling before the phone call, determined to forget about Jessica and her pencil-nibbling tendencies. Forget the overly sensitive tellers and everything else that was driving him crazy, and concentrate on something he had a measure of control over—namely, the physical security measures in this anachronism of a building.

There was plenty on the list to keep his attention; plenty of work he needed to get lined up, including some major projects like updating the computer security—Raul's specialty—as well as installing "cages" or bulletproof glass rooms at each entrance that could trap a robber inside with the flick of a switch.

Yep, there was more than enough here to occupy his attention. So it made no sense at all when he found himself watching Jessica again.

Then again, watching Jessica had become a habit over the past week, he realized, as John wandered off and she turned to make her hourly trip down the teller line, pausing for a word with each of the women. At first, he'd told himself he was merely keeping an eye on her to evaluate how she operated—to discover how lenient she actually was with her employees and how she handled the customers.

Unfortunately, that excuse could only be stretched so far. It hadn't taken him more than a day to realize that for Jessica, nurturing her employees—in fact, nurturing just about anyone who came near her—was as much a part of her as her accent and dimples.

He didn't really approve of her attitude. In his estimation, it was best to keep a distance from the people you worked with—hell, from people in general. But keeping his distance from Jessica was becoming harder and harder to do. He was constantly aware of her. Whenever she was near, his senses would shift into high gear, his lower body hardening with arousal.

Which made no sense, since she definitely wasn't his

type. He'd always been attracted to tall women with lush breasts and hips. Still, he couldn't stop fantasizing about how Jessica's slight bare breasts would look, how sweet they'd taste. How easy it would be to lift her up by her slender hips so she could wrap her legs around him while he found out.

He'd certainly never gone for sweet smiles and innocence. The women in his past had all had the same knowing look in their eyes, the same "live for the day, no strings attached" attitude. They knew the score and weren't backward in making their own desires clear. He'd never had to give chase; they'd been more than willing to make any necessary advances. But although he suspected that Jessica was aware of his sexual interest—the little Texan was no fool, after all—she refused to acknowledge the attraction that sparked between them, pretending their every contact was merely business.

And yet, twice now she'd reached out and touched him as if she'd been helpless to resist. And when she'd put her hand on his arm yesterday, he'd *felt* the responsive quiver that raced through her body. He'd *seen* desire flare in her eyes before alarm took its place and she'd snatched her hand away.

He knew in his gut that she'd continued their argument with renewed vigor in an attempt to camouflage her reaction. But why? He reached up to touch his cheekbone, a rueful grimace pulling at his lips. Maybe she was put off by his scar and battered nose. As Raul had said, he didn't have the handsomest mug in the world. There was no denying that the way the scar curved along his upper cheekbone, pulling down the edge of his eye slightly, wasn't pretty. He looked more gangster than good guy, and while some women seemed to be attracted by that, maybe Jessica wasn't one of them.

Or maybe she was simply reluctant to get involved

with someone she worked with. He could understand that. Having an affair with a fellow employee was almost asking for trouble. He'd always steered clear of becoming involved with anyone connected with his business...but never before had he met anyone quite like Jessica.

Besides, that couldn't be her only reason for acting so aloof. The ever-helpful Pam had told him the first day he arrived that Jessica had gone out with Rod. Pam had also assured him there was nothing serious between the two and Mitch believed her. Everything in Jessica's manner—or more specifically, her lack of awareness of the guy—indicated she and Rod were just friends. Which made Mitch's annoyance at the other man for putting his arm around her even more irrational. He'd never been jealous or possessive about a woman before, yet when Rod had touched her, he'd had to fight the urge to knock the other man's arm away.

Yeah, nothing was the same with Jessica. So maybe— despite the fact they worked together—having an affair in this situation wouldn't be a bad idea at all. If attraction was creating the antagonism between them, the logical solution might be to deal with the attraction and dissolve the tension.

Mitch smiled, rather pleased with that conclusion. It made sense. Because he certainly wasn't willing to put up with the hostile attitude she'd been displaying the past two days. From the start, she hadn't been shy about expressing her dissatisfaction with his methods of operating, but until the video incident, she had at least hidden her reaction from the tellers.

Until she withdrew her support, he hadn't realized how much she'd been doing behind the scenes to keep the women calm and in control. They'd even seemed to like him a little. Now, as he'd told Raul, they treated him like the carrier of some fatal disease. Partly because of the video, but even more, he suspected, because he'd argued with Jessica. With the exception of Dorothy, the women had definitely ranged themselves on their operation officer's side, tensing up around him and listening to his instructions with barely concealed impatience when they couldn't simply ignore him.

He didn't like it. He wanted the women to calm down again before someone got hurt. He wanted this job finished as quickly as possible.

And he just plain wanted Jessica Kendall.

Maybe he should call her over, set her straight about the tellers and ask her out. Get everything settled at once. He picked up the phone again and dialed her extension, watching her as she answered the ring.

"Yes?" she asked, her soft drawl stretching the word out to three times its normal length.

"I want to talk to you, Jessica. Come over here right away."

Even from this distance he could see her stiffen at the abruptness of the order and he hung up before she could protest—at least over the phone. The way she slammed down the receiver and the militant erectness of her posture as she marched across the room toward him said more clearly than words that she'd be protesting to his face soon enough. So, he didn't give her the chance. Rising at her approach, he indicated the chair across the desk.

"Thank you for coming so quickly, Jessica," he said, belatedly remembering Raul's idea of trying a little charm. "Won't you have a seat?"

She hesitated, clearly suspicious of his polite tone, but finally sat in the chair he indicated, negating the cooperative action with the remark, "I don't appreciate receiving arbitrary orders, Flaherty."

He sat down, too, and tried a smile, showing plenty of teeth. "Mitch," he corrected her. Since that just made her eyes narrow, he feigned surprise, adding, "Did I sound arbitrary? I just thought we needed to talk. To discuss exactly how to handle this small problem we're having."

A puzzled frown creased her smooth forehead. She leaned back in her chair, and he heard the slide of silk against silk as she crossed one slim leg over the other. He forced his gaze to stay on her face. "We have a problem?" she asked.

He held on to his smile with an effort. "With the tellers."

Her crossed leg swung lazily, drawing his attention along her beautifully shaped calf to her small arched foot. He jerked his gaze back up to her wide, brown eyes.

"I'm not having any problem with the tellers," she said sweetly.

Mitch abandoned his smile—and covert contemplation of her slim ankles—along with his halfhearted attempt at diplomacy. "Well, I am. Ever since that damn video—"

"Which I advised you not to show."

"Which you *argued* with me about," he corrected. "Ever since, the women haven't been cooperating. Every time I even come near them, they—"

From the corner of his eye he caught sight of Maria, sidling closer. She moved to Jessica's side and stood there. With her attention fixed on him the way a smart person would watch an unpredictable wild creature—like a snake or something equally repulsive—she said to Jessica, "Can I interrupt you for a moment? I need approval for this check...."

"Of course," Jessica said, holding out her hand.

Maria gave her the check and waited, still watching

him, both hands resting protectively on the small mound of her stomach as she shifted restlessly from one foot to the other.

Jessica perused the check. Maria perused him. Mitch wanted to peruse Jessica again, but didn't dare under Maria's unrelenting stare. Not only that, but the teller's obvious nervousness made him feel edgy.

He endured her unblinking stare for half a minute, but when another thirty seconds went by, he growled, "I'm not going to hurt you, for God's sake."

He meant to sound reassuring but Maria's eyes only widened.

He tried again. "Relax!" he ordered, slamming his hand down on the desk for emphasis.

Jessica gasped. Maria cowered. Mitch swore.

Jessica quickly scribbled her initials on the back of the check and handed it to the teller, saying soothingly, "There you go, Maria."

Maria backed away, then hurried off with one last glance over her shoulder at Mitch. He watched her depart, and when she reached the teller line, he could see her say something to Lupe, who worked next to her. Both women turned to stare his way. Mitch swore again as Lupe made the sign of the cross.

"There—that's exactly what I'm talking about," he said to Jessica in bitter triumph. "They all act like I'm the devil or something."

"'Something' is right," Jessica said dryly. "I guess desk slapping is some primitive means of reassurance they simply don't understand."

"Very funny," he growled.

Her leg swung lazily again. "I don't think you know how to handle women."

"Oh, yeah?" He'd show *her* how he handled women when he got her alone.

Before he could say so, however, Jessica added with curiosity in her eyes, "Why are you so nervous around the tellers?"

He straightened. "*I'm* not nervous around them— *they're* nervous around me. And I want you to do something about it."

She froze. Then her crossed leg began swinging again, faster this time in unconscious rebellion. "Let me see if I have this straight," she said, her brown eyes narrowing. "You ignored my advice and upset the women, and now you expect me to calm them down?"

"Yeah," he said, pleased that she'd gotten the point so quickly.

Her mouth turned down in disgust. "It doesn't work that way, Flaherty. You can't show them a terrifying video, fight with me, growl at anyone who comes near and slap your desk for no apparent reason—and then expect my tellers to trust you."

Mitch opened his mouth to argue, but before he could get started, another teller timidly crept closer. Diane, this time.

"Excuse me," she said in her soft, breathless voice. Her wide eyes—like Maria's had been—were fixed on Mitch. "I need Jessica to—"

"Yeah, yeah, we know." He gestured her forward wearily. "Go ahead. I'll wait."

He drummed his fingers on the desk impatiently. This wasn't going at all the way he'd planned. Forget asking Jessica out; they couldn't even finish a business discussion without someone interrupting.

Thinking about the problem, he looked broodingly out over the lobby, his gaze settling on a kid standing right by the instant deposit box. Some idiot in the past had located the box next to the customer service line. This meant that whenever the tellers took out the deposit envelopes, they were within reach of any lunatic who decided to grab for the money. It also meant the box was vulnerable to kids—or pranksters—who might decide to slip something inside.

The boy suddenly looked around. His gaze met Mitch's. Immediately he glanced away. Mitch's gaze immediately sharpened.

The boy was wearing the typical summer outfit of baggy shorts, raggedy T-shirt and a baseball cap pulled over his eyes, and he appeared to be about twelve or thirteen. He'd leaned his skateboard against his hip, and was holding something beneath his shirt. When he slid another quick glance Mitch's way, Mitch stood up, barely noticing that Diane had left and that Jessica rose along with him.

She glanced at his face then out over the lobby. "What's wrong?" she asked quietly, but with underlying tension in her tone.

"There's a kid over there," Mitch said grimly. "I don't trust him."

She followed his gaze. "Why? What's he done?"

"Nothing yet. But that doesn't mean he isn't going to. Kids have a tendency to act impulsively—to do strange stuff for no apparent reason."

Jessica transferred her stare from the boy to Mitch. "Of *course* they do. They're *kids*. Don't you have any brothers or sisters?"

Justifiable annoyance caused his tone to harden. "No, but I ran into plenty of kids while I was on the force and believe me, they can cause a sh—a huge load of trouble."

Hardly had he finished speaking when the boy lifted his hand to the opening in the box. Mitch didn't hesitate. He started toward him, with Jessica on his heels.

Unfortunately, the kid didn't hesitate either. Dropping

his hand, he scooped up his skateboard and hustled out the door before Mitch had taken two steps.

Mitch wanted to chase him, but a couple of tellers—Linda, the head vault teller and, curse his luck, that red-haired Pam—were walking toward the box to empty it for the late-afternoon deposits. Mitch veered their way and they all reached the deposit box at the same time.

Mitch kept his expression blank, not wanting to alarm them—especially the volatile redhead—but determined to check the box before allowing them to get near it. They obviously hadn't noticed the kid. The pretty brunette had a questioning expression on her face, while Pam stared at him—really, he was almost getting used to the expression—as though he was a homicidal maniac. She held an empty canvas bag in one hand; the other, predictably enough, was spread protectively across her beach ball of a stomach.

"Hello, ladies," Mitch said, trying to look as non-threatening as possible.

Linda nodded briefly at him, then reached up, key in hand, toward the locked lid of the box.

"Wait!" Mitch said, his tone sharper than he'd intended.

Pam squeaked and jumped, bumping into Linda, who stumbled heavily.

Mitch's hand shot out and he grasped the brunette's upper arm, managing to steady her before she fell. Sweat broke out on his forehead. What if she'd fallen? Gone into labor? Broken her water or something? Damn it, Jessica was right: he didn't know how to handle women. *Pregnant* ones, anyway.

But he'd always known that. "Sorry," he said, releasing her.

"What are you going to do, Mitch?" a soft voice drawled at his side.

He glanced down at Jessica. "I don't want them to open the deposit box until I can check it. I think the kid stuck something in there."

"A bomb!" Pam said promptly—loud enough to make a couple of customers standing nearby move back a little, uneasy expressions on their faces.

The concern in Jessica's brown eyes was replaced with exasperation. "Of course it's not a bomb, Pam," she said, her tone gently chiding. "It's probably just a—"

"A firecracker!"

"—an ice-cream cone, like last week," Jessica continued, overriding the interruption. "I'm sure it's not anything dangerous..."

The box shook. *Thump. Thump, thump.*

"Oh my God, it *is* a bomb! A big one!" Pam said, her blue eyes widening as the thumping inside the box continued. She moved back, pulling Linda with her.

A woman customer stepped out of line, and headed toward the exit.

For the briefest second, Jessica's eyes widened, too. Involuntarily, her gaze lifted to meet Mitch's. Recovering her composure, she said firmly, "Stop it, Pam. That's definitely not a bomb. It's...it's..."

She broke off, looking at Mitch rather helplessly.

"Definitely alive," he said glumly.

Pam squeaked again. More heads turned their way. Another customer left, but more crowded closer with curiosity on their faces.

Mitch assessed the situation. Okay, fun time was over; he didn't want people crowding around with the possibility of panic.

He held out his hand to Linda for the key. "Come on, let's get this—"

"Rat! Or maybe a snake!" Pam took another step back.

"Pam!" Jessica said.

"—whatever it is out of there before it hurts itself or somebody else," Mitch said. "Everybody step back."

A snake did seem to be the likeliest possibility. With that thought in mind, he unlocked the top of the box and began to cautiously lift the lid. Before he could get it open, however, Jessica put her hand on his arm. Mitch sucked in a breath, cursing beneath his breath at the heat that burned low in his abdomen at her soft touch.

He glanced down, meeting her worried brown eyes. "What?" he said rather harshly.

She immediately removed her hand, a blush rising in her cheeks, but continued to meet his eyes steadily as she said, "What if it *is* a snake? Shouldn't we call animal control?"

"Let me see what it is, then we'll decide. Now step back."

She lifted her chin but did as he ordered, moving back several feet and making sure everyone else did so, too.

Mitch cautiously raised the lid. He peered inside, prepared for the worst-case scenario.

A big, fat, toad stared up at him.

"For goodness' sake, what is it?" Pam demanded, moving closer again.

At the sound of her shrill voice, the toad's eyes bulged. Its speckled chest swelled in indignation.

"Ribbit!" it declared and leaped. Directly at Pam.

Reflexively, Mitch reached out and caught it midair—and then stood there thanking his lucky stars that he had. Pam fled, uttering small shrieks and waddling toward the stairs and the safety of the break room as fast as her plump body allowed. He shook his head in disbelief. If she panicked that much when the toad simply jumped at her, he couldn't imagine her reaction if the amphibian had landed.

He soon forgot about Pam as the animal made another desperate bid for freedom. Mitch managed to contain it, but the rest of the crowd moved back—as if he indeed held a bomb rather than a fat, frightened toad. He glanced up sharply, opening his mouth to tell everyone to get back to work, but before he could get the words out, Jessica roused from her frozen, wide-eyed stillness and said briskly, "All right, everybody, show's over. Nothing to see here but a man holding a toad. Let's get back to work."

Some of the tellers seemed to feel a man holding a toad was sufficiently entertaining to waste some time on, but Jessica didn't let them linger, shooing everyone away from Mitch and back to work.

Then, under his irate stare, she had the effrontery, the sheer gall, to smile at him dismissively—that serene smile that always made his teeth clench—before turning on her heel, obviously preparing to depart, herself.

Without finishing their discussion about the tellers.

Without giving him a chance to ask her out.

Without settling one damn thing—like what to do with this damn creature.

Just like after that video, she once again planned to go blithely on her merry way, leaving him holding the bag. Or in this case, the toad.

Not this time, sweetheart, he vowed silently. "Jessica!" he said as she started to walk away.

The note of command in his voice stopped her in her tracks. She whipped back around, her wide eyes flashing, then narrowing to slits. "Is there a problem...again?" she asked icily.

"No problem," he replied, stepping closer. "You've just forgotten this."

He thrust the toad into her hands.

5

To HER CREDIT, she didn't drop it. She was from Texas, after all. But Jessica hurriedly held the toad out at arm's length to get it as far away as possible from her blouse, her hands grasping the soft little body beneath its front legs while the long back legs dangled forlornly.

The creature wiggled a protest at the undignified position. Jessica shuddered. One side of Mitch's mouth curved up in a crooked smile. Jessica's gaze was fastened on the toad but she managed a quick glare in his direction. "Take it back, Flaherty. I don't like toads."

"Mitch," he corrected smoothly. "And neither do I."

Jessica spared him another glance, then grimaced as the toad lifted one of its back legs to push at her fingers with its webbed toes. "Uck! Mitch, I insist that you take him right now."

"Insist all you want, Jessica, but the way I see it, this little guy is your problem. Aren't you in charge of visitors, customers and personnel?"

"This 'little guy' is an intruder," she argued, "and it's your job as head of security to deal with intruders, not mine." The toad wriggled again, and she wrinkled her nose. "Especially intruders that I suspect are about to wet on me."

Mitch took pity on her; besides, they were beginning to attract attention again and he didn't want to become the center of another crowd. He needed to talk to her, and he planned to do it away from this infernal bank, where any minute they could be interrupted by hysterical tellers, robbers, even toads.

Grasping Jessica's arm, he steered her toward the door with the toad still dangling out before her like a miniature, muddy-brown hostage. "Tell you what we'll do," he said confidingly. "We'll call a truce and handle this small problem together."

Without giving her a chance to argue, he led her to the counter where the head vault teller had retreated, a reluctant smile on her face as she watched Jessica tussle with the amphibian. "Linda? Hand me Jessica's purse, will you?" Ignoring the sputtering protest Jessica was starting to make, he added, "And take over for her here, will you? She won't be coming back today."

Accepting the bag from Linda, he tucked it under his arm and headed to the door with Jessica in tow.

He managed to hustle her out the door, but Jessica dug in her heels in the bank parking lot, bringing them both to a halt. Heat shimmered up from the black asphalt, making her nylons stick to her legs, while her once-crisp blouse wilted even more. "But the bank—"

"John is there to okay any big transactions, and Linda can lock it up." He glanced down at her, lifting his eyebrows. "Can't she?"

Jessica met his challenging stare, and bit back the protest rising to her lips. Linda could, of course. The teller had done so before when Jessica had had to leave early. John would do his part, too, if no one else was there to handle things. But she couldn't help feeling fretful, like a mother forced to leave her children with a baby-sitter for the first time. And Mitch was pushing her to make a quick choice. She felt overwhelmed by his closeness, his warm hand on her arm, the soothing tone of his voice.

She glanced around, looking for another excuse to remain, and her gaze alighted on her sturdy Toyota. "My car—"

"I'll bring you back to pick it up, after we've talked." He studied her face, then heaved an exasperated sigh. "Come on, Jessica, you know I'm right. We'll be interrupted every few minutes if we stay here, and we need to discuss the tellers. And a few other things as well. Please."

His tone dropped lower on that last word and Jessica's stomach followed suit. Something in his voice and heavy-lidded gaze made her suspect that the "other things" he wanted to discuss were strictly personal. A shiver, half of apprehension, half of excitement, traveled up her spine. She glanced away, saying, "I can't leave for the day. There's too much to do."

Mitch studied her with a knowing look in his eyes, then suddenly abandoned the argument. "Okay, then release him right here."

Jessica looked around at the cars moving steadily across the hot black asphalt and the busy traffic on the streets beyond. The creature would be flattened in less than a minute if she let it go here. She gave Mitch a sidelong glance. "Couldn't you take him?"

"No."

His tone didn't leave much room for argument, so she wasn't surprised when he continued in the same uncompromising vein, "As I see it, you have three alternatives. You can take him to a pond somewhere and release him yourself…"

Jessica's lips tightened. She didn't know where any ponds were in Los Angeles.

"You can let him go here…"

The animal flinched at that suggestion and began struggling in earnest.

"Or, you can come with me to release him and then finish our discussion. I'll even treat you to dinner."

"That's blackmail, Flaherty."

His white teeth flashed in a satisfied grin. "I know."

The toad wriggled again, his small heart beating frantically beneath her fingers, and Jessica surrendered to the inevitable. Mitch was right, after all, they did need to talk. Bumping heads as they'd been doing was a waste of everyone's time and energy, and they'd get more settled away from the bank and the constant interruptions.

"All right. Let's go," she said, and held out the uninvited guest. "Now, would you please take this thing?"

"Sure." But instead of the toad, he grasped her arm, steering her toward a wicked-looking black car. Not a brand-new vehicle, Jessica noted with faint surprise, but an older-model Corvette that had been polished until the black paint gleamed like a mirror. Mitch unlocked the door, set her purse on the seat and pulled out a white bag with golden arches on the side. After dumping the trash inside into a nearby trash can, he opened a pocketknife attached to his key chain.

Briefly forgetting her fears about the toad wetting on her blouse, Jessica protectively brought the little creature closer to her chest. "What are you going to do?"

"Obviously, not what you think I am," he replied, sparing her a sardonic glance. He punched a few small holes in the bag then held it open.

Thankfully, she dropped the toad into it and wiped her hands along her skirt as Mitch rolled the top of the bag shut. "I need to wash up," she said, wrinkling her nose a little, and toying with the idea of escaping back into the bank.

"I've got some hand-wipes," Mitch said, bending over to reach into his car again and open the glove compartment. "This brand can even get off grease."

He ripped open the packet and pulled out a moist paper towel. When she reached out to take it, he caught her hand in his. With a small frown of concentration, he carefully rubbed the moist cloth over her palm and between each finger. Jessica's pulse speeded up, and heat suffused her body. It seemed like such a personal thing for him to do. She pulled her hand away, but he caught the other one and cleaned it, too. Quickly finishing up the small task, he tossed the towelette into the trash, then used another to briskly clean his own hands.

"Okay, let's get going," he said, throwing that one away also. "If we don't, Kermit here will probably bake in the hot sun."

He helped her inside the black car. Pushing her purse out of the way, Jessica sat down, making sure her skirt protected her legs from the sun-heated black leather. She put the paper bag containing the toad carefully on her lap, and fastened her seat belt.

As Mitch climbed in beside her, she said, "Somehow, I would have expected you to be driving a newer vehicle."

He shrugged. "Why waste my money, when this baby has all the punch I could want? I'll get the air-conditioning going. It's hotter than hell in here."

He turned the keys in the ignition and the car roared to life. Jessica gave a small gasp, her hands tightening instinctively on the paper bag as he pulled out of the parking lot and onto the street. The seat beneath her was shaking more than a vibrating bed in a cheap motel— heavens, where had that image come from?—while the air from the vents blew out gustily, tossing her hair into curls and flattening her blouse against her body.

The air from the vents soon turned crisply cold. She shivered a little as it cut through her thin blouse and lace bra, chilling her heated skin and causing her nipples to contract into tight little buttons.

"Oh, my goodness," she breathed, alarmed by her body's reaction and even more alarmed as he suddenly gunned the engine to zip into the next lane.

Mitch obviously didn't recognize the dismay in her tone. His white teeth flashed in the first genuinely pleased grin she'd yet seen him give. "Sounds pretty good, doesn't she? I picked this baby up when I was just sixteen. It took me two years to get her going, but she's been purring ever since."

Purring? Jessica felt as if she were astride a roaring beast. She clenched her teeth to keep them from chattering as she bounced slightly in the seat. Tucked inside his bag, Kermit bounced too.

"Great, isn't it?" Mitch prompted again.

Jessica had brothers; she could recognize a hint when she heard one. "It's something, all right," she said diplomatically.

"The park I'm thinking of isn't far from here," he told her over the low thrum of the engine, accelerating to pass a slow-moving Volkswagen bug. "We should be there in about fifteen minutes."

Faster, the way he drove, Jessica thought silently, but already her anxiety was subsiding. Mitch handled the car with ease, his big hands sure and confident on the wheel. He had nice hands, she thought to herself. Strong and tanned, just a little work-roughened but nicely shaped with long fingers and clean, trimmed nails. How warm they had felt on her own, she thought, remembering how gently he'd wiped off her hands with that towelette.

The memory made her stomach clench, and she forced her attention away from him to gaze out the window at the shops and businesses flowing past. After a few minutes, they turned off the crowded avenue to prowl among a bewildering twist of residential streets. Sooner than Jessica would have expected, they pulled up before a small park decorated with a pond in the middle. Kids were playing baseball off in the distance, and a dog barked eagerly at a man who threw a Frisbee for him to chase. Old oak trees stood in groups, providing plenty of shade and places to picnic. The whole place reminded her a little of the town park at home.

"How did you ever find this?" she asked, picking up Kermit's bag as Mitch came around to open her door.

"I grew up in this neighborhood."

Following along behind as he led the way toward the pond, Jessica glanced around with new interest at the houses surrounding the park. The homes were old and crowded together. A few here and there showed signs of recent renovation, but for the most part they were worn and run-down. It wasn't a bad place, but it certainly wasn't a wealthy neighborhood either.

"Here we go," Mitch said, interrupting her thoughts as he paused by the water's edge. "He should do fine here."

Jessica wasn't so sure. She dubiously eyed the small flock of ducks swimming around in the middle. "Don't ducks eat toads?" she asked.

Mitch sent her a sidelong glance. "No," he said definitely. "They don't eat toads at all."

"How do you know?"

His gaze reluctantly met hers again. He sighed in exasperation, and ran his hand through his hair. "Okay, I'm not sure if they do or not. But if they do, they probably eat tadpoles—not big fat toads like Kermit."

Jessica didn't quite buy that. She looked around again. "If this is such a toad haven, then why aren't there any other creatures around?" Her frown deepened. "I don't think it's dirty enough. Don't amphibians prefer ponds with—what do you call it? Moss? Algae? You know—that slimy brown stuff?''

"Jessica," Mitch said, drawling out her name persuasively. "Do you really want to drive around in this heat, looking for a dirty, slimy place to leave that darn toad?''

She did. Cursing silently under his breath, Mitch spent the next hour and a half looking for a suitably duck-free, slime-filled environment in which to release their muddy-brown friend. Jessica finally approved a storm drain—surrounded by an eight-foot wire fence that he had to scale holding the damn McDonald's bag in his teeth—as an appropriate new home.

"There, that wasn't so bad, was it?'' she said cheerily as he dropped back down beside her after releasing the toad into the water. *Near* the water hadn't been good enough to satisfy Jessica.

"Oh, that was great fun," he agreed sardonically, shaking his wet pant leg in disgust. He'd slipped on the slime and landed knee-deep in filthy water. He glanced at her dusty blouse and skirt with vengeful satisfaction. "Come on, we're both going to have to change. No respectable restaurant will let us in looking like this.''

"We don't have to go—''

"We're going to dinner. I'm hungry and we need to talk.''

His tone ended that discussion. Since Mitch's place was closest, they went there first so he could change. He lived in an apartment complex not far from the bank in terms of distance, yet it might as well have been light-years away in terms of affluence. A security gate surrounded the modern, pristine building, and once inside, Mitch pulled the car smoothly into a small garage, climbed out and came around to Jessica's side to open her door.

"I can wait in here," she suggested, looking up at him.

"No."

She didn't argue. Not only was the heat stifling in the small windowless building, his expression told her it would be useless anyway. She followed him along a tree-shaded sidewalk to his apartment, looking around with interest. The complex had lush shrubbery, smooth grass and boasted not one, but two pools. Mitch's second-story apartment overlooked the second pool, which contained a red-haired woman in a minuscule bikini sprawled on an air mattress, floating lazily around in the blue depths. A broad smile replaced the woman's rather pouty expression as she caught sight of Mitch climbing the open stairs with Jessica at his side.

"Hi, Mitch!" she called. "Are you coming out for a swim?"

"Not tonight, Bonnie," Mitch called back as he inserted a key in his door. Actually, three keys, Jessica realized. Two for dead bolts and the third for the doorknob itself. He turned to glance over the railing as he added, "Jessica and I've got work to do."

The redhead reminded her of Dorothy, Jessica realized. She had the same avid gleam in her eye that Dorothy always had whenever she glanced at Mitch. Ignoring his reference to Jessica and undeterred by his dismissive tone, the woman cupped her hand and dribbled water over her tanned stomach. Looking coyly up at Mitch again, Bonnie cooed, "Are you sure, Mitchie baby?"

Involuntarily, Jessica's gaze met Mitch's, hidden beneath his sunglasses. Raising her eyebrows, she mouthed silently, *Mitchie baby?*

She could have sworn a slight flush rose beneath his rugged cheekbones. "She calls everyone baby," he growled, and gestured impatiently for Jessica to precede him through his open door.

Sure she did, Jessica thought skeptically. Just as she'd suspected, he obviously had quite a bit of experience with women, which came as no surprise. Even Crab Apple had its share of bad boys, and Jessica had learned early to recognize the signs. If a man was as sexy as the devil, attracted women the way a hound dog attracts fleas, yet was still single past the age of thirty, you could wager the ranch that he was used to running with a herd of women—and judging by Bonnie, a pretty fast herd at that.

Well, that didn't concern her in the least, Jessica reminded herself. She had no intention of ever being just one in a crowd. Never had and never would.

Her resolve firmly in place, she stepped past him into his apartment. His living room was huge, with a gray carpet that stretched endlessly from the wall of electronic equipment at one end, to the bar stools grouped around the open counter of the kitchen at the other. Except for those items, furniture was scarce. A well-worn black leather recliner held the place of honor in front of the big-screen television, but the matching couch pushed against a wall was obviously an afterthought and looked brand-new. Mitch appeared to be big on technology and low on style.

"Make yourself at home." He nodded toward the recliner. "I'll take a quick shower and be right back."

Jessica sat down and automatically swiveled the chair to stare after him as he headed down the hallway to the bedroom at the end. He pushed the door shut behind him, but it didn't close all the way. Through the gap she could see him opening and shutting dresser drawers, yanking out clothes.

When his hands went to his belt buckle, she suddenly

realized she was staring and hurriedly looked away. She focused on the wall unit. It certainly was a fine one, made of oak and filled with a stereo and CD player, the big TV, even a DVD player, if she wasn't mistaken. A closed section at one end of the unit apparently served as a bar, judging from the wineglasses hanging above the small counter and the mirrored glass door above them.

A movement in the mirror caught her eye and she glimpsed Mitch again. The mirror was set at exactly the right angle to reflect his darn bedroom...with him undressing inside.

No matter, she didn't have to look. There were other things to concentrate on. He tugged off his shirt, and heat pooled low in her abdomen. Other things like his muscular, tanned back and broad, sloping shoulders—no, darn it. She'd look at something else. Like his great, big...television. She resolutely stared at it a moment then her errant gaze wandered...just a bit. Just enough to see Mitch's reflection again. He pulled a gun from the back waistband of his pants and set it on the dresser. He began unbuttoning his pants. She unconsciously held her breath, releasing it on a sigh as he stepped out of the jeans to reveal long muscular legs and tight, masculine buttocks encased in snug black briefs.

For a second she simply couldn't look away, but when his hands went to the waistband of those briefs, common sense finally kicked in. She bolted from the chair, haring into the kitchen and away from that mesmerizing male striptease.

Her cheeks still felt a little warm, but she managed to meet his gaze with an assumption of innocence as he strolled back into the living room a few minutes later, wearing dark slacks and polished shoes and still buttoning up the long-sleeved white dress shirt he'd put on.

He raised a questioning eyebrow. "You want a drink or something before we go?"

"Oh, no—no, thank you," Jessica replied hurriedly. "I was just admiring your...kitchen," she added rather lamely, looking around. Too bad it was the barest, most impersonal kitchen she'd ever seen. The spacious countertops didn't have a thing on them.

If Mitch wondered what there was to admire, he didn't voice the question, but said, "Let's go, then, before the restaurants start getting crowded."

They left the apartment, pausing for Mitch to rebolt his three locks. Dusk had settled in, and the pool lights were on below. Bonnie was gone, Jessica noticed, peeking quickly over the railing, and no one else accosted Mitch as they headed back through the complex to the garage.

They pulled into Jessica's apartment complex twenty minutes later. Hers may not have been in such a wealthy section of the city as his, nor was her building and landscaping quite so well kept up, but there was really no need for him to frown as she led him to her door, she thought crossly. His scowl darkened when he saw that she only had one lock on her door, but Jessica didn't give him a chance to comment.

"Come in, sit down," she commanded briskly. "There's soda in the fridge if you want some and cookies in the jar. I'll be out in fifteen minutes."

That said, she went down the hall, making sure *her* bedroom door was closed tightly behind her.

She took a quick shower, pulled on fresh panties, and then wasted ten minutes considering what to wear. Her wardrobe wasn't extensive...and not very exciting, either. She had plenty of suits, and while one of those would probably be the most appropriate outfit to wear for a business dinner, she simply couldn't bear to don it in this heat. Irritated at herself for dithering, she finally yanked a sea-green sheath off its hanger and slipped it over her head. The shimmering cotton was a little informal, but it was also one of the coolest dresses she owned. Especially since the spaghetti straps made wearing a bra prohibitive.

She slipped on high-heeled sandals, deciding not to bother with nylons. She ran a comb through her hair, retouched her lipstick and emerged a few minutes later to pause in the doorway to the living room.

When she'd decorated the apartment, she'd congratulated herself that the simplicity of her linen-covered sofa and chairs, with floral throw pillows scattered here and there, looked neither too fussy nor feminine. She'd been wrong. The hard masculine lines of Mitch's face and build stood out in stark relief against the soft lines of her furniture as he sat on the edge of an overstuffed chair, leaning forward with his elbows resting on his spread knees as he examined something pink in his hands.

He glanced up and saw her. He automatically rose to his feet, his eyes skimming her figure and his pupils darkening. She was sure he'd make a comment about her dress, but instead he held up the item, asking, "What's this?"

Jessica realized he had the baby blanket she'd started crocheting. "It's a blanket—for Diane's baby. She's having a girl."

"And you're making it with this little stick?" He brandished the crochet hook, too.

She nodded.

He looked suitably impressed, then spoiled the effect by adding, "But won't the baby fall out through these holes?" He poked a long brown finger through one to demonstrate.

Jessica marched forward to rescue her work. "Okay,

so maybe I'm not the best crocheter in the world, but those holes are part of the pattern—''

A deep chuckle interrupted her, and Jessica broke off her tirade to stare at him in amazement. Amusement filled his face, altering its hard lines and making him appear oddly boyish and appealing. He actually looked approachable, with his stern mouth curling up lazily at the corners to show his strong white teeth, a teasing glint lighting his blue eyes. Something inside her seemed to rise up in response, but she ruthlessly pushed down the unwanted emotion, saying dryly, ''You were teasing.''

''Yeah.'' He set the blanket on the arm of the chair and rose. ''Are you ready to go? I want to discuss the tellers over dinner.''

Jessica hesitated, thinking quickly. Already the amusement had faded from his face, replaced by his usual expression of stern determination and, perhaps, just a touch of weariness.

''Why don't we stay here?'' she suggested. He'd seemed a little more relaxed, kidding her about her blanket. Not as rigid as he usually was whenever they tried to talk. Maybe here—on her own turf—she could make her case more convincingly than she'd be able to do in the formality of a restaurant.

She headed toward the kitchen. ''I'm sure I can whip up something.''

He followed her, a bit more slowly. ''Are you sure? Sounds like a lot of trouble.''

''It's no trouble at all.''

It certainly didn't seem to be, Mitch decided a few minutes later. He leaned back against the counter, watching as she moved gracefully around the kitchen pulling out pans, vegetables and two boneless chicken breasts. ''Are these okay with you?'' she asked, indicating the meat.

"That's fine. Can I help?"

She glanced at him with surprise in her eyes, and he smiled slightly, answering her unspoken question. "No, I'm not much of a cook, but I'm excellent at cutting stuff up."

She handed him a knife and a head of broccoli. "Go to it, then."

He started chopping as she went to work on a sauce for the chicken. He glanced at her from time to time, intrigued by the happy, almost contented expression on her face as she stirred in soy sauce and ginger.

"You like to cook?" he asked curiously. His mom had hated cooking—and cleaning up afterward, for that matter.

"I had to like it, being the oldest of eight," Jessica said. She studied the mixture bubbling in the wok with an experienced eye and turned down the heat a little. "Since my mother and father worked out on our family's ranch most of the time, it was up to me to get dinner and take care of the younger ones."

Mitch tried to imagine what that would be like—growing up among so many siblings, being the oldest. It sure explained why her nurturing instincts were so strong, why she was so protective of everyone in her little domain—her employees, the customers, even that pitiful toad. She'd probably been taking care of her brothers and sisters farther back than she could remember.

One thing was for sure, it seemed she really knew her way around a kitchen. The smells coming from the pan made Mitch's mouth water—almost as much as the sight of her in that dress she'd put on. From the moment she'd emerged from the bedroom, he'd had a hard time keeping his eyes off her. In her business suits, she reminded him of a little colonel, marching around the bank to check her troops.

In this dress, she was graceful and lithe, pure female as she whirled about, pulling out cornstarch and more spices from the cupboards, wooden spoons from a drawer. The blue-green material turned her brown eyes even darker and set off the pearly tones of her smooth white skin. Straps no bigger than shoestrings held it up, revealing kissable hollows along her shoulders and neck. He didn't think she was wearing a bra, and when she stretched on tiptoe to reach plates from a high shelf, he was sure of it. The material skimmed her high breasts, pressing closely to accentuate slightly peaked nipples and then draping softly again over her curves as she lowered her arms to set the plates on the counter.

She glanced over at him, and frowned at his idle hands. Noticing he'd finished up the broccoli, she handed him a carrot. He accepted it and absently took a bite.

Jessica pointed a pepper mill at him admonishingly. "No snacking until the cutting's done."

Feeling absurdly guilty at his lapse, he began working again, slicing the carrot into neat orange disks. "Did you come to L.A. to get away from your family?"

She stopped peppering the chicken to stare at him in surprise. "Of course not! I came here to earn more money. The little bank back in Crab Apple doesn't pay half as much as you can get in 'the bank robbery capital of the world'." She smiled reminiscently. "At home, the closest we ever came to a robbery was when old Mr. Whitaker dropped a twenty on the floor, and Jennifer Rodgers's two-year-old picked it up and tried to eat it. What a riot! Mr. Whitaker kept shouting that the baby was trying to 'hide the evidence' while Jennifer was having fits about her daughter putting dirty money in her mouth."

Mitch shook his head in mock wonder. "More babies and banks. They seem to go together around you, don't they?'' He popped another piece of carrot into his mouth, meeting her suspicious eyes blandly as she glanced quickly over at him. ''So what are you planning to do with the extra money you'll be earning?'' he asked, to divert her attention from his small theft. ''Buy a new car?''

''Help out my mother.'' She whipped the plate of broccoli and carrots away from him before he could snag another piece, and dumped the vegetables into the wok with the chicken. ''She got into a bit of a financial bind when my father died a couple of years ago.''

A faint cloud crossed her expression as she finished speaking, and she pressed her lips together, industriously stirring the food. Mitch leaned against the counter and folded his arms across his chest, resisting the unfamiliar impulse to hug her or something. To try to offer comfort. He'd never really been good at stuff like that. ''That's pretty nice of you,'' he said slowly. ''I can't think of many people who would set aside their own life to help a parent.''

The sadness in her expression faded, replaced by faint amusement as she met his eyes. ''Don't look quite so admiring. Thousands of people help out their parents. Besides, what I'm doing isn't as self-sacrificing as it sounds. My dad gave us all shares in the ranch, so now it's a family business. Any money I contribute will benefit me as well as everyone else in the long run. Ah, this is done.''

She stirred the chicken once more, then turned off the heat. ''We'll have to eat in the living room on the coffee table,'' she said, turning around to hand him the plates. ''I didn't bother buying a dining-room set since I knew I wouldn't be in L.A. long.''

He accepted the dishes absently, distracted by her remark. "Are you planning to move to another apartment?"

She shook her head. "I'm planning on heading back to Crab Apple by the end of the year. As soon as Nita comes back to work."

He didn't reply and Jessica glanced at him. He looked as if he might say something, but instead he turned and carried the dishes into the living room as requested, returning for the glasses and dusty wine bottle she unearthed from a low cupboard. Jessica joined him a few minutes later carrying the stir-fried chicken and vegetable mixture and some white rice.

Mitch dug in as if he'd never seen food before. "This is fantastic," he declared a little while later, helping himself to seconds. When he finished, he leaned back and patted his lean stomach.

Jessica smiled indulgently. Mama always said a satisfied man was a more reasonable man, and Jessica had high hopes that Mitch would listen to her now when they discussed the tellers. Still, only someone with limited cooking skills would consider this simple meal anything out of the ordinary. Remembering his barren kitchen, she asked, "Don't you cook *at all?*"

He shook his head. "The extent of my ability in the kitchen is to poke holes in a potato and pop it in the microwave. Still..." His eyes surveyed her lazily. "My baked potatoes aren't too bad. I'll have to make you one sometime."

Jessica choked a little on the wine she'd served with the meal. If she wasn't mistaken—and she doubted she was—that gleam in his eye was distinctly sexual. It was obviously time to turn the conversation to business. She took a deep breath, girding up for battle. "Now, about the tellers..."

"Yes, about the tellers," he said before she could continue. He straightened and pushed his plate aside. "I've told you before, Jessica, and I'm telling you again. Everyone needs to follow procedure, you can't keep making exceptions. Take Linda, for example. The only people she should let into the merchant room are merchants who've been approved and that she recognizes. She can't keep letting in people from the regular line."

"She only does that when the line gets too long," Jessica protested. "She's trying to provide better customer service." She raised her eyebrows in challenge. "Surely you don't object to that?"

"What I object to is that by ignoring bank policy and making exceptions, she's putting her safety—as well as everyone else's—at risk. And it's not just your tellers, Jessie. They're only following your example." He frowned at her accusingly. "Last week you let in a customer yourself after the bank was closed."

She rolled her eyes. "Come on, Mitch—that was Mr. Weyher—he's been with our bank for over sixty-five years. We've always done special little favors like that for him. Nita did before I got here, her boss did it before that. Mr. Weyher's not going to rob us or anything."

"That's not the point. When you're lax in one area of security, it's easier to make exceptions in other areas as well." He didn't bother to try to hide the disgust in his tone as he added, "If nothing else, you have to stop treating Edwards as if he's a king every time he comes in. The guy manhandled you, and you act like he's some kind of hero."

"He's sorry about all that. I didn't want him to feel bad."

Mitch snorted in disgust. If it had escaped her notice that Edwards had developed a massive crush on her, it sure hadn't escaped his. "Well, if you make him feel any better, he'll probably sue us over that fight. It's got to stop—all of it, Jessie. I want you to promise—no more special treatment for any of the customers."

"All right," Jessie agreed reluctantly, appreciating the logic behind his request. "But you need to make some concessions, too. Robberies aren't the only way the bank loses money—you know that as well as I do. You're making too many changes, too rapidly, and it upsets the tellers. When the tellers are upset, they're more likely to make mistakes—take in counterfeits, pay out the wrong amount. After watching that video you insisted on showing, Pamela paid the check number instead of the amount on one of the checks, she was so upset—"

"Pamela upset, imagine that."

"It's not just her," Jessica said, her chin lifting at his dry comment. "Diane, and even Lupe—who usually stays cool no matter what—have been out of balance, too. You know, Mitch, sometimes the bigger banks can learn from how the small ones operate. At our bank in Crab Apple, we promoted a family-type atmosphere, and kept everyone aware that their contributions were important to keeping things running smoothly. We hardly ever suffered any losses."

He still didn't look convinced. Groping for a way to make him understand, she added, "In my experience, things go easier when people pull together. Take my family, for instance. If Mama had to raise all the money we need alone, it would be pretty much impossible. But with all of us kicking in our share, it's not as big a problem."

"You sound like you're all very close."

"Of course. Family is the most important thing in the world."

Really, that was all she meant to say...she didn't know how the conversation progressed from there to a description of her brothers and sisters—starting with beautiful Bernadette, or "Bernie," as she was called, who was next in line to Jessica—and going all the way down to mischievous little Mike, the youngest in the brood and a real handful at thirteen. Except that Mitch seemed so interested and kept feeding her questions, laughing at the kids' antics. It wasn't until she caught herself telling a story about Nancy's pet donkey that Jessica became aware of how far she'd strayed from the subject—and how terribly much she'd been talking.

By this time, they were both leaning lazily back against the sofa with wineglasses in hand, dinner dishes pushed aside so they could prop their feet up on the coffee table.

She focused on their feet, suddenly noticing how close her sandals were to his shiny black dress shoes. Her dress had hiked up higher on her thighs than was seemly for a business discussion, too. Self-consciously she changed position, turning to face him on the couch and tucking her legs demurely beneath her.

"I'm sorry," she said, embarrassed that she'd been dominating the conversation. "I don't know what came over me, rambling on like that." She gave her wineglass a suspicious glance, then took another sip.

He shrugged, dismissing her concern. He'd gotten hold of the baby blanket again and was idly wrapping a bit of yarn from the unfinished edge around his long forefinger and then pulling the string off again. "I don't mind. About the only taste of family life I ever got was hanging around with my partner, Raul—he has a pack of brothers and sisters, but we did our best to avoid them," he said. "Your family sounds interesting...and you sound like you miss them."

"I do," Jessica admitted softly.

He shot her a penetrating glance. "But not as much

as you would if the bank hadn't become sort of your home away from home, right?''

She tilted her head to the side. She'd never thought of it like that before. "I guess that's true. They've all been kind to me and I want what's best for them.''

He sat there playing with the piece of yarn, the small crocheted blanket appearing especially tiny in his big hands. "I'm not trying to upset the women, Jessie.''

The sincerity of his words was clearly etched in his expression. Her heart melted—just a little—at the concern in his blue eyes. "I know,'' she said quietly.

"I'm simply trying to make the bank safer for them, as quickly as possible.''

"I know that, too.'' And she did. She'd never thought he was cruel, simply stubborn. "But too many changes, too quickly, cause a lot of stress, Mitch. It's important to me to take care of those I'm in charge of to the best of my ability. If I promise to try and keep things more formal and businesslike, can't you make a concession, too? To let me in ahead of time on any changes that will affect my tellers? And take things just a bit more slowly?''

His dark eyebrows lowered over his battered nose as he frowned down at the pink yarn, considering what she'd said. Finally, he nodded and laid the blanket aside on the arm of the couch. "Okay, I'll take things as slowly as possible with the women.''

He glanced up, his piercing blue eyes snaring hers. "But I can't promise to do the same with you.''

6

JESSICA'S HEART JUMPED into her throat. She swallowed, trying to force it back where it belonged and resolutely set down her wineglass. No more of that stuff—it was making her hear things. "I beg your pardon?" she inquired politely.

A brief smile touched his lips, but the intent look in his eyes didn't fade. "I want to get to know you better, Jessica. Much better."

Her throat tightened even more, making it difficult to speak. Her voice sounded husky as she said, "I don't think that would be wise. There's plenty of other women you can...get to know. Dorothy—or that woman at your apartment."

"You're the one I'm interested in." His eyes scanned her face, attempting to read her reaction. He must have seen the alarm written there because his voice deepened, coaxing persuasively, "I just want the chance to explore this attraction between us."

"There's no attraction," she protested weakly.

His eyes labeled her a liar. He didn't voice the accusation, however, but simply reached out and picked up her hand, lying limply on her lap. Immediately that warm current of sensation shot up Jessica's arm and tingled through her body. She fought to keep her expression impassive, to meet his eyes steadily. To try to hide the accelerated beat of her pulse and the warm flush spreading beneath her skin.

He cradled her hand in his. Her breath hitched—just the tiniest bit. Surely he hadn't noticed. But the knowing look in his eyes said he had and his callused thumb stroked across her palm, pushing down on the sensitive center.

Her fingers curled reflexively, the small spasm echoed in the pit of her stomach. She snatched her hand away.

Then he did accuse her. "You're lying, Jessie. You want me as much as I want you. Admit it."

She wasn't about to admit anything. She knew his type. Give the man a blade of grass for his horse and he'd claim the whole range. "I'm not interested in starting a relationship right now," she insisted.

His eyes held hers for a moment longer, then he glanced away, staring broodingly down at the blanket beside him. A small grimace altered the straight line of his lips as he asked, "Is it my scar? Does it bother you?"

"Of course it doesn't bother me!" she said, too distressed by his bleak expression to mince words.

He glanced at her. "My nose then?" He tapped it lightly.

"You have a fine nose—a manly nose," she said, indignant at the thought that he could doubt it. Any other nose would be ridiculous on his rugged face. "There's nothing wrong at all with the way you look. You're one of the most attractive men I've ever met—"

She broke off, the glint in his eyes giving her pause. A little appalled at what she'd admitted, she repeated firmly, "I just don't want to get involved right now."

"Why not?"

Did the man ever quit? "I don't want to date someone I work with."

"Pam said you dated Rod. You work with him."

Thank you, Pamela. Jessica had regretted that date with Rod at the time, and she regretted it now even more.

"But Rod and I could never be more than friends," she argued without thinking.

That gleam in his eyes burned hotter. "Unlike us."

He didn't even bother to make it a question. Jessica bit her lip. *Way to go, genius. Why don't you just admit you're hot for his body and you know what kind of underwear he wears besides?*

"I'm planning on returning to Crab Apple before the end of the year," she reminded him, trying to recover lost ground.

"That's six months away," he countered. "A lot can happen in six months." Determination tightened the line of his jaw, and his eyes darkened, their expanded pupils making them appear almost black. "Why won't you give us a chance?"

She met his gaze. *Because you're a dangerous man,* she wanted to tell him, *with your hungry eyes and warm hands. You make a woman do dangerous things. Like smiling at you too often, and lingering with you over a glass of wine. Like being jealous of a chance-met red-head, and secretly watching you undress, imagining what it would feel like to stroke your tanned shoulders and muscular arms. To kiss that oh-so-stern mouth.*

He was dangerous, all right—dangerous to a woman's heart. And Jessica had no intention of leaving hers behind, broken in L.A., when she went back to Texas.

She doubted he would accept any of that as an excuse, however, so she gave him one she didn't think he would argue with. "Because there's a man who wants to marry me, waiting back in Crab Apple," she said simply.

His expression immediately changed. His eyes narrowed and the skin seemed to tauten over his high cheekbones. Jessica stiffened, her stomach swooping with alarm at the sense of menace emanating from him. She felt as if she'd just poked a mountain lion with a stick—creating one very angry big cat.

Uncurling her legs, she rose. Escape was the best way to end this discussion. Bending down, she picked up the coffee cups then strolled into the kitchen, feeling marginally safer with each step away from him. With the width of the small room between them, she even found the courage to say, "It's getting late. I'd better clean up."

His expression changed again, the dangerous glint in his eyes suddenly masked by his usual impassive expression. "I'll help."

"That's not necessary—"

"Yes, it is." He rose to his feet and picked up a couple of dishes. Ignoring her protests, he came closer, and the fluttery feeling in Jessica's stomach spread frantically, making her tremble with trepidation.

Quickly, she turned to the sink, saying over her shoulder, "So, what projects do you have planned?"

To her overwhelming relief, he allowed the change of subject, providing laconic details of the top-of-the-line security equipment and the latest computer programs he planned to install, all the while calmly wiping the dishes she washed and watching her with that disquieting look in his eyes.

He didn't say anything else about wanting her; he didn't need to. His eyes were getting the message across quite adequately. They kept snaring hers, causing her own gaze to skitter away. When she raised her arms to put the wineglasses in the cupboard, she could almost feel his gaze on her, roaming the line of her body from her breasts down to her toes. She scrubbed the dishes desperately, but nothing could distract her from that lazy, intent gaze.

You're a full-grown woman, Jessica Jean Kendall, she

scolded herself. *You can resist the silent pressure he's exerting.* The trouble was, she wasn't sure if she could also resist the pressure building inside her, the rising need to step into his arms and run her fingers through his thick hair, to feel his body pressed achingly close to hers.

She had to get away from him, and the quicker the better. Jessica raced through the dishes, her hands trembling with unwanted excitement, the fine hairs on the back of her neck prickling with wariness. Her great idea of confronting him on her own turf didn't seem quite so clever now. How did you suggest without sounding impolite—or worse yet, panicky—that it was time for a man to leave? To get into that sex machine he called a car and just—

Her car! She'd forgotten all about it. Pulling the plug in the sink, she wrung out the dishcloth and folded it neatly over the faucet, turning to face him with a relieved smile on her face. "We'd better pick up my car before it gets too late."

He dried the plate he was holding and set it on the stack, then turned to face her. "Your car should be fine where it is," he said, slinging the towel over his shoulder and crossing his arms over his chest. "The bank parking lot is fairly secure. If you don't feel like going out again tonight, we can pick it up in the morning."

He didn't add, *After we've slept together,* but to Jessica the words seemed to hover between them.

"I'd rather go get it now," she said.

He didn't argue; in fact, he hardly said a word as she gathered up her purse. He waited equally as patiently while she turned the lock on the door, and outside in the warm night air, her trepidation eased a bit. She kept a careful foot of distance between them and he allowed it, stalking silently beside her to his car, which lounged like a lazy black beast in her parking space.

He opened the passenger-side door and she slipped inside, careful not to touch him, turning away quickly to snap on her seat belt. She folded her hands in her lap in a semblance of composure as he slid in beside her. His big frame seemed to take up more than his share of space, and Jessica's nerves tightened again. He was so close. His broad shoulder almost touched her and she could smell his spicy aftershave and the fresh scent of the soap he'd used.

He switched on the ignition and the growl of the big engine throbbed through her. She shifted in her seat, then forced herself to sit still and look calmly out the windshield.

"Do you want the windows open, or the air-conditioning on?" he asked, his deep voice rasping along her sensitive nerves.

"The windows open, please," she said, remembering how the frigid air-conditioning had affected her before. Her nipples already felt tight and achy. If they contracted any more, they'd probably pierce right through her dress.

He complied, and as they drove along, the raucous music of the city's night sounds flowed in with the balmy breeze. The hot wind swirled around her, tousling her hair like teasing fingers, forcing her to abandon her rigid clasp on her own hands to push the strands out of her eyes. Light from the passing cars and street lamps slid around the darkened interior, too, gliding up Mitch's strong arms to highlight his profile—the broken nose, rugged cheekbones, his masculine mouth. He turned his head suddenly, and caught her watching him. He smiled slowly. Jessica hurriedly looked away, her heart thumping even faster at the heated sensuality in his eyes.

The tension in the car continued to build, as tangible

to Jessica's overstrung nerves as the leather seat vibrating relentlessly beneath her. In an effort to break the thick silence between them, she started to talk, possibly faster than she'd ever talked before, about any innocuous topic that came to mind—the L.A. weather, how busy the city was, the price of beef in California compared to Texas. Mitch didn't contribute much to the conversation, just made low soothing sounds of agreement whenever she paused, but for some reason those husky monosyllables didn't soothe Jessica at all. It was with almost overwhelming thankfulness that she saw the bank come into sight.

He parked. He switched off the car, turned off the headlights. Jessica glanced fleetingly at his face, half-hidden by the shadows, and pasted a falsely bright smile on her own. Just because her nerves were twanging with tension at his nearness was no reason to forget her manners. "Thank you for a…a pleasant evening and for listening to my concerns about the women. I'll see you on Monday. Have a good weekend."

She heaved a sigh of relief. There. That had gone very well, she decided. He hadn't answered, but that was fine. She didn't need an answer.

Anxious to be on her way, she reached for her seat belt. She pushed the button. The clasp wouldn't release. She wiggled it, then pushed again, harder and harder, pulling at the strap across her chest, trying to escape before…

His warm hand covered hers, stilling her frantic fingers. He breathed her name like a long, deep sigh. "Jessica…"

And she just couldn't resist anymore. She sighed, too, the small sound signaling her surrender. She turned into his arms and his mouth closed over hers.

7

JESSICA HAD KISSED plenty of men in her life. After all, in Crab Apple, the single men outnumbered the single women seven to one—a fact the men constantly groused about and the women sent up nightly prayers of thanks for. Even the plainest woman in town was courted to a certain extent, and Jessica had by no means been the plainest. She'd kissed tall men, short men, some handsome men and even more who were kindly described as having "good personalities." She'd kissed men who'd been serious about her like Tom, and others who were merely testing the waters.

But all those other men and all those other kisses fled from her mind the minute Mitch Flaherty's mouth touched hers.

She'd expected the heat, the experienced sexuality. But his tenderness took her by surprise. Who would have thought the big hands sliding into her hair could be so gentle as they tilted her face up for his kiss? Who could have known that those stern lips could be so persuasive as they brushed slowly across her own, coaxing them to part?

Helplessly, she complied. His tongue traced her trembling mouth, then slid deeply inside. He caressed her soft inner cheeks, the ridge of her teeth, the slight roughness of her tongue. He teased her with his own, inviting her to respond, and when she did, his arms tightened around her, pulling her closer still.

It felt so good, so right—all of it, Jessica thought hazily as his mouth devoured hers. The warm leather seat beneath her bottom and back. The burning pressure of his lips against hers, the exhilarating taste of wine that lingered on his tongue. She breathed in the soapy scent of his skin, stroked the rock-hard muscles of his arms. Even the sultry breeze drifting in the window was part of the dark seductive pleasure of Mitch's embrace. She'd never felt so wanton...so sexy and hot.

She'd known he was dangerous. But even more dangerous was the passion rising inside her, threatening to drown all her scruples, all her worries, in a scorching tide of desire for this man.

Alarmed by the intensity of the sensation, she broke away, half relieved, half disappointed when he allowed the small bid for freedom. She lifted her lashes to look at him in the shadowy light. Heat rose in her cheeks at the possessive look in his eyes as his heavy-lidded gaze roved over her face, studying her expression in return. His eyes—those deep blue eyes—seemed too intent on hers. She couldn't sustain that compelling stare. Her lashes drifted down again to avoid it, her head falling languidly against his shoulder.

She knew she should sit up, move out of his arms. But it felt so nice lying against his hard warm body, with his strong arms around her. Who would it hurt if she indulged herself, just for a moment?

He kissed the delicate skin of her temple. His breath flowed across her skin as he said huskily, "So, there's a man in Crab Apple, hmm?"

She felt her flush deepen. His lips moved softly along her eyelids and down her cheek, inching back toward her mouth. "Yes, there is," she said breathlessly. The sandpaper roughness of his cheek against hers caused little contractions of excitement in her belly. "His name is

Tom—Tom Hutchinson. He's a widower with two little girls.''

For the briefest second those warm lips paused, then resumed their leisurely journey across her heated skin. He probed the shallow dents of her dimples with the tip of his tongue. ''And this Tom—he didn't object to your coming to L.A.?'' He sucked gently on her chin.

Jessica shuddered, her head falling back. He kissed the smooth, vulnerable skin exposed beneath her jaw. ''Tom knew I could make more money in the city.''

His lips traveled down her neck in a series of small biting kisses, leaving small shivers of pleasure in their wake. He lingered at the sensitive junction of her shoulder to taste the hollows there. ''Why didn't he help out your mother?''

Jessica lifted her hand to slowly thread her fingers through his hair. How soft, how thick the dark strands were. ''I couldn't let him do that. He's not a rich man. Besides, this was my obligation, my...responsibility.''

Her fingers drifted down, enjoying the faint whiskery feel of his lean cheeks before settling gently on his lips. She didn't want to talk, about home or anything else that would make her have to stop this. All she wanted was to kiss him again.

He nibbled on her fingers, and she slid them upward, pressing her palm against his mouth. He kissed her palm, too, while his hand lifted to slowly slide her dress strap off her shoulder. The seat belt was in his way. He slipped his fingers beneath the belt to move it aside and the back of his hand brushed firmly over her erect nipple.

Jessica gasped. He smiled against her palm, still pressed against his lips. Her hand fell limply to his shoulder and he kissed her neck again, pushing her dress down a few inches to reveal the upper curve of her breast. His long finger slowly stroked her there, brushing back and forth. Back and forth, in a slow, sensuous glide.

Unconsciously, Jessica held her breath. His deep voice was a husky whisper in the shadows. "Have you and this Tom been…intimate?"

Her flesh burned hotter. That finger kept teasing her, moving downward a centimeter at a time to the pointed tip of her breast. She couldn't concentrate on anything but the pleasure of that seductive touch. "No, of course not." She suppressed a moan as he stroked closer to the aching peak. Her breath emerged in small gasps. "Tom…is…a gentleman."

Mitch certainly wasn't. Piercing pleasure shot through her as he reached her pebbled nipple. He pressed firmly and Jessica groaned with relief, burying her face against his neck.

He removed his hand, ignoring her faintly murmured objection and slid her other strap off her shoulder. Lost in a sensual haze, compliant and docile in his hands, Jessica made no protest. Her head lolled back against the leather seat as she waited for whatever he'd do next. She didn't try to escape the mouth that kissed her sensitive breasts. She didn't push the hand away that settled on her thigh, stroking slowly upward.

No, she didn't surface at all…but Mitch did.

He lifted his head and tensed, his arms tightening around her. Vaguely aware that a car had pulled up nearby, Jessica opened her eyes, too—only to flinch and squeeze them shut as a bright light shone in the car.

Instinctively, she yanked up her dress and burrowed against Mitch, hiding her face in his shirt. He held her there, his big hand cradling the back of her head protectively as two officers approached the car.

"Okay, folks," the first one said in a bored voice, as if he'd uttered the words a hundred times. "I need to see—'' The officer's tone suddenly changed. ''Hey, Mitch—Mitch Flaherty. Is that you?''

''Yeah, it's me, all right,'' Mitch replied, with Jessica's face still pressed against his chest. His voice rumbled against her hot cheek as he added, ''How've you been, George? Jerry?''

''Fine, just fine,'' said one, while the other muttered a response Jessica didn't quite catch. The officers had turned their flashlights away, but Jessica had no doubt that they were still watching them. One said with a trace of amusement in his voice, ''On a stakeout, Flaherty?''

''I wanted to check the outside security of the building at night,'' Mitch answered. ''We've been having a few vandals around the ATM machines. Jessica agreed to...keep me company.''

''I see.'' If the officer was skeptical about the story, he was polite enough not to say so, but only added, ''Well, be careful. I wouldn't hang around out here too long.''

''We won't,'' Mitch replied.

A second later, a door slammed and the patrol car pulled away. Jessica immediately straightened, moving away from Mitch's embrace and yanking up her dress straps.

He reached out and tugged gently on a strand of her hair. ''Jessica...''

No, not again. She pulled away and jabbed at the buckle of the seat belt with her fingers. Mercifully this time the clasp released. Quickly, she turned and opened her door, climbing out before he could stop her. ''Good night, Flaherty.''

''Jessie,'' he said again, a warning note in his voice this time.

She ignored it. *''Good night.''* If his tone was sharp, hers could have cut glass. ''Despite all this...'' she

waved her hand in the air to encompass their recent embrace "...this *activity,* I haven't changed my mind. I'm
not interested in having an affair with you. Not now, not
ever. So, good night, Flaherty, and have a pleasant weekend."

JESSICA WAS NO FOOL. She knew that a kindly fate had
intervened—in the unlikely form of L.A. policemen—to
prevent her from making a very foolish mistake. No matter how hard she scrubbed her kitchen floor the next
morning, or how vigorously she pushed the roaring vac-
uum around the carpet, she couldn't escape the realization that she'd come close—dangerously close—to making love with Mitch Flaherty.

In his *car,* for goodness' sake.

How could she have acted that way? she agonized as
she beat chocolate-chip cookie dough with a merciless
hand, uncaring that the dough would probably be tough.
She didn't like chocolate-chip cookies, anyway. But baking, her mother had always claimed, was a panacea for
a troubled mind, and Jessica's mind was very troubled.

The cookies didn't help—nor did the apple pie or
strawberry cake that followed. Maybe the kids were what
was missing. If she was back in her quiet hometown in
her mother's busy, noisy house, the kids would be
swarming around, demanding attention and the goodies.

But in her quiet apartment in this busy, noisy city,
there was nothing to distract her from her thoughts. No
way to ignore the guilty realization that she'd let things
get out of hand—that she'd let *his* hands and lips wander
where they had no business being—without uttering a
word of protest.

She spread whipped cream on the cake with lavish
desperation. She wasn't like that. She wasn't wanton, she
wasn't wild. She wanted a relationship with a man some-

day, of course she did, but a calm, dependable, *steady* relationship with someone she'd learned to respect and trust.

Not a brief affair with a man like Mitch Flaherty.

Mitch was too like this city—exciting, but ever-changing. He wasn't into permanence, or commitment. The men in Crab Apple might appear a bit dull in comparison, but at least they were stable. Mitch was as stable as the ground beneath the L.A. basin during an 8.0 earthquake.

They were simply too different to ever get along. For goodness' sake, she was a home, hearth and "kids around your knees" type of woman. The eldest daughter of a respected family, well known for her practical nature and common sense. She was a calm, competent, take-charge gal—not the kind of woman who moaned in a man's arms, then hid behind her curtain when he came knocking—as Mitch did later that afternoon.

Although perhaps *battering* was a better description of Mitch's actions, Jessica thought, wincing as he hit the door harder and harder, and even raised his voice to declare, "I know you're in there, Jessica Kendall. We need to talk about last night."

Unable to resist, she pulled the curtain back a sliver to stare at him, careful to remain hidden. He looked angry—very angry. His dark eyebrows were drawn down in a scowl, and his lips—oh, those sinfully pleasurable lips—were pressed together in a firm straight line. He wore a blue T-shirt that made his blazing eyes bluer than ever, and straight-cut jeans that showed off his lean hips. He planted his fists on those hips whenever he paused in his hammering.

Just looking at him made Jessica's heart beat harder than he was beating on her poor door. Quickly, she dropped the curtain before she succumbed to the temptation to let him in.

Because she had decided—somewhere between icing the strawberry cake and mixing lemon bars—the less talk the better. Look at what had happened when they'd talked last night. In fact, she'd come up with a plan that would take care of the whole "possible affair" thing altogether.

She'd simply pretend those kisses had never happened.

She just needed to make it through the weekend, after all. Once back in the stodgy, stuffy, sterile setting of the bank, she'd be safe again, with plenty of employees and business around to buffer Mitch's advances. It was just being alone with him in her apartment, or his car—or other perilous places like that—that she needed to avoid.

So she stayed as still as one of the proverbial three little pigs, barricaded in her kitchen behind baked goods, while at her door the big, bad wolf pleaded, cajoled and threatened to get in. She didn't emerge until he finally left—spurred on his way by an irate neighbor who recommended a place for him to go.

And to ensure she wouldn't end up in that very warm place along with him, on Sunday Jessica went to church, to offer prayers of thankfulness and praise for the exemplary job the L.A. police were doing investigating parked cars. Then she took refuge at Linda's house for the rest of the afternoon and evening, playing Candyland with Linda's two preschoolers until colored squares danced before her eyes, the kids were cranky with exhaustion and once again the risk of Mitch catching her alone at her apartment had passed.

On Monday, she rose bright and early and donned her battle gear—her plainest, most tailored, "don't-mess-with-me-I'm-a-businesswoman" brown suit and her highest "look-'em-straight-in-the-eye-or-at-least-higher-than-their-chin" brown heels—and marched into the bank armed with her platter of goodies, ready for battle.

Only to feel her pulse speed up and her resolution waver as Mitch rose from the edge of her desk where he'd been sitting to demand, "Where the *hell* have you been?"

8

"AM I LATE?" Jessica asked innocently. She pretended to look at her watch, hoping he wouldn't notice that her hands were trembling from the forbidden excitement of being near to him again.

His eyes narrowed. "You know you're not. And you also know *I'm* not talking about this morning. I want to know where you were all weekend."

Jessica set down her platter before she dropped it, keeping her expression calm with an effort. "Oh, I was out and about, here and there. I was busy—very busy." She picked up some papers from her desk, and rustled through them in an industrious fashion, to illustrate just how busy she'd been.

Mitch didn't look impressed. "Your car was in your parking space when I stopped by on Saturday."

"I went out walking," Jessica lied without a qualm.

"I could smell stuff baking in your apartment." He looked accusingly at her platter. "Stuff like that."

"I made these earlier in the day. They were probably cooling when you came by." She smiled, politely and impersonally. "Sorry I missed you. Did you want something?"

She almost winced as soon as the words left her mouth. *Not the best choice of phrasing, Jessica.*

Sure enough, Mitch jumped on the opening she'd inadvertently provided. "No, I don't want some *thing*. I want you. We need to talk, to discuss what happened before those damn cops arrived—''

"Excuse me, Jessica—Mitch,'' Pamela interrupted coming up behind them. The teller took an involuntary step back as Mitch whirled around to glare at her. "Ah, if this isn't a good time…''

Jessica reached out and grabbed Pam's arm. She hauled her closer, ignoring the redhead's attempts to escape. "It's a fine time. What is it?''

The teller quit trying to pull away but kept a wary eye on Mitch, whose expression had darkened to an alarming degree. "I just wanted to tell you that some men are here—to replace the security cameras and start working on the glass traps for the exits. Should I let them in? We haven't opened yet to customers.''

Mitch glanced at the glass doors at the back of the bank, and swore beneath his breath. Five men stood there—the crew Raul had promised to send. He growled, "Yeah, let them in.''

Pamela hurried off to do his bidding, and he turned back to Jessica, grimly noting the relief on her face. "We still need to talk.''

She smiled that serene nun smile that always drove him crazy and picked up the plate of cookies and cakes she'd brought. "Maybe later. Or even tomorrow or the next day. Don't worry about it, Flaherty. I think everything we really need to talk about has pretty much been covered.''

She walked off, heading toward the stairs to the break room before he could say anything else to stop her. Hands on his hips, Mitch glared at her slim straight back and gently swaying bottom. Even the severe lines of her god-awful brown skirt couldn't disguise the jaunty swing in her hips.

He scowled. She probably thought if she ignored him

long enough, he'd fade into the background like that poor sap back in Texas. Or be content to stare at her with puppy-dog devotion the way Rod and that idiot Edwards did. Narrowing his gaze, he sent a silent message directly between her delicate shoulder blades. *It's not going to happen, Bambi Eyes. Trying to escape me or pretending I don't exist isn't going to change a damn thing in the end.*

Especially not after the progress they'd made Friday night. He strode over to greet the men Pam had let in the door, his mind still on Jessica. Ever since he'd arrived at this bank, he'd seen over and over again how she listened and laughed with everyone else. Now he'd had a taste of what that felt like—to be friends with Jessica. And he had no intention of returning to the way they'd been before.

He shook hands with the five men who grouped around him, and then set them to work immediately, three measuring and checking out the electrical plans for the glass cages at each door; two replacing the security cameras that he'd decided were too outdated to bother with. Then he stood at a distance, his eyes on the crew but his thoughts occupied with Jessica and what to do about her.

He couldn't understand her attitude, why she was so reluctant to see where this thing between them might lead. After all, it wasn't only the hot kisses that had been so good. Until Friday, he'd never even realized how just plain nice it could feel to simply hang out with a woman. To listen to her soft voice and see the interest in her eyes while they talked and worked together making dinner, then relaxed on the sofa afterward.

Probably her family worked and talked together like that all the time. His mom had never been the domestic sort. She and Mitch had gotten along fine for the most part, but for as long as he could remember, he'd pretty much taken care of himself. Never in a million years would she bother making anything by hand, like Jessica's little pink blanket. His mom had had—still had, for all he knew—a very active social life. Staying home had been the last thing on her mind.

The women he usually went out with were like that, too. He couldn't remember the last time one of his dates had made him dinner. But Jessica had seemed to enjoy cooking for him. She'd actually seemed to like talking to him, too. And after kissing her, he had no doubts at all that she wanted him. *A lot.*

He smiled, remembering how slim and supple she'd felt in his arms. How sweet she'd tasted, how responsive she'd been. There'd been passion in her kiss, longing in the way her arms had closed around him, holding him tightly to her. If they hadn't been interrupted by those damn patrolmen he was sure she would have admitted that, physically at least, she wanted him as much as he wanted her. He was willing to settle for that.

He wasn't especially concerned—as she seemed to be—that she'd be leaving soon. He wasn't fool enough to believe any relationship lasted forever, and theirs would no doubt burn out by then. But passing up something that could be so good—better, he was sure after kissing her than anything he'd ever felt before—well, that would be just plain stupid.

He frowned. Hell, Jessica needed him in her life even if it was only long enough for him to get a decent lock on her door. And he'd tell her that. If he could ever get her to talk to him again.

His scowl deepened as he thought back to Friday night. Yeah, life was a bitch, all right. As a teenager, he'd made out all over this city for hours and hours in every damn deserted parking lot he could find, with every willing girl that he could persuade to join him in the back of his car. Not once had they been caught by the police. Not once.

Yet, nearly sixteen years later, he parks for a few minutes—a few damn minutes, mind you—and the police move in quicker than kids swarming a broken fire hydrant on a hot afternoon.

If her frozen demeanor was any indication, Jessica wasn't about to forget or forgive any time soon. She was all hung up in her small-town morals. Antarctica would probably melt before she did, and he couldn't wait that long. Not if she was planning to return to Texas in a few months.

He definitely needed the help of an expert.

He pulled out his cell phone and hesitated, considering the matter. This might be a little tricky. He needed Raul's help, but he didn't necessarily want his friend the lady-killer to suspect how much *Mitch* wanted Jessica. If Raul knew that—and that she wasn't returning his interest—his friend would make his life a living hell with his constant needling.

Diversionary tactics were clearly in order. Mitch dialed and as soon as Raul answered, said without preamble, "I'm not making much progress here, buddy."

Over the phone, his partner's voice sharpened with concern. "What do you mean? Isn't the crew there? Did the cameras arrive—"

"Yeah, yeah, all that's going fine," Mitch interrupted. "Jessica is the one who's giving me problems."

There was a familiar silence at the other end of the line. "So we're back to Miss Ball-Buster, are we? You say she's causing some kind of trouble?"

Yeah, with my sleeping and concentration, never mind the arousal that has become my almost constant companion whenever she's around, Mitch thought caustically. He was beginning to feel as if he was growing a damn third leg. "She's stalling, dragging things out and creating unnecessary difficulties."

Raul swore.

"Exactly," Mitch said, pleased with his partner's response. "Things would definitely run more smoothly if I could get her on our side." *And into my bed.*

"So do it," Raul said impatiently. "Play up to her. Be nice for a change. Try a little diplomacy."

"I am nice." *And the nicer he was, the more wary she became. Just look how nice he'd been Friday night.* "She just doesn't trust me." *Maybe with good reason, after he'd almost seduced her in his car, but still...*

"Then back off a bit. Make her feel involved in the project. You're probably using your usual run-them-over-like-a-freight-train tactics. Try being more subtle. Discover her weaknesses, her soft spots, and use them to our advantage." Raul's voice toughened. "Whatever you do, get her on our side. We can't afford any delays. We need to focus on our target date and get this project finished."

Not bad advice, Mitch decided, clicking the case on the phone closed and slipping it back in his pocket. He thought over what his friend had said about being subtle. He *had* come on rather strong the other night, maybe that was why she was running scared. Maybe he did need to back off a little, let her come to him.

Yeah, Raul could be a definite pain sometime, but he always came through in a pinch. Trust his friend to get right to the heart of the matter.

Mitch smiled, and turned away from the workers to locate Jessica. She was standing behind the counter across the lobby, talking to Diane while they waited for the customers to start coming in.

Mitch did as Raul had suggested. He focused on his

target, narrowing his eyes on her as he considered Jessica's soft spots.

Her pink lips were soft, of course, and so were her Bambi Eyes—when she wasn't glaring at him, anyway. Her silky hair had felt plenty soft when he'd stroked it, and her skin—she definitely had the smoothest, softest skin he'd ever touched.

But none of these were the softest thing about Jessica. No, the softest thing about Jessica was her heart.

And he knew just how to use that to his advantage.

JESSICA HATED peeling boiled eggs. They always gave her trouble. The shell invariably crumbled into tiny pieces and stuck to the egg. The following day she had one halfway finished, though, when Mitch came into the break room with John at lunchtime.

Jessica paused in her shelling for a moment, then resumed the small chore when Mitch, after a brief nod that encompassed all the women around the table, turned away to continue his conversation with the manager. Mitch was taking her brush-off surprisingly well, she thought, ignoring the tiniest twinge of disappointment at his new lack of interest.

"These chocolate-chip cookies you made sure are good," Pam said, sitting on her left. Pushing aside her untouched salad, the teller picked up one of the few cookies remaining on the platter in the middle of the table. "Do you put anything special in the recipe?"

"No, nothing," Jessica answered a bit abstractedly. Mitch and John had moved behind her to stand near the coffee machine. They seemed to be discussing food, from what she could hear above the low buzz of conversation from the women on lunch break. Yes, she definitely caught Mitch's voice asking John if he knew of any good restaurants nearby.

"You use real butter, don't you, Jessie?" Diane asked softly on her left.

Jessica looked at her blankly.

"In the cookies?" Diane prompted.

"Oh, yes. Yes, I do." Jessica peeled her egg more slowly, tilting her head just a little to listen to the men talking behind her. She heard Mitch say in his low baritone, "You see, John, I'm having this problem..."

Jessica's ears pricked up.

"...With my stomach. I get this burning sensation..."

She stiffened, gouging her egg in her surprise. *Mitch* was having trouble with his stomach? Why, he was much too young to have a problem like that.

Apparently, John thought so, too. "Well, well, harrumph...I must say, at your age—but never mind that. I understand perfectly what you mean, my boy. Banking is a very stressful business..."

"Do you use milk chocolate or dark chocolate chips?" Pam asked. She took a bite of the cookie. Shutting her eyes, she wrinkled her forehead in concentration, chewing slowly. "I can't tell."

"Dark—and milk chocolate, too." Jessica couldn't remember what she'd put in the dough and couldn't care less. John was saying something else and she strained to hear.

"Oh." Pamela's eyes popped back open and she regarded her cookie with renewed interest, turning it this way and that. "I never would have thought of putting in both kinds."

John's voice rumbled beneath Pam's comment. "So you think you might have an ulcer...?"

An ulcer!

"...Your symptoms sound..."

"What about nuts?"

Jessica turned her head to stare at Diane. "Nuts?"

"Those are good in cookies, too."

"I wonder if anyone's ever tried nuts in lemon bars?" Pam reached for the platter again.

"...This doctor I know is excellent..."

Jessica stiffened again. She knew John's doctor. He came into the bank sometimes. He was even older than John...possibly older than dirt. What would *he* know about modern-day ulcers?

"Did you make these from fresh lemons?" Pam asked, waving the yellow bar in her hand.

Mitch said ruefully, "I guess I'll have to cut back on Mexican food. Eat at home more..."

Definitely.

"Or do you use lemon pudding? I've tried that."

"...But my cooking isn't so great..."

He'd admitted that the other night.

"And I love those hot chili peppers they have down at the Mexicatessen," Mitch said. "In fact, I've heard that a jalapeño or two might actually be good for ulcers..."

"Pudding makes them kind of gooey, though."

"That's crazy!" Jessica burst out. Her boiled egg rolled off the table as she jumped to her feet. "You can't eat that!"

Everyone stared at her in silence.

Pam froze with the lemon bar at her mouth. She lowered it slowly, a stricken look on her face. "Honestly, Jessie, this is only my second one today. Okay, maybe my third if you count the one at morning break. But I didn't think you'd mind..."

Jessica took a deep breath. Fighting to recover her composure, she said, "Mind? Of course I don't mind. I only meant you might want to—to eat your salad first." She added a little lamely. "You know, for nutrition. For the baby."

"Oh." Pam's face brightened again. "That's true." She pulled her salad closer again and shook half a bottle of blue cheese dressing over it. Everyone else resumed their conversations.

Jessica, however, could no longer hear John or Mitch behind her. She turned to find them both watching her. John looked bewildered. Mitch had what almost appeared to be a smile on his face.

He held out his hand. On his palm was her half-peeled, now definitely dusty hard-boiled egg. "You dropped this?"

"Thank you." Jessica took it from him and threw it in the trash, along with her brown paper bag. She headed to the door, but paused there, fighting the urge to turn around again.

Every nurturing instinct inside her was screaming for her to do something. She knew intuitively that Mitch wasn't the type to complain of pain or anything else. He must have been hurting pretty badly to even mention the matter. She couldn't help remembering that he wasn't a good cook and how pleased he'd been by the meal she'd made him. Baked potatoes would get awfully boring after a while. *Anyone* would get sick eating out night after night the way he did or consuming frozen dinners. Restaurant food was either greasy or rich, in her opinion, and as for frozen dinners—you might as well eat cardboard. Home-cooked meals were much more wholesome.

She didn't want to do it; she suspected she'd regret it, but Jessica couldn't help herself. Because he was sick and needed help and for *no* other reason, she asked, "Ah, Mitch. Could I have a word with you? In the hall?"

He lifted his eyebrows in questioning surprise. Nodding to John, he followed her out the door.

Jessica moved down to the end of the hall so no one

else in the break room could hear. She looked up at Mitch, who met her eyes impassively.

"I couldn't help overhearing—about your possible ulcer." A strange expression crossed his face and, afraid she'd embarrassed him, she added hurriedly, "I—I didn't mean to eavesdrop. It's just that, well, John's voice carries, and—"

He lifted his hand to stop her stammered explanation. "It's no big deal, Jessie. I'm not even sure I have an ulcer, to tell you the truth. If I do, it's probably just in the beginning—the *very* beginning—stages. I'm sure if I eat right, it won't be a problem at all. Don't worry about it."

He turned away and she reached out to stop him, then hurriedly snatched her hand back before she touched him. Catching her movement, he paused and looked down at her again. She took a deep breath. "But it doesn't sound as if you *are* planning to eat right. I'm sure jalapeños aren't good for an ulcer, Mitch."

He shrugged. "Like I said, it's no big deal."

Trust a man to feel he had to act macho. "But it is," she said, distressed at his uncaring attitude. "Bland food is what you need. In fact—" She took another deep breath. "I meant what I said about not getting involved, but there's no reason why we couldn't have a friendly dinner together now and then. Why don't you come to my house tonight? I'll fix something light and wholesome so you can get the idea of the sort of stuff you *should* be eating."

Again, a strange, almost satisfied expression crossed his face. Jessica's eyes narrowed in suspicion. If he thought she was asking him over so they could pick up where they'd left off...

But apparently no such thought was in his mind. To

her surprise he refused the invitation. "Thank you, Jessie, but I wouldn't want to impose."

"It's no imposition," she protested. His refusal made her all the more determined to help him in spite of himself. "I have to make something for myself anyway. You know I like to cook. Doing it for one more wouldn't be a problem at all."

He hesitated. "If you're sure…"

"I'm positive."

His eyes gleamed and he smiled. "Dinner it is then. At your place tonight."

9

ANY FEARS Jessica harbored that Mitch might come on to her again were lulled that evening. He clearly enjoyed the chicken pot pie she'd made, and once again helped her chop the vegetables. They talked about work—without arguing once. He was pleasant, polite…and treated her with as much sexual interest as he would a maiden aunt.

So there'd really been no reason not to ask him over again the next night—for baked Cornish game hen this time, with nutritious green beans on the side. Again, he was a perfect gentleman. Even dull, kind Tom had never treated her with such polite reserve. Mitch had obviously gotten the message that she simply wanted to be friends.

The following night he repaid her hospitality at his own apartment, and if she felt a wary thrill race through her at entering the wolf's lair, her fears were in vain. They simply played video games then ate the biggest baked potatoes she'd ever seen.

It was while she was digging through her meal, trying to find some potato in the heap of sour cream, butter and bacon that he'd piled on top of her poor spud, that she learned Linda was right. "The tellers think you're nervous around pregnant women," she said during a pause in a conversation about work.

She made the remark idly, but she could immediately tell by the expression on his face that she'd hit pay dirt—and not in her potato.

Mitch's mouth almost dropped open he was so surprised. "Who told you that?"

"Linda mentioned it," she said. "Is it true?"

Mitch was tempted to lie...but if they'd all noticed, it probably wouldn't do much good. "Yeah."

She gave him a reproachful look. "Mitch...I can't believe you feel that way. As if they're social outcasts or something." She popped some more potato in her mouth and chewed sadly.

"I don't think they're social outcasts! They're just...dangerous," Mitch answered, his attention straying a bit as he looked down at his own potato. It was adorned with a tiny dab of butter. Because of his imaginary ulcer, Jessica had gently refused to let him have sour cream, bacon, chili or any of the other stuff he usually piled on. It seemed she'd done some research on ulcers, and to his chagrin, had learned that while remedies varied, most medical experts advised avoiding anything spicy, fat-filled or "hard to digest"—which pretty much covered his usual fare. So far he'd gone along with her restrictions to keep up the deception, but man, was he ever tired of eating stuff with no taste.

He took an unenthusiastic bite, considering sneaking a little sour cream. He glanced at Jessica to see if he could get away with it, only to discover that his timing couldn't have been worse. If he'd wanted her complete attention, his last comment had definitely done the trick. Jessica's eyes were fixed on him intently as she leaned toward him over her potato, her expression filled with curiosity. "What do you mean, dangerous?"

Hell, he'd done it now. He never should have admitted even that much. "It's hard to explain," he hedged, hoping that would end the conversation.

No such luck. Without taking her eyes off him, Jessica took a sip of the white wine he'd chosen to complement the potatoes—the wine she'd told him it would be better that he didn't drink—then set down her glass. "Oh, I see," she said, her eyes narrowing thoughtfully. "You're afraid—"

"I'm not afraid," he said, stung in spite of himself. "I'm merely cautious. And I'd rather not talk about it."

"Why not?" Her surprised expression suddenly grew sad. "Don't you trust me? I thought we were becoming friends."

"We are becoming friends...I do trust you, it's just..." Her doleful expression didn't change, and he heaved an exasperated sigh. Were all women from Texas so damn sensitive? "Okay, I'll tell you why I'm cautious around pregnant women under one condition," he said, raking a hand through his hair in frustration.

"Anything," she said solemnly.

"You have to promise you won't spread the story around."

Her expression brightened again. "Okay."

He eyed her suspiciously. "You're saying that too glibly. I really mean it. I want you to promise you won't ever, under any circumstances, tell anyone else."

Jessica held up her hand and crooked her little finger. "Should I pinkie-swear?"

"If that's what it takes." Taking a sip of water to fortify himself—and did he ever want that wine now—he began, "See my nose?"

"The one in the center of your face?"

"Yeah, that's the one. Do you know how it got broken?"

Jessica was definitely intrigued. "In a fight? With a pregnant woman?" she guessed. "That would have been something to see."

He eyed her sardonically. "Yeah, it would—but that's not what happened. I was sixteen, staying at my friend

Raul's house, when his mom suddenly went into labor with her fifth kid. There wasn't time to get her to the hospital, Raul and I were the only ones home and…well, to cut a long, not very pretty story short, I fainted at the critical moment, fell on her oak nightstand and broke my nose.''

Jessica was a little disappointed in the tale. "That's unfortunate but hardly a reason to be afraid of all pregnant—"

"That was the *first* time I broke it," he said, interrupting her. "The second time I was a rookie cop. I'd taken all the childbirth classes they offered, determined to be prepared if that sort of situation ever arose again…and it did. We got a call. A woman was delivering in the back seat of her car, which her husband had parked along South Elm Avenue. My partner and I arrived at the scene. I opened the back door and bent down to check on the baby's progress, when the woman's leg cramped. She kicked out, hitting me right on the nose. I stumbled back, fell over on the sidewalk and was out for the count. By the time I came to, the baby was there, my nose was broken again and my partner was smirking like a son of a bitch. The story made the rounds of the station for a good two months.''

She bit her lip. "Okay, I could see where you might be a *little* wary—"

"The *third* time I was around a pregnant woman was the worst. I'd learned my lesson by then, and when we responded to a 902M call in east L.A. and discovered a woman giving birth, I pretty much got out of the way. The husband was in the bedroom with her, my partner was helping—and I thought I was safe, standing in a corner a good ten feet away from all the action. Then the woman lets out this god-awful shriek. Her husband, a.k.a. the idiot, says, 'Ah, c'mon, Olga, the pain can't be *that* bad.' Apparently Olga disagreed. She picked up a glass on the nightstand and flung it at him. Unfortunately, her aim was off—maybe because the kid's head was crowning down below at the time—and the glass shattered against the wall right next to my head. A big piece flew and cut me by my eye—damn near blinding me. I had to have surgery, wear a patch like a pirate for a month, and came away with this—'' he tapped the scar ''—as a permanent reminder to avoid pregnant women like the plague in the future. Tell *me* you wouldn't be nervous around them after that.''

Jessica stared at him. So, basically, the scar and broken nose that gave him such a tough look had been acquired through run-ins with pregnant women and not the thugs she'd imagined.

She tried to keep from smiling. He was clearly defensive about it all, but she found the revelation oddly endearing. Like the news about his ulcer, his fear of pregnant woman made him seem more human...more vulnerable somehow. Safer to be around. He'd always appeared to be so sure of himself and in control. It was oddly reassuring to know he wasn't completely fearless *all* the time.

The last of her wariness eased away. This was a situation, the kind of man she was used to. Mitch might look like a mountain lion, but inside he was a pussycat in need of a friend.

She actually felt a little guilty remembering his expression when she'd abandoned him with all those crying women after that video. Talk about his nightmare come true....

Still, *he'd* been the one who wouldn't listen at the time—he never listened once he'd made up his mind about something. For instance, driving her home that night, he mentioned that the lock on her door wasn't secure enough. She replied that it was just fine, thank you very much.

But somehow she wasn't surprised when he dropped by on Saturday to change it, and installed two dead bolts. The only hint of unpleasantness that day was the stare-down between Mitch and the neighbor who'd yelled at him before for pounding on Jessie's door. But no threats were uttered this time; no displays of masculine ego or outrage. On Sunday they watched baseball on his big-screen TV. Really, even life in Crab Apple had never been so calm.

With the strict diet regime she'd drawn up for him, Mitch's ulcer appeared to be under control, but Jessica still had dinner with him almost every night for the next two weeks. After all, why shouldn't she, when she had no intention of ever getting carried away in his arms again?

Mama always said if you played with fire, you were bound to get burned. And if a woman played around with a man with hot eyes and warm hands, she was bound to get seduced.

But talking and flirting with Mitch, what was the harm in that? Just because a woman went wading didn't mean she planned to swim the ocean. She'd made her position perfectly plain, and she didn't have to worry about *his* feelings. He was too experienced to be hurt by a small-town girl, and she no longer had any worries that she couldn't keep him under control.

Besides, he was so much fun to be with. They both liked the city at night, and the beach during the day. They both loved Chinese food and video games—Mitch had them all. Jessica was the champ at Zelda, Mitch could beat her soundly at Duke-Nukem.

They also both enjoyed their work. She saw him at the bank every day, and when it closed, he'd coax her out on dates to explore "his" city. It was fun getting to know L.A. with someone who loved it so much. He showed her the gritty excitement of the crowded business districts, and the elegant sophistication of the city's famous museums. On his arm, Jessica sauntered along the tacky, flashy splendor of Hollywood Boulevard and picnicked with him in the woodsy beauty of Malibu State Park.

Life was suddenly exhilarating. But what really made Jessica's breath catch and her heart pound wasn't the city sights, but the passion she glimpsed more and more frequently in Mitch's eyes. A mixture of fear and excitement would course through her veins. Her stomach would swoop and her nipples contract into tiny peaks.

Still, nothing would come of that, she assured herself constantly. She'd proven she could handle him and she simply wouldn't let it. After all, they didn't want the same things. She liked people, the more the better. She couldn't imagine life without family, and looked forward to someday having one of her own. Mitch was a loner. His friends, although tight, were few. He and his mother didn't appear to be close at all, and he never planned to have a family of his own.

"Never?" she repeated in amazement, pausing as they walked along the beach one evening to stare at him. They were both barefoot. Mitch had taken off his shoes and socks, and she'd handed over her sandals, as well, for him to carry. He'd driven her down to Seal Beach just outside of L.A. County after work to show her what a "true" beach town was like. They'd had dinner at the small restaurant at the end of the pier, then decided to walk along the water at sunset, Jessica gathering shells, while Mitch threw stones into the foaming waves.

He smiled. "Don't look so shocked. Not everyone

craves to hear the patter of little feet and be forced to change dirty diapers.''

''No, but most people want kids to love, to build a family,'' she replied, thinking of the joy of little arms hugging tight, the milky-sweet smell of babies, the gamin grins of five- and six-year-olds.

''Yeah, well, not everyone grows up in a family like yours,'' he said, bending down to pick up a smooth black stone lying at his feet.

Surely he couldn't be talking about himself? A wave washed over her feet, feeling cool and silky in the warm night air. She glanced up at him, trying to see his expression in the dusky light. ''What was your family like?''

''Nothing like yours, that's for sure,'' he said, tossing the stone into the air and catching it neatly. ''My parents broke up when I was four and I never saw my father again. He died when I was nine. As for my mother—'' He shrugged. ''We've pretty much lost touch. She moved out of California when I was sixteen. She took off one day with her new boyfriend while I was at school. Left me a note, two hundred bucks and a bag of groceries.''

The black stone went skipping into the crashing waves, expertly flicked there by his lean, tanned fingers. He didn't sound bitter or upset, Jessica realized, just chillingly matter-of-fact. She tried to hide her shock, unable to imagine a mother who would abandon her teenage son. ''What did you do?''

''Stayed with Raul's family until I turned eighteen and could enlist.''

Jessica remained silent, staring at his profile as he looked out over the ocean. Backlit by the peachy sky behind him, he looked tough and uncaring, a hard man with a broken nose and a scar that curved along his cheek, with a gun hidden in a holster under his shirt. But she'd learned these past two weeks that he wasn't as tough as he seemed. And as a child, it must have hurt a lot to have parents like that.

"You must have been lonely," she said slowly. "If you'd had brothers or sisters…"

He shrugged again. "I'm not much for crowds. Besides, I knew Raul—we watched each other's backs." He glanced at her face, and a faintly mocking gleam came into his eyes. "Don't look so tragic, Jessie. Don't you know you don't miss what you've never had?"

She stared up at him in the fading light, and suddenly knew that he was wrong. You *could* miss what you'd never had. Because often at night lately, she'd toss and turn, tense with sexual frustration, missing his touch, missing *him*.

She'd fooled herself, thinking she'd forgotten his kiss. She turned away, too, to watch the seagulls swooping over the water. She never should have spent so much time with him, she knew that now. Never gotten to know what he was like under that tough facade.

He picked up another stone, and then turned to face her. Their eyes met. Jessica didn't know what he saw in her expression, but his eyes suddenly flared hotly with desire. He dropped the stone and pulled her close.

His lips settled over hers with possessive familiarity and Jessica shut her eyes, sinking into that whirlpool of heart-pounding sensuality that she'd felt before in his arms, unable to stifle the surge of guilty joy she felt at the realization that he still wanted her, too.

But before she could drown completely, he broke the kiss. Resting his forehead against hers, he said, "Does this mean you're willing to let me make love to you now?"

She intended to say no, truly she did. Nothing had

changed; he still wasn't right for her. She'd be going back to Crab Apple soon, and he might be moving on even sooner.

But for some strange reason she hesitated, and that hesitation made his eyes flare again and his face tauten with desire.

He cupped her chin in his hand and tilted her face up to his. "Don't play with me, Jessie."

"I'm not. I'm just not sure…"

His eyes darkened even more, then he released her. The cool, salty breeze ruffled his thick hair, while the waves broke in endless repetition behind him, washing slowly up the sand and over their feet. "Then don't kiss me until you *are* sure. Because I want you…and I'm not sure how much more of this 'just friends' thing I can stand."

When she remained silent, he turned away, gathering up the shoes he'd dropped on the sand. "And if you're honest with yourself, I think you'll realize you feel the same. Think it over and give me your answer tomorrow."

10

How HAD IT HAPPENED? How could she actually be considering having an affair with Mitch Flaherty?

Alone the next day, Jessica silently puzzled over the issue, staring unseeingly down at the clipboard in her hands. She'd come upstairs to the stockroom, partly because there was always work to be done there, putting away deposit slips, cash sheets and other paper supplies on the shelves; and partly to avoid Mitch and his searching glances. He thought she'd gone out on an errand to pick up supplies to decorate the bank for an upcoming promotion. Instead, she'd escaped to the quiet, dimly lit room because it was such a good place to think.

And she needed to think about this—about what she wanted to do, and she had to do it alone. Because whenever Mitch was with her lately, logic flew out the window and emotions took over—new, unsettling *sexual* emotions that she'd been determined to avoid feeling about a man like Mitch Flaherty. Which was why she'd told him no after that first kiss.

But maybe her change of heart about him wasn't so strange as it seemed. After all, the first time he'd made the suggestion about "getting to know her better"—his euphemism for beginning an affair—he'd been reacting on a purely sexual basis. Now, however, things were different. They'd talked. She'd told him about her family and he'd confided in her in return, and now they had something special—something Mitch, despite all his experience, had never had before.

Friendship.

The thought gave her a small glow of satisfaction. Funny, how something bad—like Mitch's ulcer—could actually turn out to be a blessing in disguise. If it hadn't been for his illness, she never would have gotten to know him better and discovered what he was really like.

But she did know him better now—well enough to realize that she couldn't put off any longer the decision whether or not to take their relationship to a new level. His words and expression the night before had made that more than clear. The trouble was, if she decided not to have an affair with him, she'd have to stop seeing him altogether. He obviously was no longer satisfied with the relationship they had now, and she...well, being with him almost constantly had only made her craving for him grow. There was no use fooling herself. She simply couldn't forget that first kiss...or the one that he'd given her last night.

But was she willing to abandon all the beliefs she'd grown up with, the old-fashioned but solid values she'd adhered to all her life, for a brief fling with a man who wasn't interested in commitment? Her mind definitely said no—such an affair would be neither prudent nor wise.

But her body—oh, her traitorous body—shivered with excitement at the thought of spending the night in his arms, of feeling him kiss and caress her all over. Of being able to touch him in return, to discover for herself where the blazing passion she'd felt when he kissed her might lead.

There was only one choice a wise woman could make. Tonight she'd tell him that she had decided—

"Are you busy, Jessie?"

Jessica gave a small start, then turned to smile at Linda, who hovered in the doorway. "Just woolgathering. What's up? Am I needed downstairs?"

Linda shook her head. Entering the room, she sat down with a sigh of relief on the stool Jessie automatically pushed toward her. "No, I just needed another vault book and thought I'd come up and get it now since you already had the door unlocked."

She watched as Jessica stood on tiptoe to lift down the required item from a high shelf. Accepting the book with thanks, Linda sneezed at the dust that rose from the cover. Sniffing a little, she asked, "Are you going to be up here long?"

Jessie shook her head. "No, I'm almost done. In fact, you and the girls can leave as soon as you all balance tonight. I'll probably be leaving early myself."

"Ah, let me guess. You're going out with Mitch again," Linda said with a knowing look on her face. Her expression turned more serious. "You two are getting pretty chummy. Be careful you're not being blinded by all that sex appeal."

Again Jessica felt that small glow of satisfaction. Not even Linda, who was usually such a good judge of character, knew the *real* Mitch. "As a matter of fact, I think you might have been right about what you told me before. That Mitch is really rather…shy."

Linda looked surprised. "He is? I know I told you that, but to be honest, I'd kind of changed my mind the last few weeks. There certainly isn't anything shy about the way he looks at you now. If that man doesn't have sex on his mind, I'll eat my shoes—worn soles and all."

"So start munching," Jessica said with a trace of smugness. "Mitch and I are just good friends." So far, anyway.

Linda didn't look convinced, but she didn't argue either. "Are you seeing him tonight?"

Jessica nodded, unable to suppress a small smile. "I made reservations at Antonio's for an early dinner." And after that, they'd talk. *Really* talk.

"Well, good for you," Linda said, standing up with a sigh. "Lately, all I want to do when I get off work is crash into bed." She brushed off a dust mark on the front of her blue maternity dress and headed to the door, saying over her shoulder, "By the way, you might want to let Mitch know how early those reservations are. I just caught sight of him heading toward the electrical room with a big pastrami sandwich in his hand from the deli next door."

Jessie stared after her in surprise. Linda must have made some mistake. Pastrami was definitely on the list of foods Mitch wasn't supposed to have. Surely he wouldn't put his health at risk like that, especially when he hadn't had a single pain lately.

Determined to find out, she hurried downstairs to find him. He wasn't in the lobby or working with the crew installing the double glass doors at the bank exits, but when she asked where he might be, one of the men jerked his thumb in the direction of the small room behind the ATM machine where the alarms were set. The electrical room—just as Linda had said.

Her heart sinking, Jessica strode quickly to the door and peeked in.

Mitch was standing there, the electrical fuse box opened in front of him. He looked up, and his eyes warmed at the sight of her. "Hey," he said, his voice low and husky with unfeigned pleasure. "I didn't expect to get the chance to be alone with you until tonight. Did you just get back?"

"I never left. I was up in the stockroom," Jessica

admitted, feeling an answering tug of warmth in her chest merely at the sight of him. The dark blue shirt he wore made his eyes shine like a clear blue sky. He had a holster-type belt filled with screwdrivers, pliers and other tools slung around his lean hips, and no-nonsense work boots on his feet.

And crumpled next to those boots was a bag clearly labeled Benedicto's Deli.

"Are you busy?" Jessica asked, looking away from the incriminating bag and back up at his face as he peered into the fuse box.

He nodded absently. "A little. I'm just at a critical point here. If I'm not careful, our lights might go off."

He turned back to the box and Jessica walked over and picked up the bag. As she had feared, only a few crumpled napkins remained inside. "Oh, Mitch..."

Mitch glanced up from the fuses he was altering, faintly alarmed at the distress in her voice. "What's wrong—oh," he said as he caught sight of the bag in her hands.

The surge of annoyance he felt quickly dissolved at the concern in Jessica's eyes. She was worried, he realized. About him.

A feeling of warmth spread through his chest. Obviously, it was time to come clean. The ulcer ruse had more than served its purpose, after all. He no longer needed to rely on it to keep seeing her. Besides, his taste buds were atrophying from all the bland pap he'd been eating lately. Yeah, it was definitely the time to tell her the truth.

So when she asked, "Did you eat a pastrami sandwich, Mitch?" he immediately confessed.

"Yeah. I did. But you don't need to worry about it, Jessie," he added hurriedly as she bit her lip. "My ulcer is gone."

Her forehead creased in puzzlement. "You think you're cured?"

"Well, actually, I was never really ill," he confessed, feeling a little sheepish. "I just used the ulcer gag to get you—to get you to go out with me."

He smiled, expecting her to smile in return. She didn't. Her fingers crushed the bag in her hands.

"Are you saying you lied to me?"

He shifted, feeling absurdly guilty. "I fooled you," he corrected, trying to ease the anger growing in her eyes.

It didn't work.

"*Made* a fool of me, you mean," she said quietly, tossing the bag aside.

And before he could stop her—explain that hadn't been his intention at all—she turned on her heel and headed to the door.

"Wait a minute, Jessie. Give me a chance to explain." He raised his voice as she opened the door. "I can't leave this right now. Come back here so we can talk."

Fat chance of that happening, Jessica thought, slamming the door on her way out. He'd had plenty of chances to explain on all those dates they'd gone on. What was there to explain now? That he'd known all along that she was concerned about him? That he'd used that concern to get past her defenses?

Any way she looked at it, he'd lied to her. And he'd played her for a fool as well.

She marched to her desk and handled her work automatically for the next hour while her mind continued to dwell on what Mitch had done. How he must have secretly been laughing at her all this time.

Thank goodness she'd realized in time what he was truly like. What if she'd made the colossal mistake of going to bed with a man like that? A man who used a person's better feelings against them? The one positive thing in this whole fiasco was she no longer had to decide whether or not to have an affair with him. He—by his despicable deceit—had made the decision for her.

Cringing at the thought of how worried she'd been, she welcomed the anger that stiffened her spine, nursed her rage for the rest of the day so that when he emerged from the alarm room, she could meet each of his demanding, seeking glances with stony indifference. How dare he think that this made no difference, that they could pick right up where they'd left off last night. *She'd* thought that they were becoming friends. That they had something special. That she knew him better than any other woman ever had.

Well, she may not have truly known what he was like before, but she sure did now. He'd proven he was as sensitive as a Brangus steer. And if he dared to come near her, she'd carve up his deceitful hide and fry his liver for dinner. And make him eat it!

Yes, she was fully armed to repulse any overtures Mitch tried to make. She wasn't quite as prepared, however, for the sneak attack launched on her defenses by her friend late that afternoon.

"Maybe you should give the poor guy a chance to explain," Linda said. The bank had already closed to customers for the day, and the two were alone in the storeroom beyond the vault, preparing a cash shipment to go out by armored truck the next day.

Jessica didn't answer. Linda watched silently as she entered the combination on the lock on the old cabinet, before adding accusingly, "You've barely said a word to him all day."

Jessica didn't look up from her task. "He made an idiot out of me. How can he possibly explain away that?"

"I think you should at least listen to him."

Jessica gave her an incredulous look. "Why should I?"

"Because you like him."

"Not anymore, I don't."

"Come on, Jessie. Who do you think you're fooling? You wouldn't be so hurt if you didn't care about him."

"I'm *not* hurt, I'm simply angry because he wasn't straight with me," Jessie declared. Ignoring the disbelief in her friend's eyes, she added, "And I don't want to discuss it. Let's just get this transfer ready."

Linda said nothing more and they counted the money, stacked it, double-checked their figures on the cash sheet, then recounted it again. It was more than an hour later before they could finally stuff the cash deposit into canvas bags, and the bags back into the cabinet, all set and ready to go when the armored car arrived the next morning.

By this time, Linda was looking exhausted.

"You go on," Jessica urged her after the cabinet lock had been reset. "Everyone else is going home early. In fact," she said, checking her watch, "it's already past seven, so they've probably already left. I know John is up in the break room. I'll walk out with him when I finish pulling in the teller carts and file cabinets."

Bringing the teller carts into the vault and storeroom to be locked up for the night was usually the head teller's job. Linda gave Jessie a smile, obviously grateful to be spared the task for once. "Thanks, Jessie. It's not so much I'm tired, but these twins keep dancing on my bladder."

She left. Half an hour later Jessie had dragged all the carts in, and the vault and storeroom looked more jammed than the 405 Freeway at rush hour. She was in the storeroom, squeezing her way through a thin path in the pile of carts to return to the vault, when she felt someone watching her. She glanced up.

Mitch.

He didn't say anything, just stared at her with the unrevealing expression he could assume so easily. Despite her resolve to maintain an icy calm, Jessica could feel her heart pound just at the sight of him. The realization that he could affect her so easily made her angry all over again. "Yes?" she said coldly. "Did you need something?"

"Yeah, I need to talk to you. To get this misunderstanding cleared up."

"There's no misunderstanding." She made a move toward him, but he didn't budge out of her path and there was no other way to get around him, trapped as she was in the small sea of carts. She halted and her chin lifted. "You lied to me."

His eyebrows lowered in a frown. "I didn't lie, exactly. I simply told a small…falsehood to get you to go out with me. So we could get to know each other better."

"It seems you were successful then. You learned I'm a sucker for a sob story, and I learned you'd say anything to get a woman into bed."

Anger pulled his eyebrows together. His chiseled lips tightened into a stern line. "That's not how it was at all, Jessie—"

"Well, that's how it appears to me," she said, cutting him off. "And since *you* can't be trusted to tell the truth, I'm afraid I'll have to go with my own version of events."

It was a fine exit line and Jessica was determined to use it. She pushed past him, ignoring the flare of heat in her belly as her shoulder brushed his arm, and headed out of the storeroom and into the vault. But there she stopped, realizing she wasn't going to be able to leave on that final scathing note after all.

The steel door had swung shut. They were locked in.

11

JESSICA STARED at the closed door for a long, stunned moment. Then she whirled around to face Mitch, who had come up behind her.

"Damn," he said, looking over her head at the locked door. "This is all my fault." Automatically, he slapped his pants pockets. "And wouldn't you know, I left my cell phone on the desk."

He glanced down at Jessica. Her brown eyes flashed as they met his. Her fists were clenched by her sides and a flush of anger stained her cheeks a rosy red. "You mean, you shut that door on *purpose?*"

Mitch's temper, already rubbed raw by her stubborn refusal to listen to reason, suddenly flared to meet hers. "Give me a break, Jessica," he said, not bothering to hide the sarcasm in his tone. "I only meant I should have had that door fixed sooner. I know I'm a liar of the worst kind—"

Color rose in her cheeks.

"—But I'm not fool enough to put us in possible danger just to get you alone."

Her bright color faded a little. "Danger? What do you mean? We have plenty of air—there's vents—"

"Yeah, and what if there's a fire in the bank? We'd bake in here like a couple of Thanksgiving turkeys."

He regretted the remark as soon as the words left his mouth. The warm color in her cheeks ebbed even more, leaving her pale and worried-looking. Cursing under his breath at himself for allowing his temper to get the best of him, he added roughly, "Hell, forget I said that. There's no reason on earth there'd suddenly be a fire, and as antiquated as this building is, it does have sprinklers installed."

Her anxious expression faded, replaced by her usual one of calm resolve. "Of course there is...and I'm sorry I accused you of closing the door," she added conscientiously if stiffly. Her expression lightened. "Chances are, we'll be out within the hour anyway. John was still in the break room when I came in here. He's bound to notice my car in the lot and realize something is wrong."

"Did you park near his car?"

She shook her head. "No...in the back lot. You?"

He hated to douse the hopeful gleam in her eyes, but he wasn't going to lie—not even by avoiding the question. Not after the chewing out she'd just given him. "I parked there, too."

She bit her lip at his reply, but said stoutly, "There's still a chance he'll notice."

Personally, Mitch thought their chances of being rescued due to John's acuity were on par with the painted angels on the lobby wall coming to life and unlocking the vault themselves. Even if Jessica and he *had* parked near the old man, Mitch doubted seeing their cars would have penetrated the fog John seemed to exist in these days.

He didn't say so, however, but nodded noncommittally and pointed out, "We'll know one way or the other within the next half hour. If John notices we haven't left, he should be able to get someone here to open the door by then."

Resigned to waiting, he propped his shoulders against the steel door and crossed his arms. Jessica, however, was unable to stay still.

The aisle created by the jam of carts was confined and narrow, but she paced it anyway while Mitch watched her broodingly. On the one hand, he wanted to continue to argue his case about that damn imaginary ulcer. On the other, he didn't want to rile her up again. She had enough to deal with being locked in.

He studied her face, trying to determine how well she was holding up. Her slim eyebrows were drawn down with worry, but at least her color was good. A faint shade of pink still tinted her cheeks and her brown eyes looked anxious but bright.

Sometime during the day, she'd unbuttoned down to that teasing third button again, and half of her blouse had pulled out from her skirt. She had a rumpled look that Mitch found completely endearing, it was so unlike the prim-and-proper image she always tried to maintain. She looked as if she'd just been thoroughly kissed—and he wished he'd been the one to do the job.

As if she sensed his thoughts, she suddenly met his gaze. Her steps faltered, then stopped, and the color in her cheeks deepened. Catching his glance at her waist, she tucked her blouse in more firmly and straightened her skirt. She straightened her slender shoulders and back as well.

It didn't help. Mitch still wanted her like the dickens.

But instead of reaching for her as he yearned to do, he merely glanced at his watch, and pushed away from the wall. "Looks like John didn't notice anything wrong. Which means we're stuck here for the night."

She clasped her hands together. "All night?"

His jaw tightened at the dismay he glimpsed beneath the determinedly calm expression on her face. "It could be worse. What if today was Friday instead of Thursday? We'd be locked in here over the weekend. As it is, since the cleaners are gone, we just have to stick it out until Rod or John and Linda open the vault in the morning.''

She nodded slowly, and he looked around, considering their situation. ''We might as well get as comfortable as possible—especially before the lights go out.''

He looked up at the fluorescent lights in the recessed ceiling of the vault as he spoke. The lights were set on a timer which, he knew as well as Jessica, would turn them off at 7:00 p.m. and on again at seven in the morning. The lights in the storeroom were on the same system except for an old bare bulb hanging in a back corner that was operated manually by pulling on its dangling string.

Mitch picked his way through the pile of carts back into the storeroom and glanced around. The room was divided into three sections by floor-to-ceiling shelves filled with boxes of old banking transactions that the bank was required to keep for a certain number of years, and a few cartons of decorations used in the lobby during the holidays.

He made his way to the middle section of shelves. Once he moved the carts shoved in there, he decided, they'd have an area of approximately five feet wide and eight feet long to stretch out in. Plenty of room to make a bed for two people, he thought with a certain amount of satisfaction.

''I'll clear this out,'' he told Jessica, who had trailed him into the storeroom. ''That way we'll get some light from that bare bulb in the back when the others go out, but not enough to bother us if we manage to get comfortable enough to sleep.''

He looked at her blandly as he made the last comment and Jessie met his gaze just as impassively. She had no intention of ever getting *that* comfortable. She acquitted Mitch of purposely trapping them together, but she wasn't naive enough to think he wouldn't try to use their enforced intimacy to his advantage. He'd shown he was willing to use anything to his advantage when necessary. The speculative gleam in his eye as he glanced over their proposed sleeping area made that more than clear.

She didn't challenge his assumption, however. He'd discover his mistake soon enough.

He glanced around at the boxes. "I'll see what I can find for us to sit on. Why don't you see if there's anything for us to eat?"

She nodded and moved off to see what she could discover.

Her search proved surprisingly fruitful. Almost all the women kept bottled water handy on the top of their carts, and she borrowed a bottle from Thelma and one from Pam. Pamela also had almost a full roll each of butter rum and peppermint Life Savers—a very appropriately named candy to eat when trapped, Jessie decided, adding the hard candy to her hoard. Diane had a banana on her tray—a bit overripe, but not inedible. On Lupe's, who was more of a heath nut than the others, Jessica discovered an apple and a granola bar as well. All the tellers had packets of moist towelettes on their carts, since handling money was a grimy business. She scooped up those also.

Cradling her booty in her arms, she made her way back through the carts to Mitch. She paused at the cubicle-like area he had cleared, staring in surprise.

He *had* created a bed of sorts. He'd spread canvas money bags on the floor and covered them with the Christmas-tree skirt the bank used to wrap the base of the thirty-foot pine brought in every year for the lobby. The skirt, which John's wife had made over twenty years ago, was huge and thickly quilted. Folded into fourths it looked quite cushiony. An inviting place to lie down...with Mitch. Her lips tightened. Did everything come back to sex with this man?

Pushing the unsettling thought aside, Jessica knelt at one end of the makeshift bed to set down the things she'd gathered. Mitch sat at the other end, stretching out his legs and leaning back against the rough plaster wall behind him.

"Here's some paper towels for our hands, and a water for you and one for me," Jessica said, handing them over. She broke the granola bar in half. Mitch wiped off the blade of his pocketknife and divided the apple and banana.

She held up the two rolls of candy. "Do you like peppermint or butter rum?"

"Butter rum."

She tossed the roll to him, and picking up her half of the banana, began to eat.

She'd finished that, and her granola bar as well, when the lights went out. For a second Jessica tensed, and then slowly took another bite of her apple. As Mitch had said, they could still see, but the light was dim, the shadows darker. Suddenly, it felt as if they were having an intimate midnight picnic out in the woods somewhere, instead of trapped in a musty room.

Not liking the direction of her thoughts, she put her banana peel and granola wrapper in the canvas bag Mitch has set aside for trash, then tossed in the rest of her apple, too. Feeling restless, she stood up and stretched—stopping in mid-bend when she realized Mitch's eyes were on her.

"You'd probably feel more comfortable if you took off your nylons, and your skirt and blouse. You *are* wearing a slip under all that, aren't you?"

She was—not that it was any of his business—and she intended to keep her slip on, along with all her other clothes. More comfortable—hah! Who did he think he was fooling with that line? He'd slipped off his shoes and she'd discarded her heels—her aching feet had made that almost a necessity—but that was as far as she planned to undress with him around, thank you very much.

Without answering his question, she scooped up her candy and water, deciding to sit on top of the cart at the end of their cubicle for a while. It would be easier on her back, she told herself. The fact that it was also farther away from Mitch was only incidental.

She jumped up on the cart and popped a peppermint into her mouth. She sucked gently on the small disk, enjoying the zing of the minty sugar on her tongue.

Mitch had already finished his meal and was eating his candy, too. One after another he tossed the small gold candy into his mouth and crunched them up with his strong white teeth, his eyes fixed broodingly on her face.

He wouldn't quit staring at her. He was trying to un-nerve her again, that's what he was trying to do, Jessica decided, avoiding his gaze. Well, it wasn't going to work this time. She had his number now. He couldn't scare her anymore with that sexy, "I-want-you-and-I-want-you-now-babe," look in his eyes, and he wouldn't fool her with another sad story, either.

"I wasn't trying to make a fool of you, Jessica. Like I said, I just wanted the chance to get to know you better," he said suddenly in that low coaxing tone that always made her insides melt.

Ignoring him, Jessica took another small sip of water from her bottle. She wanted to go easy on the liquids. Mitch had scrounged up a black plastic cauldron from the box full of decorations that had been used to hold candy for the customers at Halloween. He'd put it in a dark corner to be used as their "chamber pot" if necessary, but Jessica sincerely hoped it wouldn't come to that.

She took another drink of water—almost choking on it when Mitch said suddenly, his tone more demanding now, "Talk to me, Jessie, before you make me lose my temper, too. This is the perfect opportunity to straighten things out between us."

He paused. When again she didn't respond, he added, "You can't stay mad forever, you know."

Jessica didn't see why not. She was from Texas, after all, where long memories and grudge-bearing were a matter of civic pride. Hadn't he ever heard about the Alamo?

She ate another candy, swinging her legs and staring at the boxes on the shelf above him. Which one would fall on his stubborn head first if California had one of its famous earthquakes? she wondered. Probably that big one, right on the edge.

"C'mon, Jessie. Is what I did so terrible?"

Silence.

"Or are you just using my small deceit as an excuse to turn me down?"

That made her so angry she couldn't stay quiet any longer. "I don't need an excuse to tell you no. I'd already realized before discovering the truth about your ulcer that an affair between us would never work."

"Oh, yeah. And why's that?"

"We're just too different." She met his eyes steadily. "You live for today. To you everything is temporary and constantly changing. Everything is 'no big deal.' If a lie gets you what you want, then why not tell it? You don't care about anyone, and that's how you run your love life as well." She took a deep breath. "I, however, believe commitment is necessary to make a relationship worthwhile."

"And how did you become such an expert on relationships?"

"I learned from my mother, who knows more about life than you ever will."

He made a scoffing sound. "Are you telling me your mother, a woman with all those kids, doesn't believe in sex?"

"She believes sex without commitment isn't worth it," Jessie said. She looked at his skeptical face, but in her mind she saw her mother's kindly, careworn one. Gripped with sudden homesickness, she told him, "There's this burned-out old house in the lot next to ours. It used to belong to my grandparents, but now all that's left is a few crumbling walls and a two-story staircase that somehow survived. None of us kids are allowed within ten feet of that lot normally, but whenever one of her girls reaches that certain age when boys are suddenly the most interesting creatures on earth, Mama takes us over to that old lot to have a talk."

Jessica drew a deep breath, remembering how quiet, how still it had seemed standing by the tower of rickety planks with her mother. "She tells us that making love without marriage is just like climbing that old staircase. It's dangerous, you can fall anytime, and even if you do make it to the top, it leads nowhere. You might be high for a while, but sooner or later the only place to go is back down. That's why I won't have an affair with you, Mitch Flaherty."

Mitch stared at her in the shadowy darkness. Jessie met his eyes unflinchingly, sure that now he'd finally abandon the issue, leave her alone.

He didn't.

His low voice drifted out from the shadows. Her skin prickled in wary alarm. "Your mother sounds like a very clever woman, Jessica," he said slowly, "and that's a very edifying story, complete with a neat little moral designed to keep teenagers on the straight-and-narrow path. The only problem is—you're no longer a teenager. You're a woman. And you're tired of being so restricted.''

Her pulse speeded up. Her back stiffened. With anger—and a strange, rising panic. "That's not true—"

"Of course it is," he cut her off ruthlessly. "And I bet, no matter what your mother told you—that you climbed that old staircase anyway, probably in the dead of night when none of your brothers or sisters could see you. You went right up it and stared out as far as you could see, enjoying every guilty, exhilarating, dangerous minute of being up there. *Didn't* you, Jessica?''

How did he know?

Her throat felt dry. Her heart beat faster. She tried to stop him. "That's ridiculous—"

"Is it, Jessie?" he cut her off again. "Why else did you come to L.A.? Not because of the money—you can't tell me you couldn't have found an equally well-paying job closer to home. No, you came to the most dangerous city you could think of, to work in one of its most run-down banks, because you were tired of being the perfect example, the eldest of eight in a town where everyone knew you. You were tired of being the dutiful daughter and never taking any risks.''

"No!"

"*Yes*. And you knew all along—somewhere deep inside—that I still wanted you. You had to know. But you wanted to experiment with me, to see where things between us might go, so you jumped on that story I told because it gave you a respectable reason to pursue our relationship.''

She wasn't like that. She couldn't be—

But a chill chased up her spine as he added with dark

certainty in his deep voice, "You might fool everyone else with your prim-and-proper facade, your straitlaced little suits, but I've held you in my arms. I've *felt* the excited tension in your body. I've *tasted* the passion in your kiss. You want me, Jessica Kendall, just as much as I want you."

His eyes snared her panicky gaze and refused to release it. "In fact, I'm *exactly* the kind of man you traveled to Los Angeles to find."

12

His words hit Jessie like a kick from her sister's donkey. She gasped, her chest aching as she tried to get her breath. She felt stunned, unable to think straight, knocked from her pedestal and off balance.

His eyes refused to release hers and she stared helplessly at him in return. His gaze seemed to be the only steady thing in a world that had turned upside down and inside out.

Because he was right. He hadn't fooled her; she'd been fooling herself. Her anger had only been an excuse to avoid the real issue: that no matter how dangerous, how temporary, how wrong it might be, she wanted—more than she'd ever wanted anything on this earth—to make love with Mitch Flaherty.

And she simply couldn't deny it any longer.

Mitch sucked in a breath at the acceptance, the unhidden desire that suddenly softened her expression. He held out his hand, her name emerging hoarsely from his suddenly dry throat. "Jessica…"

Without another word, she climbed down from the cart and walked toward him. To Mitch it mattered—almost too much—that she came to him. He felt as if he'd been chasing her for years, instead of only the few weeks that had actually passed.

But now, when he finally had her within reach, he hesitated. How ironic that he'd used a trick to bring her to this point only to discover that he wanted her to be sure that she wanted this as much as he did. That it wasn't simply a new experience, a taste of the forbidden unknown that she craved, but *him*—Mitch Flaherty.

He started to ask her, but changed his mind. If she didn't feel that way, he really didn't want to know. Because he needed her so very much. His heart, his whole body, felt like one big ache of painful yearning.

He reached out and she placed her hand in his. He looked up at her in the shadowy light. Her eyes were solemn, her lips slightly parted. A small pulse beat frantically at the side of her throat. His hand tightened around her small fingers.

"Jessie..." he said huskily. He tugged a little and she kneeled beside him. "Jessie..." he repeated. And she came into his arms.

He held her gently, but as closely as he dared, careful not to scare her with the need raging inside him. She felt so good, so right in his arms, with her small, soft breasts crushed against his chest and her slender arms around him. Surely she felt it, too? How well they fit together?

She had to know that *this* was real.

His hand slid through her hair, tugging on the satiny strands to pull her head back so he could kiss her. His mouth lowered. He touched her lips once, then twice, lingering longer this time. Her mouth was silky soft, her tongue slightly rough. He groaned, his lower body hardening with excitement.

Their tastes mingled—butter rum on his tongue, peppermint on hers. He kissed her deeply, thoroughly, wanting to claim every part of her, filled with a primitive need to erase any lingering reservations she might have. To bind her to him, closer than she'd ever been to anyone before.

He kissed her until she was pliant, with her arms

draped around his neck. Then he lifted his head to look down at her as she lay across his lap.

Her lips were swollen and red. Her eyes were closed. He kissed her delicate eyelids and her lashes fluttered against his chin with butterfly delicacy. He nuzzled her soft cheek and explored the shell of her ear with his tongue. When he placed small, biting kisses along the slender column of her throat, she moaned and clutched him closer. He smiled against her skin.

Eager to taste even more of her, he lifted his hand to her blouse and struggled to undo the tiny pearl buttons. Her hand came up to cover his and his heart dropped with dismay. Surely she wasn't going to stop him now?

Her eyes opened. She stared up at him beneath heavy eyelids. "Let me do it. They're so small and tight, they're hard to get open," she told him softly.

He buried his face against her hair with a groan as her slender fingers pushed his aside. *Small and tight.* The words, in her sweet, sexy drawl, made him hot all over.

She sat up and began undoing the buttons one by one. Mitch rose, too, watching her as he pulled off his shirt. Her eyes darkened as she stared back at him, her gaze roaming his tanned chest. His body hardened in response. He undid his pants and shucked them off, taking his briefs along with them. Her eyes widened even more at the sight of his arousal and her fingers faltered to a halt.

Mitch was a little amused, then puzzled by her big-eyed stare. "Jessie?"

Her gaze didn't even waver.

Comprehension dawned. He slowly picked up his jeans and held them in front of him.

That broke her transfixed stare, and she glanced away. "Yes?" she asked in a husky voice. She cleared her throat and added, "Did you say something?"

She sounded calm enough, but his usually straight-talking little Texan seemed to be having a terrible time meeting his gaze. And she was being very careful now not to let her eyes wander anywhere else on his body. Keeping his jeans strategically placed, Mitch crouched beside her and caught her chin in his hand. He tilted it upward until her reluctant eyes met his. "Jessie...are you a virgin?"

She pulled away. "Yes."

Now she sounded almost hostile, and Mitch's heart sank—he didn't want to hurt her. Yet, at the same time, his possessive soul rejoiced at the news. She'd never been with any man—*he'd* be her first. He'd always heard a woman never forgot her first time.

Now she'd never, *ever* be able to forget him.

His muscles tensed with heated excitement. His loins throbbed. He resisted the urge to grab her, kiss her all over and throw her back on that blanket to cover her body with his own. But even with all his senses clamoring for him to do just that, there was one thing he wouldn't risk—her welfare.

He said slowly, "Is birth control a factor here?"

Jessica realized he was asking if she was on the Pill. She wasn't. But although this was the perfect excuse to back out, she didn't take it. She was almost positive she wasn't at a fertile stage in her cycle. Surely one time wouldn't hurt.

She looked down, undoing the final button of her blouse as she said, "We're okay."

It probably wasn't the most rational decision she'd ever made, but how could she be rational when she could feel the heat of his hard body beckoning her nearer? How could she think straight when his hot eyes were making her insides melt with desire?

And then he didn't give her a chance to think at all.

Catching her mouth with his, he slipped her blouse off her shoulders. He broke the contact just long enough to lift her slip up over her head and off, then he kissed her again—more deeply this time, pulling her down to lay beside him until her head rested on his muscular arm. His mouth moved on hers, while he coaxed her closer still, his big hand sliding down to cup her buttocks and draw her against him.

His mouth took hers, over and over again until Jessica's head spun. It spun even more when he rolled suddenly, carrying her with him until she lay atop his hard length.

Jessica lifted her head to look down at him, trembling with excited trepidation at the feel of him beneath her. He gazed back up at her and gave her a slow, sexy smile. Her lace-covered breasts lay against his chest. His flat hard belly rubbed against her smooth one. His arousal, so alarmingly big, pressed demandingly against the crotch of her panties.

He held her gaze while his warm hand swept over the smooth skin of her back in a long slow stroke. He did it again, moving over the curve of her bottom this time. Again his hand stroked her, and this time his fingers slipped under the back waistband of her panties.

Slightly shocked, Jessica stiffened and his mouth caught hers, distracting hers with a deep searching kiss, while his hand cupped and stroked her bottom. Then those clever fingers moved lower, lower, searching for the core of her. He touched her and she gasped, the sound swallowed by his kiss.

He probed gently and she moaned at the warm, melting feeling deep inside her. She squirmed a little, trying to adjust to the strange sensation, and he groaned into her mouth.

He moved his hand away to sweep off her panties. He

undid the clip of her bra and tossed that aside, too. Then he rolled again, until she was underneath him, his body lying along hers.

Myriad sensations bombarded her. The taste of his searching tongue. The spicy, musky scent of his body. His lips covering hers, making them feel swollen and so sensitive. The soft feel of the quilt beneath her. The hard strength of his body along hers, the exciting roughness of the hair on his chest and legs against her skin. His warm hands exploring her breasts, his mouth following to kiss the soft curves and taste her nipples before moving down her stomach, and then lower still, making her moan with unbearable delight.

But then he moved back up to kiss her lips again. And all the feelings swirling inside her coalesced into a moment of piercing clarity as Mitch slowly, carefully entered her body.

Jessica bit her lip to keep from crying out. He felt so big, so hard. She couldn't help tensing at the tight, burning sensation, and he paused to kiss her deeply, over and over again, until she was once again pliant in his arms.

He thrust again, then stilled. Jessica froze, too, alarmed at the tearing pain. She felt too stretched, too invaded. Instinctively, she tried to push him off. He wouldn't move, but only kissed her cheeks and temple soothingly, whispering, "Just stay still a moment, sweetheart. Let your body adjust to mine."

She tried. And gradually, the pain faded, eclipsed by building passion. She clung to him as the tightness in her lower body grew more intense. Then suddenly, she couldn't bear to remain still a moment longer. She writhed, and gasped at the stabbing pleasure the movement caused. She twisted again, and more aching pleasure rippled through her.

Then he moved, too. Faster and deeper he thrust, each

stroke increasing the intensity of the pleasure, pushing her higher. She couldn't bear it, she couldn't take any more.... She reached the top. For a long, endless moment she hovered there before she shattered among the stars.

A split second later, he shattered too, and her body pulsed helplessly around him as he sank into her warmth.

Slowly, they drifted back to earth and simply lay there for a time, with Mitch's head resting on Jessica's breasts, her arms draped across his back.

Lifting her hand, she lazily combed her fingers through his hair, enjoying the silky feel of the thick, short strands. He sighed, relaxing more fully against her. His body grew heavier with sleep, but Jessica didn't care. She shifted to make him more comfortable and continued to stroke his hair, staring up at the pitted tiles in the ceiling. So this was what she'd been missing all these years. What she'd waited for, been searching for. She sighed with contentment. She'd made the right choice— choosing him.

"Jessie?" His voice was deep with sleep. He stirred, then turned over, carrying her along with him, until she lay across his chest again, with his strong arms wrapped around her. She nestled her head contentedly on his shoulder. His hand stroked lazily down her back and over the curve of her bottom in a big long swoop of warmth. "Are you all right?" he asked huskily.

She smiled against his skin. "I'm fine."

But fine, it seemed, simply wasn't good enough. Not that night. He placed his hand on her breast and kissed her swollen lips. Then he took her up to ecstasy once again.

13

THE STEEL VAULT DOOR creaked open at precisely eight o'clock the next morning. A bewildered John and a horrified Linda peered in, immediately catching sight of Mitch and Jessica waiting to be released.

"Were you locked in here all night?" John asked, his faded blue eyes rounding with surprise.

"Yes," Mitch answered.

"Good Lord, locked in all night…I…harrumph… never heard of such a thing," John mumbled, his bushy white brows waggling up and down as they did whenever he was particularly distressed. "Although, once…back in 1959, I believe it was…the stall door in the bathroom got jammed, and I had to wiggle that little knob…hard to hold on to, you know, those little knobs—"

"For goodness' sake, John, move out of the way so they can get out," Linda said, gently shoving him aside to open the door farther. But before Jessica had a chance to take more than two steps, Linda waddled in to hug her—not an easy task with the teller's swollen stomach between them—and to say with heartfelt sympathy, "Oh, Jessie, you poor thing—locked in all night like that. Are you *okay?*"

"I'm fine," Jessica said, patting her friend's shoulder before pulling away. "But I'm desperate to get to a bathroom, and then go home and change. I'm sure Mitch is, too."

Jessica glanced at him as she spoke and almost winced. *She'd* agreed, after another hour of irresistible persuasion early this morning, to continue their affair a while. *He'd* agreed, after threats of extreme violence if he didn't comply, to keep their relationship a secret. They'd cleared away all evidence of their makeshift nest, but although the man looked tired, he also looked ridiculously satisfied. He might as well be wearing a sign that said, "I Had Sex in the Vault" across his forehead, she thought crossly.

She frowned, hoping to make him look more tense before Linda noticed. He only smiled lazily back at her, then started out the door. "I'm going to run home and get cleaned up," he said, his voice dropping to a murmur as he added, "I'll see you later, Jessie."

Despite herself, the suggestive tone of his final sentence made her shiver with anticipation for the night ahead. Trying to hide her reaction, she said briskly, "That's fine, Flaherty."

She resisted the urge to stare at his departing back. She turned to Linda, who now had a distinctly speculative gleam in her eye, and John, who still merely looked vague, and said, "I hope you won't mention this to anyone else. I'd prefer that it doesn't get around that I could do something so stupid as to get locked in the vault. I'm sure Mitch would prefer to keep it secret, too."

"Of course we won't tell anyone, Jessie," Linda assured her immediately, and John made harrumphing sounds of agreement.

They both kept their word, as Jessica knew they would. Linda never broke a confidence, and John was a gentleman to the core. Not once in the following days did anyone—not even Pam—mention Mitch and Jessica's night-long sojourn in the vault together.

Yes, there was no reason in the world for anyone to

suspect anything had changed, that she and Mitch had become lovers. Yet Jessica couldn't escape the feeling that everyone knew, that everyone was watching.

If she saw the tellers whispering together, she was sure they were talking about her and Mitch. When Maria said something to Lupe in a long string of Spanish that contained the word *idiotas,* she was sure again their affair was the subject under discussion. The faces of the angels in the mural held regal rebuke, and those darn cherubs looked downright gleeful. When she counted money, Washington, Lincoln and Jackson all stared up at her accusingly, while Franklin seemed to have a conspiratorial air. She put him at the bottom of the pile.

Approval and disapproval seemed to flow around Jessica with every swing of her conscience. She knew that she should break off her affair with Mitch. That what they were doing wasn't right.

Yet, she couldn't bring herself to do it. He was addictive, making her high with delight. Simply catching sight of him across the lobby made her heart beat faster. Sharing a smile in passing or talking with him about the bank, while all the while his eyes told her he was thinking about other things as well, made her days bright and exciting.

And the nights. She shivered with remembered ecstasy, just thinking about those hot, passionate nights. Mitch certainly knew how to make a woman's toes curl—Jessica was only surprised that hers hadn't acquired a permanent kink. He'd make love to her until she was reduced to a blissful puddle of exhaustion. The only thing as good as his lovemaking was the secure, contented feeling she had each night, falling asleep in his strong arms.

He never went home afterward. Her apartment became the place he spent most of his nonworking hours. His shirts crept in to nestle among her dresses. Her tooth-brush leaned against his in a cup. For three weeks Jessica floated on a joyful cloud, high above the usual worries and concerns of life.

She came crashing down to earth again the morning nausea forced her from her bed in a frantic rush to reach the bathroom.

There was nothing like hugging a toilet bowl to make a woman face reality, she thought wearily, staring down at the white porcelain in between vomiting bouts. The only good thing about the whole wretched performance was that no one was there to see it. Mitch had left half an hour earlier to work on another job down in Orange County, just outside L.A. As the work wrapped up at First Saver's, he spent more and more time at the new bank, getting things started. Which left Jessica—and her commode—all alone to consider the ramifications of her sudden illness.

She tried to tell herself she had the flu. Or maybe food poisoning, or that temporary ulcer that had plagued Mitch. But the practical common sense at the bottom of her nature—the same common sense she'd buried for the past three weeks—wouldn't buy it. She'd been around too many pregnant women for far too long now not to know what this sudden illness probably meant.

With relentless precision, her logical mind laid out the facts. She and Mitch had made love that night in the vault without protection. Mitch was a healthy, apparently virile male. She was a healthy, apparently fertile female. Ergo, she was probably pregnant.

The thought brought joy, confusion and more nausea. She bowed over the toilet bowl again.

Thankfully, the sickness proved as brief as it was vi-olent. Within a few minutes, she managed to stagger back to bed again. Fifteen minutes later, she forced down two soda crackers and when they stayed down, she dressed and went to work.

On the way there, she stopped at a drugstore for a pregnancy test. At lunch, hidden in a bathroom stall, the little stick inside told her that her suspicion was correct: She'd be hugging a lot of toilets for the next month or two.

She wasn't sure what to do. At least, she was sure what *she'd* be doing—having a baby. She just wasn't sure how Mitch would react. After the major scene she'd staged over him lying about an ulcer, how could she admit that she'd misled him about birth control—and become pregnant as a result?

For three days, she kept the news to herself despite her alarm at how quickly he seemed to sense something was wrong.

"Are you okay, Jessie?" was his constant query, concern in his eyes.

"I'm fine. Everything's great," was her repeated reply, given with wide-eyed sincerity.

She suppressed her sudden tendency to burst into tears every time he kissed her goodbye in the mornings. She resisted the desire to cling tighter during their lovemaking at night. But she couldn't overcome the need to talk to someone about all this. Her mother came to mind, but with wistful regret, Jessie discarded that idea. Her mother had enough to worry about right now. Linda was the next obvious choice, and she broke the news to her friend as they counted the night deposit bags the fourth morning after Jessie confirmed her condition.

"Pregnant? Oh, Jessie, how did that happen?" Linda exclaimed, looking up from a jumbled mass of cash and checks from the Sunshine Bookstore down the street. "Why weren't you more careful?"

If she was looking for sympathy, she'd obviously

come to the wrong place, Jessie thought dryly. "There was only one night that we didn't use birth control and that was the night we were locked in the vault. Condoms were the one thing I couldn't find on any of the teller carts."

"I swear, it must be the water in this place that makes us all so fertile," Linda muttered. She began counting out the coins, making small towers of dimes, nickels and quarters. "So what are you going to do? What did Mitch say?"

"Nothing."

Linda knocked down her pile of quarters. "The jerk," she said, her eyes narrowing.

"He might very well be, but not in this instance," Jessie admitted. "I just haven't told him yet."

"Jessie!" Linda looked at her in dismay. "You *have* to tell him. He has the right to know he's going to be a father."

"I'm planning on telling him, I just wanted to wait a while." Jessie glanced at her friend, and tried to smile. "I thought I'd try to find out first exactly how he feels about me and marriage, without the complication of a baby."

"That's a good idea," Linda said thoughtfully. "You'll discover his true feelings, which will help you decide how to handle the situation. What could go wrong with that?"

SOMETHING WAS WRONG. Mitch couldn't quite figure out exactly what the problem was, but the tense, uneasy feeling he'd had for the past five days wasn't something he could argue with.

He'd had the feeling before, and it always presaged trouble. He'd had it as a uniformed cop, just before he and his partner walked into a robbery in progress at a local drugstore one day. He'd had it as an undercover detective, just before a drug buy went sour and the dealer he'd been trying for a good three months to catch got away.

The first time he'd had the feeling he'd been sixteen. He'd returned home to find some groceries, two hundred bucks and a note telling him his mother had left him behind.

Yeah, he'd learned not to argue with his instincts. But he wanted to—*man,* did he want to. Because this time they kept telling him something was wrong with Jessica.

She acted different lately. Not as happy. When they'd first gotten together, there'd been this glow about her. She'd look at him across the bank and the light in her eyes would make his heart leap. He'd feel warm, and strong, and wanted. He'd almost feel…loved.

But for the past five days that had changed. She seemed tense and preoccupied. They'd make love at night—that, at least, was still great between them—but afterward, instead of snuggling closer the way she used to, she'd turn away, leaving him feeling confused and worried. She no longer went around the bank smiling for no reason. Her face no longer lit up at the sight of him— hell, now she hardly looked at him at all. Worst of all, when she did, she wouldn't meet his eyes. She'd glance away quickly as if she felt guilty, or was trying to hide something.

With any other woman he'd suspect she was cheating. But Jessica wasn't like that. What he suspected Jessica yearned for wasn't another man, but her hometown in Texas.

And why wouldn't she? Her people were there, plenty of family and friends who loved her and that she loved and cared about in return. Still, he'd thought, for a little while, that she was starting to care for him, too.

But what did he know about family or caring or love? He obviously wasn't the kind of man a woman built her life around, and Jessica was more independent than most. He'd known all along that their affair wouldn't last, that he wasn't the kind of man she wanted. That she planned to return home soon. She'd told him all that up front. If he'd started to hope she'd changed her mind...well, that was his problem.

Yet, he couldn't stop hoping that maybe he was wrong, that she wasn't thinking about leaving, about going back to Texas yet. But that hope pretty much faded when she brought up the subject later that night.

He didn't even see it coming. They were sitting together on the sofa in her apartment, with his arm around her, her head on his shoulder, while they watched baseball on TV. The Dodgers had just tied the game, making up a two-run deficit in the bottom of the ninth inning, when she said, "Isn't it funny, how in different parts of the country, people do things differently?"

"Yeah," he said. "The Dodgers have a tendency to try to slug it out in a situation like this, to go for the big home run, while most other teams try to finesse a win, taking a walk or a sacrifice."

"I'm not talking about baseball," she said with a shade of annoyance in her voice. She sat up straighter, moving away from him a little. "I'm talking about values. How what matters to a person—oh, say a person born in L.A., for example—might be different than what someone who comes from a small town like Crab Apple might want."

At the mention of Crab Apple, Mitch's gut twisted. Damn, she *was* thinking about her hometown. He didn't say anything. He didn't want to talk about that place, didn't want *her* talking about it. He wanted her to forget it altogether, to just enjoy being with him. And to watch the game.

But she persisted. "Do you agree, Mitch?"

"Yeah," he said, hoping whatever he was agreeing with would end the discussion.

Jessica's heart sank at his answer. He agreed, then, that they didn't want the same things in life. She moved a little farther away, tucking a foot under her bottom and turning to look at him. She tried to read his face, but his expression was at its most impassive as he gazed at the TV. "I guess to people in L.A...people like you...a career is what's important. While in Crab Apple—"

Crab Apple, Crab Apple, Crab Apple, Mitch thought. *God, he was sick of that town.*

"—Most people put family first. Like my friend Tom, for example. He married rather young."

Mitch stiffened. *Tom!* So she was thinking about going back to that jerk, was she? Funny, how much he could hate a man he'd never even met. "Yeah, and look where it got him," he said cuttingly. "Widowed, with two little kids and not enough cash to help you out when you needed it. He should have stayed single—" should *still* stay single "—and worked a while to earn some money. The guy's a loser."

Jessica stiffened, biting her lip. So! He thought a man who chose love over money was a loser. "Marriage is important to Tom." *Isn't it important to you?* she thought.

Mitch tried to control his rising anger. He'd just *bet* marriage was important to the guy. Tom no doubt wanted to marry Jessica so he could have her in bed every night and get a mother for his kids into the bargain. "There are a lot of things in life that are more important than marriage," Mitch told her. *Like us. Like what we have right here.*

Jessica stared at him in silence. Her plan to find out where she stood had worked out all too well. He wasn't interested in marriage, not at all.

What a time to realize she'd fallen in love with him.

Her heart ached, and tears burned behind her eyes. *Oh, Mama, you raised eight kids, and this one is a fool. Why did I think I could give this man my body, and not lose my heart as well?*

She stood up and headed to the door. Keeping her voice from trembling with an effort, she said over her shoulder, "Like I said, different people want different things." *And obviously you don't want me.*

She left the room, but Mitch stayed on the couch, staring blankly at the television long after the Dodgers had lost the game.

14

"HE'S NOT INTERESTED in marriage," Jessica told Linda the next day in the merchant room as the teller unlocked her cart, getting ready for customers. "He said plain as day that marriage is for losers." Her eyes filled, but Jessica blinked back the tears, refusing to let them fall. She blew her nose fiercely.

Linda patted her arm. "Oh, Jessie, I'm so sorry. What did he say about the baby?"

"I didn't get the chance to tell him. I was so upset, I just went to bed and he didn't join me until later." Until three o'clock to be exact. She'd lain there for hours, looking at the clock. When he finally did come to bed, instead of taking her in his arms as he'd always done before, he'd turned his back. She blew her nose again. Not only didn't he want to marry her, he was obviously tired of her as well.

"He'll be horrified to hear about the baby," she told Linda. Remembering his fear of pregnant women, and what he'd said about children at the beach, she added, "I don't think he likes children at all."

"Well, too bad, since he'll be supporting one," Linda said grimly. Jessica looked up to protest, and her friend raised her hand to stop her. "He did the crime, he can pay the fine."

"I don't think that's quite how the saying goes," Jessica said. She didn't want Mitch paying for a child he didn't want. She remembered how she'd thought that night in the vault that it would be okay, just once, to make love without birth control. How she'd virtually lied to him, and how once had become twice, then three times before morning.

It wasn't the smartest thing she'd ever done, and yet... She laid her hand over her abdomen and the tiny life nestling there. And yet, she couldn't help thinking that it was the luckiest.

Because she wanted this baby. And she had plenty of family in Texas who would welcome this baby, too. At the thought of her family, a sudden painful longing welled up inside her. She wanted to go home right now, this second, to see her brothers and sisters and the mother who loved her no matter what.

This baby was a blessing, and if Mitch Flaherty was too stupid to realize that...well, he was dumber than a retarded tadpole.

She gave her nose a final blow and threw away her tissue. She tucked in her blouse and straightened her spine.

"What are you going to do, Jessie?" Linda asked, looking at her with concern in her eyes. "Pam heard you throwing up in the bathroom this morning, you know. The word about your baby is already starting to spread."

Jessica lifted her chin. "I'm going to unlock the doors and let the customers in. When Mitch gets here, I'm going to tell him about the baby, and then I'm going home to Texas. But before I leave, I'm going to make him promise—by fair means or foul—to recommend to the new operations officer that each and every one of you women be kept on until you're ready to go out on leave."

Linda's worried expression eased into a smile. "You get 'im, girl."

Unfortunately, Jessica couldn't get him because Mitch

wasn't there yet. The lunch hour came and went and still no Mitch. It wasn't until nearly closing that Jessica looked up from her work and saw he had finally arrived.

He was standing across the lobby by the back doors, talking to one of his crew. He looked tired. He hadn't gotten much more sleep last night than she had, she thought, her heart aching with unwanted concern.

"He's here, Jessie," Linda said, appearing by her side.

"I know."

"The longer you wait the harder it's going to be."

Jessica knew that, but her nerve still wavered a little. Once they talked, everything would change. Oh, she'd miss him so much! Shaking off her despair, she straightened her shoulders, determined to get the unpleasant task done. "I'll talk to him just as soon as I can get him alone."

Linda began, "It's only fair—" then broke off, a spasm crossing her face as she clutched her side.

Jessica supported her arm. "What is it? A labor pain?"

"No, I'm sure it's not," Linda said, but her face looked pale. "It's way too early yet."

"Still, I think you should go home—or to the hospital," Jessica said, remembering the horror stories Mitch had told about babies coming suddenly in houses and cars.

But already Linda's color was looking better. She shook her head. "No, I'm fine. One of the babies must have just kicked extra hard."

"At least get off your feet a while. Go on upstairs and lie down for a few minutes." Jessie smiled wryly. "I'll come up, too, and see if I can keep some crackers and tea down as soon as I finish my teller check and talk to Mitch."

Linda headed for the stairwell, and Jessie strode to the

line of tellers, pausing beside each woman, making sure everything was okay, that they had enough cash and, most importantly, that nobody needed a bathroom break. Resolutely, she refused to glance in Mitch's direction, but she could feel him watching her, and her shoulders stiffened a little as she kept grimly at her task.

She'd just finished talking to Lupe and had reached Diane, when she glanced up and noticed that something was wrong with Pam. She'd avoided Pam all day, not wanting to answer questions about the baby until she had the chance to talk to Mitch. The red-haired teller was stationed at the end of the line and the customer in front of her had a big smile on his face. But Pam's smile looked strained, her skin pale. Maybe she was upset because Jessie hadn't talked to her. Or maybe…

Oh, please, God, don't let her be having labor pains! Jessie thought with a sinking feeling. She was already dreading confronting Mitch. She simply didn't feel up to also dealing with the commotion Pam was sure to cause if she had started labor.

Shaking off her foreboding, Jessie walked briskly toward the red-haired teller. The closer she got, the more her heart sank. Something was definitely amiss. Pam looked like a wax doll, the stricken smile frozen on her lips and her hands crossed protectively across her stomach. Pam was the farthest along in her pregnancy, due to be the first one to deliver. Her belly was simply huge. At this stage, labor was a real possibility.

She'd help Pam take care of this customer and then send her home—or to the hospital if need be, Jessie decided. She was so focused on Pam's condition that it took her a moment after she reached the teller's side to realize Pam's pregnancy wasn't the problem at all.

It might have been the customer's nervous eyes that tipped her off. Or the scared look in Pam's face.

But the biggest clue to the real trouble here was the rubber duck sitting on the counter.

It didn't look strange at first—at least, no stranger than any other little yellow duck sitting on a bank counter with its cute orange beak curved into a big smile. It wasn't until Jessica noticed the silver rod sticking out of the top of the duck's head that she realized something more was going on than a customer with a toy fixation.

She glanced at Pam. "What's that?"

"An antenna. He stuck it in the duck."

"I can see that," Jessica said. "But why?"

"Because I'm robbing the place," the man declared in a fierce whisper. "And this here bird's a bomb."

Jessica looked at the rubber duck's owner. He didn't look like a robber. Or a man who'd gone crazy. He had an unremarkable, almost nondescript face. Ordinary brown eyes and hair, and ordinary clothes, just blue jeans and a white T-shirt. Nothing about him would stand out in a crowd.

Unless you counted his duck.

"I want money—big money, not only what she has in the top drawer but in the bottom as well," he said, waving the duck threateningly. He shoved a paper bag across the counter. "If you don't give it to me, I'll squeeze the duck and the whole place will blow."

Jessica definitely didn't want the duck squeezed. Pushing Pam gently aside, she started stuffing—ones, twenties, hundreds—whatever money her hands touched in Pam's cart she thrust into the bag. The dye-release bait money went in with everything else, not because she would have remembered to include it, but simply because it was wrapped with the other money as Mitch had insisted.

She wanted to glance toward Mitch. She didn't dare. He might notice something in her expression. Come over and try to help. She didn't want to take the chance of him getting hurt—of anyone getting hurt.

"Hurry up," the man hissed.

She worked faster. She'd shoved the last of the money in the bag and wrapped it closed, when a cheerful masculine voice said, "Hello, Miss Kendall."

Jessica looked up. Edwards was standing next to the robber, plaster powdered over his hair and work clothes, his round cheeks bulging with a big beaming smile. "I thought you might like to know I just got a promotion at work. You aren't talking to just a member of the construction team anymore. You're talking to a crew *leader*."

"How...how nice," Jessica faltered. Obviously, Edwards hadn't seen the duck, which the robber had shoved inside his jacket. Jessica could see its little eye, however, peaking out by the zipper.

She glanced back at Edwards. "Congratulations! Well, as you can see, I'm helping this customer—"

Edwards spared the man a cursory glance. "Go ahead. I don't mind. Being a crew leader requires patience, you know, and smarts. Plenty of smarts."

Jessica clutched the bag tighter, uncertain whether to hand it over to the robber now or wait until Edwards left. Best to wait, she decided, to keep him from getting involved.

But judging by how he was chatting away, it didn't appear Edwards would be leaving anytime soon. He'd traveled from the "plenty of smarts" theme to telling about how the other men on the job were jealous of his new position. And envious of how much money he'd be making now. "I can afford to do a few things I wasn't able to before," Edwards said, puffing out his chest a little. His belly automatically followed. "We might even be able to go out sometime. What d'ya say?"

Jessica wasn't sure what to say. She wanted to say something, *anything* to get Edwards to leave, but nothing came to mind. The robber apparently reached the same conclusion she did—Edwards was pretty much here to stay.

From beneath his jacket, the thief gestured impatiently with the duck, making it bob up and down, as if it was nodding at her. Jessica started to slide the bag over, but stopped as Edwards reached out to grab her hand.

"We can maybe get a burger, a bag of fries—" he said, waggling his bushy eyebrows in what he no doubt considered to be an enticing gesture. "I'll even treat you to a milk shake."

"Jessica…" Pam said, agitation making her bounce a little on her stool.

Jessica swallowed, trying to ignore the bobbing duck, the waggling eyebrows and the bouncing teller, and marshal her thoughts. Forcing a smile, she shook her head at Edwards and tried to free her hand. He wouldn't release her.

The duck was bobbing more urgently now; the robber was starting to look as desperate as she felt. "Thank you, Mr. Edwards," Jessica said firmly. "But I'm afraid I'll have to refuse your invitation—"

"Because she's sleeping with me. So why don't you take your hands off her?" Mitch said suddenly from behind her.

Jessica stiffened in alarm. Help had arrived—at the worst possible moment. She glanced at Mitch's face as he stepped up beside her. His lips were pressed in a straight line, his eyebrows were drawn down with anger as he glared at Edwards.

Oh, good Lord, he was going to do something stupid!

He did. Reaching down, he grasped Edwards's wrist, forcing the bigger man to loosen his grip on Jessica's hand. Edwards jerked violently away, hitting the robber's arm.

The rubber duck fell onto the counter. Everyone froze.

"What the hell is that?" Edwards demanded.

Both Edwards and Mitch stared at the yellow toy. The antenna had gotten bent in the scuffle, Jessica noticed.

"A duck bomb," Pam declared with an excited bounce. "That man is robbing us."

"The hell he is!" Edwards declared.

Mitch stepped between the two women and the duck, but Edwards stepped toward the robber. With one mighty blow, Edwards knocked the robber out.

"JUST THINK," Jessica said in a marveling tone a few hours later, sitting on the edge of the long table in the conference room. "Edwards is a hero!" She swung her legs happily.

Leaning back against the door facing her, Mitch nodded curtly. She must have made the remark at least ten times in the last ten minutes. "He sure is."

"He was so brave! So daring!"

Mitch's jaw tightened. He'd waited for over two hours for the police and FBI to take everyone's statements and leave. He'd paced outside the conference room where they were taking Jessica's statement in private, anxious to talk to her, to take her in his arms and know—*really know*—that she hadn't been hurt.

As soon as the feds left, he'd strode into the room and, thankfully, found her alone. Shutting the door on all the gawking women trying to crowd in behind him, he'd leaned back against it to keep them out and taken her in his arms for a tight hug.

A hug that had been all too brief.

She'd pulled gently away almost immediately, saying, "We *are* at work, don't forget. Someone could see us."

And instead of accepting the comfort he was aching to give—"I'm fine, Mitch, honestly"—and going home to rest—"I'm not upset! Everything happened so quickly I didn't have time to be scared"—all she wanted to do was talk on and on *and on* about how wonderful Edwards had been.

How quick-thinking. How brave.

Mitch was the one who was getting tired—of hearing about Edwards's derring-do. Honest to God, he was thankful that everything had turned out okay. But listening to Jessica, you'd think Edwards was Arnold Schwarzenegger instead of a not-too-bright construction worker who was a shade too ready with his fists.

"Can you imagine knocking someone out with just one blow to the chin?" Jessica asked him.

"Yeah," Mitch said and glanced at her. She was perched on the edge of the huge polished table, swinging her legs, her face full of admiration for Edwards's slugging abilities.

Mitch couldn't take it anymore. He had to add, "But it really wasn't the smartest thing for the guy to do. He could have gotten hurt. Or worse yet—" *definitely worse yet* "—the duck could have gone off, blowing up the place."

"But I thought you said it was simply a rubber duck with an antenna in its head."

"It was. But we didn't know that at the time."

"Of course we didn't. But you have to admit, Edwards moved like lightning."

Mitch gritted his teeth. Whoever heard of a three-hundred-pound streak of lightning? "The smart thing to have done in this situation," he explained patiently, "was to follow procedure. Let the robber leave with the money and simply trap him in the cage."

She looked at him, lifting her slim eyebrows in surprise. "But I thought the cages weren't working correctly yet."

"Well, yeah, but—"

"Weren't you storming around just yesterday, cussing under your breath because it took you over two hours to reopen the doors once you'd flipped the lock?"

"There was a bit of a problem—"

"A bit!" Jessica rolled her eyes.

"It wouldn't have hurt if the thief stayed locked in a couple of hours." She opened her mouth to say something else, and he added quickly, "The point is that it would have been the safer way to go."

"I can't imagine any totally safe method to deal with a crazy man with a rubber duck," Jessica said, waving her hand dismissively. "I think Edwards's method worked just fine."

Seriously annoyed now, Mitch straightened to continue the argument, forgetting about the door behind him. As soon as he moved away, it cracked open and Pamela peered in. She pushed at it, forcing him to step forward, and bustled into the room before he could stop her. Lupe and Maria were right behind her. Before Mitch could tell them he wasn't through talking to Jessica yet, the whole group of tellers pushed into the room, chattering and surrounding her, and forcing him to move to a corner to avoid getting jabbed by gesticulating hands or bumped by rounded bellies.

They crowded so closely around Jessica that soon all he could see was the top of her silky brown hair. That's what always seemed to happen lately, he thought with piercing clarity. He'd try to get close to her and he'd be pushed away. Most often by Jessica herself.

"Oh, Jessie, thank goodness you came over when you did. I couldn't move I was so scared," Pamela said.

"That duck had such a menacing expression on its face."

"That robber was wicked, positively wicked." Thelma's voice rose above the clamor.

"He'd have to be, to use a little duck that way," Diane agreed.

"He was on drugs probably," Lupe deduced with morbid satisfaction. "I'd like to drug *him*, the *bastardo*, and stuff that duck down his throat!"

All he'd like to do was to get Jessica alone, Mitch thought morosely. She was getting ready to leave him, he just knew it. After that conversation last night, he had no doubts left. He'd thought all day about talking to her, making her change her mind, but he wondered now if he'd even get the chance.

His chest ached with a familiar pain, but he pushed his anguish down, letting anger flow in to take its place. How could she just walk away from something that was as good as what they had together? Walk away from him?

"Pam pushed the alarm button, you know," Diane's soft voice could be heard during a mild lull. "The whole thing is on tape."

Jessica was caught up in some idealistic vision of the perfect relationship, that was her problem, Mitch decided. She thought she wanted some perfect guy, who'd live with her in a little white house in Crab Apple—Crab Apple, what kind of stupid name was that for a town anyway?—and have the required two point five kids. She'd probably marry that jerk Tom just because he had two kids already made. Didn't she realize that what they had could never be as good with anyone else?

"The police had surrounded the place," Maria said excitedly. She crossed herself. "I swear, Jessie, until I saw the police rush in I didn't realize a thing was going on.''

Jessica chuckled ruefully. "Neither did I. If I had, I would have told Linda to push the alarm instead of— Linda! Oh, my goodness, I forgot all about her." Jessica jumped to her feet. "I sent her upstairs to rest!"

"She is," Thelma said. "I was up there an hour or so ago and noticed she'd fallen asleep on the couch in the women's lounge."

"She did?" Jessica's forehead wrinkled with concern. "That doesn't sound good."

The only thing that would sound good was the news that Jessica was staying, Mitch thought morosely.

Pamela patted her shoulder. "Don't worry, Jessie. When your pregnancy gets a little farther along, you'll see how tired you can get—"

Mitch stiffened, his heart jumping in his chest. "When her *what!*" he bellowed.

The women gasped and cringed. They all turned to stare at him. Silence filled the room.

Mitch didn't even notice. His whole attention was fastened on Jessica's wide eyes. Guilt was in those eyes...and confirmation of what had just been said.

Jessica was *pregnant.* She was going to have *his* baby.

His lips felt so stiff he could hardly speak. "Exactly *when* were you planning to tell me?"

"I, ah...I—"

He sucked in a deep breath. His voice grew stronger. "Today? Tomorrow?"

"Well, actually..."

"When the kid arrived?"

He started toward her. Jessica instinctively moved to the other side of the big conference table to avoid him. Like a herd of anxious sheep trying to protect an innocent lamb from a hungry wolf, all the women moved with her, surrounding her with their bulky bodies.

Mitch stopped, his jaw tightening in frustration. Unless he planned to start shoving pregnant women aside, there was no easy way he could reach her. Her name emerged on a low growl. "Jessica..."

Jessie shivered in excited fear. He sure looked angry. It might be best if she talked to him later. When he'd calmed down a bit.

Using Pam as a shield, she feinted to the left. He followed. But Jessie had practice avoiding charging bulls; one angry man wasn't too hard to escape. She darted back to the right, whirled around Pam and out the door.

She headed for the stairs. Partly because she wanted to check on poor Linda, but even more because she hoped Mitch might think she'd done an Elvis and left the building. She wasn't quick enough, however. He saw her enter the stairwell door and he came after her, bellowing all the way. "Jessie! You stop right there!"

She didn't think so. She reached the top of the stairs. He was right behind her, still yelling at her to stop before she hurt herself.

Linda wasn't in the break room. Jessie headed for the women's bathroom and safety. He wouldn't follow her in there.

She opened the door and raced into the lounge. Mitch barreled in behind her...and stopped dead.

Linda was lying on the small couch in the entryway, panting for all she was worth.

15

LINDA'S FACE was pale and strained, her eyes panicked as she breathed in small gasps. "Oh, thank God," she said when she saw them. "Everything's happening so quickly. Not like my other kids at all. No one heard me calling—" She broke off, shutting her eyes and leaning her head wearily back against the couch.

Mitch grasped Jessica's shoulders and gave her a small push toward the door. "Go call 911. Tell them we have a medical emergency here and then see if any of the women have medical experience."

She hurried off. Mitch strode toward Linda. He took her hand and her eyes opened. He hunkered down beside her, hoping she wouldn't hit out unexpectedly, but trying to make it easier for her to see his face. "How far apart are your contractions?"

She glanced at him, but her eyes were glazed and unfocused. "One minute. Two, at the most," she said, beginning to pant again.

She panted faster as another contraction hit. She grabbed his hand, squeezing his fingers as the contraction peaked. Mitch sustained the pain without a word, simply thankful she hadn't caught hold of his nose or any other vulnerable body parts. For fifteen seconds Linda's grip tightened, then slowly released.

Her head fell back in exhaustion. Her eyes closed, and she released his hand. Gingerly, Mitch shook his fingers to restore circulation and then patted her shoulder in awkward comfort. Damn, he wished he was better at this. Where the hell was Jessie?

He heard the door open and looked up as Jessica came in.

"I called, the paramedics are on their way," she said before he could ask. She walked over and he stood up, thankfully relinquishing his place by Linda's side.

He watched as Jessica took her friend's hand and gently patted it. She was so good at that kind of stuff. "Don't worry, Linda, help will be here in just a little while," she said softly.

Linda nodded wearily.

Jessie looked back up at Mitch as he asked, "Do any of the other women have medical training?"

Jessica was shaking her head before he even finished speaking. "No." Her big eyes searched his face. "Can you handle it?"

A familiar feeling of dread washed over Mitch. Not, he realized with sudden clarity because he was afraid of getting hurt, but because he was afraid of hurting Linda, or her baby. And letting Jessica down.

She knew as well as he did how he'd always botched this stuff up in the past. He glanced at her, expecting to see in her expression the same dismay he was feeling. He didn't. Complete trust was in her eyes.

"I know you can do this, Mitch," she said quietly. "We can do this. Together."

He nodded grimly. After all, what other option did they have? He was the only one with training. "I'll get washed up."

Giving birth was hard work. Mitch barely had time to finish scrubbing his hands before things started happening real fast. The women waiting anxiously outside passed in a pile of clean dish towels. Jessie spread a few beneath Linda and helped her off with her soaked nylons and panties. Then she took up position by her friend's head to act as coach.

Mitch took up his position at the other end of the couch. The baby's head was crowning. The teller's contractions were coming faster and harder now, and it wasn't more than a few minutes when she announced she had to push.

Mitch had hoped to wait for the paramedics, but if there was one thing he'd learned, it was that you didn't argue with a woman in labor. "Okay, let's do it then," he said, his jaw clenching with determination.

By the time the first baby arrived a mere five minutes later, he felt as if he'd sweated buckets and aged ten years.

Linda wasn't looking too good either. Her wan face broke into a smile, however, when he said, looking down at the tiny mite who had slid out into his hands, "We've got a winner here. It's a girl!"

"Oh, Linda, she's so beautiful," Jessica said, tears bright in her eyes.

Looking down at the baby, Mitch started to correct Jessica—he didn't want Linda to get her hopes up too much—but then he paused. There *was* something awfully endearing about the little one who was stretching, just like a real person, in his hands.

Her head was smaller than his palm. She had lashless eyes, a button nose, chipmunk cheeks and pursed lips. To top off the package, the thatch of hair on her head stuck straight up, punk-rocker style. She kept waving around hands no bigger than a dime, as if trying to get his attention.

Yeah, maybe she *was* beautiful at that.

He wrapped her in the dish towel Jessie gave him and handed the baby over to her mother.

Linda's face glowed. "Oh, thank you—thank you

both,'' she choked out. She dropped a kiss like a blessing on the baby's head.

Mitch glanced at Jessica's face. Her eyes were smiling gently as she looked at her friend and the little one. Her eyes met his. It didn't take a mind reader to know that she was imagining holding their baby in her arms like that.

The paramedics arrived a few minutes later, beating the second baby's arrival. Again, Jessie stayed by Linda's side, giving encouragement while her friend went through the whole procedure a second time.

Mitch had it easier this time. He was in charge of holding the first baby—who he'd secretly dubbed Number One. He stood on the sidelines, watching the medics' performance with a critical eye. They did fine, he thought indulgently, as Number Two made his appearance, wailing at the top of his lungs. A boy—not bad-looking, but nothing like the girl *he'd* produced. And of course, it took *two* paramedics to handle the job he'd done alone.

The paramedics didn't linger after that. As quickly as possible, they carried Linda down the stairs, past all the waiting women, and loaded her into the ambulance. Mitch handed his baby over, and Jessica passed in Number Two.

The doors slammed shut. The ambulance took off, sirens blaring and lights flashing in the gray evening light. Dusk had fallen during all the commotion upstairs. It was past time for everyone to go home. The chattering women all went back into the bank to gather their stuff, but Mitch remained in the parking lot.

He stared down the street at the flashing lights until they disappeared from view. Funny, how quickly a person could get used to holding a baby in his arms. Funny, too, how empty those arms could feel when the baby was gone.

Almost as empty as his heart would be when the woman he loved went away.

He heard heels crunching on the pitted asphalt behind him. He didn't need to look around to know that Jessica had joined him.

Her voice reached him softly from where she'd stopped, a few feet away. "You were wonderful, Mitch."

And he had been wonderful, Jessica thought. Calm and in control, not a hint of indecision in any of his actions. If he'd been worried or scared, it certainly hadn't shown.

He hadn't turned to face her and she stared at his broad shoulders, asking curiously, "Were you worried?"

His broad shoulder lifted and dropped in a shrug. "Yeah, I was worried," he admitted. "I didn't want to hurt Linda, or her baby. And beyond that, I guess I didn't want you to see how bad I am at this kind of stuff."

"What kind of stuff?" Jessica asked in surprise.

"Family stuff. Being the kind of man a woman depends on."

"You are that kind of man."

He turned. A tiny chill ran down Jessica's spine and her smile faded as the parking-lot lights illuminated his face. Not since the day he'd arrived had she seen such a grimly determined expression on his face. "Oh? If you really feel that way, then why didn't you tell me about the baby?"

"I was going to tell you," she admitted. "Today in fact."

"So why did you run away like you did?"

She shook her head, clasping her hands in front of her. It was so hard to explain. "I don't know. You just looked so angry. And I guess I don't like to be pushed...." Her voice trailed off. It seemed so stupid, so futile now to have acted as she had. "But I never really thought you were undependable. I've always known, deep inside, that you would take care of your responsibilities."

And it was true, she realized. She had known that—and she also knew why she'd run. Because she hadn't wanted to simply be a responsibility. She hadn't wanted to discover that he didn't love her.

She didn't know what reply she expected. But certainly not what he said.

"Well, that's good. Because your running days are over. I'm not about to let you leave, take my baby and go back to Crab Apple."

His tone was so matter-of-fact that it took a moment for what he was saying to sink in. When it did, Jessica stiffened. "Who are you to tell me what I'm going to do?"

He smiled, but there was no humor in his expression. "Like I told you before, I'm the man you came to L.A. to find. The man—the *only* man—that you've ever made love with."

Again his tone was almost pleasant. And for some reason, that made Jessica even angrier. "That doesn't give you any rights over me."

He seemed to consider that. "No, it doesn't, does it? At least, not that alone." He took a step toward her. "But that *is* my child you're carrying, isn't it? I believe that gives me some rights."

He took another step, and the light revealed his expression more fully. Again Jessica suffered a shock. He looked so implacable.

She told him, "I'm not intending to keep your baby from you. If you want to be involved, that's fine with me."

"That's good, because I *do* intend to be involved—fully involved." He paced closer. "I intend to be there, watching you grow big and round and probably cranky with our child.''

He came closer still. "I plan to be there when our baby is born, and to still be there as he or she grows up. In fact, I intend to father your next child, too, and however many we decide to have after that."

He grasped her shoulders, looking down into her face. His lips curved in a sardonic smile at the stunned surprise he saw there. "That's right, Bambi Eyes. When it comes to our relationship, I'm calling the shots now. Not you."

He pulled her into his arms and his mouth closed over hers. Jessica expected the heated sensuality, the teasing excitement, but the yearning hunger in his kiss took her by surprise. She felt almost consumed by his searching mouth, the warmth of his tight embrace.

He held her as if he never planned to let her go.

By the time he did release her, she was trembling with rising need. She leaned weakly against him, and he rested his chin on her hair. "Don't you know I love you, Jessie?" His voice was so hoarse it was almost unrecognizable. "That I never ever want to let you go?"

She couldn't believe it. She pushed away a little to look up at him. "Me, too? And not just the baby?"

He hugged her close again, rocking her gently in his arms. "Yeah, you, too. The baby is a fantastic bonus, but I think I fell in love with you the first day I walked into this damn bank. I've certainly never felt this way about anyone else before." He rested his forehead against hers, looking intently into her eyes. "Do you love me?"

Her arms tightened around his neck. "Oh, Mitch, of course I do."

That was all she got to say. Taking charge again, Mitch lowered his mouth to hers.

Epilogue

FROM THE RELATIVE ISOLATION of the doorway, Mitch surveyed the cluster of women gathered in Linda's living room eight months later. All were chattering happily, almost all had babies on their knees. Automatically, his gaze sought out Jessica.

She was sitting in a big armchair by the fireplace, excitedly opening the baby-shower gifts spread around her. Mitch liked these showers that women appeared to enjoy giving. He and Jessie had gotten some pretty good stuff at the wedding shower the women had thrown for them, too. But it wasn't the gifts that made him smile, but the sight of Jessica and how much fun she had, opening the presents.

Her round basketball of a stomach made the task something of a challenge these days. She didn't have much lap left to put things on. But she seemed to be managing with Pamela's help, despite the little red-haired baby Pam was holding who kept grabbing at the brightly colored wrapping paper heaped around their feet.

"Would you like to hold Michelle for a while?"

Mitch glanced down at Linda, who had paused by his side. She'd just laid down Number Two, and was holding Number One—who looked as if she never planned to sleep again. The baby's eyes were wide open, her little arms waving excitedly at the sight of him.

Linda smiled. "She certainly seems happy to see you."

She sure did. Still, Mitch hesitated. He was gratified that Linda and her husband had named Number One Michelle in his honor, and even more pleased that they'd chosen him as the baby's godfather. But the little one was so fragile, so helpless. So damn wiggly. Every time he held her he was afraid he might inadvertently drop her or something.

But Linda didn't give him a chance to refuse. She plopped the baby in his arms and went over to join the group by Jessica.

Mitch was trying to arrange Michelle in a more comfortable position against his shoulder when Raul strolled over. "Nice party, huh?" his friend asked, stopping beside him with a piece of cake in hand to watch his struggles with interest. "That one's the girl, isn't it?"

"What clued you in?" Mitch asked. "The pink bow in her hair?"

"Naw, the way she's grabbing on to your big old beak," Raul answered, taking a bite of his cake.

Mitch gently removed the small hand tugging at his nose as Raul added, "So the rest of the kids are boys, huh?"

"Yeah," Mitch answered, a little preoccupied. Michelle had grasped his ear now, and was trying to see how far it would stretch. He pried her tiny fingers loose, thanking God he'd never pierced his ear like his more debonair friend, then winced as she latched on to his hair.

"And all the women named their kids Jesse?"

Mitch merely nodded this time. Michelle was holding his lower lip with the hand that wasn't buried in his hair. It was hard to talk.

Raul gave a low whistle. "They sure must like your wife."

"They do," Mitch said. He'd finally managed to anchor Michelle against his shoulder, burying her fists between her tummy and his chest. In this position, all she could do was kick at his stomach while she gnawed on his shirt. He could put up with that.

He glanced over at the man at his side. If Raul felt any uneasiness at being only one of two males present at a baby shower it certainly didn't show. His friend had donned a suit for the occasion. His white shirt was crisply ironed, his dark hair neatly combed. A gold ring in one earlobe gleamed against his golden-brown skin, and his dark eyes glinted with satisfaction as he looked around the room while taking another big bite of cake.

You'd think he was a sheik surveying his harem, Mitch thought sardonically, patting Michelle gently on the back as she kicked happily.

He looked around, too, and noticed that several of the women were smiling at his handsome friend. Dorothy appeared almost enraptured. Mitch wasn't surprised. Raul had always had that kind of effect on women. From the first time they saw him, the tellers had all given him their unqualified seal of approval.

Mitch glanced at Jessica, expecting her to be gazing at Raul, too. She wasn't. Her eyes were fixed on him with that warm glow on her face that always made him feel ten feet tall.

She smiled. Mitch smiled back, then grunted in pain as Raul suddenly elbowed him in the ribs.

"Less than a month to go now, right?" Raul jabbed again. "So, pal, are you up to being a daddy?"

Mitch winced a little and nestled Michelle closer. Trust Raul to poke at a sore spot. No, he wasn't sure he was up to it. He worried constantly about doing the wrong thing, about letting Jessica or his unborn child down. He worried about the birth. He worried if they'd both be okay. Most of all, he worried about being a good father and husband in the years to come.

After all, he didn't have much experience of family life to draw on.

But no way was he going to admit his fears to the lowlife at his side. "Yeah, I'm up to it," he said, adding for good measure a saying he'd heard Jessica's mother use when they'd gone back for the wedding. "Any fool can sow the seed. It takes a real man to take care of the crop."

Raul choked on the last of his cake.

Pleased with his friend's reaction, Mitch called out, "Hey, Linda. Can Raul hold Michelle a while?"

All the women looked their way again. Linda beamed, pleased at Raul's apparent interest in her daughter. "Of course he can!"

Sheer, unadulterated terror crossed Raul's face. Ignoring his friend's stuttering protests, Mitch carefully passed the baby over—just in time for Michelle to spit up on Raul's immaculate suit.

"Holy hell, she's vomiting," Raul said, a hint of panic in his voice. He stared at Michelle, who smiled toothlessly back with baby barf trickling down her chin before making a grab for the ring in his ear.

She caught it, first time trying, Mitch noted with satisfaction. *That's my girl.*

Raul grimaced, trying to escape. "What should I do?"

"Take her into the bedroom and put clean clothes on her," Mitch advised, adding after a judicious sniff, "better change her, too. I think she pooped."

"Holy sh—"

"And don't cuss. She's a baby girl, damn it."

Raul's mouth snapped shut. Leaving him to his struggles, Mitch headed toward Jessica. Yeah, he didn't have all the answers, but he'd certainly learned more in the past few months about babies than the lady-killer king knew.

He sat down on the arm of Jessie's chair. She looked up at him with such love in her brown eyes that he could feel his throat tighten as he reached down to take her hand. At least there was one thing he was sure of: day by day, baby by baby, with Jessica by his side, he'd get this family thing licked.

Yeah, with love helping him out, everything would be just fine.

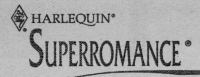

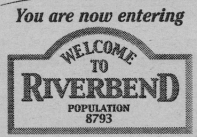

You are now entering

WELCOME TO RIVERBEND
POPULATION 8793

Riverbend...the kind of place where everyone knows your name—and your business. Riverbend...home of the River Rats—a group of small-town sons and daughters who've been friends since high school.

The Rats are all grown up now. Living their lives and learning that some days are good and some days aren't—and that you can get through anything as long as you have your friends.

Starting in July 2000, Harlequin Superromance brings you Riverbend—six books about the River Rats and the Midwest town they live in.

BIRTHRIGHT by Judith Arnold (July 2000)
THAT SUMMER THING by Pamela Bauer (August 2000)
HOMECOMING by Laura Abbot (September 2000)
LAST-MINUTE MARRIAGE by Marisa Carroll (October 2000)
A CHRISTMAS LEGACY by Kathryn Shay (November 2000)

Available wherever Harlequin books are sold.

HARLEQUIN®
Makes any time special ™

Visit us at www.eHarlequin.com   HSRIVER